FREDERIC REMINGTON
AND
THE NORTH COUNTRY

FREDERIC REMINGTON
AND
THE NORTH COUNTRY

Atwood Manley
and
Margaret Manley Mangum

E. P. DUTTON · NEW YORK

Published in the United States by E. P. Dutton,
a division of NAL Penguin Inc.,
2 Park Avenue, New York, N.Y. 10016.

Published simultaneously in Canada
by Fitzhenry and Whiteside, Limited, Toronto.

Library of Congress Cataloging-in-Publication Data

Manley, Atwood.
Frederic Remington and the north country / Atwood Manley and
Margaret Manley Mangum.
p.   cm.
Bibliography: p.
Includes index.
ISBN 0-525-24647-9
1. Remington, Frederic, 1861–1909.   2. Artists—United States—
Biography.   3. Remington, Eva Caten, d. 1918.   4. Artists' wives—
United States—Biography.   I. Mangum, Margaret Manley.   II. Title.
N6537.R4M36   1988
709'.2'4—dc19
[B]   88-11936
                                                   CIP

Designed by Earl Tidwell
Map of the North Country by Joseph P. Ascherl

1 3 5 7 9 10 8 6 4 2

First Edition

Grateful acknowledgment is made to the
Frederic Remington Art Museum of Ogdensburg, New York,
for permission to reproduce certain illustrations in this book.

This book is gratefully dedicated
to Betsey Caten Deuval,
great-niece of Eva Caten and Frederic Remington

CONTENTS

Sixteen pages of illustrations follow page 114.

ACKNOWLEDGMENTS

We may be listed as official authors of this book, but the names of many others deserve to be added to ours. Our grateful appreciation goes to all, living and dead, whose special knowledge and insights have enlarged our understanding of Frederic and Eva Remington, especially the following:

Our family: especially Alice Reynolds Manley (Atwood's wife and Peg's mother), who died in 1986 and who knew we could do it, who throughout our lives encouraged, criticized, edited, proofread, and added factual source material for all of Atwood's writing and for this project.

Also, Janet Manley Labdon for help with illustrations and photographs and attention to countless details; Megan Mangum for photographs; John A. and Scott R. Mangum; Kenneth C. and Catherine Labdon; all the John A. Reynolds, Falcos, and Labdons; John M. Mangum; and last but assuredly important, George and Ebony, the family dogs, who waited patiently to go out, come in, and eat when Peg was at the computer.

Betsey Caten Deuval, Gouverneur, New York, for opening her private store of recollections of Eva and Frederic Remington and of Emma Caten; for sharing family memorabilia and treasures; for friendship, soup, and sandwiches; and Ernie Deuval, her husband, who listened patiently to us.

Dr. Allen P. and Marilyn D. Splete, Damascus, Maryland, Remington buffs, scholars, authors, for sharing their unpublished draft of *Frederic Remington—Selected Letters,* for giving encouragement and counsel, and for sharing numerous phone conversations.

Dick and Margaret Myers, Canton, New York, who were always there to encourage, counsel, answer questions, search for details, and urge on the flagging junior author.

Persis Boyesen, Ogdensburg, New York, member of the Free Library staff, who gave her personal time and her historical knowledge so generously.

St. Lawrence County Historical Association staff, past and present, Canton, New York, who helped and opened archives and photograph files to the authors: John Baule, Rick Rummel, Jon Austen, Janet McFarland, Betty Coots, and all the volunteers at the St. Lawrence Historical Association who compile genealogical materials.

Staff of the Owen D. Young Library, St. Lawrence University, especially rare book librarian and university archivist Lynn Ekfelt, whose enthusiasm, friendship, knowledge, and facilities helped more than anyone will ever know.

St. Lawrence University administration and faculty members, past and present, and their spouses: Dr. Frank (former president) and Ann Piskor, Priscilla DiAngelo, Lisa Cania, Neil Burdick, Frank Shields, Richard and Ruffina Holliday, Robert and Betsy Matteson. William and Nadine Axtell, Dr. Paul Jamison, Andrew K. Peters, George Raica (director of Brush Art Gallery), Rachel Sadinsky.

Remington Art Museum staff and board members, past and present, Ogdensburg, New York, especially present director Lowell McAllister, Mark VanBenschoten, Joseph MacDonald, Allen Newell, Mildred Dillenbeck, Melody Ward, and all the hardworking and helpful secretarial staff and volunteers.

Canton Free Library staff and the Benton Board, especially Susan Sheard, Virginia Witherhead, Karen Enns, Janet McFarland.

Peter H. Hassrick, director, Buffalo Bill Historical Center, Cody, Wyoming, for help, support, and friendship.

Michael Shapiro, St. Louis, Missouri, author and curator at the St. Louis Art Museum.

Mildred Dillenbeck, Ogdensburg, New York, longtime Manley family friend and former Remington Art Museum staff member, who reviewed the completed manuscript for factual errors. Muriel Heineman, Baltimore, Maryland, and Jeri Donovan, New York, New York, who read and criticized the manuscript.

Sally Gross, Allentown, Pennsylvania, who introduced Peg to

late-nineteenth-century American artists and shared her research and teaching materials freely.

Robert and Hertha Rockwell, Corning, New York, gracious hosts who taught and encouraged.

Also, Jeff Dykes of College Park, Maryland; David Dary of Lawrence, Kansas; William and Judith Diehl, Dave Baker, Allen and Kate Newell, Howard Scott, Mary Ellen and Ted Erickson; Bernadette Stillo; the staff of the Adirondack Museum; the staff of the Kansas State Historical Society; the staff of the Rockwell Museum of Western Art; Tom and T. J. Wilkins of I/O Computers in Stroudsburg, Pennsylvania; R.K.R. Hess Associates owners, staff, and facilities in Stroudsburg; John Kirk; Betty Rine, postmaster, Henryville, Pennsylvania; Charles W. Appleton, Dorman Priest, Helen Rogers, Maurice Bloch, Dr. Harriett Chaney, Evelyn Carpenter, Dr. John Miller, Susan Dogan, Judy Bush of Eagle Valley Printers, Dr. Douglas Ziedonis, Dr. John Beamer, Rudolf Wunderlich, William Remington.

Finally, and most importantly, our literary agents and friends, Paul Bradley and Martha Goldstein. And the staff at E. P. Dutton, especially our editor, Joyce Engelson; Trent Duffy, the managing editor; Pat McCormack, the production manager; Nancy Etheredge, the art director; Kathy Ward, the manager of Text Processing Services.

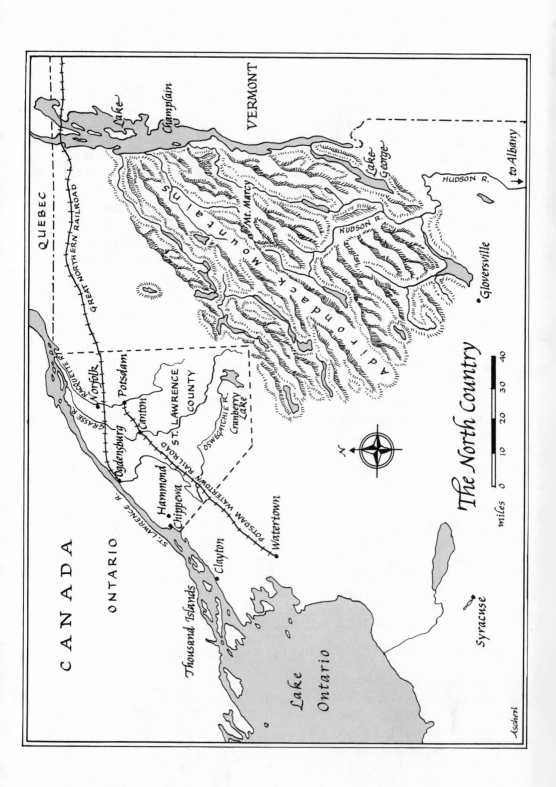

The North Country

miles

0   10   20   30   40

Ascheri

FOREWORD

Over the years we have generally been drawn to consider Frederic Remington in a western context. So highly regarded has he become that most observers are oblivious of the significance of the artist's eastern attachments. Despite his spiritual and inspirational affinity with the West and its rich store of historical narrative, Remington was at heart an easterner. If we look at Remington from the perspective of his North Country (upstate New York) associations, we discover a new side of his character—facets heretofore masked by the heroic proportions of the western myth he strove to perpetuate and with which he was so strongly identified.

This book is written with that new perspective as its guiding principle. Because Remington was raised in the North Country and throughout his life retained firm ties there, the authors have set out to persuade us to regard the artist in a north-south orientation. And they succeed in doing this—in providing a fresh understanding of Remington as set within the familial, geographical, and cultural context of upstate New York.

As a painter of the North Country, Remington was part of the continuing tradition of interpreting the people, life, and place begun in the mid-nineteenth century by Arthur F. Tait. Especially inviting was the wilderness that Tait had artistically explored in the Adirondacks. Winslow Homer later discovered a creative unity in that region, and Remington was far more at home there than in the West.

There he was one with the wilderness, informed by her imagery, vested in her wealth, and strengthened by her constancy.

On another level, one more psychological than geographical, this volume explores the "inner" Remington. We are so accustomed to seeing the external manifestations of the artist—his paintings, his writings, his bronzes—that we often miss the man himself as an involved and engaging personality. The authors reveal the underlying personal forces that drove Remington throughout his life. By observing the everyday activities of the man and the fabric of his personal character, we are able to gather insights into his extraordinary creative process as well.

And within these pages Eva Remington is featured as never before. Not just the Victorian woman who resided in the shadow of her spouse and his fame, Eva emerges with a strength and persona of her own. We see that without her force of character and her determination Remington might well have slipped into oblivion both during his lifetime and after.

PETER H. HASSRICK
Director, Buffalo Bill Historical Center
Cody, Wyoming

INTRODUCTION

The aging Chevette chugged eastward on I-80 toward the George Washington Bridge and New York in early June 1984. Nature, with complete disregard for the calendar, was welcoming me (Peg Manley Mangum) to the city with a summerlike heat wave. Moist air pressed down as New Jersey's hill country leveled to the coastal plain. Westward behind my little car, thunder grumbled as an angry sun sank into the horizon. Musing, I imagined how Frederic Remington would have reacted to the sight of that eerie sky. He was so fascinated by light.

With threatening thunder, dimming sky, and enervating heat, I now wondered why a remark of Robert Rockwell, founder of the Rockwell Museum of Western Art, had pried me from a cool Pocono retreat. Two weeks before, in Corning, New York, the Western art collector had advised me to attend a Sotheby–Parke Bernet auction of American art at which a painting by Frederic Remington, artist of the Old West, would be auctioned. "That Remington will bring at least half a million," Rockwell had predicted.

At the time, I had restrained a gasp of surprise. Now, while lights blinked on in the greenish twilight, I mulled over the project that first had taken me to Corning and currently was carrying me to New York: in October 1983, my father, Atwood Manley, and I had agreed to write a book together about Frederic Remington and his relationship to the North Country, the little-known region in north-

ernmost New York State where the artist—and my father and I, also—
had been born and raised. We planned to use Atwood's unpublished
research materials and new information that I would unearth.

The Sotheby auction would help confirm the current status of
the art created by the fat man from Canton whom Atwood remembers vividly from childhood and who was a contemporary of Williston Manley, Atwood's father and my grandfather. Nearly three decades had passed since Canton and the North Country celebrated the
1961 centennial of the artist's birth; in that time, Frederic Remington's work had achieved an artistic immortality that far surpassed
any acclaim the artist of the Old West had received during his own
lifetime. Indeed, after his death in 1909, Remington and his works
had descended rapidly toward oblivion.

By the time I reached Sotheby's dignified portals, I looked like
a drowned city rat. The eastbound storm had overtaken me as I parked
on Manhattan's Upper West Side, then headed down Broadway and
crosstown to the famous auction house in the East Seventies. A stalled
bus, torrents of rain, and resulting traffic snarls had made me late.
The auction was in progress. Every seat was taken by well-bred, well-
clad New Yorkers.

Instead of sinking into a seat, and pretending invisibility, I edged
through tiers of standees at the rear of the hall toward a side pillar
where I hoped to hide. The throng of young men and women through
which I moved, many with catalogs in hand, talked in stage whispers. Shamelessly, I began to eavesdrop and soon realized that young
successful New York was garnering future cocktail conversation about
what American paintings had been sold for how much, and who
were the important people present that evening. Here and there,
whispers identified the real art lovers.

With leaning place achieved, I turned attention to the auction.
That evening's catalog listed well-known and lesser American artists
of the nineteenth century. At the front of the hall, efficient attendants
replaced canvases that had gone under the hammer with other canvases yet to be sold. In the seated rows, people raised white, numbered standards up and down to indicate their holders' bids. The
auctioneer droned on with upward-bound prices, hesitated, stopped
as standards ceased to wave on high. No sign of the Remington
painting yet. Bemused, I succumbed to the spell of auctioneering
that had lured me as a teenager, although Sotheby's is a far cry from
the rural auctions of northern New York that I had attended as a girl
with Atwood.

When a Winslow Homer painting was placed on the easel, anticipation rippled through the crowd. This, obviously, was one painting New York had been waiting for. The standard waggling accelerated, bids mounting ever higher. Feeling the undercurrent of excitement, I wondered what would happen when the Remington arrived—and, finally, the moment I had come to see occurred. Again, the wave of anticipation swept through the hall, as it had with the Homer, this time with more intensity. The attendant took away a minor painting that had hardly been noticed. In its place was the Remington canvas Robert Rockwell had bidden me to come to see.

Strangely, I hardly heard the auctioneer's voice. Instead my attention was riveted by *Coming to the Call*. There, against the lemon yellow sunrise stood the great moose, his magnificent rack of antlers silhouetted against the glow of sky, on a marshy point that jutted into the cold, dark lake. Almost hidden in the shadows beneath the point lurked the cedar canoe, its hunter poised, ready to pull his rifle trigger. In that instant, I was no longer in the crowded Manhattan auction hall. Instead, I was young again, feeling the chill of Adirondack dawn, scenting the dank sweet perfume of forest earth and balsam needles, while mists wisped above the black waters of Cranberry Lake, ghosts that walked so lightly on the surface they left no ripple.

With a start, I returned to Sotheby's as the auctioneer intoned, "Gone, for five hundred thousand dollars." No one was surprised, especially not me. I slipped out of Sotheby's into the wet and noisy Manhattan night. The flight into memory was replaced with wonder. As I tramped along the wet street, Bob Rockwell's voice echoed once again: "There are dead artists, deceased artists, and old masters."

What, I wondered, would Fred Remington have thought of the prestige that high price represented—he, who never had been welcomed as a full member into the National Academy of Design, where the artistic Olympians of his own time lived, although he had stood poised on the threshold in the last two years of his life. How, I fancied, his widow, Eva, and her spinster sister, Emma, would have rejoiced at this affirmation of their faith in Fred's talents. After he died so suddenly, they had devoted the rest of their lives to working to prepare the place of honor they believed the man they had loved and admired, nurtured and understood, better than any others deserved in history.

Fred Remington never "fitted in." Not into the mold of North Country conventionality to which he was born and bred and that his mother vainly hoped he would adopt. Not even into the frontier world he strove to record and idealize for his admiring public. Nor, really, into the publishing world that courted him and published his work for twenty-five years. Certainly not into the New York circles of the social elite of one hundred years ago. He was too big, too brash, too elemental—too talented, perhaps—to "belong" in his own time.

In our time, his biographers, scholars, and the growing number of people who view his vast body of work have had only hints of the complex person of Frederic Remington. In his own lifetime, it was the same: Frederic Sackrider Remington, although a prolific communicator through his art and articles, remained a hidden man. Physically, the artist was well camouflaged, hiding behind his boisterousness and good humor, his ever growing corpulence, his "small boy" countenance and demeanor. Only his wife, Eva Caten Remington, knew or sensed most aspects of this complicated human being. His New Rochelle neighbor and close friend, Augustus Thomas, the playwright, called him a "mental hermit."[1] His cronies at the Players' Club in New York City knew him as a bon vivant. His business associates respected his astute bargaining powers. And his enthusiastic fans and readers pictured a former cowboy, who had lived an adventurous and dangerous existence on the frontier, although the truth is that he spent only one year in Kansas as a sheep rancher. For Frederic Remington presented many faces to his worlds. And he lived in several worlds at once.

Of one of Remington's several worlds, little has been written or recognized. This is the North Country—the region ranging from the northern tier of the Adirondack Mountains to the St. Lawrence River and Canada—where Frederic Remington was born, spent his youth, and returned seasonally throughout his life. Here, his relatives lived and from here came his wife and his closest, lifelong friends—the men and women who helped launch him on his career and who remained loyal long beyond his lifetime. The North Country molded him, nurtured him, and impressed its customs and culture upon him. He departed the region as an unhappy and rebellious youth, who soon discovered the depth of ties with people and with place that drew him back year after year until he was returned finally, in death, to be cradled in the earth beneath a great pine tree through which the northern winds he loved sang and above which spreads the pale, clear azure of northern skies.

Fred Remington's friend, writer Irving Bacheller, was the first to name his and Remington's homeland the "North Country." During Fred's and Irving's childhood in the 1860s and 1870s, the region was a "howling wilderness," a place that seemed hardly touched by human habitation. Bacheller, who had lived on a remote farm in the Adirondack foothills rising to the horizon south of Canton village, heard wilderness cries "many a time . . . in the voices of wolf and panther."[2]

Humankind had arrived late in the North Country. For uncounted centuries, it had belonged to the River (the majestic St. Lawrence) and the Woods (the Adirondack mountain wilderness) and to the wildlife that sheltered there. In the Woods were moose and elk, panther (called "catamount" or "painter" by old-timers when Fred and Irving were young), lynx and bobcat, bear and deer, wolves, raccoons, beaver, otter, and other small forest creatures. Ponds, lakes, and streams teemed with trout, pickerel, great northern pike, large- and smallmouth bass, and "punkin seeds."

Even in pre-Columbian times, the North Country was almost uninhabited. A few archaic groups had lived beside St. Lawrence tributaries and then, finally, ancestors of the Iroquois had hunted and fished in the region. Even after the coming of the white men— the French, who discovered the St. Lawrence River and claimed its bordering lands for France—the Adirondack wilderness remained the traditional hunting grounds of the Mohawk Iroquois far to the south. Along the River's southern bank lived only the Oswegatchies, a small group from the Mohawk nation who had wandered north to settle near the point where the Oswegatchie River ("black waters," in the Indians' language) feeds into the St. Lawrence.

For more than a century, the French, too, left the North Country to its isolation. Then, in 1749, upon the urging of the French priest Father François Piquet, they founded Fort La Présentation, at the confluence of the Oswegatchie and the St. Lawrence (where the city of Ogdensburg now stands). Between 1754 and 1760, during the sporadic battles of the French and Indian Wars, Piquet and the Oswegatchie braves he had won as French allies became the scourge of British settlements far to the south and west.

The British never guessed how their French enemies had penetrated to the heartland of the New World to establish and guard their affluent fur-trading empire. The secret of the French inland waterway—up the St. Lawrence River to Lake Ontario and thence through the other Great Lakes—was revealed only when British general Lord Jeffrey Amherst led his army of ten thousand north to Lake Ontario and then down the River to Montreal in 1761.

That watery highway became the route by which New Englanders moved westward after the American Revolution (until the Erie Canal was opened in 1826). Some of those adventurous pioneers became the first permanent North Country settlers after the new state of New York sold vast tracts of unappropriated land that were its only wealth to Manhattan speculators and financiers. In the late 1790s, one of these men, Samuel Ogden, sent his agent north to the moldering Fort La Présentation to build the village of Ogdensburgh (the *h* was dropped in 1868 when the community became St. Lawrence County's only city). In 1800, an itinerant vagabond named Daniel Harrington stopped off beside the Grasse River sixteen miles east of Ogdensburg to plant a field of wheat. A year later, tired of tilling his land by hand, he traded his meadow for Stillman Foote's horse and bridle and rode off out of history, leaving the town of Canton's first permanent settler.

To these isolated communities and to other villages that sprang up on northerly flowing St. Lawrence tributaries came the men and women who brought the customs and dialects that make North Country culture unique ("They think differently—see life differently," a twentieth-century observer has commented.) Even in the 1860s, when Fred Remington and Irving Bacheller were born and after railroad lines began to snake across the North Country's flat river plain, North Country people were shut in by the Mountains and the Woods, and the River's water boundary. "I remember well the mental boundaries of these people in my youth," Irving Bacheller wrote late in his lifetime:

> In the east was history, in the west mystery, in the north the British, in the south the Democratic party, while above them was a difficult heaven and beneath the wide-open and capacious hell.
>
> The men stopped now and then to swap horses and stories and political opinions, but the women were always busy. . . . They were a wonderful race of women—each a spinner, a weaver, a knitter, a sewer, a tailor, a cook, a washer-woman, a nurse, a doctor, a wise and tender mother. They went to the neighbors for a visit or an evening of frolic . . . but their hands were busy even while they played. . . .
>
> Their lives were lonely. They were often thinking of old friends and beloved scenes they had left forever, and yet

they were not more than a hundred miles from them—a journey so long and difficult that they dared to think of it only in dreams. They found diversion in work. They worked and saved and sang of rest, but seemed never to be taking it. Their songs were streaked with the note of melancholy. It was like the sound of the wind in the chimney on a cold day.[3]

Here, on October 4, 1861, in the bustling, postpioneer village of Canton, Frederic Sackrider Remington was born to Clara Sackrider and Seth Pierpont Remington. In Canton, and later in Ogdensburg beside the River, he spent most of his childhood years and grew up attuned to the mysterious primordial forces that crouched beyond the villages and their surrounding farms. Fred and the other boys cherished that wonderful place. It was—and remote portions still remain—a wild world of beauty "with its many lakes and ponds . . . its ancient green trails . . . its wild life . . . its mighty hunters . . . for here were rivers walled and often roofed with pine and birch and tamarack and bordered with lilies; and there were torches of blue iris flaming above the reeds, and wild rose crowding to the water's edge."[4]

Fred Remington was born six months after the eruption of the Civil War, a factor that strongly influenced his formative years and much of his later art. He lived only forty-eight years, dying at Ridgefield, Connecticut, the day after Christmas in 1909. Although he became the highest paid, most successful illustrator of his day, in that little-known North Country world of his youth, Fred Remington was viewed, first, as the rambunctious and rowdy only child who was heir to two of Canton's leading families, and, later, as the roistering fat man who painted pictures. With only a few—like his childhood chum, John Howard of Ogdensburg; or his uncle, "W. R." Remington of Canton; or his New York City financier friend Barton Hepburn, who also hailed from St. Lawrence County—did Remington share his dreams and frustrations, his successes and failures. None of these people knew him totally, and only a few glimpsed the inner man who yearned for beauty and harmony, yet was compelled to hide his sensitivity behind a brash and sometimes abrupt exterior.

Both in his own time and in the present day, Frederic S. Remington and his art always have elicited strong opinions from all who came into contact with them. People in his own day were, by account, of two minds about the artist: they either had no use for him or were exceedingly loyal friends who believed firmly in his talents.

His advocates have never been able to define clearly the secrets of his success. In his own time, Remington's work provided images of heroic endurance and victory over threatening forces of nature for a people concerned to subdue them on behalf of an expanding economy and rapid national growth. Today, perhaps Remington's art attracts because, both at home and abroad, we have been snared by the myth of the cowboy and his horse, captured by the mirage of a vanished golden age of the nineteenth-century frontier, the more automated our lives have become. We yearn for courage and heroism, traits Remington so effectively recorded and glorified.

By some authorities and historians, Frederic Remington's art has been called "romantic" and "harmonious." Some have criticized him for an ineptitude in the use of color, but never of form. Others have labeled the painterly work of his final years "impressionistic"; indeed, one Western art authority has claimed that Remington would have become the country's outstanding Impressionist if he had lived beyond his forty-eight years—an opinion forecast three-quarters of a century ago by a reviewer of Remington's last New York exhibition three weeks before his death. The artist has been called a genius; or dismissed as merely a good draftsman.

Without doubt, Remington's bronzes catch and balance action in a unique and highly skilled way. Lacking formal training in either sculpture or engineering, Remington nevertheless managed to produce miracles of balance in mass and weight. And though he may never have lived the life of a working cowboy or cavalry soldier, he did plug along with these actors and their steeds in the great western drama, recording in his mind's eye subtleties of movement, anatomy, and composition that high-speed photography was later, in fact, to prove uncannily accurate. Above all, in the dimensions of his work, he did reveal glimpses of universal aspirations that all men yearn for, so that the "ordinary" may be invested with a hint of meaning.

No one as compulsive as Remington was in his work—or in his pursuit of travel, sport, or conviviality—could possibly have been easy to live with day by day. Yet his wife, Eva, lived contentedly through twenty-five years as his marriage partner and afterward mourned her loss. Almost nothing has been written about Eva and few have troubled to search out facts about her. The truth is that she was Fred Remington's hidden strength, one of those sustaining women who stand beside individuals the world has acclaimed as successful, particularly in earlier times.

The couple first had to survive severe stresses during their long courtship. They had to weather conflict and difficult adjustments in their first year of marriage. It was no coincidence that Frederic Remington was able to focus his impressive energies on his art only after he and Eva married and could share life together. Remington's letters and diaries reveal how much he missed Eva when she was absent: he yearned to return home to her from his western trips; he bemoaned an empty house when she was gone. Eva dosed his digestive complaints in later years and he, in turn, always nursed her tenderly during illness. He called her "Missie" or "Kid," in the rough style he affected, and he welcomed her younger sister Emma to his home and hearth, winning from this diminutive, persevering woman a loyalty that helped to save his work from obscurity long years after his death.

No one yet knows the actual number of paintings, bronzes, sketches, and illustrations the artist produced in those forty-eight years. In 1947, Harold McCracken, his first serious biographer, estimated the total to be more than two thousand. Recent authorities have raised the estimate, conservatively, to well over three thousand. And the total number rises as more of Remington's work is unearthed. We include some of these, published for the first time, in this book. For Fred Remington was as profligate in giving away his sketches and paintings to friends, relatives, townsmen, and admirers as he was in his habits of ingesting food and beverage. In the homes and attics of North Country residents and in near forgotten hiding places and storerooms of far-flung descendants of North Country old-timers or late-nineteenth-century Remington fans are "undiscovered" Remington drawings, sketches, and paintings still awaiting the light of this new day of Remington popularity and collectibility. We know, because we have seen some of these hitherto unseen, unpublished, and unexhibited examples of Remington's art in the homes of our own relatives, friends, and new acquaintances. Even as this book was being edited, Peg Mangum looked with amazement at two "unknown" wash black-and-white Remington paintings, the property of longtime New England residents. The very same afternoon, she talked with the owner of an unlisted Remington oil painting and of a hitherto unlocated Remington bronze.

Fred Remington's large body of work, which includes his journalistic writing and his novel, *John Ermine of the Yellowstone,* was of course the product of his genetic and emotional heritage, as well as of the era in which he and Eva lived. Of the artist's forty-eight hard-lived years, twenty-five were spent recording in ink, oil, and bronze the unsung heroes (Indians, cowhands, soldiers, Mexican peasants) of the vanishing frontier who fought, resisted, dared, and died in the

wild lands of the West. Remington's own life spanned years of tremendous change in the larger life of the American nation. As well as
recording and idealizing history, Remington actively participated in
events that hastened pell-mell through the waning years of the nineteenth century, although his profession often forced him into the
observer's role. Yet, in many ways, he typified his times.

Like so many others, Remington left his native roots in the
Northeast, bitten by the frontier bug. Like so many others, he encountered and experienced the frenetic activity of New York City,
drawn there in his pursuit of success. Like others also, he found that
he needed surcease from his own and from the urban center's intense
stress and rapid pace. With economic means eventually at his disposal, Fred was able to enjoy his island retreat, called Ingleneuk, in
the Thousand Islands region of the River—his beloved St. Lawrence—or in the forested Adirondacks. Finally, he and Eva built their
last home together, which they named Lorul Place, between the two
extremes of city and North Country, in Ridgefield, Connecticut.

Despite his inaccuracies and his personal eccentricities, and beyond whatever critics have made of his professional technique or personal habits, the events and achievements of Remington's life are
worth exploring further. Frederic Remington, who was so little
understood in his own time, exemplifies in his life and artistic development the two faces of creativity: its conflicting, sometimes even
destructive effects upon those who possess it, and, at the same time,
its ability to generate works of art that speak to all of the human
condition.

The following pages record the results of our pursuit of the truth
about this man as we perceive it. We believe that Frederic Remington's art and his adult life will be understood more clearly if placed
against the backdrop of his own family geography and culture—the
North Country. He carried the invisible stamp of this region with
him onto the larger stage upon which his adult life was enacted.
Furthermore, we are convinced that Eva Adele Caten, who became
Fred Remington's wife in 1884, was crucial to his development as an
artist. In addition, in the years of her widowhood, Eva quickly and
intuitively sought the best means to preserve for posterity and to
augment the value of the products of her husband's skills.

We two authors have a personal investment in this chronicle, as
well, because, as father and daughter, we are ourselves of North
Country heritage. Our loyalties are further focused by the fact that

the weekly newspaper founded in 1856 by Frederic Remington's father became our family enterprise in 1873, when our ancestor, Gilbert Burrage Manley, purchased the *St. Lawrence Plaindealer* from Pierre Remington and became its proprietor.

Gilbert's son Williston Manley, Atwood's father, was Fred Remington's contemporary. Like Fred, as a boy, he skylarked with his pals on Canton's Fairground, explored the neighboring fields and woods, learned to swim in the Grasse River, which flows through Canton. As a man, Will Manley, too, loved the forests and lakes of the Adirondacks and fished the waters of the St. Lawrence River. Both men absorbed the strengths and the weaknesses of the culture from which they sprang and both played their roles in the burgeoning, adolescent nation. Once grown, Williston remained in the North Country at the *Plaindealer* and Fred departed to a different and wider arena. But the people and the places and the times that molded them were similar.

We—Atwood Manley and Margaret (Peg) Mangum, Atwood's daughter—have both absorbed the oral and written North Country history and tradition from Williston and his peers. The mantle of editorship of the *St. Lawrence Plaindealer* fell to Atwood. Peg, Atwood claims, grew up on printer's ink at the *Plaindealer* office, serving her writing apprenticeship under grandfather and father. Through the *Plaindealer*'s editorial office came the parade of men and women who returned from the wider world beyond the North Country again and again to regenerate their spirits in the land of their youth, and who paused to share their lives and their adventures with Will and Atwood. And into the *Plaindealer* went items and articles of all they did, and of their comings and goings.

Atwood can remember, as a lad, having his mother identify Remington's portly form skillfully maneuvering a cedar canoe with a double-bladed paddle on the St. Lawrence River. He is probably the only person left who can articulate his memories of the burly artist, or who can weave together the multitude of myths and tales that accrued to that complex man. Upon retirement from publishing the *Plaindealer,* Atwood delved into North Country history, long a hobby, which he was able to indulge thereafter. In 1961, he was asked to write a four-page pamphlet about Frederic S. Remington for Canton's celebration of the centennial of the artist's birth.

What was originally intended as a chronology and biographical sketch of the artist of the Old West emerged as a sizable manuscript. By dint of searching laboriously through old newspaper files and contacting old-timers still alive at that time who remembered Remington, Atwood unearthed a wealth of fact and anecdote. He also was able to authenticate details of the artist's life that had hitherto remained unclear. The results of his research were published in a monograph, which included on its cover a four-color reproduction of the Remington oil painting that Atwood himself had discovered in an old Canton home he had been asked to appraise.

The 1961 Remington monograph reaped a host of intangible returns for Atwood. The booklet found its way into the hands of museum curators and directors, art dealers, Remington buffs, editors of historical and art publications, and writers about Remington and Western art. As a result, Atwood began a vast correspondence that has lasted to this day. Many of the country's leading Remington authorities have found their way to Atwood's den in the Manley home on Judson Street in Canton. His visitors have included people such as Peter Hassrick of the Buffalo Bill Center of Western Art in Cody, Wyoming; Michael Shapiro of the St. Louis Art Museum; Rudolf Wunderlich, then head of New York City's Kennedy Galleries, and now an owner of Chicago's Mongerson-Wunderlich Gallery; Robert Rockwell, whose assiduously collected Remingtons and Russells form the basic collection of Corning, New York's, Rockwell Museum of Western Art. Authors Allen P. and Marilyn D. Splete spent hours with Atwood when they began their own five-year project of collecting Remington's voluminous personal correspondence for publication in *Frederic Remington—Selected Letters.*

Until recently, when age and failing eyesight have restricted his activities but not his enthusiasm or interests, Atwood was often asked to examine sketches and artworks that owners and dealers believed to be products of Remington's talents. He has never considered himself an art authority, but he has gleaned enough through his studies to be consulted by professionals. Since 1961, Atwood has continued his research on Remington and on other North Country men and women whom he admires. At age seventy-six, he published *Rushton and His Times in American Canoeing,* the biography of a Canton canoe builder who gained international renown. In 1986, Atwood's Remington monograph was reprinted as part of the catalog of a New York State Remington exhibition, sponsored by the Adirondack Museum, Blue Mountain Lake, and the Frederic Remington Art Museum, Ogdensburg.

Atwood's files bulge with notes, photographs, manuscript drafts, and carbon copies of numerous letters. Peg has examined additional bits of Remington memorabilia tucked in odd drawers or mounted carefully in scrapbooks. Some items may be of dubious value, but most document a detail in the life of the artist, his family, or his North Country associations that would otherwise have gone unnoticed.

The search for information about Fred Remington has been like a treasure hunt. In addition to the structured and systematic, chance and happenstance, luck and serendipity have played their roles throughout the years of research.

In our numerous stacks of papers are information and anecdotes from varied sources: a copy of Pierre Remington's will, still on record in the St. Lawrence County files; facts long ago discovered for a writing assignment about a meeting of Presbyterians and Congregationalists in New England in the early 1800s that explain the background of North Country religion and education; the transcript of a conversation with friends that revealed how and why Fred Remington's ancestor Christian Sackrider of Philadelphia traveled to Dutchess County, New York; Eva Remington's diary reference to "Teddy and Madeleine Burke" of Hartford, which lends credence to a Spanish-American War story about the artist; old clippings stored in Ogdensburg's Public Library and old books of Fred Remington's in the vault of the Canton Free Library; a pile of papers in the basement of the old Kipp house in Canton; letters unearthed in estates of deceased North Country residents.

Having North Country relationships, past and present, has been a boon to both of us. We have access to people and to sources that other Remington students have not used. Both Fred and Eva Remington left diaries of their last years, for instance, which hold special meaning for this book. In those diaries are numerous terse clues about people or places that make sense only when set in the North Country context. One fascination in preparing our narrative has been the search for these choice, revealing insights into the artist's private life. A nickname or an abbreviation may be meaningless to scholars unfamiliar with North Country history, but they have provided us with information that makes Fred and Eva all the more real and more human. In addition, our knowledge of familial relationships and marriages among Remington's contemporaries has helped us to establish a pattern that was most important to his life. An influential, invisible North Country "network" extended to metropolitan New York and, as such, lends meaning to vague references found in letters, diaries, and articles. We have found clues in other writings about

Remington that have led us to new revelations about important events in the artist's life.

Although the Remingtons moved in more monied, more sophisticated social circles, Eva and Fred were contemporaries of Atwood's parents and of his in-laws. Their shared life-style basically was middle-class, small-town, Victorian. In addition, they shared common attitudes and a similar worldview. Having known these people intimately, as parents and grandparents, we have a wealth of related details and additional insights into a way of life that now is gone.

Both of us have been intrigued by the events that followed the artist's death. To our knowledge, no writers have yet detailed Remington's slide to oblivion after his death, nor the slow rise to a permanent place among the nation's most acclaimed artists. First Eva, and then her sister Emma Caten, took as their mission in life the establishment of Remington as an American artist for all time, and their goal has finally been attained. Atwood's own experiences and friendships, coupled with information made available to us by Caten heirs, have enabled us to add the women's story to the written record.

In a 1986 visit with Atwood, then ninety-three years old, Michael Shapiro, curator of the St. Louis Art Museum and a committee member for the Remington Masterworks Exhibition that opened in 1988, rocked gently in the crowded Manley den while Atwood wove tales of the artist's North Country adventures and contemporaries. In an aside, this Remington scholar said to Peg, "He is as much an expert and a scholar in his chosen field as I am in mine."

The pages that follow are our attempt to provide a slightly different perspective on Frederic Sackrider Remington. We hope that the portrait of the artist that we present will help readers to integrate and appreciate more fully the climate of the culture and of the forces that formed the man and propelled him both in his life and in his work. Perhaps, against this background, viewers of Remington's art will better sense some of the underlying themes common to us all, then and today. For Fred Remington's life and work, and the times in which he lived, were no doubt as contradictory and complex for him and his contemporaries as are those in which each of us is engaged today—or as simple. Here is our account of this great American mythmaker: his great strengths and his great human shortcomings.

FREDERIC REMINGTON
AND
THE NORTH COUNTRY

1

CALAMITY
IN KANSAS CITY

In Kansas City, Missouri, shortly after Christmas 1884, young Frederic Remington, stocky and powerful at twenty-three, with the build of a prizefighter and the soul of an artist, awaited the arrival of his mother by railroad from faraway northern New York State. Only a few days earlier, the chubby little widow who still sought to control her only child's life had notified young Remington of her plan to visit a girlhood friend, Mary Russell, now the wife of Kansas City lawyer Watson J. Ferry. Clara said she wanted to escape the bitter subzero cold of northern New York's winter.

Fred Remington knew better. Clara Sackrider Remington, widow of a Canton, New York, Civil War hero and North Country political leader, Seth Pierpont Remington, was on her way to Kansas City to bring her son back into line. Although Mrs. Remington's face was round and placid, her plump features veiled the set, stubborn tenacity with which she pursued her desires. Fred Remington knew this better than any other living person. Clara had bequeathed both features and obstinate self-will to him.

An efficient and far-reaching North Country network had set his mother's travel plans in motion. The young man should have recognized that word would inevitably filter back to the little village in the isolated St. Lawrence River valley that Frederic Sackrider Remington was teetering on the brink of disaster. Mary Russell Ferry could easily have written something to her lawyer brother, Judge Leslie W.

Russell, in Canton. By now, all the Remingtons and Sackriders, as well as their Canton relatives by marriage, must know that Eva Caten Remington, Fred's bride of three months, had left Kansas City for good shortly before Christmas, and that his fledgling hardware business had failed. Perhaps even the rumor that he was a silent partner in a Kansas City saloon had reached northern New York ears.

Only two years before, young Fred Remington, finally twenty-one and in control of his inheritance, had flaunted his intention to head west to find adventure and quick success like a battle flag before a Canton audience. Less than a year before this expected visit from his mother, on a quick trip back to that St. Lawrence County village, he had assumed the posture of success, announcing to Canton newspaper editor Gilbert Manley the "profitable" sale of his Kansas ranch and declaring his intention to move to bustling Kansas City, to set up in business, and then to take his longtime sweetheart Eva there as his bride.

Now, ten months later, for the first time in his short adult life, Fred Remington was shaken to the core, his happy-go-lucky manner lying in shreds about his ego after the events of the past month. Eva Caten Remington, the diminutive, dark-eyed beauty he had adored since 1879 and married October 1, 1884, had departed bag and baggage for her paternal home in Gloversville, New York, as one revealed calamity after another rudely shattered Fred Remington's shell of careless optimism. The young Remington would have to face his nemesis—embodied in the short, plump person of his own mother—alone. It would be the most important confrontation of his twenty-three years.

After their wedding in Eva's hometown Presbyterian church, Fred and Eva Remington had traveled directly to Kansas City. They spent their honeymoon in the little house Fred had bought for Eva in the Pendleton Heights section. The first weeks were blissful. The young man doted on his slight, wistful-eyed bride. Neighbors, peeking through lace curtains, watched as morning after morning the stocky, blond Fred departed down the front path for work. Eva would follow him to the front gate to kiss her big husband farewell. Sometimes Fred would reach back down over the fence, lift the tiny Eva off her feet and over the four-foot fence, to carry her down the street with him.[1]

They were together, finally, after five years of separation and tragedy. Fred had swept away the obstacles and objections that Lawton Caten, Eva's father, had raised four years before when the rack-

ety youth first formally sought Eva's hand. Fred was no longer a
callow would-be artist. He had reached legal majority, left his two
guardian uncles behind, obtained his paternal inheritance, and was—
according to his own glowing reports—succeeding rapidly in business in the West. Even Eva, who knew that Fred's only real ambition
was to become an artist, believed him. Quick financial success first,
he had persuaded her, then he would pursue his artistic grail. On the
surface, all seemed at first to be as her new husband had explained.

The honeymoon came to an abrupt end only eight weeks after
the wedding. Aspiring artist Frederic Remington persuaded a not
very reluctant Eva to model for a painting. Still enveloped in an iri-
descent bubble of romance, Remington posed his adored and ador-
ing model and set to work. Eva, who was convinced of her husband's
talent, followed his instructions patiently, waiting in happy anticipation for her first view of her portrait. When Fred finally threw down
his brushes and led her around the big easel to see his work, she was
speechless.

Eva expected to see a traditional portrait of herself like those
that hung in homes in Gloversville and Canton. Perhaps she had
remembered the painting of Fred's grandmother, Mary Sackrider, that
hung in the parlor of the Sackriders' Miner Street home in the little
North Country village where her young husband had grown up. That
picture of Mary showed a winsome and still youthful matron, wearing a pink satin gown, with her face crowned by chestnut hair. Eva
knew that Fred had painted in the same traditional, nineteenth-century
style when he had transformed his grandfather Sackrider's likeness
onto canvas, so that he seemed to have breathed life into his painting
of the old man.

Now, for the first time, she was face to face with the way her
new husband saw life and intended to immortalize it through his
brushes and pigment. Instead of being the subject of his painting,
she was merely a vehicle by and through which he could paint what
gained reality in his imagination. She had hoped and expected to see
at least a likeness of her own dark-eyed, creamy-skinned countenance
with its crown of shining dark hair. As she posed, she had imagined,
even, that an idealized version of her own attractive self was being
born. Instead, she was confronted by a watercolor of an unidealized
desert-dwelling Mexican woman.

After the first long moment of dead silence, instead of offering
the encouraging critiques Fred was used to, the erstwhile supportive,
loving, and ladylike Eva blew up. The fragile bubble of romance

burst irrevocably before her anger as she told her young artist husband exactly what she thought. Fred was appalled. At twenty-three, he was new to the intricacies of feminine vanity, blithely unaware of the hidden veins of fire and iron in his bride's character. He could not believe that Eva, the only person who saw him as the artist he wanted to become, would react so violently to his work. He had expected encouraging, objective criticism but, instead, the sight of the painting had transformed her into a Fury. Fred Remington was so shattered that only months later was he able to confide to his best friends in Kansas City, Franklin and Nellie Hough, that his painting of Eva had almost cost him his "Missie."[2] In the following twenty-five years as a painter, Frederic Remington never again attempted seriously to portray a woman on canvas.

Until that moment in their little Pendleton Heights home, only Eva, of all the relatives and friends of Remington's youth, had really recognized the artistic demon that hovered beneath young Fred's jolly, headstrong exterior. No one from his North Country past ever took Fred Remington's artistic ambitions seriously. They saw only a hedonistic young giant who thought the world was his oyster and whose whirlwind energies swept him heedlessly in first one direction and then another.

In New York State's austere North Country villages, where physical survival still played a dominant role, painting and painters were held in low esteem. Itinerant artists did wander into Canton or Ogdensburg occasionally in the nineteenth century, rendering portraits in return for room, board, and a small fee. One such anonymous and talented vagabond had painted Fred's grandmother, a younger Mary Hutchins Sackrider.

For most people in that still sparsely settled region, life retained a pioneer, even puritanical spirit that allowed only a few the leisure or motivation to dabble in the arts. Of these few, most of the women turned to creative needlework or inventive quilting. Fred's own mother, Clara Remington, whose impending arrival he now awaited, was among these. Of North Country male artists, amateur or professional, Canton had produced only two by 1884. Both were contemporaries of Fred Remington's now deceased father, Pierre. Canton Village accepted Henry DeValcourt Kipp's hobby of painting with tolerant skepticism; after all, Kipp was gainfully employed as Canton's main coffin builder and part-time cabinetmaker. The other, Salathiel Ellis, had long since disappeared from the North Country to find his place in a wider world, first as a cameo cutter, later as creator of U.S. Mint medallions and coins.

In Canton, in the 1860s and 1870s the Sackriders, the Remingtons and their neighbors had watched with fond amusement the rambunctious child, Freddie Remington, sketch horses. As the years went by, few, if any, in Canton or Ogdensburg (where his family later moved) took Fred's knack for drawing seriously. Neither, in fact, did the young Remington. At first, the boy set his sights on West Point, hoping to emulate the military exploits of the father he worshipped as a hero. In his teenage years, Fred switched his career plans to journalism and politics, still influenced by his father, Pierre Remington, who, after the Civil War's end, had gained regional acclaim as a newspaper publisher and influential state Republican political force. Fred's young uncle, "Mart" Remington, had become a journalist in the state capital at Albany. Both father and uncle urged Frederic, the Remington heir-apparent, to follow in their professional footsteps. In their minds, and in those of North Country manhood, becoming an artist spelled both financial and personal ruin. Because the idea of having an artist in the family was unthinkable, neither relatives nor hometown neighbors gave serious thought to young Fred's artistic ambitions, even when he applied to and attended Yale University's Art School.

Only Eva Adele Caten, whom Fred met and loved on sight in 1879, sensed his ever present, ever growing need to draw and to paint. But even her steady encouragement could not help nineteen-year-old Fred when he was thrust out into life prematurely, in 1880, at his father's death. For two frustrating years, the up-to-then overindulged and still immature youth subjugated his bursting energies to the family will, working in clerking jobs in the state government, but chafing for the time when he would reach legal age and could claim his inheritance and his freedom. While rebellion festered, however, young Frederic Remington kept drawing, sending sketches off to popular publications, hoping unsuccessfully at that time for acceptance.[3]

Family and North Country culture set Fred Remington's priorities, helped in part by his own desires for quick and easy affluence and a sumptuous life. First he would make his fortune; then he would draw and paint. All that was necessary was for the youth to obtain the capital with which to launch the ventures generated by his fertile mind. That capital became available when, at twenty-one, he received the modest inheritance left him in his father's will. In February 1883, four months after his twenty-first birthday, he quit the desk job he hated in Albany. By March 1883, Frederic Sackrider Remington owned a sheep ranch in Peabody, Butler County, Kansas. By summer, he was writing home for more money.

The frontier and the West awakened an elemental vein of sympathy deep within Frederic Remington, its unrecognized source in part his own North Country heritage. After all, civilization had barely touched the virgin forests of the Adirondacks and the silent power of the mighty St. Lawrence River. In the clusters of villages perched near a virtual wilderness region, he had spent his childhood, unconsciously nurtured and influenced by the forces of nature. In Kansas City, at the edge of the frontier, he was at the gateway to great reaches of primal grandeur stretching to the sunset, wild lands that drew him like a magnet. As yet the young man was unaware that these were the forces he would later struggle to reproduce on canvas. Instead, because he was a brash, opinionated, overindulged, rebellious, romantic young man, Fred Remington persuaded himself that he was at the frontier for financial success. Until December 1884, he looked on his father's bequest of $13,000[4] (a considerable sum in those days) as his open sesame and a never-ending stream of financial security.

Fred Remington had deluded himself. His gifted tongue had persuaded only those in faraway Canton. Eva Remington's anger, roused by his painting of her, ripped away the façade with which the bumptious young Fred Remington had heretofore faced the world and had screened himself from reality. The truth came out, as Eva, stimulated now by her righteous indignation, began to question him about everything. In actual fact, Fred had failed three times at earning his living in less than two years. As a rancher, he had been ignorant and irresponsible and he recovered only part of his initial investment there. He had fled Butler County and rural life after he and other young men had disrupted a public gathering by shooting spitballs at a baldheaded performer. The immature prank had had legal consequences, when he and fellow mischief-makers were hauled before a magistrate.

His Kansas City success was a house of cards, too. By December 1884, the eight-month-old firm of Ashley and Remington, dealers in bar and sheet iron, was a fiction. Charlie Ashley had departed for parts unknown and Fred, rather than going off to business on Sixth Street each day, was, instead, frequenting Bishop & Christie's to play pool and to help persuade customers to spend their money in that popular saloon. For Fred Remington had carried out the intention to put his money "in hardware and whiskey" that he had confided in a letter at the end of 1883.[5] His hardware business never got off the ground and he had sunk what remained of his inheritance, after starting the hardware firm, into Bishop & Christie's as a silent partner, with no real guarantee of return. Even the little Pendleton Heights house was his only on paper.

How Eva Caten Remington received all that her husband revealed in the hours after he unveiled his apparently shocking "portrait" of his young wife, no one but Fred ever learned for sure. Roused as she was to anger and disillusion, Eva may possibly have packed her bags and left Kansas City, threatening to have nothing more to do with Fred unless he straightened out his life. This act, however, was inconsistent with her character in the light of her later continuous support and nurture of her artist husband.

More likely, the moment of truth that the young couple shared brought into the open Eva's own disappointments and difficulties in adjusting to life in the semifrontier town so unlike anything she had ever known and certainly never had expected from Fred's former glowing reports. Years after Remington's death, Harriet Ferry Appleton, whose mother was Mary Russell Ferry and who was ten years old that year, commented that Eva must have been homesick for the tree-lined streets of the settled old northeastern villages. Kansas City, Harriet remarked, was new and raw in 1884.[6] Their friend, Nellie Hough, who was a key observer in the events of Fred and Eva Remington's life that winter, felt that Eva was never really happy in Kansas City.[7]

Both Fred and Eva, as products of their own time and place, had married "for better or for worse," and through their wedding vows affirmed the religious and cultural expectations of lifelong commitment. When the heat of Eva's rage and Fred's despair over the humiliating truth of his financial condition were past, it is much more consistent with Eva's practical character and with the dependency on Eva revealed by the whole of Fred's later life that the two should have worked through a plan for the future together, before she left town.

Eva, by her own standards, was no saint. She loved the good life and expected her husband to become its provider. Yet her code also excluded self-pity and complaint. She was gentle and at the same time firm.[8] The eldest of the five Lawton Caten offspring, she had assumed the maternal role for her younger brothers and sisters when

Flora Caten died in 1880. Beneath Victorian surface behavior and values was a pragmatic young woman who looked out at life through her wistful brown eyes with lively interest. She was neither moody nor domineering, and for the most part moved serenely and surely along the paths that life opened to her. Eva was, in fact, the antithesis of Clara Remington, whose visit to Kansas City she had left Fred to face alone.

Until his mother's arrival, Fred Remington, all evidence to the contrary, clung to the hope that he could magically recoup the inheritance that had slipped through his fingers. Eva, practical beneath her femininity, knew better. Her husband, Frederic Remington, the business entrepreneur, did not exist. Frederic Remington, the overindulged and underloved son of his mother, Eva rejected. In Frederic Remington, the artist-to-be, Eva still firmly believed, and for him she packed her trunks and returned to the quiet village in central New York where she had waited for Fred the five previous years and now prepared to wait again.

Eva's departure just before Christmas signaled to watching Kansas City that the affairs of Frederic Remington had reached a crisis. Eva left, Nellie Hough later recorded, because of the young couple's plan that would allow Remington to reorganize his financial resources.[9] In all probability, Eva's departure for her father's home was the first step in the program the two had evolved. Fred, still hoping for financial return from his silent partnership in the saloon, remained in Kansas City to dispose of their house, to build his portfolio of sketches and paintings, and to retrieve what he could from his disastrous investments.

Although Nellie Hough's statement did not spell out details, she probably knew better than most of Kansas City what was happening in the young Remingtons' lives. She was in a special position to watch the stormy events that whirled about Fred Remington in those raw winter months. Her recollections form one of the few written records we have of this vital turning point in Frederic Remington's life.

Frank and Nellie Hough, who were older than Fred Remington, were already established in the busy young city's middle class. Frank Hough, a banker, had ushered Frederic Remington up the front steps of his house soon after Fred took up residence in a Kansas City boardinghouse in April 1884. Watching their arrival, Nellie Hough had marveled at the sense of power and energy that the stocky blond man beside her husband emanated.[10] The friendship grew. Fred showed his sketches to the couple and soon asked Frank to model for some of his drawings. Nellie, it is obvious from her reminiscences, did not take to Eva as warmly as she did to Fred. Perhaps Eva's eastern ways placed Nellie on the defensive.

After Eva's departure before Christmas 1884, the depressed young husband visited the Houghs more and more often for friendship and support. Early in the New Year, when the Pendleton Heights house was gone, he moved his remaining possessions to the kindhearted Houghs and lived there for the months he remained in Kansas City. Before he finally departed, he gave Nellie and Frank Hough six paintings in gratitude for their kindness and friendship.[11] One of the paintings was the calamitous watercolor for which Eva had modeled. He had named it *Gracias, Senorita, May the Apaches Never Get You.*

The future artist of the Old West did not recognize one other group of Kansas City supporters at the time. Instead, he had at first placed the Ferry family among the forces with which he must contend: allies of his domineering mother and proponents of the conservative North Country philosophy he had hoped to escape.

Mary Ferry had remained quietly in the background during Fred Remington's stay in Kansas City. She and her husband were in their fifties. Watson Ferry was a law partner of Mary's brother-in-law, Wallace Pratt, another North Country man, who had married Mary's older sister, Adeline. The Ferry's son Wallace was nearly Fred's age and little Harriet was ten in 1884. The Ferry family returned to Canton periodically to visit relatives and friends, among them the Sackriders. Mary's parents, John Leslie and Mary Wead Russell, had brought up three daughters and a son in Canton's Presbyterian church, where Fred's grandfather Sackrider was an elder. On visits home to Canton, Mary had often visited the Sackrider home and had watched young Frederic Remington grow up.

When Eva arrived in Kansas City, the Ferry family had come to the little house in Pendleton Heights to welcome Fred's bride. They looked long and carefully at the paintings and sketches Frederic displayed and listened attentively as the bridal couple explained that Fred was sending his work to the famous publishing house of Harper Brothers in New York. At least two drawings, the Remingtons explained, had been accepted, although these were redrawn by staff artists (and neither was credited to him by name when published).

Perhaps the most loyal Ferry family supporter of hulking, blond Fred Remington was the little girl, "Birdie," as Harriet Russell Ferry was nicknamed. Visiting the young Remingtons in their tiny house, Birdie stood quietly at her mother's side, her eyes wide with wonder and fascination at the drawings she saw. An obedient child of that strict era when children were seen and not heard, Harriet Ferry stored her impressions in a quick, retentive memory. (And she recalled these memories of the handsome young giant, the dainty and lovely young wife, and the vital and even disturbing action in the drawings years later in letters written in response to the queries of Remington scholar Dr. Robert Taft.)

Whether the initiative for Clara Remington to visit Kansas City originated with Fred's mother herself or with Mary Ferry was never recorded. Mary, who was the daughter, sister, and wife of lawyers, was certainly discreet, and her daughter Harriet's later memories of those 1884 events reveal her parent as a thoughtful, objective woman.[12] In the light of what occurred when Fred and his mother confronted each other, it is much more likely that Clara Remington herself suggested the visit to the Ferry family.

After Eva was gone from Kansas City and Fred's mother Clara had arrived to visit, the little girl kept listening. Although Fred Remington, who never related well to children, hardly noticed her at the time, Harriet never forgot him. She was entranced by the young man's robust presence, "his gaiety and agreeableness."[13] Harriet Ferry's life continued to meet and mingle periodically with Frederic and Eva Remington's, both in Canton and in New York City, where the fates would send both her and the Remingtons.

Kansas City art dealer William W. Findlay was as important to Remington the artist as were the Houghs and the Ferrys. Fred bought his art supplies at kindly William Findlay's store. As his funds dwindled, Fred lugged three of his paintings to show the art dealer, who liked them so well that he took them on commission. Years later Findlay's son, Waldstein, recalled that the art dealer sold the paintings for $150. "Later a man came in and offered $100 to Remington to duplicate one of the three," Waldstein Findlay remembered. "Father told him, 'You've got your start now. Don't duplicate anything. Keep conceiving new pictures.'"[14]

Neither Kansas City nor his friends nor his paintings impressed Fred Remington's mother, Clara. She saw nothing good in the raw, busy frontier city where East and West met in a network of steel railroad lines, where plodding wagonloads of settlers set out to homestead prairie farms, and to which cowboys, on the spirited western ponies Fred Remington so loved to draw, went to carouse after long cattle drives. Clara Sackrider Remington had gone to the frontier to rescue her foolhardy, rascally child and to bear him home to Canton as a prodigal son. Chubby little Clara Remington had the will of a Titan.

Ten-year-old Harriet Ferry, playing in the parlor of the red house on Broadway, kept still as a mouse to hear the adult conversations going on above her bent head. Her parents and Uncle Wallace reasoned with Mary's guest that losing his money might do Fred Remington good. It could help to further the young man's artistic career, they believed, for the Ferrys had become persuaded of Fred's talent.[15] But Frederic Remington's mother had not traveled to Kansas City to be rational. The idea of her son as an artist was unthinkable. Clara, moreover, was irate that her child had squandered his fortune, risked his reputation and his good family name, even his wife—but most important, his financial inheritance.

Reason fell on the deaf ears of stubborn resolve. Clara was convinced that once she could talk with her son he would be persuaded by maternal wisdom. That meeting took place in Nellie Hough's parlor, which Clara viewed with sniffs of disdain and remarks about the crudities of life on the frontier. (Years later Clara told the *Carthage* [N.Y.] *Evening Press* in an interview that she objected to Kansas City "because it was not a western custom at the time to wash dishes and keep otherwise clean."[16]) Nellie Hough, who had opened her home to the mother of her husband's friend, bristled in silent indignation. The confrontation between mother and son did not progress as Clara intended. Nellie, who was present, later wrote, "She pleaded with him to give up his foolishness and take 'a real man's job.' She did not have one word of encouragement for his art studies, but made every inducement in a business way."[17]

To his mother's surprise, Frederic Remington did not yield. Nor did he erupt into a rage, as he usually had in the past when Clara's iron will confronted his own less mature obstinacy. This time "he turned a deaf ear to all her pleading," Nellie wrote,[18] and Clara Remington discovered that some new quality and resolve had infused her son. None of her ploys, so successful in bygone years, aroused the responses they had evoked in Fred's boyhood. For the first time in his life, Fred Remington, who had always come round to her way of thinking, who had always loved and admired her, and who had always given in after childhood tears or adolescent rages were vented, had become a stranger.

A defeated Clara Remington returned to her northern New York village home, baffled, angry, and as obdurate as ever. She left behind the son who had failed in three business enterprises in less than two years, whose wife appeared to have deserted him, and who now was off on an even more "destructive" course of painting pictures. Fred Remington's mother also left behind a man standing firmly on his own resolve for the first time in his life. Never again would Clara Remington feel the close affection of the child she had cradled and smothered with attention during the lonely years of the Civil War. The bond between mother and son was as dead as was his father, the man who had been a loyal yet distant husband to this frustrated, lonely, and unhappy woman.

The effort to sever the emotional apron strings that had bound him to his mother used up every ounce of Frederic Remington's own will. He dallied in Kansas City throughout that spring of 1885, living with Frank and Nellie Hough, using Frank as a model for his sketches, waiting—so he claimed—for his refund from the now relocated Bishop & Christie saloon.[19] Some days he hired a horse to ride out onto the prairie to the west of the city to sketch. At other times, he dropped in on Al Hatch, who ran a disreputable establishment at the edge of town that would today be called a "roadhouse," for a round or two of boxing. Although he was a skilled fighter, Al Hatch was hard put to protect himself from Fred Remington's bull-like strength. In an interview after Remington achieved fame as an artist, Hatch said that Remington could have succeeded as a prizefighter if he had chosen that route instead of painting. Describing Fred's prowess, Al Hatch said, "he was not a bully, mind you, but a nervy kid with bull strength. I stayed sorry two weeks because I put the gloves on with him once."[20]

Except for his boxing bouts and his sketching, Remington seems to have existed in a state of dreamy paralysis during the spring of 1885. By early summer, all hopes for regaining even a portion of his lost inheritance were gone. In its new quarters Bishop & Christie's listed a new third partner. When Fred went around for his dividends in early 1886 there were none. "That made a great change in him," Waldstein Findlay recalled in 1911, "realizing that he was dependent on himself."[21] What happened from now on would be the result of his own struggles. His old, careless self-confidence had temporarily vanished, along with dreams of easy success. He had only his own goals for his art, his faraway wife's belief in his abilities, and the tremendous fund of energy that would fuel his talents in the years ahead. But he still had to find the means to rebuild his shattered reputation, discover a way to establish himself as an artist, and provide Eva with a decent life.

One answer to Remington's dilemma lay back East, either in the North Country homeland to which he could return or in the rapidly expanding city of New York, where the country's publishing empires were. Another possible answer lay farther west, where the final days of conquest of the frontier still were being played out by settlers, cowboys, the military, and the native Indian tribes. In early summer, Fred Remington suddenly and impulsively made his decision.

> He was standing on the corner of 9th and Main streets, which, about that time, was beginning to be the center of town, when Shorty Reason—a house painter—drove along in a spring wagon behind a little fleabitten gray mare, a tough animal.
>
> "Wait a minute, Shorty," called Remington. "Do you want to sell that mare?"
>
> "Nope," replied Shorty, being wise in the ways of horse trading.
>
> "Is she good in the saddle?" asked Remington.
>
> "Try her," said Shorty. So right in the center of town Remington and Shorty together unhitched the mare from the wagon, borrowed a saddle and Remington tried her.
>
> Shorty fixed the price at $50 and the next morning Remington rode, companionless, . . . out of the life of Kansas City.[22]

He carried with him onto the western plains a pack containing a minimum of clothing and as many sketchbooks and paints as he could cram into his kit.

Unlikely as it seemed, he was now on his way to success as an illustrator/artist and was unknowingly initiating the pattern he would follow for the rest of his life. In the next few months, he would travel through frontier lands, sketching and recording in his photographic mind the materials that he would transform by his talent and imagination into illustrations that soon would be in demand in popular eastern periodicals. In the East, Eva waited for him, as she would wait throughout the years ahead for his return from his western trips. And in the North Country remained the people and the places to which he would return in the future as faithfully as to his wife.

From that time on, Remington would live out his life in those three widely separate worlds—the West, where his adventurous dreams could be transmitted onto paper by pen and paintbrush; the commercial and publishing center of New York City, which would provide a livelihood; and the North Country of his youthful memories, where his great gifts originally were generated and thenceforth were periodically renewed. For Frederic Remington in the Far West rediscovered the vital influences of his North Country heritage. Again and again in later life, he returned to the Woods and the River (the Adirondack Mountains and the St. Lawrence River) of his homeland, where he found the inner harmony that eluded him in every other setting. Although his rejection of maternal domination was final, North Country relatives and friends remained the primary relationships of the artist's life, and this included Eva, whose roots were similar to his.

Somehow the New York City world, and even his fascination with the frontier life into which he rode now from Kansas City, could not nurture or sustain the man's inner needs. Certainly, almost none of the people in these other settings understood the person who hid behind his jovial and ever increasing physical bulk. Even in New York City, the adult Remington's closest intimates, with one or two exceptions, were men and women whose roots lay in the North Country and who had known him throughout childhood and adolescence.

Fred Remington soon recognized that he would, after all, always be deeply tied to that isolated postpioneer region in northern New York State. His own tremendous energies and drives may have been inherited, but his adult role models were men who grasped hatever opportunities the North Country's stern culture and harsh climate afforded and from them carved success. From those men and from those patient, sustaining North Country women, endlessly busy with households and families, Remington formed his own ideals of excellence.

2

EARLY CHILDHOOD: "I ALWAYS LIKED HORSES"

« 1861–1869 »

Frederic Sackrider Remington was born on October 4, 1861, nine months after his mother and father, Clarissa Bascomb Sackrider and Seth Pierpont Remington, were married. When her son was born, blond, round-faced Clara was almost twenty-five and slender, dark-eyed Pierre, as he was called to distinguish him from his Universalist clergyman father Seth W. Remington, was almost twenty-eight. Their baby boy was born in the white clapboard Remington house on Court Street in Canton, where the newlyweds lived with the groom's family.

A month and a half later, Pierre (pronounced "Peer" in the North Country) Remington—newspaper publisher, ardent Republican, and fiery patriot—sold his weekly newspaper to his foreman, Joseph Van Slyke, and enlisted in the newly formed cavalry regiment known as "Scott's 900,"* for which he had stormed the North Country to en-list recruits in the Union cause. Two months after their son's birth, Clara bade her husband farewell at Canton's new railroad depot as the steam locomotive spit cinders onto the December snowfall that shrouded Canton. Then, as the "cars" took Pierre south to Staten Island and a staff position as major in the new regiment, the young woman packed up belongings and baby and returned to her parent-

---

*Scott's 900 was named for Assistant Secretary of the Army Thomas Scott. The "900" referred to its irregular number of men (one hundred in each of nine companies, instead of the usual ten).

al home on Miner Street to wait out the long, uncertain months of war.

No one knows what precipitated Clara's move back to Deacon Henry and Mary Sackrider's comfortable house. Chances are that Clara, who became a strong-willed, stubborn woman whose ambitions encompassed her husband, her child, and her social position, had locked horns with her mother-in-law. Maria Pickering Remington was strong-minded and dominating, too, and was known to have a temper. Clara's father-in-law, the Reverend Seth Williston Remington, was seldom home. He traveled throughout New York State as a fund-raising agent for the new Universalist-sponsored St. Lawrence University, whose redbrick building stood on a hill at the southern edge of Canton. In addition to newlyweds Clara and Pierre, the household also contained Pierre's twenty-two-year-old brother, W. R. (William Reese) or Bill, who already was proprietor of a little stationery store, as well as young Mart and Josie (Lamartine Zetto and Josephine), fourteen and twelve, respectively. (Pierre's elder sister Maria had married at age sixteen and lived in Geneva; older brother Chauncey, an invalid, lived with relatives far downstate in the hamlet of Smith's Mills.)

Life with the Remingtons could not have been easy for a new bride with a character like Clara's. Although Canton was a cosy, interdependent community in the mid-nineteenth century, with liberal Universalists living jaw to jaw with Bible-thumping Presbyterians, unexpected differences in Remington and Sackrider philosophies and styles demanded major adjustments for the new Mrs. Remington. Despite being raised in the stern Calvinistic ethic of her Presbyterian parents, Clara had left a home of warmth and nurture. She found herself among a hardworking, business-minded group who, for the most part, lacked humor.[1] Mild Reverend Seth Williston may have preached the universal fatherhood of God and brotherhood of all humankind during the two years he spent behind Canton's Universalist Church "desk" when he first brought his family to Canton in 1854, but at home forceful Maria ruled supreme.

Maria Remington owned the Court Street house, an unusual circumstance for a woman in those days, but she came from a New England tradition that allowed women to assume leadership in a Victorian society that demanded wives to dwell in their spouses' shadows. Her own aunt had been a renowned Quaker preacher, and the Universalist movement, in which her uncle David Pickering was a well-known minister, advocated the education of women.

As time proved, Seth and Maria Remington were not a congenial couple and most of the family seems to have lived by reason and will rather than by the heart. Clara's own serious and ambitious husband, Pierre, was preoccupied with his weekly newspaper, the *St. Lawrence Plaindealer*; politics; and recruitment of volunteers for Lincoln's Army of the Republic, which he himself now had joined. Of the entire "tribe of Remington," as Fred Remington later referred to that branch of his family, in those days only young Mart exhibited wit and imagination.*

In returning to her own family, Clara could not have expected a less crowded household than she had experienced during her first year of marriage. Both Sackrider and Remington families—as was customary in that day—contained multiple members, no matter what their age or status. Like W. R. Remington, Clara's bachelor brother Horace Sackrider, who was Pierre's age and a partner in the Sackrider hardware business, lived at home. The rest of the Sackrider household included fourteen-year-old Rob, Clara's younger brother, and her maternal grandparents, Roswell and Sally Hutchins, who spent part of their time with the Sackriders and part with their other daughter, Sarah Hodskin, whose husband, Barzillai, was a prominent Canton businessman.

Clara Remington may have wanted to return home in part because her own parents, Henry and Mary Sackrider, were grieving. In 1860, during Clara's own courtship with Pierre, Mary, then forty-five, had given birth to an infant girl, Frances. Baby Fanny died before Clara's own child was born, and Clara may have hoped that her own robust son could help fill the chasm left by her baby sister's death. Probably her own frustrations with the Remington household, however, were as important as her parents' needs, for Clara's own desires remained paramount to her throughout her life.

At the Sackriders' Miner Street home, Henry Lewis Sackrider was the acknowledged head of the household, supported and seconded by his wife, Mary, a gentle and caring woman. Deacon Sackrider, as respectful fellow townsmen called him, appears to have been bequeathed the religious zeal and dedication of a remote European ancestor, a Protestant clergyman in Alsace. Henry's deep love of his

---

*According to Irving Bacheller in his *From Stores of Memory,* young Mart was imaginative, brilliant, and witty. As a lad, he wrote a humorous satirical poem, now lost, about a local political situation, the memory of which Bacheller treasured all his life. Mart put his writing talents to work first on his brother Pierre's newspaper and later as a journalist in the state capital at Albany.

Savior and God permeated every aspect of his life. The Sackriders were not intellectual, finding their intangible needs met through their religious faith and practice within family and church. Strict Calvinistic tenets of that day did not burden Deacon Henry and Mary. Instead, they found their faith a source of joy and strength that carried them through their lives.

Only a block east up Main Street in the Presbyterian Church where he was an elder, Henry looked after the common spiritual welfare. On lower Main Street and a stone's throw from home, at Sackrider & Sons, the family hardware business, Henry cared for his fellows' material and social needs. Sackrider & Sons became an informal social center for Canton menfolk. Irving Bacheller remembered it as a genial gathering place where small boys could hear "many a good story and much hearty laughter" from the bewhiskered men who gathered around the wood stove in the center of the store. For "there were miles of whiskers in those days and nowhere was the head of a Yankee more fertile inside and out."[2]

The big house to which Clara brought the infant Frederic Remington rose two stories high, with a big attic and a deep dug basement, where Mary kept root vegetables in winter. In Canton homes, built as airtight as skilled carpentry could devise, fireplaces were being replaced with iron stoves. Like many other Canton homes, the Sackrider place had an entrance hall, off which were the front parlor and the back parlor (sitting room), with the dining room opening on the opposite side of the hall. Most dining rooms were separated from the kitchen quarters by a pantry with built-in cupboards, where china, glassware, and cutlery were stored. Upstairs bedrooms were unheated, unless a stovepipe happened to rise through a room from the first floor. It was customary for the eldest household members to have the bedroom above the family kitchen, where painful rheumatic bones could be soothed by heat rising from the wood range on which family meals were cooked. In the long winter months of northern New York, the kitchen, where a pump graced the wooden sink, was the center of family life.

The Sackrider house, in common with other Canton homes, had a front veranda, from which a path led to the street. Between the village footpath and the hard-packed dirt street, Mary and Henry had planted American elms, as well as sugar maples that they tapped in spring for their sweet sap. Behind the house stood a small barn where Freddie Remington played as a little boy and romped with his pals on later visits from Ogdensburg (where his parents moved in 1872).

Well-to-do Cantonians had their own horse, cow, and chickens. In mild weather, cows were driven to pasture in meadows outside the village. Near the barn, tucked away unobtrusively, was the family outhouse.

Although no photographs of Frederic Remington as a baby have been preserved, he must have been a sturdy infant, because he avoided or survived early childhood illnesses that swept away many nine-teenth-century infants, including his own aunt. Undoubtedly, his early months were like those of every baby, cuddled and coddled by his mother and grandmother, fed and burped, bathed and diapered, swaddled tightly in the "binders" and other voluminous wrappings used on babies of that era. He grew rapidly into an obstreperous, round-faced youngster, the indulged only child in a household of adults. A half-mile away on Court Street were his equally fond Rem-ington relatives, who, although not as demonstrative as the genial Sackriders, nevertheless doted on the child of absent Major Pierre. The little boy had a surfeit of attention from relatives and from a mother who apparently began early on to plan for his future success and affluence.

As he grew into a toddler, young Frederic Remington was roughhoused and teased by his uncle Robert Sackrider, a lad only fourteen years his senior. As a young adult, the artist Remington still jokingly addressed letters to "Unkie Yob," who remained the artist's favorite uncle. Clara's older brother, Horace, who married in 1863 and who became one of Fred's guardians when Pierre Remington died, dropped in often at his parents' on his way to or from the hardware store.

Little Fred Remington soon learned that Grandfather Henry Sackrider, known to his sons and later to his grandsons as "the Gov-ernor," was in charge of the household's economic and spiritual wel-fare. Grandmother Sackrider took care of the kitchen, household health, and family hygiene, but Deacon Henry made sure that his religion was the focus of family life. The Sackrider family Bible had the place of honor on the parlor table. In it, Henry or Mary conscientiously recorded births, marriages, and deaths.* Daily family prayers were part of the routine in homes like that of the Sackriders.

Family members were expected to attend midweek prayer ser-

---

*Atwood found the exact date of Frederic Remington's birth in the Sackrider Bible, correcting an error that had long been accepted as truth. Another page contains the aging Deacon's message to his family, written shortly before his death in a shaky hand and commending his "dear children" to his lifelong faith.

vices at the Presbyterian Church, as well as the two Sunday worship services and Sunday school (a nineteenth-century addition to American Protestantism), which filled most of the Lord's Day. Parents in those days expected as much of their children as they did of themselves in the practice of religion. Little Fred Remington was taken to church regularly, first as an infant in his mother's arms, then to sit and squirm through the long services on the hard Sackrider pew beside Clara and his grandparents while the stentorian tones of the Presbyterian dominie resounded above the boy's blond head.

Life in the Sackrider home and in Canton itself was, however, anything but bleak for a little boy. The Deacon was a happy man, and Mary, busy about her eternal household tasks, radiated comfort and love. Some of his grandfather's happy nature rubbed off on the first grandson, for Fred Remington became an optimistic, buoyant youth who expected life to bring him good fortune and good fun. Fred was full of mischief and his pranks often plunged him into trouble, but, no matter what the consequences, Fred took his punishment in good spirit. Even as a man, in the company of cousins and former schoolmates, Fred could not resist a practical joke.

During his first four years, little Fred Remington could peer from almost every window of his grandparents' house out on the wonderful and secure world of that isolated, bustling postpioneer village. Still semiraw from its recent frontier days, Canton was tiny (a population of fifteen hundred) but proud and self-sufficient. It boasted an ashery, a sawmill, a foundry, a smithie, box and carding factories, flour and feed mills, plus two prospering new manufacturing concerns: Levi Storr's recently invented steam clothes-pressing device and David M. Jones's new St. Lawrence Box Stove. These small industries, and the new Watertown-Potsdam railroad line, had brought on a local business boom. Canton's only other claims to fame were its position as the St. Lawrence County seat and the new coeducational St. Lawrence University.

The Sackrider house stood just off Canton's main thoroughfare, called "the Street" by Cantonians and Main Street by the uninitiated, and one block east up the hill that rises from the Grasse River. Over a covered bridge that spanned the Grasse just above the dammed rapids rattled what traffic there was en route to or from Ogdensburg sixteen miles distant, or Potsdam to the east, or south to De Kalb, Gouverneur, and more distant points on the road that forked off from Main Street west of the bridge.

Barzillai Hodskin's cows still grazed in his meadow behind homes and small stores located on the north side of the Street. "Bar-*ZILL*-ey," as his name was locally pronounced, was little Fred's great-uncle by marriage, an enthusiastic entrepreneur who owned the prosperous, newly enlarged, big brick Hodskin House, which the child, who looked from the Sackrider parlor window, could see down by the covered bridge. Across from that hotel, Water Street stretched north beside the Grasse, providing access to Canton's busy little industries, surely an intriguing byway to the curious child. On lower Main Street's north side stood the Union Block of businesses and stores. The office of the *St. Lawrence Plaindealer,* the weekly newspaper Fred's own father had founded (as his proud mother repeatedly told him), was located there on the second floor.

Around the corner up Main Street stood Canton's second oldest house, where Dr. Daniel Campbell had held the very first village dance early in the 1820s, when his two daughters were young. Mary Sackrider and his mother often took the sturdy, kilted, long-haired little boy there to see Mary Sackrider's friend, old Eliza Campbell Miner, who still lived in her family home with her husband Ebenezer and her youngest daughter, Mary. Eliza was famous for original needlework designs, and in the parlor hung her oil painting of Canton's county fair, which Ebenezer had helped to found. Young Mary, or Minnie as she was known, was still in her teens, but Clara told Fred to call her Aunt Minnie, and Aunt Minnie she remained to Fred and much of Canton all her long life.

Peeking from that Main Street house while the ladies visited, or from his grandparents' windows, Freddie Remington could feast his eyes on a village full of horses. In the 1860s, the North Country lived in the age of the horse, the only local transportation available except one's own sturdy legs. Down the Street plodded teams of heavy workhorses, dragging wagons or sledges heavy with grain or piled high with logs for the gristmill and sawmill on Water Street. Up the Street from the covered bridge trotted horses pulling rattling buggies. Lawyers on horseback urged their sleek steeds toward the county buildings on Court Street. Up and down the Street at hitching posts at the edge of the plank sidewalks, patient horses snoozed or stamped, whisking away flies in summer or enduring cold winds as winter approached, awaiting the flick of their masters' reins.

Across Miner Street from Grandfather Sackrider's and behind the Hodskin House were the Hodskin House livery stables. Up behind the Deacon's barn, beyond the rear of the rambling Campbell/

Miner house, and close to Bridges Hotel at the corner of Park and Main were more stables. On Court Street, on the way to Grandmother Remington's house, behind yet another hostelry, were more livery stables. In all of these, travelers staying in town tethered and fed horses, unhitched from buggies and wagons. And here Canton folk, too poor or too old to own their own horse and rig, could rent good horseflesh and the surrey, buggy, or wagon they required for a trip to Ogdensburg or Potsdam, or into the surrounding countryside.

In winter, a team of heavy workhorses, Percherons or some mixed breed, pulled the weighted snowplow to clear village streets. Snowbanks soon were piled high in those days of a more severe climate. On hot summer days, a team hauled the village sprinkler to damp down the thoroughfares that passing wheels and hooves churned into hovering dust clouds. Also in summer, the village ice wagon clanked and dripped along streets and lanes, its patient horse tossing mane and tail to whisk off flies during frequent stops while the iceman shouldered the great crystal blocks delivered to waiting households.

Horses and talk of horseflesh took priority over politics and the weather in most conversations at the Sackrider store and other male gathering places in Canton. Since 1853, when Ebenezer Miner, with two other prominent county men, founded the St. Lawrence County Agricultural Society, the annual county fairs held at the new Canton Fairgrounds had heightened village interest in horses. The fair's races had become a big event at the end of each summer, when farmers and village people from St. Lawrence County hurried to the fairgrounds. Men, women, and children alike thrilled to see sleek trotters stretch to their utmost, urged on by drivers hunched on the fragile-looking sulkies. Even nonbettors, such as Deacon Sackrider, could hardly help speculating as to the chances of their favorites.

Doubtless little Fred, playing at his elders' feet in the Sackrider sitting room, heard many tales about horses, including the steeds who bore his own cavalry officer father and other soldiers into battle somewhere far beyond small Fred's horizon. The child could relate to an absent father through what he knew: the spirited horse his officer father rode that looked like those fine saddle horses he saw on Main Street.

Curvetting horses, a current of excitement that swept through Canton when victories were won for the Union, the mock warfare of village boys who drilled with wooden rifles, were all a child under four could possibly comprehend about a war being fought hundreds of miles away. The child Frederic Remington must however have sensed the undercurrent of anxiety present in his mother, during the long periods between the infrequent, scrawled letters that arrived from Pierre after his regiment went into action. Like all children, although seemingly oblivious of adult conversation and absorbed in his own play, Frederic absorbed the fear, dismay, and grief his elders experienced when bad news arrived, and it penetrated the sturdy child's external play. In small Fred Remington's imagination the combination of war excitement and anxiety formed fantasies of larger-than-life heroes, peopled by his dashing father and the other young men from Canton. Some fantasies he transformed into childhood mischief and play. Many he harbored into adulthood until finally he was able to combine talent, later observation, and those latent memories into form and color in his paintings and bronzes.

Although young Fred Remington may have imagined his father as larger than life, his adulation had a basis in fact. Pierre Remington was a courageous officer in the eyes of the men who served under him. One of these, Lieutenant Arthur B. Holmes, later described his former major as an "honest and brave soldier, always kind to his men, and generous to a fault,"[3] and Major Remington became a hero to more than his young son on a hot, sultry day in 1863.

On June 26, 1863, Major Pierre Remington was in charge of a skeletal squadron ordered by regimental commander Colonel James B. Swain to ride into Virginia's countryside on reconnaissance.[4] Remington crossed the Potomac and rode beyond Fairfax County Courthouse. Having found nothing, the eighty men and five officers headed back toward headquarters the next day. Then, over a hill, an advance detail spied what they took for Confederate General John S. Mosby's "bushwhackers," who had been harassing the region. Suddenly, one of the detail galloped back toward the main body of Remington's men, yelling, "Don't go over that hill or ye're a goner!" The trooper had seen a mass of mounted graycoats on the other side of the rise.

One of Remington's young lieutenants crept to the hill's crest to stare openmouthed at the area around Fairfax Courthouse, where hundreds of Confederate cavalry were milling about in apparent confusion. The Southern troops' disorder was the result of a few comrades' encounter with the Union detail. Remington's officer hastened to his commander to urge Remington, as he wrote later, "that we would all be gobbled up if we did not get to the rear. I said, 'Turn back! Turn the other way and run, there is a whole rebel brigade under the hill!'

"Instead, Remington ordered, 'Front into line—March!' " With his handful of men "yelling like wild Indians," some armed only with sabers and others brandishing empty pistols they had already fired, Pierre Remington and his troopers charged, unknowing, into the midst of Hampton's Brigade, the cream of Confederate Jeb Stuart's celebrated regiments. The Southern force numbered fifteen thousand and hauled eighteen pieces of artillery. Under orders from General Robert E. Lee, Stuart was circling Union forces near Washington in a swift forced march north to join the main Confederate force, which already had penetrated well into Pennsylvania. The battle of Gettysburg was in the making at that very moment.

The headlong charge of Remington's tiny group threw the vastly larger Confederate force into confusion. Remington, quickly realizing that his command was outnumbered, rose in his stirrups and called for his troops to cut their way out of the melee. He and eighteen men managed to escape.

Because of that brief hostile encounter, Jeb Stuart ordered his columns back southward in order to seek a more roundabout course, away from what he ascertained to be a Union threat. Remington's sortie, coupled with Stuart's decision, was "General Lee's excuse for his failure in the Gettysburg campaign. . . . Lee is reported to have said that had Stuart joined him one day sooner, a different tale would have been told."

After the battle of Gettysburg, the remaining years of war took Scott's 900 and Pierre Remington into the Deep South. He and his men fought in Tennessee, Mississippi, and Louisiana. At war's end, they were in Kentucky. Pierre Remington was mustered out in the summer of 1865, returning home to Canton to a wife who could not have had any real perception of what her husband had lived through and to a round-faced little son fairly exploding with excitement. Time had moved slowly on Canton streets. Pierre Remington, now age thirty-one, had survived several lifetimes of experience, by comparison, in places his North Country neighbors had learned about only from scanty news reports or hasty letters written by husbands and sons.

If Clara, now twenty-eight, had hoped that Pierre would settle into a normal Canton home and future, her aspirations were soon shattered. Soon after her husband's return, she and the son who had been the focus of her existence for four years were uprooted by the returning cavalry officer and moved far from all they knew of life. For the next three and a half years, the little family had to adjust to the husband and father they hardly knew, and to strange surroundings that Clara tolerated and young Fred hated.

Their first move was to Albany. Pierre Remington, now promoted to the rank of brevet colonel on the strength of his army record and earlier political accomplishments, was appointed to a position on the quartermaster's staff in army headquarters in the state capital.[5] He received this position at the end of the war, but nothing is known about the Remingtons' lives in the ensuing months.

In late 1866 or early 1867, the Colonel received a second job offer that brought an even more radical change to the small family. His former lieutenant, Arthur Holmes, of Bloomington, Illinois, proposed that he and his former major form a partnership to edit and publish the *Bloomington Pantograph*. Pierre Remington agreed and the family moved to the Midwest. Holmes, an enthusiastic Republican like Remington, wrote in an 1880 letter, "He [Pierre Remington] was editor of the daily and weekly Republican [newspaper] for that year [1867]. . . . His wife and son Fred, both of whom we learned to love dearly, came with him."[6]

Bloomington may have loved Clara and Fred, but young Fred, at least, detested Bloomington. In 1877, when he was attending Highland Military Academy in Massachusetts, sixteen-year-old Fred Remington referred to that year in a letter to a friend: "I lived in Bloomington, Illinois, once in my life and never want to live there any more."[7]

In Bloomington, five-year-old Fred had only his mother and a busy father to relate to instead of familiar village children and numerous grandparents, uncles, and aunts. He had been transported rapidly from one alien environment to another. Illinois was nothing like the North Country. The midwestern town was new and strange. Instead of playmates he had known all his life, he had to find new friends—and he may not have liked his Bloomington playmates. His mother, who was always rigid and had difficulty adapting to new situations, was forced to make similar adjustments. Only Pierre Remington, used to new environments and now back in harness in his former profession of newspaper editor, was entirely comfortable. We know nothing about the relationship between husband and wife, nor why young Fred was their only child. The couple may not have made a good adjustment to each other, separated as they had been for four years and both accustomed to extended family relationships, rather than life as a nuclear family. In any event, the Pierre Remingtons stayed in Bloomington less than one year.

Arthur Holmes's 1880 letter, which eulogized Pierre Remington after his early death, claimed that the Remingtons returned to Canton because Pierre had received an "appointment" there. Probably he was referring to the position of Canton postmaster, which we know Pierre Remington held from late 1867 to 1874. Canton postmasters in that day took on the position as an addition to their regular work. The job was a political plum because Civil Service had not yet been instituted, but the salary was a pittance and could not have supported even a family as small as Pierre Remington's. Pierre, therefore, repurchased the *St. Lawrence Plaindealer,* and by early 1868, the small family had returned to the North Country for good.

Pierre resumed an editorial mantle he had first donned at age twenty-two, when he and a young Canton lawyer, William B. Goodrich, had hitched their political and professional ambitions to the ascendant star of the new Republican party. As a teenager, Pierre Remington had been apprenticed as a printer in Buffalo and Binghamton, near where his clergyman father held pastorates before coming to Canton's Universalist Church. His Canton partner in 1856 had county political connections, and little capital was needed to launch a small-town weekly in the mid-nineteenth century. All they required were a case of used wooden type; a secondhand manually driven press (at first provided to the new publishers by the *Plaindealer*'s ailing rival, the *Democrat*); and newsprint.

On August 12, 1856, the first issue of the *St. Lawrence Plaindealer* came off the *Democrat*'s old Franklin press. The weekly—with its name shortened and with Pierre its sole owner when he bought out Goodrich later that year—consisted of small pages of crowded hand-set type. Titles, not headlines as we know them today, preceded essaylike prose. Its publisher was openly opinionated, and, what is more important, the readership expected what would later be considered flagrant editorializing.

In 1868, after he resumed editing his paper, Pierre hired his youngest brother, Mart, a student at St. Lawrence University, to write and help with editorial responsibilities. The Colonel, as he now was known, plunged back into his former political activities, as well as fulfilling his role as village postmaster. In addition, he helped his parents manage their affairs, including payment of his father's personal financial pledge to St. Lawrence, for all was not well with Maria and Seth Remington.*

Among the first features Colonel Remington added to his newspaper were regular reports about the dirt track and harness racing. For as long as the Colonel was at the helm, the *Plaindealer* columns carried an abundance of news of the equine world. The former cavalryman, like his Canton peers, had always been a horse lover. Now he began to invest in horseflesh, buying trotters and pacers rather than real estate. When "Van" (Walter) Van Valkenburg moved down to Canton from Hermon in the late 1860s to set up his racing stables near the fairgrounds at the county seat, he and the Colonel began a happy partnership, which contributed substantially to the lifelong love of horses of the Colonel's young son.

Van trained horses for the North Country racing circuit and became the best of his kind in the North Country. When Colonel Remington moved his family to Ogdensburg in 1872, he persuaded Van to relocate his stable to quarters at the Ogdensburg Fairgrounds racetrack east of that city. His racing career extended long after Pierre's death.

How much time the busy Colonel spent with his young son in the years after they returned to Canton is a matter of speculation. At about the time of his new racing partnership, the Colonel, who, like Clara, indulged their only son, bought Fred a pony and in the next years the boy and another youthful racehorse enthusiast, Pete McMonagle, could often be found at the Canton Fairgrounds or at Van's stables. A natural athlete, Fred became a skilled rider and even learned to handle a racing sulky. No wonder the adult Fred Remington said, "I always liked horses, from the time I was a small boy."[8]

In all probability, the Colonel—who had racing cronies and political friends throughout the North Country—took his young son along with him on some excursions. We do know that Fred went with his father to see racing enthusiast Perley Malterner, a farmer who lived several miles out of the village on the old De Kalb Road.

---

*This may be one reason for Pierre Remington's return to Canton. Fred's cousin, Henry M. Sackrider, before his death in the 1950s, told Atwood that Pierre's parents withdrew from community life, becoming "eccentric." A family schism had certainly occurred by Maria's 1878 death. When Seth Williston died and was buried at Henderson Harbor in 1881, none of his surviving sons was present, although they erected a monument for him in Canton's Evergreen Cemetery.

Perley admired Fred's father so much that he named his own son Pierre. Years later, when he was a successful artist on his yearly North Country vacations, Fred continued his friendship with the Malterners. He always rode out to the farm at least once during these stays, an admitted enticement being Mrs. Malterner's salt pork and gravy.

Beyond going on occasional exciting outings with his father and hanging about Van's stables, Fred's life as a young boy was full of other activities. Canton was a wonderful place for boys in those days. Once family chores and lessons were out of the way, youngsters like Fred Remington escaped watchful mothers to join in boyhood fun and pranks. In summer, "small boys followed the older boys down to the swimming hole below Princess Rock in the Grasse River near Jerry Travers' tannery, were dunked and told to sink or swim; so they swam. While the beginners dog-paddled, the old boys tied their shirts and pants into knots and soaked them in the water. The small fry had to crawl out and go to work with teeth and finger nails, trying to unknot their clothes to the taunting chant of 'Chaw raw beef! Chaw raw beef! Chaw raw beef!' "[9] One legend about Fred Remington may or may not be true (because tall stories are the privilege of every Yankee tale-teller). It is said that after one such hazing the chubby youngster sped home over Water Street, up Main, to Miner and the Sackrider house in the buff. This probably did happen, because Fred Remington, child and man, never paid much attention to what more staid people thought of him. Fred became an expert swimmer. Years later he taught his young cousin, Henry Sackrider, Uncle Rob's son, to swim; Henry later told Atwood that his cousin Fred "was like a fish in the water."[10]

In autumn and winter, the industrious among Canton boys set traps for muskrats or hunted gray squirrels in Davis' Woods or sent their pet mongrels chasing rabbits in the Morley swamp. Every boy wanted a gun exactly like his father's, but most had to earn pennies to buy a secondhand muzzle-loading shotgun, probably from Deacon Sackrider's hardware store. Every little boy dreamed of the time when he would be old enough to go to the Big South Woods and Cranberry Lake with Canton men on a real deer or bear or moose hunt. In the meantime, they sharpened their skills on small game. Now and then, a boy would come upon a baby rabbit or even a 'coon and carry it to the home barn to raise as a pet. Sporting skills and facility with guns and other equipment came readily to young Fred. He had natural aptitude for sports of all kinds, and his parents indulged him although they were no more affluent than other middle-class Cantonians.

When snow came, boys and even sometimes the more adventurous girls crowded to Carl Gully's toboggan slide near the riverbank, vying for places on those flat, fast-moving, hard-steering contraptions, then hanging on to the ropes for dear life, red-cheeked and tuqued, for the breathless, death-defying ride down the snow-packed slide and out onto river ice or snowy field. At other times, they slid down Ansel Watson's slide at the head of University Avenue on "the Hill" (where St. Lawrence University stands) on wooden sleds, some made of barrel staves, others more intricately constructed and painted.

No one skied in those days; snowshoes were used instead. Or they swept the river ice clear of snow with twig brooms, then strapped their makeshift skates to cowhide boots with thongs. The skates most often were manufactured from flat, hand-whittled wooden plates to which were screwed cast-iron blades made at David Jones's foundry. The more adept learned the intricate grapevine or figure eights or skating backward, but most just slipped and slid and fell.

Spring meant mud season and fishing. Canton springs were not (and still are not) beautiful. The hard-packed snowdrifts shrank slowly. Spring rains created miniature rivers where ordinarily streets and lanes provided footing for village feet. The boys splashed along in their heavy boots, seeking the deepest puddles in the way that every boy in every age has always done. Little River and the Grasse turned to torrents of angry water, swollen by melted snow racing down from the Adirondack hillsides. The water was icy cold then and dangerous. The flats outside the village were sheets of water. But ardent fishermen could hardly wait for the miserable weather. It meant that soon trout would rise to bait and flies. Little boys cut willow sticks for rods to which they tied oiled string or heavy linen thread snitched from their mothers' sewing baskets. Worms were free for the digging. Fishhooks could be begged from fathers or purchased for a pittance, but some little boys relied on bent pins and faith. There were chub and perch and punkin seeds, and even the occasional bass, although they ate the fingerling trout. In summer, sometimes fishermen hooked huge muskellunge in the Grasse, and even in Little River.

Fred Remington's lively imagination made him a ringleader in Canton boys' escapades. Although the family moved to Ogdensburg when he was eleven, he was in Canton after that, almost as much as at his new home, especially during vacations. He was a tease, too.

Alice Pettibone Helme told Atwood late in her life that, as a girl, she had hated young Fred Remington. At age nine, Fred, apparently succumbing to her feminine charms, had shown his appreciation by yanking her pigtails and then painting her doll a horrible shade of green.[11]

While the Pierre Remingtons lived in Canton those brief years, Fred went to a private, or as some call it, a "dame" school. It was run by Miss Sarah Randall and was located in a modest wooden structure beside her home on land at the rear of what is now a Park Street florist shop. These private establishments were the way all Canton youngsters learned their elementary course work, and Canton had at least two such schools.[12] Only a few public elementary schools had been founded in the 1870s, and in the 1880s only six hundred such public institutions were in existence in the entire United States.[13]

Like other Canton youngsters, Fred Remington was expected to take part in the social life of his parents. Families and friends spent considerable time visiting one another, sometimes invited, sometimes dropping in to chat informally. Some friendships were the result of church connections; others resulted from kinship or marriage. In a community as small as Canton, everybody knew everyone else, but interfamily friendships appear to have developed in clusters.

Family interrelationships in Canton became increasingly complex during the ensuing years of Fred Remington's life as young men and women from the village and the growing university paired off. Fred Remington was related by blood, marriage, or affection to many of Canton's leading families. Later, relatives of his wife, Eva Caten, further complicated the intricate web by marrying into Canton–St. Lawrence families. Several such Canton families were crucial to events and decisions that affected young Fred's near future (such as the Miner family; see chapter 3), and many remained as major participants in Frederic and Eva Remington's adult lives (the Russells, for example; see chapter 1).

One group of intermarriages with far-reaching implications for Fred and Eva is worth detailing, because the participants will be reintroduced several times in the course of our narrative. While Pierre Remington was at war, his younger brother William Reese married Lavilla Everest, daughter of the local butcher. When the Pierre Remingtons moved back to Canton in 1868, young Fred made friends with his four-year-old cousin George. The two grew into great pals, sharing the practical jokes both loved to pull on more dignified relatives and friends. They had a third partner for their boyhood and later crimes: young Frederick Gunnison. The "other" Fred was son of the Reverend Dr. Almon Gunnison and Lavilla Remington's older sister, Ella. Both Lavilla and Ella had studied at St. Lawrence University, where Ella met and fell in love with the young ministerial student who eventually became St. Lawrence's president. The Gunnisons now lived in Brooklyn, where Almon was minister at All Souls Universalist Church, but they regularly returned to Canton, where all their relatives lived.

Like all children, Fred Remington lived in the present, playing hard, studying only a little, full of mischief and fun. Unlike most of his playmates, he remained an only child who was overindulged by his mother and who his father hoped would follow in his own military or professional footsteps. Fred grew into a sturdy, rather plump youngster whose blond coloring was like his mother's and other Sackriders', but whose quick intellect—directed mostly toward pranks in those days—resembled his father's. He and his parents had every reason to assume that a comfortable and secure future lay ahead, now that the war-torn, disruptive early years of family life were over.

(Courtesy of Frederic Remington Collection, Owen D. Young Library, St. Lawrence University, Canton, N.Y.)

3

THE YOUTH: ENDINGS MAKE NEW BEGINNINGS

« 1869–1879 »

Sometimes life changes in the twinkling of an eye. That happened to eight-year-old Fred Remington in the middle of one night in 1869 when "he and the entire community of Canton were routed from bed by the cry of 'Fire! Fire! Fire!' Canton's Union Block, which stood at the foot of Main Street near the covered bridge and diagonally across from the Hodskin House, was ablaze. On the second floor of the three-story brick building was the *St. Lawrence Plaindealer* office and printing plant. With no formally organized fire department, Canton's "sole defense in 1869 . . . reposed in its two bucket brigades, the 'Wooden and Tin Pail Companies.' "[1] Village men and the older boys, nightshirts half-tucked into trousers, passed bucket after bucket of Grasse River water along a human chain in a vain effort to save Canton's most imposing business structure.

On the veranda of the Sackrider house on Miner Street, chubby Fred jumped and jigged with excitement, held firmly by his protective mother so that he would not scamper toward the inferno a block away. With her husband's hasty departure from the Remington home, Clara had dressed quickly, ordered young Fred to do the same, and then scurried, her heart pounding with fear, toward the pillar of smoke and flame. Her parents' home was safe, but now she watched her husband's business, and the small family's main livelihood, being devoured.

The orange glow from the roaring blaze lighted a chaotic scene straight from the nether regions, and somewhere in the melee was Pierre Remington, his face glistening with sweat and streaked with smoke and grime. Clara and the other women, many clutching shawls about their shoulders to cover long muslin nightgowns, stood anxiously in doorways, peering toward the eerie scene with hearts in mouths, their little children peeking around their mothers' skirts. Some of the more practical among the womenfolk dressed hastily, stoked up stoves, began to brew steaming pots of black coffee, and rummaged in their larders for meat and bread and leftover berry pies.

By dawn, the Union Block and the entire lower half of the Street lay in smoking ruins of tumbled brick walls and charred timbers. All that Pierre Remington saved of the *Plaindealer* from the fire of 1869 were his subscription lists and ledgers. As the weary men downed coffee, sandwiches, and pie, plans were already afoot to provide temporary quarters to businesses victimized by the fire. An isolated community like Canton understood the need for interdependence. Energetic Pierre Remington soon reestablished his newspaper up the Street in more modern quarters, then turned his editorial pen to establish and organize the St. Lawrence Fire Department. Pierre became the assistant chief engineer of Canton's new defense against the fiery demon: a primitive hand-pumped, hand-drawn "machine," that had been purchased secondhand from the City of Ogdensburg. The magnificent machine enchanted small boys like Fred, who frequently visited the tiny stone shed on Water Street that became the "Engine House."[2]

The new fire department was hardly trained when, in 1870, men and machine were put to the test in Canton's second great fire. This time fire hit the upper half of Main Street's north side. Afterward, Colonel Remington reported in the *Plaindealer* that "the firemen arrived on the scene promptly with their machine." Unfortunately, he was forced to admit, "there was an insufficient length of hose to reach the flames."[3] Once more, Cantonians confronted ruin. In less than two years, the entire business district and some homes on the north side of the Street were leveled. The village rallied under Colonel Remington's leadership, this time enlisting sixty-seven of the most able-bodied men of the village in the fire department. From then on, the St. Lawrence Fire Department, made up of three companies—Hose, Hook and Ladder, and Engine Company Number One—became the pride and joy of the community, and especially of young Fred Remington.

The two great fires presaged the end of Fred's early boyhood in the village and terminated the Remingtons' three years of normal life as a tightly knit family. In 1870, after the first fire, Pierre Remington took on a second full-time job. His Republican editorial policies and his war record won him appointment as collector of revenue for the District of Oswegatchie, with headquarters in Ogdensburg. For the next two years, the Colonel shuttled back and forth between the two communities: in Ogdensburg, supervising the collection of charges levied on goods arriving at the largest United States port of entry from Canada then in existence; and in Canton, working with his youngest brother Mart to rebuild his newspaper business. Pierre Remington's new position brought a welcome twenty-five-hundred dollars[4] a year to reestablish the *Plaindealer* and to provide his only child with the luxuries upon which Clara insisted. For Clara Remington made sure that young Fred was the best dressed child in Canton and had his every childhood wish satisfied. Somehow, in addition, Pierre Remington, a kindly man, made personal loans to friends in need and continued his own racing pursuits.

During the next two years, Clara saw that Fred's life in Canton continued undisturbed, filled with school and church, romps and mischief with friends, expeditions to explore the fields and woods, odd moments watching men building sand casts in Jones's iron foundry, and idle attempts to draw the horses he so loved. At school, autograph books were the current rage. When asked for his signature, young Fred always drew a horse, sometimes adding a smart remark, and signing his name with a flourish.* For Fred, the Colonel had once more become a misty background figure who appeared and disappeared from his childhood world, but whose presence brought special excitement into life.

For a brief spell in 1871, Fred stayed with his Sackrider grandparents while his mother and father were absent on a western trip. Possibly, the Colonel hoped to find business opportunity out west again. Atwood has discovered that many North Country men had invested in a silver mining venture in the Rockies at about this time. He believes that Pierre Remington, ever with an eye to new business ventures, was one of these men. On this trip, Fred's parents returned to Bloomington, Illinois, for a visit, and then traveled on west, although none of this was mentioned in the letter Fred received from

---

*Every so often someone in the North Country turns up another early Remington autograph book signature and sketch, found among musty old papers stored in attics. Sometimes the autographs of other youngsters are preceded by a jingle or verse. Others are simply a scribbled signature, but Fred Remington even then always identified himself by drawing a horse and adding a jocular, brash phrase or two.

his father during his parents' absence. Instead, while stopping in a Chicago hotel, Pierre wrote to his young son, "Your mother has bought you some soldiers, and they are no little 'peanuts' but regular 'square-toed' veterans." Pierre admonished the youngster to "say your lessons and be a nice boy so that when she [Clara] gets home there will be nothing to mar the pleasure of your meeting." He signed the letter, "from your 'Venerable Papa.' "[5]

In 1872, young Fred and his "venerable papa" participated in what was surely a red-letter day in his youthful life.

> On July Fourth that year, the Fire Department proudly led the [annual Independence Day] parade through Canton's streets with its new Hose Cart, its two-wheeled Ladder Cart, [while] four stalwarts of "Engine Company Number One" gallantly tugged at the ropes of "the machine," the hand-pumper. At their fore strutted one of the proudest boys in all Christendom, gaily decked out like them in his brand new parade fireman's uniform, visored cap, white gloves, and all. Freddie Remington had become the official mascot of Engine Company Number One and later posed with its four hero-members for the local photographer. His father, the Colonel, by then had been promoted from "Assistant" to "Chief Engineer."[6]

How Pierre found time or energy for still another activity is impossible to guess.

Fred's father, even on his swift black mare or by the slower roundabout railway journey, had to make the grueling trip between Ogdensburg and Canton several times each week year-round. And in the North Country, winter begins in November and lasts well into April. Although Mart Remington toiled on at the editor's desk of the *Plaindealer,* the pace became too strenuous for Pierre. Reluctantly, the Colonel decided to move his family to Ogdensburg and to put his newspaper up for sale.

By late 1872, Pierre Remington's printer, our cousin, George Manley, wrote a letter to his uncle and our ancestor, Gilbert Burrage Manley, a schoolteacher in Homer, New York, that the *Plaindealer* was for sale. Gilbert made the long trip to Canton and decided to buy the paper. The sale was finally consummated in 1873. In the meantime, before the end of 1872, Clara Remington once more packed up Fred and their possessions to move into the white house that her husband had rented on Hamilton Street in Ogdensburg. In 1874,

Pierre, with the proceeds of the *Plaindealer* sale, purchased an interest in the *Ogdensburg Journal and Republican* and again became an editor.

Young Fred Remington did not appreciate one by-product of Pierre Remington's new job until years later when he and Barton Hepburn became close friends. In the 1870s, Hepburn was only a name mentioned frequently by the Colonel when he recounted his Ogdensburg experiences to family and friends in Canton. Originally from a farm near Colton in the Adirondack foothills, Hepburn had moved to the river port to teach at the Ogdensburg Educational Institute, the city's secondary school, which young Fred later briefly attended.

The soft-spoken, brilliant young Hepburn quickly drew the attention of county Republican leaders, of whom Pierre was one, through recommendations of Stillman Foote and Colonel Edward C. James, two prominent Ogdensburg attorneys under whom, in his spare time, Hepburn studied law. A year after he was admitted to the New York bar, with the influence of county Republican leaders, Hepburn was appointed school commissioner for the second county assembly district. By the time Fred Remington was playing havoc with discipline in Ogdensburg school classrooms, Hepburn had departed for the state legislature at Albany to lay the foundation of his later brilliant career in the state government and, finally, in finance. Although Fred knew and was helped by his future friend during his two unhappy years in Albany in the early 1880s, Hepburn's and Remington's lasting friendship was forged during the years of their professional prime, in Canton and New York City.

Fred was eleven when his family moved to Ogdensburg. He may have missed the attention of his many Canton relatives, but in no time, the cocky, mischievous, outgoing boy set forth to explore his new surroundings and to find friends in the new neighborhood. Not far from the Remington house was the Patterson Street volunteer fire company station, where the youthful firebuff felt right at home. Fred could glimpse the St. Lawrence River beyond the head of Hamilton Street every time he stepped out his own front door. The River, he soon discovered, dominated nearly every Ogdensburg life and activity. Most businesses at the center of town on Ford and State streets had some connection to the River, or to the cargoes offloaded at the docks that lined the waterfront. The docks, railroad yards, steamers, barges, and steam locomotives made the river port a busy, thrilling place.

Fred soon found that boys in Ogdensburg spent as much time on or in the cold river waters as they possibly could. Once the new schoolmates had become friends, the boys explored the River in St. Lawrence skiffs, fished for bass and pickerel and perch, always hoping to hook a giant muskellunge. "Upriver" lay the Thousand Islands, where Ogdensburg families began to build summer "camps," as North Country people have always called the cottages and hunting lodges, sometimes commodious and comfortable, that are found on the St. Lawrence and beside Adirondack lakes and ponds. In summertime, excursion steamers plied back and forth to the Thousand Islands, laden with day passengers from Ogdensburg. Daily, when the River was free of ice, ferries bustled back and forth between the city and its Canadian neighbor, Prescott.

The business district lay five blocks west of Hamilton Street. Here, some wooden sidewalks boasted board roofs and gas street lamps glowed at night. Fred discovered some streets bore girls' names: Elizabeth, Caroline, Isabella, and Catherine. His new pals told him that in Ogdensburg's old days, Nathan Ford, Samuel Ogden's land agent who laid out the original village streets in a grid, had named some streets for Revolutionary War heroes and others for his nieces. Most boys that age thought naming streets after girls was silly; Franklin, Knox, Hamilton, Washington, and Fayette (after Lafayette) were more to their liking.

When young Fred went to visit his father at work at the Customs House, he walked through history. Traveling westward on Washington Street he passed the porticoed Parish Mansion, built by David Parish, who left Europe for his North Country landholdings in the early 1800s, began steelworks at Rossie, and established a shipyard in Ogdensburg. Less than thirty years before the Remingtons arrived in Ogdensburg, David Parish's nephew, George Parish, had lived in the big house with the mysterious Ameriga Vespucci, whom Ogdensburg called "Parish's Fancy." Some old Ogdensburg residents could remember the foreign lady who tossed exotic oranges to them in childhood as they scampered past the mansion wall, and a few had even attended the famous "Pic-Nic" when she entertained village children shortly before she left Ogdensburg. Grown-ups still spoke of Parish's Fancy in whispers in front of their own children in 1873.*

---

*Young George Parish was supposed to have won the Italian beauty as his mistress in a card game from rakish John Van Buren, son of the United States president, and to have settled her in rooms connected with the rest of the mansion by a secret door. The Italian beauty, rumored to have been a courtesan, had appeared in the

David Parish had built a big fieldstone warehouse and store not far beyond his mansion; this warehouse was now the Customs House. Fred Remington's father presided there over the inspection of incoming cargoes, immigrants, visitors from Canada, and Ogdensburg ladies returning from shopping trips to Prescott. The Customs House, the oldest federal customs building in the nation, stood near "The Crescent," which ran along the curved eastern bank of Ogdensburg's harbor, where the Oswegatchie joins the St. Lawrence. The United States–Canada ferry slip was nearby and from the Customs House, young Fred could look across the harbor to Van Rensselaer Point; from its end each night a warning light blinked from the newly renovated federal lighthouse. On the point, no signs remained of Fort La Présentation. Stones from its tumbled walls had long since been hauled away for use in other buildings.

Fred learned more about Ogdensburg's exciting past at the private school on Green Street where his parents enrolled him. Stories about Oswegatchie Indian scalping parties fueled his imagination. Some of his classmates were descendants of British loyalists who fled the American Revolution, then returned from Canada to build the new village. He discovered that the Seymour House, the local hotel, stood on the very spot where the battle of Ogdensburg was fought in the War of 1812, when the border city was captured by the British. Ogdensburg's Preston King was supposed to have encouraged Canadians to revolt from Great Britain in the so-called Patriots Rebellion in 1837–1839. Famous men had visited Fred Remington's new city. Gouverneur Morris, the financier of the American Revolution, had traveled north to visit the Parish family and to see his landholdings. Washington Irving, creator of Rip Van Winkle, had arrived on a trip through the North Country. More recently, General and Mrs. Ulysses Grant had been honored guests.[7]

Whenever visiting dignitaries appeared in Ogdensburg, Fred's parents were included in official and social gatherings. By virtue of

nation's capital to petition Congress, unsuccessfully, for a land grant. She based her claim on her descent from explorer Amerigo Vespucci, inspiration of the name *America*. George Parish returned to Europe in 1859, leaving his then-middle-aged mistress, who soon departed also.

In late 1915, the widowed Eva Remington and her sister Emma Caten moved into the Parish Mansion at the invitation of George Hall, then owner of the historic house. Across Washington Street, in the former Joseph Rosseel house, the Ogdensburg Public Library housed Remington's Indian artifacts, given by Eva to the city. In 1922, after the two women had moved (and after Eva's death in 1918), the Remington Art Museum was established in the Parish Mansion.

Pierre Remington's official position and his political leadership, the Colonel and his lady moved among Ogdensburg's elite, a more affluent and more cosmopolitan group than any in Canton. Among these families were descendants of the earliest leaders of Ogdensburg, when it was the first incorporated village in the county and, for a time, the county seat. Descendants of the Fines, Hasbroucks, Judsons, and others were among those with whom the new collector of the port rubbed shoulders.

For the Colonel, there were racing cronies and political circles. He and his partner, Walter Van Valkenburg, became friends with other racetrack enthusiasts at the city fairgrounds, where horses were stabled. After the day's work in office or store, men like Pierre Remington gathered at the Seymour House, or in one of the private men's clubs where they could play cards or billiards, drink and talk together. This was a far more sophisticated group than the circle who gathered around Deacon Sackrider's hardware store wood stove in Canton.

Seasonally, Ogdensburg men—and their sons, as the boys grew older—made pilgrimages, in spring and autumn, to a little-known lake in the southern part of the county, in the Big South Woods, to fish and hunt. Sportsmen from metropolitan New York City and other parts of the state began to frequent other parts of the former Mohawk Adirondack hunting and fishing paradise after the Civil War, but in the 1870s Cranberry Lake was still the province of native North Country men. In the 1850s, a few hardy souls had hacked their way into the wilderness to find the big lake from which the Oswegatchie flows and of which they had heard rumors. Now, Ogdensburg and Canton sportsmen regularly trekked to Cranberry to pursue the abundant game and cast for gigantic trout.

In Ogdensburg, Clara Remington quickly discovered that the women she met lived in a far more complicated, and often more convenient, style than that of the simpler life she had known in Canton. Ogdensburg ladies were preoccupied with household responsibilities, clothes, shopping, social engagements, and cultural activities. Help was plentiful and cheap, drawn from new immigrants who arrived in the country via the River. Hired girls carried the burden of heavy cleaning and laundry, but the lady of the house washed her own heavy silver, delicate china, and crystal.

The ice harvest from the River each winter assured housewives of cold storage for perishable foods in summer. But canning, pickling, and preserving the winter food supply was a major endeavor with each summer harvest. Food that would keep was often bought in quantity: bushels of apples or potatoes, great sacks of winter onions. Prices in the 1870s and 1880s were ridiculously low when compared to those of one hundred years later: a pound of coffee was about thirty-five cents. One "linen collar" from Nathan Frank's Foreign and Domestic Dry Goods Store on Ford Street cost twenty cents, and a pair of gloves, seventy-five cents. A spool of thread cost a nickel. Six square yards of carpet, including matting to go under it, cost fourteen dollars. Five dollars paid for a pair of boots. Raisins cost twenty-six cents a pound. "Soup meat" was twenty cents and the butcher did not bother to weigh it.[8]

Clothing was a complicated matter, because almost everything a woman or her children wore was made by hand: muslin and cambric underwear sewn with tucks and gathers and ribbon inserts, voluminous petticoats, day and "best" dresses for women and girls; elaborate kilts for little boys (whose hair was shorn only later in childhood), shirts and knickers as they grew older, knitted socks and knee-length stockings. The women did, however, purchase milliners' bonnets and shawls, gloves and parasols, as well as heavy coats and boots for themselves and the children. Excursions to Canada on the local ferryboat tempted the more audacious to conceal purchases under their clothing in order to elude Pierre Remington's customs inspectors.[9]

Formal calls were important, with cards left at the door. Teas and "at homes" were frequent among Ogdensburg's elite. In fact, as Canton's W. A. Poste commented in his memoirs, North Country social codes were rigid, of paramount importance, and strictly observed.[10]

Clara Remington was always ambitious, we know, for her rambunctious, intelligent child. She intended that Frederic would attain success and security in a position of social prominence. With the unruly boy's future in mind, she enrolled him in private studies that included deportment and social graces. In Ogdensburg, dancing lessons were conducted by an aging German dancing master, called "Professor" Bowen, a relic of early Ogdensburg times who had instructed at least three generations of Ogdensburg's prominent families.[11] Professor Bowen, who presided at dancing classes in a modified court costume straight out of Revolutionary times, was a figure of fun to Fred and his pals. The instructor wore black satin knee breeches, white silk stockings, and black patent-leather pumps with silver buckles. The dances he taught, in keeping with his costume, included the minuet. In Remington's youth and young adulthood, the schottische, the polka, the gavotte, and waltzes were becoming popular. A stout, perspiring Fred was forced to propel a self-conscious, pigtailed girl around the hall while Professor Bowen shouted the time above the tinkle of the piano accompaniment and the shuffle of awkward feet. Fred developed an aversion to formal social gatherings and balls that lasted his lifetime.

On Green Street in Ogdensburg, the brick building where Dr. Nelson W. Howard had his private school still stands. Here, in 1873, Clara and Pierre Remington enrolled their son to ensure his academic future. And here young Fred cemented lifelong friendships, learning some subjects well and a few not at all. Young Jonathan Childs Howard, or John, as he was always called, was among his father's students and became Fred Remington's closest, lifelong Ogdensburg friend. Also in school with Fred and John Howard were Ned Strong, Jim Westbrook, and Al Herriman, all friends throughout Fred's life.

Fred was taught by Professor Nelson W. Howard* himself, although the doctor's wife was also a teacher in the school. From the start, Fred was disruptive. His high jinks were the delight of fellow students and the despair of his teachers in every school he attended. Probably, the boy was too quick and too intelligent for many of his instructors. He always was impatient and easily bored with people whose minds worked more slowly than his own. Fred soaked up knowledge with little effort, except for mathematics, which he later admitted had eluded him throughout his life. The boy had a high opinion of himself—partly the result of his mother's constant petting and attention—and was vain and a dandy. Irving Bacheller remembered that, during this period, "Fred Remington came often to visit his relatives in Canton. He was a rather short, fat boy, and always 'terribly dressed up,' we boys used to think, in spotless garments and a straw hat with two or three colors on its band. He was a lively boy who talked in a loud voice."[12]

Professor Howard brought his medical enthusiasms and knowledge into the classroom. Each Friday afternoon, he lugged in an entire skeleton from the doctor's offices where he worked after school hours, hung it from the ceiling, and lectured the boys on anatomy

---

*Howard, according to local oral history, received his training through apprenticing to local doctors. Everts's *History of St. Lawrence County,* however, states that he had graduated from the University of Pennsylvania, gone west to Wisconsin to practice, then become homesick and returned to the North Country.

and human physiology; this instruction may account for Fred's later skill in depicting cowboys, Indians and soldiers. On several occasions, Howard appeared with a human arm (pickled in formaldehyde) to demonstrate anatomy. He planned to dissect a cat to teach even more to his students and deputized an unidentified lad to secure a specimen from one of the city alleyways. The good doctor never carried out his experiment: indignant fellow students waylaid the cat-napper and freed the would-be scientific subject.[13]

Unlike his serious father, Fred had a rollicking sense of humor. He viewed life around him with droll amusement and had the knack of caricaturing his teachers and fellow students. At the Green Street school, Fred's artistic abilities were encouraged by Dr. Howard. A former classmate recalled years later that young Fred used to "delight the scholars and teachers as well with his natural drawings in chalk on the school blackboard, which seemed to the youngsters as feats of magic."[14]

Fred's artistic talents in these formative years were only a source of fun for him. We do not know whether he had art lessons in either Canton or Ogdensburg. There were accomplished amateurs in both communities who may or may not have influenced the boy. Clara herself is reported to have been a talented quilter and later painted china, an acceptable hobby for "artistic" ladies in those days. Once Fred moved on into the Ogdensburg Educational Institute, "he was continually in trouble with the faculty," as Eva Remington reported to an Ogdensburg audience, in 1916, after the artist's death.[15]

Fred's "mischievous disposition together with his aptitude for characterizing the teachers and pupils on the black boards" drove his mother and father to seek advice from Canton family and friends.[16] Doubltess the subject of Fred's future was an important part of the Canton families' conversations and gentle Mary Sackrider or Clara herself may have sought help from neighbors Eliza Miner and her daughter Minnie, now Mrs. Richard Ellsworth.

In all likelihood, the choice of the Vermont Episcopal Institute in Burlington as a school for Fred resulted from the influence of Minnie Miner Ellsworth's eldest sister, Elizabeth. The eldest Miner daughter had moved to Burlington upon her marriage to Delazon Wead, and now Elizabeth's own elder daughter, Mary Wead, had married an Episcopalian clergyman, the Reverend William Weeks (later to become bishop of the Vermont Diocese). In 1875, when young Fred was to turn fourteen, his parents packed him off to attend the institute. Before he left his Ogdensburg schoolmates and teachers, he collected autographs in a new book (which now is in the Remington Art Museum in the old Parish Mansion). One message is from his old schoolmaster's wife, Mrs. Nelson Howard, who wished the adventurer well and hoped he would emulate the popular cartoonist Thomas Nast.

The Vermont Episcopal Institute was run on strict disciplinary lines similar to those of a military school (and this is probably why Colonel Remington agreed to send his son there). There, for the following school year, Fred starved, suffered pangs of homesickness, played more pranks, and was sternly punished for them. The school had been founded in 1860 by the Reverend Theodore Austin Hopkins, who was Fred's headmaster and provided the usual secondary subjects of that time. In addition to work in Latin and geometry, the institute gave the boy his formal introduction to art education in a course taught by Hopkins.[17]

Fred's wife later remarked that the school's diet of "dry toast did not exactly agree with the young student."[18] His letters to Ogdensburg chum John Howard refer to frequent surreptitious midnight gatherings with fellow students to feast on boxes of goodies sent from home. Fred's parents' hopes of curbing his talent for mischief came to naught. For those midnight feasts and for other pranks, including pelting a teacher with snowballs, Fred gained an amazing number of school disciplinary "hours" of punishment and then boasted of this dubious accomplishment in his letters to John Howard. In addition he described constant pangs of homesickness for his parents, his friends, his pony, and Ogdensburg. He wrote often to John, wistfully asking what the Ogdensburg boys were doing, what the weather was like, whether ice had formed on the River. The only things he liked at the institute were Latin (he was a bright enough student when he so desired), wrestling, and football.[19]

The Colonel now decided that a genuine military academy might solve the problem of settling young Fred down to serious study and perhaps might point him toward a military career. Even the overprotective Clara finally agreed. For the next two years, Fred attended the Highland Military Academy in Worcester, Massachusetts. The uniforms, courses in military tactics, and fellow students at this preparatory school were more to young Fred's liking. Although he never became an outstanding student, he was no longer nostalgic for home and friends. He had finally adjusted to life on his own away from Clara's pampering.

The courses in military history and tactics challenged him, but

Fred never was more than a mediocre student. Although his grades did not reflect his intelligence, the boy was an omnivorous reader. He devoured books by Joseph Gregg, Washington Irving, Lewis and Clark, and the artist George Catlin. Drawing came as naturally as breathing to teenage Fred Remington.[20] He covered textbook margins with sketches of soldiers and horses, his own kind of schoolboy doodles. Some time during his Highland days Fred began consciously to improve his drawing techniques, the first indication that he now considered his sketches more than fun. His fellow cadet and friend Julian Wilder put Fred in contact with another young amateur artist, Scott Turner of Augusta, Maine, whose drawings Fred had seen and admired. The two boys corresponded about their mutual talent, although they never met.[21]

During these years, Remington filled ledger books with sketches. Luckily, some of these have been preserved. In his research in the 1970s into the artist's early life, Atwood made two significant discoveries in one such sketchbook that relate directly to Frederic S. Remington's later work. The old ledger (now the property of the Robert Norton Galleries, Shreveport, Louisiana) came into Atwood's hands through art dealer Rudolf Wunderlich, then president of the Kennedy Galleries in New York, who asked Atwood to ascertain its authenticity. In leafing through the young artist's drawings, Atwood noted a pyramidal composition fifteen-year-old Fred had drawn, depicting Custer's defeat at the battle of the Little Bighorn, an event causing a public rumpus in 1876. Atwood quickly looked up Remington's *The Last Stand* in his copy of the artist's 1895 anthology, *Pony Tracks*. The basic composition was the same, whether from Remington's unconscious memories or from recollection of this boyhood sketch.

The second discovery about the teenage Remington's evolving technique was reported in Atwood's letter to Wunderlich:

> I let my grandson [Kenneth C. Labdon], who has helped me with some of my Rushton and Remington research, look through the ledger-sketchbook the other evening.
> "Gramp," K.C. said, "look, he has all four of that horse's feet off the ground."

Atwood's letter identifies this sketch: "Right hand page 56, bottom. The work done in colors: Some in crayon, some in watercolors, none in oils." (The Ogdensburg Remington Art Museum owns another early sketchbook of the artist from this period. Fred labeled one of the pages of this book, a picture of a soldier's head, "My first attempt at oil. Rem.")

All his young life, Fred's keen eyes had watched galloping horses race down village streets, around oval racetracks or stretch out along country roads. Unconsciously, his photographic memory recorded each detail. Remington's later work, which often showed horses at full gallop with all hooves off the ground, caused raised eyebrows in his own time. The speculation ended when the instantaneous, electric-shutter photographic techniques, developed by Eadweard Muybridge in 1886, proved that Remington's eye was accurate.*

At home on vacations during his cadet years, Fred Remington often visited his Canton relatives, renewed ties with cousin George Remington and his little sister Ella (Fred's only female cousin), played with Rob Sackrider's infant son Henry (Rob had married Emma Merkley in 1873), spent carefree hours with his Ogdensburg chums, and gradually became aware of—and increasingly concerned about— his father's declining health. Letters to his mother and his Uncle Horace Sackrider in his last term at Highland speak of the latter. To Horace he wrote, "I guess the Col. is going up in the woods with me this year. It will do the old boy good. . . . I'll put a tan on his 'phiz'. . . . Darn him, I'm disgusted so is Mama. We have concluded that the old boy don't know enough to take care of his precious corpse and we are going to do it for him."[22]

About his own future, the young Remington was less concerned. He had definite aspirations:

> I am of quite too much of a speculative mind to ever make a success at the solemn reality of a book-keeper. No sir, I will never burn any mid-night oil in squaring accounts. The Lord made me, and after a turn of mind which would never permit me to run my life from the point of a pen. . . . I never intend to do any great amount of labor. I have but one short life and do not aspire to wealth nor fame in a degree which could only be obtained by an extraordinary effort on my part.

---

*After Remington's death, the controversy continued, but in a different vein. Some Remington students believed, and still believe, that the artist painted horses in mid-air only after he himself had viewed Muybridge's work.

He continued in a letter to Uncle Horace, "No, I am going to try to get into Cornell College this coming June and if I succeed will be a Journalist. I mean to study for an artist anyhow whether I ever make a success at it or not."[23]

Instead of attending Cornell, Fred matriculated at Yale University and entered its art school in 1878. In an 1894 interview, the adult Remington told a reporter that he had originally planned on a military career, but that his weak mathematics skills prevented his applying to West Point. He also had thoughts, he said at that time, of politics, as well as of journalism.[24] Clearly, the young man did not know what profession he wanted to follow, but he was patterning his interests on his father's. His mother had aspirations for him as a businessman. His father, and later his Uncle Mart, expected him to follow in the family footsteps. Although Eva Remington later claimed that her husband had won honors in art during his student days, no such records are to be found. She may have referred, in her lecture given to the Ogdensburg Chapter of the DAR in 1916, to a later honorary degree, which Yale conferred upon her husband at the peak of his artistic career. As these youthful decisions and nondecisions began to shape Frederic Remington's future, other events were in the making that would lead the future artist of the West along pathways he had never foreseen.

myself at work

(Courtesy of Frederic Remington Collection, Owen D. Young Library, St. Lawrence University, Canton, N.Y.)

4

EXIT CHILDHOOD; ENTER EVA

« 1879–1884 »

The summer of 1879 in St. Lawrence County was, for Fred Remington, much the same as others he had enjoyed during vacations from boarding school and now from Yale. Fred's eighteenth birthday would be on October 4. He was big and blond, with an open expression and rollicking disposition. He had plenty of friends in Ogdensburg with whom to skylark and to whom he could boast of his college athletic prowess: he was a "rusher" on the Yale football team and continued to win boxing bouts. In Canton, where he could stay at Grandfather Sackrider's whenever he wished to visit, he had a multitude of friends and fond relatives. Grandmother Remington, the intrepid Maria, had died the previous year, and his clergyman grandfather had vanished from the Canton scene. Uncle Bill and Aunt Lavilla, however, remained for the time being in the Remington house on Court Street with young Ella, the only Remington girl of the coming generation, and Fred's favorite cousin, George. He and George, now a teenager and three years Fred's junior, became inseparable companions in crime when Fred forgot his college-born dignity. They teased the younger Ella, and Fred taught George all kinds of mischief. His young uncle, Mart Remington, had moved to Albany, where he was now a journalist, was married, and had become father of a little boy, Charles. Fred's only other cousin was also small. He was baby Henry Merkley Sackrider, son of Uncle Rob and Aunt Emma.

Life that summer of 1879 was easy for the young Remington.

He gave scarcely a thought to the future. Although at Yale he was supposedly studying art, much the easiest subject he had yet encountered, he still dreamed of quick success in business or journalism or politics. His family and friends had welcomed him home from Yale with open arms and hung on to his tales of college fun, for Fred was a true Yankee spinner of yarns. His mother and Grandmother Sackrider plied him with good hearty fare to make up for so-called dreary Yale meals that these two good cooks disdained. All was well except for one nagging concern: his mother's anxiety over his father, whose thin form was racked continually by a deep, dry cough.

In a letter home the previous spring, Fred had buoyantly suggested a fishing trip in the Big South Woods at Cranberry Lake as the solution to his father's health problems. Instead of lounging on the porch at Bishop's Hotel at Cranberry or casting for trout in Brandy Brook, however, the Colonel spent every spare moment that summer at Walter Van Valkenburg's stables east of Ogdensburg, watching his partner put their trotter, Mars, through his paces. Both men thought Mars a "comer," and Fred forgot his mother's worry and his hidden fears about Pierre Remington's health in the excitement growing around the big bay horse as summer waned and time for the annual St. Lawrence County Fair in Canton drew closer.

Each year a current of excitement and anticipation spread through St. Lawrence County's sparse population as fair time approached. Colonel Otis of Massena, David Judson in Ogdensburg, and Ebenezer Miner, had founded the St. Lawrence Agricultural Society in 1853 to promote better farming methods and to foster pride in North Country farm products. County fairs had become a North Country institution by 1879: a chance for hardworking farmers to gain recognition for their backbreaking labors, a joyous social occasion for isolated farm wives and children, and a wonderful excuse for everyone else within hailing distance to declare a holiday and join the fairbound crowds. Family reunions were scheduled at summer's end, bringing relatives home from as far away as Albany and New York City. But the horse races held during Fair Week had become the apogee of every fair.

As September 1879 approached, prefair excitement was at high pitch throughout the county. Farm wives brooded long hours over secret recipes, wondering for yet another time whether to enter bread-and-butter or sweet icicle pickles (made with maple syrup) this year, or whether Grandma's sixteen-egg pound cake would take a ribbon. In Pierrepont, Waddington, Madrid, and Edwards, village women worked feverishly to finish quilts or embroidery. Farmers hovered over the coddled livestock they hoped would win prizes, plying the animals with feed, currying, cleaning, and trimming hooves; rubbing sleek coats till they glistened; brushing tails; and plaiting manes. Most of the harvest was in, because North Country winters creep down early from the Arctic. Barns were full and corn shocks, like miniature tepees, still stood amid the stubble in shorn fields. Great haymows, sometimes topped with tarpaulins, created miniature hillocks in meadows. Carefully stowed away were squash, pumpkins, and other garden produce, even gigantic cornstalks, all carefully preserved in hopes of a ribbon. In farm pantries stood colorful jars of the tastiest vegetables and the most succulent fruits of the summer harvest, awaiting careful packing for the trip to Canton.

When Fair Week arrived, a mass migration occurred, with farmers urging along herds of cattle and flocks of sheep, followed by horse-drawn creaking wagons filled with excited women and children, crates of cackling fowl, boxes of preserves, and precious needlework—all making their way along weary miles of dirt roads spreading through the country like spokes of a gigantic wheel. From every direction of the compass, they journeyed toward the hub, the county seat, located nearly in the center of the vast North Country county. Canton children woke before dawn to hear the lowing of cattle, the bleating of sheep, creaking of wagon wheels, and plodding of feet making their way down every major village street (Main from east and west, Park, State, and Judson streets), then moving in slow procession out Water Street to the fairgrounds.*

Although he looked forward to another year of fun at Yale, Fred Remington delayed his return to college in 1879. He was determined to watch his father's horse Mars run the Premium Races at the Canton County Fair. All St. Lawrence County would be in the stands or leaning on the fence beside the oval dirt track on the third Wednesday in September to watch the fair's most popular event. In Ogdensburg on Hamilton Street, in the house the Pierre Remingtons rented, Clara Remington began packing bags for the yearly county fair visit home to her parents, Henry and Mary Sackrider. Although she and her horse-loving, politically minded husband moved among Ogdensburg's affluent and sophisticated elite, Clara was more comfortable

---

*Atwood's wife, Alice Reynolds Manley, could remember waking in that darkest night hour that comes before dawn to listen to the sounds of the invisible procession. The timid little girl thrust aside her fears of the dark as she listened to the tramping feet and the voices of men and animals.

at the top of the social heap in Canton and welcomed any chance to accompany the Colonel and their son on frequent trips to their hometown. At the Ogdensburg train depot, Van Valkenburg gently blindfolded Mars in order to lead the big horse up a ramp into the waiting boxcar for the railroad trip to the fair.

On Main Street in Canton, the daily hustle and bustle of business activities accelerated each year as fair time approached. Merchants, with an eye to the hordes of visitors, stocked shelves with new merchandise. At the *Plaindealer* office, Gilbert B. Manley fed the rising tide of anticipation by carefully including items about the coming fair in the weekly's tightly packed columns. The Hodskin House by the bridge and the American House at the top of the Street made ready for visitors who could afford hotel rooms and thus avoid camping out in fields near the fairgrounds. On Chapel Street, next door to the big house where a century later Atwood turned over a dusty canvas to discover an original Frederic Remington oil painting, the local artist Henry DeValcourt Kipp readied paintings for the fair.

Up Judson Street, a quarter-mile east of its junction with Court, Mrs. Theodore (Sarah) Caldwell finished airing one of the bedrooms she and her husband let out to female students attending St. Lawrence University.* One of the new students was Eva A. Caten from Gloversville. Up on the Hill at St. Lawrence University, Dr. Ebenezer Fisher pondered the future of the university over which he and Dr. John Stebbins Lee presided. Somehow, the little school had weathered financial hardships and the disapproval of North Country conservatives, and now, nearly a quarter of a century after its founding, the pink brick walls of Richardson Hall, this academic year, nurtured forty-nine young men and thirty young ladies,[1] among them Eva A. and William L. Caten, siblings from central New York.

Water Street, which led north from Canton's Main Street to the fairgrounds, had taken on a rakish air of pseudo-respectability, although throughout the rest of the year it was grubby and disheveled. Its saloons were strangely neat, with new sawdust strewn on barroom floors. Except at the time of the annual county fair, Water Street was pointedly ignored by the more fastidious of village

---

*Until well into the twentieth century, St. Lawrence University had no official student dormitories. Some men students were housed on the third floor of Richardson Hall, the original college building, where each room was warmed in winter by its own wood stove. Other students, including all the women, found housing in Canton homes.

churchgoers. Along the east bank of the Grasse River were located Canton's industries, and here community riffraff loitered. The fairgrounds itself was alive with activity for weeks before the fair opened. A swarm of workmen, made up of locals who did odd jobs or else frequented the saloons on Water Street, put the exhibition buildings, Floral and Faneuil halls, to rights. Stables and cow sheds were swept, readied for sleek inhabitants whose owners dreamed of local fame and fortune, should the coveted ribbons be bestowed upon their livestock. The oval track beside the wooden grandstand had been dragged and rolled, the grassy plot in the center scythed and mown, and the fence surrounding the track inspected and strengthened to support the weight of racetrack fans who would lean against or perch atop it to watch the North Country's finest horseflesh race down the home stretch to the finish line.

Fair officials kept an anxious eye to the weather as the day for the Premium Races neared. Sometimes in September in the North Country, the equinoctial rains come early. Occasionally, an August frost will herald an early winter. Once in a while, however, the North Country is treated to a late, moist heat wave. Throughout the county, men, women, and children used to keep watch for their favorite weather signs: the width of woolly bear caterpillar stripes, the spectacular sunsets that North Country folk are sure have no rival elsewhere in this world, the way the breezes rattle aspen leaves, whether the dairy cattle lie down with tails to the wind blowing north from the lake country down beyond Watertown, the sound of the steam locomotive whistle that changes to a hollow note when a storm is coming.

In 1879, dairy cattle and the locomotive whistle had predicted rain. And rain it did, on Wednesday, the scheduled date of the fair's harness races. Sopping wet visitors had drifted away from fair events and the fair's committee postponed the races until Thursday, the final day.[2] Thursday, September 18, 1879, dawned warm and clear. The crowds who had flocked to the fair's opening and then evaporated when the rains came swarmed back to the fairgrounds at the north edge of Canton. Farm families, villagers from every county hamlet, visitors from as far downstate as New York City, and almost the entire student body at St. Lawrence University crowded through the entrance gates, cheerfully ignoring wet grass and mud.

Urchins darted through the crowd, chasing one another, ducking under elbows and hiding behind voluminous skirts. Ladies, with broad-brimmed hats and parasols raised to ward off the sun, picked their way over the wet, rutted turf, holding skirts modestly around their ankles, chattering together, or leaning dependently on the arm of a male escort. Bearded, mustached men in tight suits and high collars, cigars in hand, strolled in groups or bent attentively to the wives or sweethearts they escorted. Mothers clung to excited aproned, pigtailed little girls. Freckle-faced, kilted little boys begged for balloons, or noisemakers, or sticky "vinegar taffy." There were fat farm wives and lean farm wives, faces beaming with delight at this annual outing that would provide happy memories and many a conversation for long, cold winter evenings ahead in their isolated homesteads. Their mates, gathered near the animals' quarters, talking laconically about crops, pulling on an occasional pipe, sometimes chewing a blade of timothy grass or a cud of tobacco.

Toward the back of the grounds was the great open-sided tent, under which the ladies from one of Canton's churches were setting up tables for the hearty spread of food that they sold to fill church missionary-fund coffers. Homemade corn chowder steamed on outside fires in gigantic kettles ordinarily used to boil laundry or to make apple butter or sausage meat. Juicy pink slices curled away from great smoked hams under the carving knives honed razor-sharp. Fragrant loaves of bread, jars of pickles, crocks of potato salad and slaw, and the famous cold vinegared baked beans of the North Country stood ready to serve. Piles of cookies, rows of home-baked cakes and pies were waiting in reserve. Kettles of steaming coffee, pitchers of lemonade, gallon jugs of creamy rich milk awaited thirsty fairgoers, although some racetrack touts had surreptitiously carried flasks of whisky with which to refresh themselves.

At Floral and Faneuil halls, the coveted blue, red, and white ribbons adorned prize needle- and craft work. High on the walls above the fine needlework hung rag and braided rugs and colorful hand-pieced quilts with equally colorful pattern names. Jars of pickles, jellies, and jams crowded the plank tables, each carefully labeled with owners' names. Sweet-smelling cakes and cookies and pies perfumed the air with mouth-watering aromas. Corn, still in husks and still attached to gigantic stalks, formed green shocks near displays of great hubbard squashes, cucumbers, bunches of maroon beets—and every other vegetable then known to St. Lawrence County vegetable gardens. Phlox, nasturtiums, veronica, roses, daisies, and asters in a last blaze of summer color stood in vases, sending their perfumes into the mélange that tickled nostrils even outside the halls. Livestock lowed, bleated, grunted, cackled, hissed, and quacked. A bantam rooster, mistaking the time of day, threw back his head to let out a cock-a-doodle-do that belied his size. The great Percherons shifted weight from one great foot to another in the long row of stables, resting after sledge-pulling contests. Close by, prizewinning dairy cattle contentedly chewed their cud, tails whisking away pesky flies. Giant Poland sows and porkers rooted in the muddy ground, burying themselves to keep cool with happy grunts.

The beauty and opulence of harvest and of herds added to the heady excitement and anticipation of the chattering crowd. These were people of pioneer parentage, and the local culture was still largely agrarian, dependent on the toil of the farm families in the great crowd. Also there that day were old-timers who could recall the untamed wilderness and the herculean efforts that only seventy years earlier had harnessed the streams to build the farms and villages now successfully sprinkled throughout the county.

Pushing his way toward the oval track with the crowd that day, young Frederic Sackrider Remington had set his mind on finding the best vantage point from which to watch his father's horse run. Jolly, brash, indulged, Fred took for granted the panorama of the fair and the greetings of men and women he had known all his life. He responded with a ready grin, shouting responses in his high tenor as he shoved his stocky frame through the crowd. He may have been in the company of friends from Ogdensburg or Canton. He may have been with relatives—perhaps his mother or father, perhaps some of his other kin. Absorbed in the fair's excitement, the young man could never have dreamed that he was about to meet the tiny beauty who would become his wife. Eva Adele Caten, whom Frederic Remington married five years later in 1884, was also at the fair. Newly arrived in Canton, she was enrolled as a special student at St. Lawrence University, taking courses in French and history.[3] She had come to watch the harness races, we believe, either with college friends and her brother Will, or with her landlady, Sarah Caldwell, who had already become her friend.*

The future artist and his future wife were from similar backgrounds, but had unique differences. Fred was an only child, and the apple of his parents' eye, pampered as a child and indulged in every way throughout his nearly eighteen years. He was the eldest grand-

---

*Eva's friendship with Sarah Caldwell continued for over thirty years. During the Remingtons' frequent visits to Canton, Eva and Sarah always had good times together. After Fred's death, Eva continued to make annual pilgrimages to Canton. Her diaries mention Sarah Caldwell as one of the women she always visited.

child in both the Sackrider and Remington clans. Eva Caten was the responsible eldest daughter of Flora and Lawton Caten's brood of five.* Fred came from two established, prominent Canton families, and his father had gained acclaim for political and military achievements. Eva's father was a self-taught engineer, whose ingenuity and hard work had made him a director of two small private railroad lines in central New York. Young Fred had been away from home at boarding schools or at college since he was fourteen and thought himself a man of the world. Eva and her brother William were on their first independent venture. They had traveled north by railroad from their home in Gloversville the last week of August to matriculate at St. Lawrence University, which was gaining renown as a liberal pioneer in coeducation. Eva was nineteen years old, tiny, and beautiful by any standards, but especially lovely when measured against the Victorian ideal of her time. Her waist was incredibly tiny, her complexion smooth, her dark eyes clear and soft. Fred was blond and round-faced like his mother, five feet ten inches tall, stocky and powerful, and already beginning his lifelong losing fight against corpulence. Fred was cocky and Eva was demure.

The fair-goers, with Eva and Fred in their midst and unaware as yet of each other's existence, pushed toward the grandstand. Excitement ran high; as the time for the premium heats drew near, county dignitaries made their way to the judges' stand. After shaking his partner Van's hand and wishing him good luck, Colonel Remington ran his eyes over their great hope in a final appraisal of the sleek bay. Then he joined the group of dignitaries, to be clapped on the shoulder and greeted as a prominent political figure and a newspaper editor as well. His usually gaunt countenance was flushed with anticipation. Whether Clara Remington joined her husband in the judges' stand, dallied in the big dinner tent talking with Canton friends, or accompanied her son to the grandstand, we have no way of knowing. Without doubt she was present, and as excited and happy as her nature allowed, although the undercurrent of fear for an ailing husband curtailed full pleasure in the day.

At the Premium Races each year a bugle sounded, calling horses and sulkies to the starting line. The crowd hushed momentarily to listen for the starting gun. When it barked, an answering roar mounted

---

*Lawton Caten was originally from Howlitt Hill near Syracuse, attended Onondaga Academy, taught mathematics there, and eventually became a surveyor in the western Pennsylvania oil fields and worked for small, private railroad companies. Flora, his first wife and the mother of five children, died in April 1880. Later he remarried.

from the excited mob at racetrack fence and in the stands. Anyone who remembers attending rural country fairs and who has watched harness racing knows the special excitement that the Premium Races elicited on that day. The big-wheeled sulkies bowled around the oval track, sleek racers stretched to their utmost, riders hunched on high seats, with reins and crop clutched in their guiding hands. From trackside, those horses seemed incredibly fluid and smooth, flowing down the track like taffy being pulled out strand by strand.

That afternoon, Mars's long legs moved in graceful, effortless rhythm. With Van at the reins, crouched on the high and awkward sulky, Mars soon pulled away, his flashing legs stretching the distance from the other racers. When he crossed the finish line, the enthusiastic crowd sent forth a mighty paean of joy that set echoes ringing across the nearby Grasse River, up the hill to State Street and throughout all Canton, northward over the flat, empty fields. Van and the Colonel had their winner. Mars had won hands down in all three heats. His winning time was two minutes, thirty-four seconds.[4] Money changed hands among bettors. Fred Remington, like his peers, beating their straw boaters in excitement, shouted his joy at the top of his high, reedy voice. Then he joined the mob swarming down the grandstand steps, intending to join his father and the victorious horse at the finish line.

Instead, somewhere en route—no records having been saved to detail the event—Fred Remington was introduced to Eva Caten, by whom we do not know. We have some verification from Eva Remington's own statement about her first meeting with her husband, quoted in an Ogdensburg newspaper more than thirty years later.[5] In North Country lore, the legend persists that Fred Remington fell in love with Eva Caten at first sight at the St. Lawrence County Fair in 1879. Neither Frederic Remington nor Eva Caten fulfilled the educational dreams and expectations they probably took for granted on September 18, 1879. No matter what the truth of their first encounter, the course of their lives took on a new dimension in the following months and, moving them toward the future, began to mold the youthful Frederic into the complex personality who became the adult and the successful artist.

The five ensuing years, after that hot September day at the 1879 St. Lawrence County Fair, were fraught with loss, frustration, separation, and painful failure for both Fred Remington and Eva Caten. On February 18, 1880, the day before his forty-sixth birthday, Colonel

Pierre Remington died. He had continued to ignore his failing health and in late autumn 1879 traveled south to New Brunswick, New Jersey, to watch his son play in the Yale-Rutgers football match. Within a few weeks, he was desperately ill, a victim of either "catarrh," "galloping consumption" (common terms in those days for cancer and tuberculosis, respectively), or pneumonia.

On his death, the North Country hero was transported to Canton aboard the train, to lie in state at the Sackrider house, where the Reverend Almon Gunnison conducted the funeral service. With full military honors, the Colonel was taken to Evergreen Cemetery for burial (although not in the present Remington plot).

Within the month after her husband's burial, Clara moved back to live in Canton.[6] Her rambunctious, spoiled son grieved privately behind surface bravado. "I am not a stoic yet," he wrote to his Aunt Marcia Sackrider later that year. The modest estate left by Pierre, half of which the Colonel had stipulated was to be Fred's when he reached his twenty-first birthday, prohibited a return to Yale. Instead, these circumstances thrust Fred out into a workaday world to earn his living in occupations for which he was sadly unprepared and that he repeatedly rejected. Remington's carefree college days were over, but he could not comprehend that to survive he must give up, at least for a time, some of his goals. The quick and easy success he had envisioned for himself had to be postponed.[7] For the next five years, Fred continued to live in the optimistic dream he had conjured up as a teenage youth, and that, unfortunately, both his parents had helped him to weave under fairly auspicious circumstances.

The Colonel left his widow and his eighteen-year-old son an estate that amounted to a little over twenty-one thousand dollars, a good but moderate sum in those days. (His share in the champion trotter, Mars, was listed in his will at one thousand dollars.[8]) The Colonel owned no real estate, but had instead lent out several thousand dollars in personal notes to friends and acquaintances. In his will, Pierre Remington named his brother-in-law, Horace Sackrider, and his younger brother, Lamartine Remington, as his son's guardians. They would supervise the young man's affairs until he reached his majority on October 4, 1882.

A fateful, and for young Frederic Remington also tragic, irony lay in the Colonel's choice of guardians. Pierre Remington's death was only the first loss of loving, supportive relatives. By 1882, Horace's wife, Fred's Aunt Marcia, was dead. Mart Remington died in 1884 and Horace was gone in 1890, before the demise of his elderly parents, Henry and Mary Sackrider, who were both dead by 1895. Of the entire tribe of aunts and uncles who had represented security and continuity through Fred's childhood, only Uncle Bill and Aunt Lavilla Remington, together with Rob and Emma Sackrider, remained. In counterpoint to their continuing support, Fred's dominating, ambitious, and unhappy mother, Clara, continued her efforts to mold her son into her own image of his future.

In 1880, however, Uncle Horace and Uncle Mart soon discovered that they had their hands full in attempting to guide their nephew. Although they tried to point the Colonel's son toward a career they believed would provide security and would have been acceptable to Pierre Remington, Fred continued to sketch and to paint. Even more difficult for his uncles, the immature and formerly indulged Fred pursued his hedonistic dream of enjoying life to the hilt, doing as little work as possible and—at the same time—living comfortably with no hardships and no noticeable economies.

Of these two uncles who now had loving jurisdiction over Fred, Uncle Horace was the formerly jolly but now conscientious son of the old deacon. He and the other Sackriders had almost none of the creative imagination so prominent in his nephew's personality. Horace and Marcia's loving worries for Fred's future elicited the artist's loyalty and affection. But Fred had paid no attention to their efforts to make him settle down and adopt the North Country work ethic that governed their solid, small-town, business-oriented lives. Fred, who must have sadly strained Marcia and Horace's patience—especially as Marcia's own health failed—always answered their letters light-heartedly and in good humor, but he did not take their advice seriously.

Uncle Mart, with his wife, Florence,* and little son, Charles, lived now in Albany. When he moved to the state capital, Mart was first a government employee in the Department of Public Instruction. Barton Hepburn, now a legislative representative from St. Lawrence County, and the former county commissioner of education, may possibly have recommended Mart for that job. Hepburn knew all the Remingtons through his former contacts with the Colonel in Republican county politics. Brilliant Mart soon moved on to become a political reporter for the *Albany Morning Express*. In a short time he was listed as part owner on the daily's masthead.

---

*Mart Remington married Florence Stevens of Malone, New York, in the mid-1870s. Charlie was born in 1876. Their second son, named after the dead Pierre, was born in 1882.

In 1880, within weeks after his brother Pierre's death, Mart persuaded his wife to take his young nephew Fred into their home. Then he began what became the ongoing task of finding Fred a job. For the next two years, Fred took each new job that Mart found for him through Mart's contacts in one or another government office, only to quit each new position or to be fired.

Atwood, whose Albany friends in the 1960s searched nineteenth-century records, found that Frederic Remington first worked as an aide in the governor's offices. Later, he was a clerk in the Department of Public Instruction, where Mart himself had worked. In 1882, Fred wrote to his Uncle Horace that he was in the actuary offices of the state Insurance Department. In addition, he is supposed to have been a reporter on the *Albany Morning Express* for a short time— Mart probably persuaded his partners to take Fred on in that position out of desperation.

During and between each new foray into the state bureaucracy, Fred made frequent trips to Canton. His lonely mother followed him to Albany and stayed with her in-laws for extended periods of time. She may have taken up residence there for a while, if Atwood's memory for old orally transmitted information is correct. This seems likely, for Clara continued to hover over her lone offspring until the end of 1885. During one Albany stay, Clara was engaged in piecing a crazy quilt. These quilt tops were constructed from random scraps of worn-out family garments and other bits of fabric. According to one record, Fred found the half-pieced quilt left on a table when he arrived home one day.[9] Mischievously, he decorated several quilt pieces with pen and ink caricatures of a cat and dog engaged in battle. Clara, instead of giving Fred a piece of her mind, included her son's mischief in her quilt and later bragged to her friends about his artistic abilities. The only other information that remains from Fred's years in Albany is that he became a friend of A. A. Brolley while sparring with him in a boxing bout at an athletic club that was frequented by both young men. Brolley and he maintained contact through letters; eventually, this former boxing partner became a New York State judge, who purchased one of Remington's paintings.

During his two Albany years, Fred courted Eva Caten assiduously, both by the U.S. mails and in person because the trip by railroad from Albany to Gloversville was short and involved only one change of cars. He and Eva had reached a private "understanding" as early as August 1880. At that time, Fred formally requested her hand in a short letter to her father, Lawton Caten:

Albany, Aug. 25, '80

Mr. L. Caten

Dear Sir:

I pen these lines to you on a most delicate subject and hope they will at least receive your consideration. For a year I have known your daughter Eva, and during that time have contracted a deep affection for her. I have received encouragement in all propriety, and with her permission and the fact of your countenancing my association, I feel warranted now in asking whether or not you will consent to an engagement between us. If you need time to consider or data on which to formulate I will of course be glad to accede either.

Hoping this will not be distasteful, allow me to sign.

Your Obd. Servt.

Fred'c Remington
Ex. Chamber
Albany
NY[10]

The stiff little note is in marked contrast to the breezy epistles he wrote to his Canton relatives. (We wonder whether Fred was really its author.) Eva's father summarily refused the young man's request for a formal engagement. Fred exhibited none of the accomplishments a Victorian father wanted in his eldest daughter's spouse. Not yet nineteen, Frederic Remington was immature, and he still appeared to see life as a continuous, lighthearted frolic. In addition, he sketched and drew, a further indication of frivolity to a nineteenth-century, middle-class self-made businessman. Fred's future marriage prospects seemed dim.

Nevertheless, throughout these transitional years, Fred pursued his artistic goals and began to search for a market for his drawings. In an 1882 letter to Uncle Horace, he mentioned traveling to New York to see whether *Harper's Weekly* would publish "some work of mine." He added, "It would be a good scheme if I could get something in there."[11] Fred went to New York to see *Harper's Weekly* editor George W. Curtis, who, indeed, purchased one of Fred's drawings, which was redrawn by William A. Rogers.[12] Eva, who firmly believed in her suitor's artistic ability, did everything she could to help

Fred. In 1882, the Beta Theta Pi fraternity chapter at St. Lawrence, of which Eva's brother Will was a member, published the first St. Lawrence yearbook, which they titled the *Gridiron*.* It contained a page of Remington drawings. Fred also is supposed to have placed some illustrations with J. B. Lippincott Company in Philadelphia in 1882.

Somehow, Fred Remington managed to get through the two years until he reached his majority, changing jobs frequently and visiting the North Country whenever he could. In Canton, he always made his headquarters at the Deacon's Miner Street home, where his mother lived, or with his Uncle Bill Remington. In the summer of 1881, Eva traveled to Canton to visit Sarah Caldwell. A highlight of that summer visit was a camping trip in the Big South Woods. The party included Eva, Clara Remington, and Fred, as well as others of Fred's relatives and friends. That summer Fred, who was apparently again between jobs, also spent time on the St. Lawrence River with his Ogdensburg cronies. In late summer, the impatient youth persuaded his uncles to advance him a small portion of his inheritance with which to make his first western foray. The *Plaindealer* that August carried a brief item stating that "Fred Remington, son of the late Col. S. P. Remington, expects to start . . . for Montana. We understand that he intends to make a trial of life on a ranch." This is the first intimation of Fred's own ambitions for his future. According to Atwood, the young man headed west by railroad via St. Paul, eventually visiting the site of General Custer's last stand. (Years later Fred casually passed on to his friend and Adirondack guide Has Rasbeck a rusted Colt .45 revolver that he claimed to have picked up on that battleground.[13])

Of the North Country relatives and acquaintances of Fred Remington in these difficult years, not one seems to have taken his goals for success as a professional artist seriously. Only Eva was faithful to his dream for his future, and she was busy in Gloversville during this period. Her brief college days had ended after that first semester in 1879. She, as the eldest daughter, was needed at home. Flora, her mother, died in April 1880, only two months after Fred lost his father. The twenty-year-old woman became her father's housekeeper and hostess as well as surrogate mother to her siblings. Will remained at St. Lawrence. Her younger brother and sister, Frederick

*The *Gridiron* is now a St. Lawrence institution. Its name refers to the gridiron on which the original San Lorenzo was martyred by being burned.

and Clara, were adolescents. Eva's closest family relationship, however, was with little sister Emma, nine years her junior, who turned to Eva for nurturing thereafter. The ties formed between the two during these years only strengthened in years to come.

William L. Caten later married and lived in Dayton, Ohio; Frederick A. Caten eventually became a businessman in Pittsburgh. Each brother fathered two children. Eva visited her brothers' families periodically during her marriage and returned again during her first years of widowhood. Clara Caten married Horatio Burr, called "Hote" by the family, and remained in Gloversville. In later years, Eva and Fred frequently stopped to visit the Burrs when traveling to the North Country, and Eva returned to Gloversville regularly while Fred was away on professional trips.

Only Emma Caten remained single, living at home with her father, who later married Sarah McCollum. According to Betsey Caten Deuval, great-niece of Emma and Eva and granddaughter of Will Caten, Emma and her stepmother were not congenial and Emma was unhappy at home, both in Gloversville and later in Syracuse, where Lawton Caten moved his second wife and spinster daughter. Emma grasped every opportunity to visit Eva and Fred Remington, both in New Rochelle and later at Ingleneuk in the Thousand Islands. She was the person to whom Eva turned upon Fred's sudden death in 1909, and the two sisters eventually lived together in Ogdensburg. After Eva died in 1918, Emma remained on in the city until her own death nearly forty years later.

Remington's first serious attempts at oil painting began during these years, with Eva's encouragement. *The Captive Gaul* has been dated circa 1883–1885, and we believe that it was painted in Canton before Fred went west to Kansas in 1884.[14] Both portraits of his grandfather Deacon Henry L. Sackrider date from about the same time and are painted in the traditional style Fred used during this early period. The Sackrider portraits must have been painted when he was in Canton on one of his frequent escapes from Albany and the desk jobs he found so boring.

In the twentieth century, Atwood Manley visited his friend Henry M. Sackrider, in the old Miner Street house when Henry's mother, Fred's Aunt Emma, lay dying. Henry's parents, Bob and Emma Sackrider, had taken over the home after the deacon's death in the 1890s. Three of Frederic S. Remington's paintings hung in the house at the time of his visit. Atwood remembers:

I can recall seeing at least two—*The Captive Gaul* in the hallway, and *The Water Hole*. It hung in the front parlor, to the right as one entered from the front hall, near a front window. Then there was another well-remembered Remington oil which graced that home down through many, many years. This was the portrait Remington did of the old Deacon, then grizzled, wrinkled and gray. It was painted on a piece of board. Although Remington has been never been rated as a great portrait painter, that likeness of Deacon Sackrider had something which left one with an indelible vision of the old man. *The Captive Gaul* is now [1968] in the Remington Art Museum in Ogdensburg; [*The Fight for*] *the Water Hole* is in the Richard Norton Memorial Museum in Shreveport, and St. Lawrence University owns the Deacon's portrait.

None of Fred's and Eva's courtship correspondence has survived. We believe that Eva herself destroyed these letters after her husband died or directed Emma Caten to do so during her final illness in 1918. The hopes, dreams, aspirations, and affections of the young couple come to us only from the circumstances within which they lived, both personally and as products of their age.

In the early 1880s, Fred and Eva were young and ambitious, their lives seemingly stretching into a future of limitless horizons, like their young contemporaries' and the nation's itself. The late nineteenth century was an age of optimism, expansion, and success, as the American people eagerly sought to make themselves masters of the new Eden into which they had been born or to which they had flocked from across the Atlantic. The nation swept headlong in pursuit of the Manifest Destiny its leaders and innovators dared and plotted to realize. In these characteristics, Frederic S. Remington and Eva Adele Caten were very much a part of their times and culture. With the omniscience of hindsight, we can look back, a century later, at that younger nation and at the younger, would-be artist from a totally different mind frame to evaluate and criticize. The nation was adolescent in the late 1800s and so, coincidentally, was Fred Remington in the mid-1880s. Both moved impetuously on with the great experiment, making a good many mistakes—as we now realize only in retrospect.

Fantasy, myth, and reality have become totally tangled with factual reports and writing about Fred Remington's life in the years 1883 through 1885. Accounts in the sources we have discovered contain sketchy or contradictory evidence about Fred Remington in his unsuccessful roles as Kansas rancher and as entrepreneur. The young Remington himself contributed to some myths and misrepresentations of actual events, in efforts to save face. Some result from gaps in historical records. J. Henry Harper's editors, and even the publisher himself, further added to the resulting confusion with the ballyhoo of nineteenth-century public relations, helping to create the legend that their rising young illustrator had been one of the cowhands he portrayed. Then, down through the years, each student or biographer of Remington has contributed his or her own speculations, which add to the mystique and sometimes reinforce error. After all, we each come to these tasks with the unconscious baggage of individual bias, no matter how much we hope to achieve objectivity! To spin a readable tale, as Fred himself well knew, all of Frederic Remington's biographers, including us, have sometimes resorted to conjecture in order to make sense of time gaps or sparse facts that do not fit the Remington we have perceived.

Remington's 1883 experiences may have formed the basis for that later legend that he was a cowpuncher, but here reality is definitely at odds with the myth. Every piece of evidence we can find points to our conclusion that Fred played at sheep ranching, was profligate in spending his inheritance, and experienced only failure. We have also concluded that Fred could have matured into the future artist he became only through these private and public humiliations. Once stripped of his false conceptions of self and life, Fred found he possessed an inner core of determination and grit and was able to harness these to his artistic talents. Once beyond the final throes of adolescence and with his sights set firmly on his goals, he never wavered. Only then could he find the success that was so important to his ego.

But first Fred Remington had to try his wings and learn how to fail. In February 1883, four months after Fred reached his majority, the *Plaindealer* columns announced to its readership that Frederic S. Remington had "resigned a government position" at Albany and had returned to Canton. In March 1883, Frederic S. Remington purchased a 320-acre sheep ranch in Peabody Township, Butler County, Kansas, for which he paid out most of his inheritance. To many easterners, *ranch* conjured up the image of miles of grazing range for cattle or sheep. Fred's family and friends in northern New York, if he had shared the facts about his purchase with them, would then have called his ranch merely a "good-size" farm, and they would have

raised eyebrows at the idea of Fred the rancher. The Fred Remington they knew had no farming experience and certainly no knowledge of sheep, whose seeming idiocies and herding instincts require
skill and patience. The nearest Fred had come to working with animals was helping out occasionally at his father's and Van's stables,
and owning and riding his own horse. His only professional discipline had been pushing a pen at Albany desk jobs, which he had quit
or from which he had been fired with regularity.

Nevertheless, Fred appeared to have had a wonderful time for
most of that year on his ranch. He enjoyed himself with other ranch-
ers and largely ignored the daily grind of hard work that might possibly (and the possibility was still remote) have spelled success. One
day of sport and fun, for instance, saw Fred and other local men
hunting jackrabbits on horseback on the neighboring ranch owned
by Robert Camp, a former Yale classmate of Fred's. In 1887, Fred
put that experience to good purpose by writing and illustrating
"Coursing Rabbits on the Plains" for *Outing* magazine, of which
another college mate, Poultney Bigelow, was an editor. His contacts
with Bigelow later ripened into friendship; an extensive correspondence, now owned by St. Lawrence University, tells of a partnership
including two working trips abroad.

There are intimations, however, that in reality Fred was running
away from loneliness, from having to cook for himself (he is supposed to have lived primarily on canned beans!), and from his igno-
rance about ranching. With the habitual lifelong bravado behind which
he hid his true feelings from the world, Remington wrote only the
sketchiest of letters home to Canton, most containing requests to
Uncle Horace for additional funds from his St. Lawrence National
Bank account.[15] As Fred's Canton account dwindled, family anxieties
for the welfare of the adventurer mounted. For all they knew from
Fred, he was off on his own, really on his own, in an adventurous
frontier life, exploring Kansas prairies, riding his favorite horse, Pinto,
hell-bent across the plains, sketching and painting, and—of course—
doing well. His relatives, however, reached other conclusions: Fred,
that eldest heir to family name and honor, was obviously failing, and
he was brushing aside any thoughts about his real future. Among
the North Country family, perhaps one or two sensed that Fred
Remington was still in flight from his father's death and from some
of life's realities.

In October 1883, Fred had a visitor from home. His uncle, Mart
Remington, arrived at the Peabody ranch. What prompted his visit,

we can only surmise. It seems likely that he was the emissary of both Remingtons and Sackriders. Probably of all Fred's relatives, he had had the most satisfactory relationship with Fred at that time. No one knows for sure what transpired between Mart and Fred during the October visit: whether Mart tried to talk sense to his nephew or whether his purpose was to persuade Fred to sell out and return home. The family—especially Clara—hoped for the latter. Perhaps Mart Remington tried to reach beneath the stubborn, self-willed optimism and the desire to paint to find out what his nephew was really experiencing; more likely he urged Fred to return to an occupation like his own or like those of Fred's other relatives. Mart's younger son, Pierre, stated in a letter (now the property of the Kansas State Historical Society) written many years later that Mart, like Colonel Pierre Remington, wanted Fred Remington to be a journalist or politician and had vigorously opposed having a male artist in the family.

When Mart left Peabody, he did not take Fred back East with him, but he did take the vehicle of his own death. Atwood has discovered that Fred's young uncle, only thirty-four during his stay, fell prey to a cold or the flu while in Kansas. He already apparently had the dreaded tuberculosis bacillus in his system when he visited his nephew, and, later that winter, the disease forced Mart's resignation from the *Albany Morning Express*.[16] Mart was dying, just as had his oldest brother, Fred's father, Pierre, only four years before. Soon after his thirty-fifth birthday in December, the young man moved his wife Florence, seven-year-old Charlie, and baby Pierre, born in 1882, home to her parents, near Malone in the North Country's Franklin County. Then Mart went into the Adirondacks to Cranberry Lake to "take the cure" of cold mountain air that so many other tuberculosis victims in the late nineteenth century hoped would restore health. The hope was vain. Fred's Uncle Mart, thirteen years the young man's senior and as much an elder brother as an uncle, died May 15, 1884.[17]

By late December 1883, Fred—for whatever reasons—was ready to quit his ranch. He referred to this in a letter written to Arthur Merkley (which is in the collection of Sackrider letters and thus probably identifies Merkley as a younger brother or nephew of Rob Sackrider's wife, the former Emma Merkley). In that letter, Fred wrote of selling out, moving farther west, going into business ("I don't care whether it is stock, mercantile, either hardware or whisky—or anything else.").[18]

The tone of the letter is despondent, an unusual mood for Fred. Perhaps Fred let his real feelings about ranching show. He may have voiced suggestions urged on him by Mart Remington, who could easily have suggested the hardware business as one occupation Fred knew enough about to survive in. As a boy, Fred had often frequented Deacon Sackrider's and Uncle Horace's Main Street store. Both those worthies, however, would have been horrified at the idea of their young relative's selling whisky. Also, by late December, Fred may have learned how serious his Uncle Mart's "cold" had become and begun to run from fear of another impending family tragedy. More probably, Fred Remington was trying to escape the results of a disastrous prank that had occurred a few days before.

That thoughtless mischief, of which he had been a ringleader, certainly contributed to Fred's desire to get away from Peabody. Twenty-two-year-old Fred's final exploit in Butler County, in company with other young roisterers, was to break up a community Christmas Eve program in nearby Plum Creek by pelting a performer's bald head with spitballs. He and his fellow mischief-makers were arraigned at the bench of the local justice of the peace, but the case was dismissed after two days. Fred took responsibility for all legal expenses incurred.[19] Then he put up his livestock and implements for sale and left ranching for good. His only bequests to the community of his first business investment were the future *Outing* article and two paintings. One, according to papers in the Kansas State Historical Society, he gave to the Peabody Library; the other, his depiction of a cowboy painted in oil on the inside of his ranch barn, is now gone forever.

The overindulged, immature boy in Remington was still in the ascendant. Everything had gone his way materially so far—excepting, of course, two years in Albany and one year at sheep farming. Optimistically, he clung to his former hedonistic goals. To rush headlong and precipitously into another adventure was one way to forget the finality of separation from his father and the fear of pain to come as he learned of Mart Remington's serious illness.

He returned home to Canton briefly in February 1884 and in all likelihood was finally able, in concert with Eva in Gloversville, to persuade Lawton Caten to let him marry Eva. Doubtless, he impressed Eva's father with his new plans, which he later optimistically announced on the Street in Canton to either Gilbert or Williston Manley. Naturally, the *Plaindealer* editor included this "news item" in the paper's Personal column. This time, however, the *Plaindealer* was a bit more cautious about Remington's ever changing future.

"He has sold out his lands and appears to have done well," Gilbert wrote, adding that Fred was entering business in Kansas City. What Fred did not tell the Manleys was that he had yet to realize the proceeds of the sale of his ranch. All that remained in his pocket of his inheritance was the cash he had realized from selling off his sheep and horses.

A gap occurs in the records that has made us speculate about whether or not Fred Remington had a final visit with his uncle, Mart Remington, during this 1884 visit to the North Country. Here again, as with extant material from the period of Fred's father's death, we can only assume that the young Remington had difficulty accepting the impending death of the other man who had been a primary role model in his formative years. A few years later, he would lose his close friend of the late 1880s, Lieutenant Powhatan Clarke. At that time, Remington also seems to have assumed stoicism, but he quickly turned to Poultney Bigelow and later to Owen Wister as sources of friendship and perhaps of affection. By the last decade of his own life, Fred had become a private and solitary figure, completely absorbed in his art. Perhaps through his work, the adult Remington found a way to come to terms with loss and death, as well as with himself. This may partially account for the intensity with which he later was to work—and for the outpouring in art, in articles, and in private correspondence that characterized him for most of the rest of his life.

But Fred Remington was not yet ready for any of this in 1884. By April, he was in the hardware business in Kansas City, using most of the proceeds he had finally received from sale of the sheep ranch. He had lured a former Ogdensburg schoolmate, Charlie Ashley, to join him in the supposedly limitless opportunities blossoming in this up-and-coming community near the western frontier. They hung up their sign, "Ashley and Remington," on Kansas City's busy Sixth Street, informing the passing public that the firm dealt in sheet and bar iron. Whether or not the brave new firm ever realized any sales, we do not know, but young Ashley soon pulled out of the venture and disappeared from Fred Remington's life.

In May, word came from the North Country that Mart Remington was dead. By June, Fred had invested the rest of his capital in a one-third partnership in Bishop & Christie, the popular saloon near his erstwhile hardware business. He kept quiet about this investment, but from then on spent most of his "business" hours shooting pool and spinning yarns with the customers there. Bishop & Christie's was popular with the city's sports. Leaning on the bar, Fred could find people of the kind he admired. Noted poet Eugene Field frequented the saloon when he was in Kansas City, and so did artist John Mulvaney, whose *Custer's Last Stand* had brought him temporary renown.

That spring, Fred must have paid his respects and told his marriage plans to his parents' old friends, the Watson Ferrys and their brother-in-law, Wallace Pratt of the firm of Pratt, Brombeck and Ferry. The Ferrys were distressed when they learned about Fred's saloon partnership. What Frank and Nellie Hough, Fred's new and best Kansas City friends, thought about this latest business venture, no one knows. Nellie never gave her opinion about it in her 1926 memoirs about Fred, which were published in *International Studio*.

Actually, most of Fred's time in Kansas City was spent riding out into the countryside to sketch and paint, or drawing from models like his willing friend Frank Hough, rather than in the more prosaic pursuits of earning a living. Nellie Hough said later that she never knew anyone so preoccupied with work as Fred was with his art. His other preoccupation was Eva. He bought the house in Pendleton Heights for her. Then he went East to marry Eva, buoyant with his usual optimism, besotted with love, and completely oblivious of mounting bills and impending disaster. The two did not take a honeymoon. (Probably Fred did not have enough funds, but persuaded his bride that their new life in their little home in Kansas City would be an unending honeymoon.)

In the last months of 1884, young Frederic Remington was forced to reveal his financial situation to his new wife. Then, in the later confrontation with his mother, he was able to stand firm on his determination to make his way as an artist. Finally, when he failed to recover the remnant of his inheritance that had been invested in Bishop & Christie's saloon, Remington abandoned once and for all his halfhearted efforts to meet his family's expectations. His delusion of achieving easy financial success was burst forever. When he rode out of Kansas City to the West early in the summer of 1885 on Shorty Reason's old plug, he was stripped of illusion, as well as of his patrimony, and ready to begin his lifework.

All unknowing he took with him, however, an intangible inheritance. He had absorbed from the postpioneer culture of the North Country an ability to survive and to make the most of circumstances.

From that region he had gained an innate sense of harmony with the elemental life in nature. From his own hardworking predecessors, he had inherited an as yet unexploited ethic of work and achievement. And somehow, he had been bequeathed the seeds of great creativity and artistic talent.

(Courtesy of Frederic Remington Collection, Owen D. Young Library. St. Lawrence University, Canton, N.Y.)

5

"HE GOES LIKE THE WIND"

« 1885–1886 »

Fred wandered through Oklahoma and other regions of the South-west during the summer of 1885, filing away in his memory the land-scapes, people, animals, action, and color that would later spring to life again in his drawings and paintings. His pockets emptied of his scant hoard of coins and bills while his sketchbooks filled to over-flowing. During these months, he may have hired on as a cowhand or other ranch worker to keep going. By late August, he was broke and miserably homesick for Missie, as he called his new wife, but his mind's eye teemed with all he had seen. He appeared on Frank and Nellie Hough's doorstep in Kansas City one day in early September. That evening, he confided to Nellie and Franklin that he wanted to go back East to be with Eva and to find a market for his art so that he could support her. Frank Hough lent him the railroad fare for the journey (although Fred later told a far more romantic story about the source of his carfare to J. Henry Harper, head of Harper Broth-ers Publishing Company, which Harper put to good use in publiciz-ing his new illustrator.)[1]

As the train racketed eastward, the young Remington's new life pattern was already emerging. All unaware, he had finished his first field trip. In his sketchbooks was a record of cowboys, Indians, mil-itary troopers, Mexican hovels, and horses—always horses and more horses. He was heading home toward Eva and the North Country, as he did thereafter with unfailing regularity. Around a short bend in time lay the first professional and public recognition of his talents, and from then on his rise to success and financial security would be rapid. Never again did Remington actually live in the West, but yearly, and sometimes more often, he returned to refill bulging sketchbooks, shoot countless photographs, gather a unique collection of artifacts for his work and for Eva's pleasure, and record for eastern periodical readers a vanishing frontier that they perceived mainly through his eyes. This would, in addition, become his contribution toward a national identity and his bequest to future generations.

Fred Remington joined Eva in Gloversville in early September 1885, a few weeks before their first wedding anniversary. After paying respects to Lawton Caten and regaling Eva's sisters and brother-in-law with accounts of his adventures, Fred swept Eva north with him to Canton. Here, Remingtons and Sackriders welcomed the prodigal back into the family fold. Canton and family moved at a slower, less frenetic pace than did the energetic Frederic Remington, but the quiet village pricked up its ears and quickened to a livelier beat whenever Fred strode down Main Street or paused to greet friends near the replica of a big shoe box that stood in front of Ellsworth's shoe store. Because rumor of his Kansas City debacle had preceded Fred's homecoming, raised eyebrows and clicking tongues were a minor accompaniment to the more enthusiastic welcomes he received. Beneath the surface confidence Remington exuded, and in spite of preoccupation with his own future, he and Eva noted changes in Canton, but, especially and more poignantly, in the families.

Grandpa and Grandma Sackrider were old and ailing now. The Deacon and his Mary were living out their days in the Miner Street house, cared for by Fred's mother, Clara Remington. Since Aunt Marcia's death in 1882, Horace, whom Eva lovingly called "Dude," lived alone in the house on State Street and carried on the family hardware business without the zest of former years, as his health steadily declined. Bob Sackrider was a fixture now at the First National Bank, growing more dandified and less effectual with each year, but just as loving. At his home, Emma, Eva's confidante and friend, watched over their only child, Henry, now eight years old. Next door, and practically family to the Sackriders, lived Aunt Minnie Ellsworth and her racehorse-loving husband, Richard. Childless Aunt Minnie mothered nieces and nephews, including her nephew by affection, Fred Remington. She adopted Eva immediately. In later years, Aunt Minnie pasted every clipping about Fred's career that came her way into a scrapbook that she kept for the rest of her life (that scrapbook, and another compiled later by Aunt Minnie's spinster niece, Fanny Wead, came into Atwood's hands and provided valuable clues for our research).

Change was even more apparent in the dwindling tribe of Remington. Of the original seven who arrived in Canton in 1854, only Uncle Bill remained. The two Remington daughters, Maria and Josie, were married and long since gone from Canton. Strong-minded Grandmother Maria had died in 1878. Grandfather Seth Williston was buried in Sackets Harbor in 1881. Two of the three fine Remington sons were dead, and Bill Remington had moved into his brother Pierre's shoes as Canton postmaster and now was a rising force in county and state Republican circles. Eventually, Bill was named county clerk and ultimately collector of the port in Ogdensburg. He had purchased the clothing emporium formerly owned by Ezekiel Willson and Richard Ellsworth, now renamed the Remington Clothing Store and located in the Miner block at the corner of Court and Main streets. George, Fred's favorite cousin, was living in Brooklyn and training in merchandising at Brooks Brothers men's store in Manhattan, with plans to return to Canton to manage his father's new business enterprise. Having George in Brooklyn added pleasure to Fred and Eva's own plans. (George carried out his goals and Remington's clothing store became a North Country institution. Later, he and his father opened a branch store in Watertown, sixty miles down the line, which George managed until his early forties, when he, like so many Remington men, suffered ill health and was forced to resign.)

In 1885, however, George had left Canton only weeks before Fred and Eva arrived, so that of Fred's Remington cousins, only teenage Ella, now emerging as a beauty, remained in Fred's old home village. Ella walked out with young men but showed no inclination to marry yet, and for this she was teased unmercifully by Fred, who affectionately called her his "old maid cousin." She and Mary Atwood, a relative newcomer to Canton and third of Isaac M. Atwood's family of five, were good friends.* The Bill Remingtons now lived in the former Hodskin House annex on the corner of Main and Miner streets, which Uncle Bill had bought and refurbished as a private home. As a result, Fred Remington's Canton relatives mostly lived in cosy proximity to one another and to the brand-new gray granite town hall and opera house, which had been built in 1878 directly across Miner Street from the William Remington's and beside the big red

*Mary Atwood married Will Manley; she was Atwood's mother.

brick Miner house where Ebenezer's old widow, Eliza, still lived. Regularly, the town clock, pride of the entire village, bonged out the hours from its place in the tower.

Although there was a dearth of Remingtons in Canton, the family was enlarged through marriage and affection. Whenever the Reverend Almon Gunnison took his family back to Canton on regular visits from Brooklyn, they stayed with the Bill Remingtons, because the two sisters, Lavilla Remington and Ella Gunnison, were close. Almon's younger brother, Herbert, was also in Brooklyn, working on a newspaper. The third Gunnison brother, Walter, had elected to stay on at St. Lawrence University to teach, although he later followed his brothers to Brooklyn and became headmaster at Erasmus Hall Academy. Almon's son Frederick, third of the prank-playing triumvirate of Remington, Remington, and Gunnison, now worked in a Brooklyn bank.

Up on the Hill in Canton, Fred and Eva could see how St. Lawrence University was growing. Two new college presidents, Dr. Absalom Graves Gaines and Dr. Isaac M. Atwood of the Theological School, presided over a student body that now boasted more than one hundred men and women. A second classroom building, Fisher Hall, stood near the school's original brick building, now named Richardson Hall, on the crown of the Hill. Close by was the red sandstone Herring Library. Dr. Henry Priest, college dean and professor of physics, had his young sister-in-law, Emily Eaton, living with him and his wife Flora in the old Willson house that they had purchased on Judson Street. Emily had come from Montpelier, Vermont, in 1882 as one of the young men and women who made up the St. Lawrence student body. She was gray-eyed, blond, and statuesque, with a lively intellectual curiosity that did not hamper her reputation as the best dancer at college balls. (Emily even taught her professors how to waltz!) Eva and Fred learned all about Emily from family talk about the Canton Cribbage Club, which Barton Hepburn had organized, and of which Emily was the only other member.[2]

A. Barton Hepburn, now prominent throughout the state, had quit his legislative career and returned to the North Country after his wife, Hattie, had died, leaving him with two small sons to raise. Now he was in the lumber business. He had already added the *A* (for Alonzo) to his name (nobody knew why) and had entered the lumber business backward, after rising quickly through the state government. From a penniless youth who had to drop out of Middlebury College, he was now becoming a North Country tycoon and a wealthy man by northern New York standards. Barton had achieved statewide recognition during his legislative years when he was appointed head of a commission to investigate malpractice in the piratical private railroad industries in the Empire State. His outstanding report and recommendations for fair regulation of the railroads brought him the appointment of superintendent of the state banking department in 1880, where his just and careful work then won the support of the very officers whose banking institutions he had to examine.

When he quit his political career on his wife's death, Hepburn returned to the North Country to practice law. His outstanding defense of some of his Colton neighbors—whose land titles were challenged by a large absentee landholder who intended to harvest lumber from the properties—won him admiration from his opponents, plus an offer to join their business interests. Now Barton himself owned large tracts of northern Adirondack forest and was busy working to initiate improved lumber harvesting techniques and better means of floating his log crops down the Grasse River to the Canton sawmills.

Barton had moved from Colton to Canton before Fred and Eva's 1885 early autumn visit. That summer, he had hired a crew of carpenters to build a ten-room home near the university on College Street, along which Emily Eaton walked each day on her way to class. It was no coincidence that the former St. Lawrence County assemblyman formed the Cribbage Club. The whole village knew that Barton Hepburn was smitten with the girl from Vermont. But Emily went blithely along, unconscious as yet that the quiet, bearded man so much older than she who often visited the Priest home intended to marry her and in later years would, in fact, carry her off to social and financial prominence in New York City.[3]

Hepburn was nineteen years the senior of both Emily Eaton and Frederic Remington. Outwardly, he was the antithesis of the aspiring artist, slight, cautious, and quiet, with dark brown hair and beard and blue eyes. Hepburn gave courteous consideration to every person who crossed his path, while Fred was often abrupt and even rude, driven by his inability to feel completely at ease in the company of others. But in years to come Barton Hepburn and the adult Frederic Remington shared certain characteristics and loves: both were thorough and hardworking; they had common ideals and values; and both loved forest and stream, hunting and fishing. That fall in Canton their paths often crossed, and they renewed the ties that had begun with Barton Hepburn's regard for Fred's father, the Colonel, in Ogdensburg and in county political affairs. In Albany, Barton had quietly watched the scatty youth during Fred's unhappy days in government work and had lent a hand to help him out when he could. Now Hepburn and Remington measured each other's worth, liked what they saw, and moved slowly toward the twenty-four-year friendship that would end abruptly at Fred's early death in 1909. The same kind of relationship occurred between Emily and Eva, although Eva Remington was the quieter and Emily the more forceful of the two women.

By October, Fred and Eva Remington were ready for New York City, Fred to invade and conquer the world of periodical publishing with his Western sketches, Eva to enjoy the excitement and attractions of the great city. When they climbed aboard the Pullman car at the Canton depot, the young Remingtons had won Uncle Bill Remington's support for Fred's artistic aspirations, either through Eva's gentle persuasion or because Uncle Bill was impressed with Fred's work. In addition, the couple had promises of a warm welcome from North Country family and friends now located in New York: Cousin George Remington; Almon and Ella Gunnison, who lived in the parsonage beside All Souls Universalist Church at the corner of Ocean and Ditmas avenues in Brooklyn; Fred Gunnison, now on Brooklyn's Dime Savings Bank staff and making a name for himself; Herbert Gunnison, a reporter on the *Brooklyn Eagle,* although he and his 1881 St. Lawrence classmate, John L. Heaton, had first found jobs on the *Brooklyn Times;* and Irving Bacheller, also on the *Times.*[4]

These young reporters had begun working at five dollars a week, a salary that gives an indication of the standard of living then. All eventually were successful: Herbert Gunnison's business talent made him the *Brooklyn Eagle* publisher; John L. Heaton moved to Pulitzer's *New York World* and became a renowned editorial writer who helped to found Columbia University's Pulitzer School of Journalism. Irving Bacheller eventually, with backing from Herbert Gunnison, founded the Bacheller Syndicate, moved among the literary elite, and was the first to read Stephen Crane's classic *The Red Badge of Courage.* The Bachellers were friends of the Fred Remingtons and the Barton Hepburns.[5]

Other men and women followed the first group of ambitious people from the sparsely populated North Country. Fred Remington had at least a nodding acquaintance with most of them. Before long in New York, the St. Lawrence County Association was organized with the sole purpose of giving transplanted North Country people opportunities to get together socially. An annual dinner, which the Remingtons usually attended (and which Eva continued to attend after Fred's death, as her diary records), became a traditional event.

The young Remingtons and their North Country friends moved to New York at a time when throngs of other people also were arriving—including thousands who filtered through Ellis Island each year. Optimism and prosperity sounded the dominant theme in the last decades of the old century, against a minor counterpoint of apprehension and anxiety. The new age of industry was ushering out old, familiar customs of a vanishing era. From the 1880s on, the entire nation was swept along on swift currents of change, but in New York City great concentrations of humanity intensified the energies of that current.

One great force for change was those individuals who saw a new Eden in the country's vast horizons and seemingly limitless resources. These men and women believed firmly that within themselves, as well as the nation's own young history and resources, lay the American genius. Although he had yet to prove so, Frederic Remington belonged to this group. Others, and these included prominent literary and artistic leaders, looked back to the glories of Europe's past civilizations for models after which to design the new American identity. Led by them and fueled with the fortunes of America's new industrial elite, New York and its sister cities rushed to create an American renaissance that would vie with the glories of Italy's ancient city-states, and perhaps the even more distant classic ideals of Rome and Athens.[6]

Of the two who arrived at Grand Central Terminus on the morning train that early autumn day, Frederic Remington maintained a frenetic pace that echoed that of the city. But he, not Eva, balked at its massed humanity, unable to assimilate and adapt comfortably to the many stimuli, the cacophony of city sound, the multitudes, and the confusion. Remington reacted to New York as author William James did when he first visited: "The first impression of New York . . . is one of repulsion to the clangor, disorder and permanent earthquake conditions."[7] Fred, whose muse was art, not poetic language, used more pithy words when he commented on New York. Although he lived, worked, and played in or near New York for most of the rest of his life, he never became a true city man. He may have dressed the part, he may have acted the role, but at best it was a sorry compromise. Remington yearned for forest and stream and a more elemental life. The frontier or the North Country, where man conquered or lived in harmony with nature, would provide not only the subjects for his art but an environment for which his own nature longed.

For Remington, the city was the means to an end. Henry Adams, that great commentator on nineteenth-century America, could have been describing the Remington of that New York world when he said that the average American was "a pushing, energetic, ingenious person . . . always awake and trying to get ahead of his neighbors" whose stimulants were "work and whisky."[8] As with other Americans of his time, "work became a form of vice," and Fred "never cared much for money or power after he earned them," although he pursued both assiduously.[9] From the time he and Eva first arrived in New York, Frederic was absorbed in making his mark in the world of publishing and later in climbing to a professional pinnacle among the art world's elite. He achieved the former in a short time, but only attained the artistic Olympus near the close of his life.

Eva Remington typified many late-nineteenth-century women. Her home was her domain, whether it was their first Brooklyn walk-up on South Ninth Street, the two-story house they later moved to near East 150th Street in the Bronx, "Endion" in New Rochelle, or their final country home at Ridgefield, Connecticut. Throughout her life with Frederic, Eva Caten Remington made their home his haven of comfort and a center of pleasant social life for their North Country and New York friends. She was, above all, a nurturer who protected Fred from the worst parts of himself and from the alien forces in life that he could not comfortably endure. Eva always "enjoyed the good life" and expected Frederic to provide it for her. She, of the two, exhibited a lively interest in, and took full advantage of, the city's cultural life: the opera, the latest play of David Belasco, Mark Twain's last amusing book, romantic novels like *Ramona,* exhibitions at the Metropolitan or Brooklyn museum.[10] She and Frederic followed city, state, and national politics enthusiastically, and Eva became a gentle advocate of women's suffrage.

Like her contemporaries, Eva loved to shop with friends at the city's new department stores, to order custom-designed hats from a milliner, to cut and sew dresses at home. She was appalled at New York food prices and a great bargain shopper. Eva was the shrewd observer in the marriage; later in her diary she commented on such people as leading illustrator Howard Pyle or writer J. Montgomery

Flagg. Her artist husband, on the other hand, reacted to those he knew or met far more emotionally than did Eva. Although Eva seldom traveled with Fred on his western journeys to collect material for his art, when she did, she was as involved as he in the new scenes and people. And—as time proved—she absorbed enough of Fred's business acumen to be able, after his death in 1909, to negotiate and conduct business affairs concerning his artwork.[11]

In one habit, the Remingtons were not typical of their counterparts. The leading book of etiquette at that time dictated that the wife should always pen family letters because "women always write these best," according to author Mrs. E. B. Duffy.[12] Although Eva did write faithfully to the family, Fred was as prolific in his correspondence as he was in sketching and drawing. Remington scratched out innumerable letters to family, business colleagues, military friends, literary and artistic contemporaries, and his wife. He was by turns terse or loquacious, and he cared not a whit for spelling or grammar—and sometimes he did not care what he said.*

In autumn 1885, Frederic and Eva Remington were strangers to the big city that later became so familiar. The New York they entered was already a great urban center, and about to become even greater if its financial and artistic leaders had their way. It was no longer Old New York, huddled at the foot of Manhattan with small communities farther north separated by cow pastures and picturesque country roads. Urban sprawl was creeping steadily north to encompass Morningside Heights and what once were summer homes in Harlem. On Fifth Avenue, palatial mansions of the new aristocracy, the titans of industry, were rising in Baroque, Renaissance, or Classic grandeur. In that modern wonder Central Park, gentlemen and ladies decked in formal riding attire posted sedately on English saddles. That newfangled contraption, the bicycle, was gaining popularity, too: bold young men and even young ladies wheeled precariously along drives where New York's fashionable took the air in open carriages. On the eastern park perimeter facing Fifth Avenue and the Eighties, the Metropolitan Museum of Art loomed foursquare and

*Much that we know of the artist has been found in the hundreds of his letters that have survived, most now in university and museum collections. During his early research, Atwood located some sources, but we are fortunate that Allen P. and Marilyn D. Splete, formerly affiliated with St. Lawrence University, have been collecting, sorting, and editing the masses of Remington letters. They frequented Atwood's den for long hours of Remington talk and have shared their work, *Frederic Remington—Selected Letters,* with us.

On the artist's spelling and grammar, see also note 23 to chapter 3 (page 244).

solid, as yet ungraced by the façade of terraced steps and fountains that later made it a classic cultural mecca.[13]

Farther downtown, horse-drawn trolleys, called horsecars, transported shoppers and businessmen on the grid of cross streets and north-south avenues that were supposed to order traffic. Vans and carts vied with buggies and surreys amid noisy confusion. Occasionally, a wild driver broke away from the mass to race at breakneck speed along residential streets lined with brownstone dwellings. New York did not yet have a speed limit, and harried policemen were the only traffic control.[14] On the Ladies Mile, merchandising marvels like B. Altman & Co. and Arnold Constable department stores were fast drawing customers away from small establishments that still specialized in hats or tobacco or fabrics or gloves. Here, too, was Brooks Brothers, where Cousin George Remington worked. With the advent of mass production, ready-made clothing was beginning to appear. At the base of the island, Wall Street's financial district had crowded into the unplanned lanes and byways of a former era, swallowing up most old private homes. It was not yet the era of the skyscraper.

Ladies had discarded hoopskirts for bustles. Gentlemen wore derbies in winter and straw boaters in summer, high detachable celluloid or paper collars, and tight-fitting suits. Clerks perched on high stools in accounting houses pulled on half-sleeves to guard their boiled shirts and protected their eyesight with visors. Fashionable ladies were preoccupied with long kid gloves, which they purchased by the dozen. They gathered to lunch at the Plaza or at Delmonico's. At night, gaslights glowed along the populous streets where New York's fashionable traveled in carriages to glittering balls or dinners, the opera or theater. Gargantuan, multicourse meals were the style at all-male dinners. Ladies sometimes indulged in the "vapors" and smelling salts when alarmed (or angry). Edith Wharton's fastidious society moved in dignified and stately tread alongside the less glamorous middle-class citizenry. The stereopticon graced almost every middle-class parlor. Painting china or seashells was a ladylike artistic craze. Gentlemen inhaled fine Cuban cigars, and a growing number were puffing on cigarettes at their clubs, as they quaffed rich port or swirled French brandy in snifters.

This was the New York world its middle- and upper-class inhabitants chose to know and see. Absorbed in their own goals and energetically pursuing their own interests, they largely ignored the rows of cold-water flats that blighted the Lower East Side and slowly crept northward along the East River front. Into these pestilential places crowded the immigrants, to labor at home doing piecework or in factories; to serve in homes, stores, and offices of the established owners of the city. The accents of foreign tongues rose above the cacophony of other city sound. Exotic odors of southern European cookery filled dingy tenement hallways, mixing with the sour smell of poverty that hung everywhere in those streets. Yet the people who filed through the U.S. Immigration offices were fueled by hopes and dreams for their own future. Many had left behind fear, war, and poverty that made their new life in New York seem affluent by comparison. Only a few individuals, like Jacob Riis, himself an immigrant, had begun to write about this side of the city that demanded social reform.

Near midtown of the 1880s (centered close to Fourteenth Street) lay the publishing world that Frederic S. Remington was prepared to conquer. Of all the magazines, Fred wanted most to have his work appear in the periodicals of Harper Brothers, one of the city's largest, best-equipped publishers. Harper's had been founded in the early nineteenth century by brothers James, John, Joseph Wesley, and Fletcher Harper, who first published *Harper's Monthly* (highly respected in the 1880s), then followed this successful venture with *Harper's Weekly* and other publications. Undismayed when their original plant had burned in 1853, the brothers immediately constructed the nation's largest, most industrialized publishing house, completed in 1855. The firm was located in two seven-story buildings, one fronting Franklin Square, the other facing Cliff Street, each occupying a quarter of an acre of land. These contained the first American mass-production publishing plant, with production located in the Cliff Street building, and the business, editorial, storage, and bindery facilities on Franklin Square.[15]

Since his Albany days, Fred had been submitting sketches to Harper's, still a family business and headed in 1885 by J. Henry Harper. In Kansas City, the child Harriet Ferry had peered over her mother's elbow to look at sketches Fred Remington was sending off to Harper's.[16] At least two of Fred's early sketches had been accepted, but they had been redrawn by *Weekly*'s staff artist Thure de Thrulstrup, and neither was signed by Remington when published.[17]

If Fred's luck with Harper's failed, the young Remington could make appointments with other New York magazines and newspapers. At *Outing*, which was devoted to the sportsman's world, Fred's Yale college mate Poultney Bigelow was now an editor. The Century

Company also published a periodical. In addition, New York's newspapers (the *World, Herald,* and *Sun*) sent illustrators such as Rufus Zogbaum into the field to give visual representation to events that Richard Harding Davis and other journalists reported in words. Photographic journalism lay in the future.

Fred and Eva Remington's journey to the city ended at the Almon Gunnison home after a rented hack took them across the Brooklyn Bridge. On the other side of the East River from Manhattan, Brooklyn neighborhoods retained their own homey atmosphere although the city of Brooklyn would soon yield independence to become absorbed into greater New York. Neat, prosperous houses stood on Brooklyn's tree-lined streets. The Brooklyn Museum, founded in the 1870s, was a cultural center, and plans were afoot to build a monumental structure that would rival museums elsewhere in the nation. Here was prestigious Erasmus Hall Academy (where Walter Gunnison would be headmaster), the Long Island Hospital (where *Plaindealer* publisher Gilbert Manley's son Mark would study), the new Brooklyn Law School (where St. Lawrence men would study for law degrees).

The young Remingtons, short on cash but long on vision, were helped by the Gunnisons and their parishioners to find a tiny walkup on Ninth Street. Here, Eva set up housekeeping with Frederic working at home finishing the sketches by means of which he intended to enter New York's periodical world. The couple remained in Brooklyn for nearly two years, but their precarious financial situation forced them to move frequently during their residence there. At one point, they were forced to live in a rooming house on Ross Street. Their last year in Brooklyn they spent at 60 Broadway.[18] In the midst of these moves, Fred plugged along with his work and his visits to Manhattan editorial offices across the East River.

Remington's big moment came in December 1885. *Harper's Weekly* purchased two signed sketches. The first, *The Apache War: Indian Scouts on Geronimo's Trail,* appeared on the cover of January 9, 1886. The second, *The Apaches Are Coming,* was published in late January. Fred's work had caught the eye of J. Henry Harper himself. Harper later described what Fred Remington showed him that day: "The sketches which he brought with him were very crude, but had all the ring of new and live material." More than Fred's work attracted Harper's attention. In his memoirs, Harper also stated that when Remington first appeared at Harper's "he looked like a cowboy just off a ranch." Fred, whose dress was ordinarily carefully reviewed by fash-ion-conscious Eva and probably had been obtained through Cousin George, must have orchestrated that aura of the West. He threw himself so wholeheartedly into the role of cowhand/artist that he for-got where truth ended and fantasy began. In *The House of Harper, A History,* J. Henry Harper, no mean storyteller himself, recorded Fred's tale of how he got back East from his western adventures. Fred's outrageous portrayal of himself as a tried-and-true western cowhand became the image the house of Harper used to promote their new and rising artist. Although western regalia may have helped Fred to consummate the sale, the effort eventually boomeranged: in later years he found himself trapped by the stereotype he had created and *Harper's* had foisted on the public. Harper wrote:

> He was anxious to get to New York but was at a loss to conceive where the funds were to come from to pay his carfare over. As he entered an unprepossessing little inn in the evening he noticed that there was a game of poker in progress in the open barroom, and he took the situation in at a glance: two professional gamblers were plucking a man who looked like an eastern drummer.
>
> Remington watched the players for a few minutes and then suggested to the commercial traveler that he had bet-ter stop and go up to bed. The savage looks of the two gamblers put Remington on his guard and he whipped out his gun, told the cardsharpers to hold up their hands and covered his retreat until he and his befriended companion were safe in the man's bedroom and had locked and barri-caded the door. Remington guarded, and his new-found friend was overwhelming in his gratitude and begged to know what he could do to recompense. Remington said he desired to go to New York but lacked funds. The upshot was that his new acquaintance, who was also on his way to the same city, invited Remington to accompany him at his expense. On his arrival Remington promptly called at Franklin Square.[19]

On the strength of Remington's first sale, Uncle Bill Remington offered to finance courses at Manhattan's Art Students League. Fred duly enrolled early that spring, but, true to his usual style, he quit in April when *Harper's* offered to send him to New Mexico on assignment to report on Geronimo's battles with the U.S. Army. Fred's brief stint at art school did generate important contacts. One of his teachers at the League was Julian Alden Weir, younger brother of his Yale art professor, John Ferguson Weir. Both Weirs, although they were fine artists of a different school, remained in contact with Remington throughout his life. Among the students was Edward Kemble, who later illustrated Mark Twain's *Huckleberry Finn* and Joel Chandler Harris's popular *Tales of Uncle Remus*. Fred also met Charles Dana Gibson and Ernest Thompson Seton. In addition, he learned about the group of Philadelphia and Delaware artists whose leader and teacher was Howard Pyle. In later years, Fred exchanged letters and paintings with Pyle, who, like Remington, believed that American-trained artists should paint the American scene. As time passed, these new acquaintances led to further introductions in the metropolitan art world. Fred's friendship with the Kembles, however, remained the closest, since the two wives enjoyed each other's company. Then too, Remington's and Kemble's careers as successful illustrators of two different regional cultures ran comfortably parallel to each other.

Fred became squarely perched on a low rung of the ladder to success that spring. In addition to the *Harper's Weekly* assignment, he snagged another editor's interest. Richard W. Gilder of *The Century Magazine* hired him to report on his proposed trip to the Southwest. Fred stirred up the entire Brooklyn apartment in his flurry of preparations. It was always so when the excitement of a proposed trip spurred him. In a letter to "Dear Dude" (Uncle Horace back in Canton), Eva later confided, "You know how he is. He goes like the wind when he gets excited about a trip."[20] Eva's role during preparations was always to anchor Fred's whirlwinds of excitement. She became practical about things like flannel shirts and long union suits in direct ratio to the degree that Fred's schemes threatened to take him entirely off the ground.

In June, while Fred was in the Southwest on his *Harper's* and *Century* assignments, Eva probably went home to Gloversville to Clara Burr, her married sister. By late June, both Remingtons were back in Brooklyn, Fred full of stories about his adventures and about the cavalry lieutenant, Powhatan Clarke, who had become his friend. Through Clarke, he had met and observed the black cavalry troopers, known as "buffalo soldiers," who became subjects for some of his paintings. On this trip, Remington also met General Nelson Miles, whose memoirs about military life he illustrated in 1896.[21] *Harper's* began to publish the illustrations from this first official reporting trip that same July.

Once more, money ran out. Again, Uncle Bill Remington came to the rescue, this time with a job obtained through his political contacts. Senator Thomas Platt, state Republican boss, was persuaded to take Fred on in the American Express Company business offices. Fred found himself tied to a desk again and to columns of figures. He lasted a month; then one day at lunchtime he put on his straw hat and departed, never to return. Later, he confided to Barton Hepburn that he could not have handled a bookkeeping or accounting job in business or a bank, confessing that he could never add or subtract accurately.[22] Fortunately for their finances, Fred was able to tell Eva in late August that *Harper's* wanted him to illustrate the Charleston earthquake. He continued busy all fall, working on the illustrations that appeared in *Harper's Weekly* and *Century* in the ensuing months. In addition, he scouted for more work. He landed an assignment to illustrate an article for the children's magazine *St. Nicholas,* and at *Outing,* editor Bigelow commissioned him to draw sketches to illustrate articles about the army campaign against Geronimo. Eva's later description of Fred's being "busy as a bee" applied to his life from late 1886 onward.[23]

The young Remington's tremendous drive was finally coming under the control of his will. From 1886 on, Remington was devoted to artistic excellence as he saw it—which meant salable products in his early professional life. Well aware of art trends both in America and in Europe, Frederic Remington pursued his own path. He insisted always that an artist must look to his surroundings for inspiration, search his own soul for the style that best expressed his artistic vision, and then work like fury. At that time in his life, Remington believed fervently that his art should tell a story, not concentrate on emotions or impressions. During those long-ago Ogdensburg anatomy lessons from Nelson Howard, he had sopped up knowledge of the human form. From early childhood, also, he had absorbed everything his pen and pencil now used to bring his horses to life. Courses at Yale and the Art Students League undoubtedly helped to hone his skills.

Fred kept right on drawing running horses with all four feet off the ground, as he had first sketched them at Highland Military Academy in the old ledger book. By 1887 Fred had a camera, which he used on trips to augment his sketches, notes, and memory.[24] At first, Fred Remington worked mainly in black and white, because the age of color reproduction arrived only in the new twentieth century. Although he made careful notes about color in the journal he kept on his trips, his early watercolors and oils were experiments for his own satisfaction at first. Fred soon was searching for means to market these paintings. He wanted to produce the best of which he was capable and, at the same time, he needed to support himself and Missie, in their version of the good life. Remington concentrated on draftsmanship, the subjects he did best, and works that would sell.

In his pursuit of excellence, Remington, the son of a printer, learned all he could about printing techniques. He visited the Harper printing plant on Cliff Street to learn how his drawings were transformed to the printed page.[25] There, he watched young women feed large sheets of damp paper into the big Adams "bed-and-platen" presses in the basement, then climbed the stairs to the drying rooms, the cutting and sewing rooms, and finally the light and airy top floor where staff artists and compositors prepared drawings and text for the flatbed presses. There, he carefully watched men laboriously hand-etch on metal plates the drawings that would appear on the printed pages. Although cylinder presses, electrostereotyping, and equipment to produce halftone, or shaded, drawings were beginning to be introduced by this time, they were not yet in common use in the 1880s. These and other improvements would soon give more freedom to illustrators and lead eventually to full-color reproduction. But in 1885, as Remington began his career, his illustrations were limited to line drawings. Fred's thoroughness, however, made him one of the illustrator/artists of his day who understood the limitations of the printed page; that knowledge may have partially accounted for his mounting success in his field.

Always, Fred was an omnivorous reader. Now his reading helped him in his work. Throughout his life, he added continually to his library, but he never took time to organize his books well, by subject or by author. (Eva and her sister Emma had to catalog the mass of books after Fred's death.) He collected books on military history and tactics. He read everything he could about Indians, although cultural anthropology was a social science of the future. In later years, he studied European history and then delved into philosophy and even religion, although he never viewed himself as a scholar and avoided church whenever he could.

On his assignments from this time on, he also collected cowboy apparel and Indian and Mexican artifacts, to provide more authenticity to his pictures, as well as to decorate his and Eva's home. (This

"Indian collection," as Eva called it after Fred's death, was rare among private collections. In 1910, Eva was approached by a number of museums that were interested in obtaining Remington's artifacts, which she finally gave to the city of Ogdensburg. Today, they are owned by the Buffalo Bill Historical Center at Cody, Wyoming.[26])

In spite of his growing knowledge of details of Indian and military life, Remington took poetic license on occasion, and for this, he has been criticized by purists. Ordinarily, he shrugged off such criticism. He was preoccupied with creating the mythic as much as the factual, so that criticism did not usually worry him. Only once, in his 1908 journal, have we discovered his disgusted and resigned comment about the *New York Sun*'s harsh criticism of his painting of the Rough Riders' *Charge up San Juan Hill*.[27] By then, though, Fred was both too wise and too ill to erupt in anger or indignation.

In his midtwenties, the young man was bound to pay a price for his drastic turnaround from undisciplined irresponsibility to the dictates of creativity and professionalism. The forces that had sent him hell-bent toward pleasure and the mirage of easy success, though, still lurked behind the emerging artist. Fred's early misadventures in ranching and business may partially be attributed to his youthful search for identity, as well as a hope of gaining approval from an overindulgent but demanding mother, and an absent, preoccupied father who died when he was only eighteen. But other factors should be considered in light of behavior that now appeared in the man.

Remington's determination to create demanded intense concentration, consistency, and discipline. Shadows of the past emerged now in abrupt mood swings and pent-up frustrations that occasionally generated behavior which was criticized in his own time and would probably still provoke disapproval today. In addition, from 1886 on, the harder Remington worked, the higher the expectations he set for his professional performance, the more he ate and drank. Although he was similar in these habits to other men of his era—among them Theodore Roosevelt, William Howard Taft, and his own friends Julian Ralph and General Nelson Miles—overindulgence took its toll emotionally during these ascendant years. Later, the price he paid was physical.

From 1886 on, Fred worked furiously in fits and starts. Then he would throw down brushes and palette to rush off on a trip or to take a commuting train from New Rochelle to New York to drink and eat with cronies of the art world. He seems to have had surges of creativity, then to have moved temporarily into a period of relative calm. At those latter times, he enjoyed good company and was himself the buoyant, jovial companion.

When he was moving in calm waters without the pressure of deadlines or when a new venture loomed on the horizon (whether it was a trip, a family visit to Canton, or planning with Eva for home life at New Rochelle, Ingleneuk, or Lorul Place), Fred's appetites were reined. But in his journals and in his correspondence with friends, he confessed repeatedly that he had fallen prey to the twin predators that haunted him. Again and again, he would vow to diet and stay on the wagon, and ever again he failed. Without Eva's soft scolding and constant nurture, Fred Remington might not have kept to his lifelong struggle against appetites and moods he could neither understand nor control.

Although Remington was often jolly and amenable, an adroit storyteller and jokester, the restless energies that drove his creativity hid inner turmoil that left him feeling incompetent in conventional social interchange with people he did not know well. He could be courteous and even dignified when entertaining in his own home, but he was also sometimes rude and abrupt.[28] Fred was maladroit at social chitchat, uncomfortable on occasions of formal visits and dinners, in dread of balls and dancing.[29] All these made up the order of middle-class urban and suburban society that courted and wished to include the rising artist and his petite and charming wife in their circles. In all these settings, Remington was dependent on Eva's social grace and her genuine interest in her fellow human beings.

Remington hid his malaise under the façade of being "a man's man," who preferred a rough-and-ready outdoor life. He liked to sit with cronies around a table, glass and bottle at hand after a huge and hearty meal, while the talk ranged from politics to moose hunts to government to tall tales of life in the raw. Periodically, Fred had to escape ordered middle-class life and creative pressures for the Woods of the North Country, the remnants of the frontier, or an assignment to record a military campaign. Even in the two latter environments, he was not an active participant, although he never admitted this publicly or, possibly, even to himself. He was cast by his profession and his hidden dis-ease, in the role of observer and recorder.

Only with his wife, or in company with a few whose love and acceptance he could sense, or close to nature—whether on the River or in the Woods of the North Country, in the Canadian wilderness or in the West—was the man truly at ease. And only at work was he able to curb the destructive frustration and despair that had once made Nellie Hough fear for his well-being.[30] The forces that drove him found a focus only when he was completely absorbed in creating his art. For, hidden under bluff manner and rotund form and deep within the driving energies and frustrations was a soul that yearned after beauty and sought a pattern of harmony.

An ordered home life with Eva at the helm helped to create outer peace and harmony. Eva moved serenely through life, her dark eyes viewing the human condition with kindness and realism. The relationship that grew between Eva and Frederic Remington was essentially private, reflecting the Victorian reticence of their times. Frederic's hidden sensitivity and Eva's dignity further guarded their intimacy, and in these traits they reflected the emotional climate of their own families and of those remote little northern New York villages where they had grown up.

Letters written by Fred to Eva, when he was on trips away from home, are as brief and breezy as those he wrote to friends.[31] But at the conclusion of almost every letter he expressed homesickness and longing to be with her. When he was at home alone in Endion in New Rochelle, while Eva visited relatives in Gloversville or Canton, the house was empty in her absence. The fear of losing Eva, resulting from the stresses of their first few months together in Kansas City, as well as from the loss of many close relatives, showed in his devotion to his wife whenever she became ill. This burly man, boisterous in public, nursed his wife gently and tenderly, lifting her into his arms as necessary to ease her pain; Eva, on her part, nurtured him constantly.[32] These private, tender moments at home were observed only by family intimates and relatives. To the outside world, Remington was the vital, unconventional artist, given to excesses, and riding his artistic steed in full cry toward success. To outsiders, Eva remained nearly always in her huge husband's shadow, seldom emerging in full view as the strong and loving person she really was.

6

DREAMS SOMETIMES COME TRUE

« 1886–1890 »

In 1886 and 1887, Fred Remington climbed quickly to public popularity as his work began to appear in *Harper's Weekly* and *Century*. The nation was eager for word of the vanishing frontier, and Fred's illustrations helped to portray it, making it visible and real. He soon found himself the illustrator of the moment. His work was in constant demand among the periodical publishers, and he had more than enough assignments. He might have settled permanently into this role, for it enabled him to begin to provide the good life for Eva.

Remington's inner creative demon was not being satisfied, however. In 1887, he made his first forays into the world of fine arts. In February, he entered a watercolor in the American Watercolor Society's annual exhibition, and that spring another watercolor survived the jury that picked paintings to be hung in the 62nd Annual Exhibition of the National Academy of Design. Neither painting won a prize, but Remington's work was now recognized officially by these two prestigious organizations. In April 1887, *Harper's Weekly* sent him to the Canadian Northwest, where he concentrated on sketching Indians and the Royal Canadian Mounted Police. Back again in Brooklyn, Fred and Eva thankfully made plans to head north for a summer in Canton.

According to Gilbert and Williston Manley in the *Plaindealer* columns, the Remingtons were in town that summer of 1887 "for the season." Fred and Eva sometimes stayed at Grandpa Sackrider's, but as his and Mary's health declined, they would take a room at the Hodskin House, around the Miner Street corner. In 1887 and 1888, however, they stayed with Rob and Emma Sackrider. Fred set up a studio in the barn behind Uncle Horace's State Street house, where he worked on the illustrations generated by his Canadian trip. Remington sketched and painted with his usual speed and intensity, clad in white duck pants and white shirt, which became liberally dabbed with colors, as he wiped brushes and hands absentmindedly on his clothes.

While Fred worked, Eva rested and chatted with Em, for she was very close to this aunt of Fred's. She sometimes went with Fred to State Street to see "Dude," who was in poor health and forced at times to remain home from work. At other times, she walked to the big Miner Street house to see Grandpa and Grandma and to help Clara in the kitchen. Sometimes Fred would throw down his brushes, call for Missie at Emma and Rob's house, and the two would head downtown supposedly on a stroll. What usually happened was that Fred, in his smeared painting regalia, mind in the clouds, quickly outstripped his tiny wife's gait. By the time they reached the Street, he would be yards ahead of Eva, who followed calmly along in his wake. Although he kept putting on the pounds as years passed, Fred still went ahead full steam.

Modern-day Canton and the world at large have no appreciation of how often Fred used North Country friends, neighbors, and family as his models. That summer, he lured his young cousin Henry Sackrider into stripping to the buff, then decked him in a loincloth and feathers and perched him on a sawhorse in lieu of a mustang. Henry was transformed into a young Indian brave in *Harper's Weekly*. The same happened to John Mills, a neighbor of Horace's on State Street, who became his model for cavalrymen. John had served in Scott's 900 in the Civil War as a lieutenant under Pierre Remington and later became Canton's first Democratic postmaster. Charley Rodgers, another Cantonian, became a regular model, too; in fact, he was so good a model that Fred inveigled him, in the 1890s, to return with Missie and him to New Rochelle, where they then lived. Charley agreed but became so homesick after a week away from Canton that he took the train back to the North Country. In later years, Fred took numerous photographs of Cantonians, as he did on his working trips and everywhere else he went. Some went into an album along with clippings and other photographs of horses, bison, and Indians in every conceivable position. He used bits and pieces of these pictures in his paintings and illustrations. After he died, Eva had the chore of sorting through his photographs, most of which she destroyed.[1] (Any that remained, including Fred's working scrapbook, ultimately became the property of Ogdensburg's Frederic Remington Art Museum.)

Canton social life consisted mostly of visiting around, often for meals. Having Fred and Missie in town was an excuse for all kinds of parties. They were good company, with lots to tell of a world Canton folks usually only read about in *Harper's* or in one of the other periodicals. Eva lunched and visited with her women friends. She always spent time with her former landlady, Sarah Caldwell, now living on Pine Street south of the Miner Street Sackrider house. Or she and Aunt Minnie might stroll up the Street from the Ellsworths' to poke through the shops, occasionally dropping in to pass the time of day with Uncle Bill or George at Remington's clothing store. Invariably, Eva compared prices with those in New York and usually ordered tubs of lard and butter to be sent to the city.[2] She found food to be considerably cheaper in the North Country, but rugs and furniture, curtain and dress goods were better buys in New York. Eva took on the task of buying new carpeting for Uncle Horace in 1889, which she found for less than eight dollars for three square feet.[3]

When he had pushed as hard as he could at his work and his genius needed refueling, Fred would head for the Street to find cronies with whom to exchange yarns. He would join the group who had chosen the big shoe box in front of Ellsworth's store as a gathering place. Or he and some of his friends would head for the American House bar. Some Canton men, such as Dr. Joseph Willson, had been in the Southwest, and Fred and they vied to tell the tallest tales of Wild West adventure. Fred's tales could make the group laugh uproariously.[4] Of the older men, Fred's favorites included Civil War veterans who had served with his father, one of them John Mills, and the artist added every memory these veterans could recall to others he treasured.

Invariably, Fred would hire a horse and buggy from one of the livery stables. Then he and Missie could take drives out into the countryside they both so loved. When Fred was too busy, Missie persuaded her favorite, Uncle Horace, to take her for buggy rides.[5] Eva had taken Dude on as her special mission. Her kind heart ached for the lonely, ailing man. She was always writing to him from New York, making plans for the next summer. Some Sunday afternoons, as they became more prosperous, Fred and Eva dressed up and Fred put Missie in the buggy's backseat while he played coachman, shaking the reins vigorously to whip the plug to a stylish trot along Canton's Sabbath-quiet, elm-lined streets.

The major social event for Canton the summer of 1887 was the wedding of Emily Eaton to A. Barton Hepburn. The ceremony was performed at the bride's family home in Montpelier, Vermont, on July 14. That did not stop Canton from celebrating. When the bride and groom arrived at the big College Street house Barton had built for Emily, the town put on its best bustles and boaters, washed the best china and silver, and went all out in a rash of parties for the newlyweds. Fred and Missie were part of those celebrations. The friendship between the two couples grew that summer, for Emily, who was the same age as the Remingtons, had need of women friends to help her learn the mechanics of household management and stepmotherhood. At twenty-six, she was now in charge of two little boys, one in poor health, and was expected to manage all the housekeeping affairs in a ten-room house.[6] In addition, she found out why Barton had built the spacious bedroom and bath on the first floor: her octogenarian mother-in-law came at his invitation to live with them. Eva, by nature maternal, had helped bring up her own four younger brothers and sisters. And she had considerable experience with a mother-in-law. Emily, it turned out, had a far easier time with her ancient relative by marriage than Eva did with Clara.

Although the new Hepburn house on the east side of College Street was a place of rejoicing and liveliness, across the street at the big Leslie W. Russell mansion (which later belonged to the University fraternity Alpha Tau Omega) sadness reigned. The Remingtons called to offer their condolences to fourteen-year-old Harriet Ferry Russell and her uncle and aunt. Harriet was now partly orphaned. Mary Russell Ferry of Kansas City had died, and her body was borne home to Canton to lie in Evergreen Cemetery beside her husband's father, Moses Jared Ferry. Young Harriet had elected to remain in Canton with the Leslie Russells, instead of returning to Kansas City. She preferred her Canton relatives, who included girl cousins nearly her own age, to a lonely life in Kansas City with her widowed father and much older brother.[7] She was a plucky girl and already had determined to earn her own way as a primary school teacher as soon as she finished school at Canton Academy.

Part of every summer in the North Country, Fred and Eva spent time in Ogdensburg and on the River. They were invited to visit

Fred's old friends John and Charlotte Howard and Al and Lizzie Herriman, or they took rooms at the Seymour House. Fred and Eva and other young couples planned excursions upriver to the Thousand Islands, where Ogdensburg families were fast purchasing island camps. While the Remingtons were in Ogdensburg their hosts would sometimes drive them up the River Road that runs along the St. Lawrence between Ogdensburg and Morristown. Sometimes they took one of the two steamboats that plied the river daily. These two passenger/freight boats were named the *Island Belle* and the *Riverton*. One would head up from Ogdensburg and the other down from the islands each day. They tooted cheerfully to each other when they passed at midpoint.

Among the families owning River camps in Chippewa Bay were the Strongs and the Knaps of Ogdensburg. Cedar Island helps to guard Chippewa Bay and its archipelago of smaller islands. The Phillips Inn, a little hotel, was located on the bay side of Cedar; there Canton folk often stayed for vacations. (Williston Manley took his wife and two children there in 1904, when young Atwood had an unforgettable glimpse of Remington paddling his canoe.) The William Sudds family of Gouverneur had a camp on Cedar Island, on the point across from Snug Island (the Strongs bought this) and what later became Remington's Ingleneuk. Fred Remington knew the Suddses because old William had been director of the Scott's 900 regimental band during the Civil War; now he owned a music store.*

The River seemed to beg for vacationers to fish and to canoe its waters. Fred was in his element there. Missie learned to paddle a Rushton cedar canoe and handle a rowboat. She soon came to love the River as much as Fred, so that they occasionally stayed at Phillips and, in the 1890s, rented a Cedar Island camp for at least one summer.[8] There, writer Irving Bacheller visited them, and Fred showed him how a plainsman talked as he drank from a jug of whisky held over his shoulder.

Although Remington worked hard, and both he and Eva played hard as well, the pace in the North Country was leisurely in 1887. They were rested and ready for what was to prove a winter even

---

*At the music store, Sudds gave lessons to aspiring musicians, including Charlie Reynolds, who became Atwood Manley's father-in-law some time after Fred's and Eva's deaths. Charles Reynolds later took his wife and three children to the Phillips Inn, too, and the middle child, Alice, also saw Remington in his canoe. That was one of many childhood memories she and Atwood shared during sixty-three years of marriage.

more full of work and recognition than the last one. That fall Fred landed his most prestigious illustrating job thus far. Theodore Roosevelt, already prominent in state and national political life, had written his outdoor book, *Ranch Life and the Hunting Trail.* The Century Company was to serialize it, and Teddy Roosevelt wanted Fred Remington to be its illustrator.

This assignment, added to his other commitments, put Remington under great pressure during the next year, because *Century* editor Richard Gilder and Roosevelt planned nearly fifty illustrations for the five articles. On the strength of this substantial additional income, at the end of the year, Fred and Eva moved to an apartment at the Marlborough House on Manhattan's West Fifty-eighth Street. They were past their worst financial times. Fred jubilantly signed a letter to Uncle Horace "The Duke of Marlborough" and wrote to Powhatan Clarke that he finally had contrived a small studio area for the first time since Kansas City days. "We'll do for the present until I have my home somewhere in the country where I can have a large and worthless collection of dogs & horses."[9]

Fred and Eva's goal of a home outside the city was closer to realization in early 1888, only months after they moved to Manhattan. Edward and Elsie Kemble, who had been good friends of the Remingtons since the two men had met at the Art Students League, lived on Mott Avenue in a part of the Bronx then called East Harlem, near 150th Street. When the house next door became vacant they persuaded the Remingtons to lease it.

Eva entered into a flurry of furniture buying and home decorating. Bird's-eye maple and golden oak were the rage in the 1880s and 1890s. Her kitchen had refrigerated storage built into the wall, and she kept it stocked with North Country cheese and butter. But cold storage for the potatoes and apples sent her by her father was a problem. She complained that she had to store them in her sewing room on the unheated second floor. Eagerly, she prepared guest rooms for the family, repeatedly urging Uncle Bill and Uncle Horace to visit and happily providing weekend quarters for George Remington when he came to New York on buying trips. And she and Fred acquired the first in a series of dogs: Toto, a miniature canine of unknown heritage.[10]

Fred now had a real studio on the second floor, which he soon stacked with paintings for *Century's* serialized Roosevelt book, his work for *Harper's,* and projects for the other periodicals now clamoring for his Western illustrations. He and Edward Kemble took regular hikes, because Fred topped the scales at 220 pounds that year and needed the exercise. On one such ramble, Fred and Kemble, who was light, willowy, and a sprinter, argued amiably about who was the better runner. A level stretch lured them into a race, and "at the end of about 75 yards," Fred joyfully wrote to Powhatan Clarke, "Mr. Kemble had learned not to trust always to appearances."[11]

The Fates now tossed a wild card into the young Remingtons' lives. In Canton, "Mother Remington," as Eva called Clara, had found herself a beau in the person of Orrin S. Levis, the hotel clerk-manager of the Hodskin House. Most of Canton and the whole family looked askance at the growing relationship between Pierre Remington's widow and a man they did not know or trust. Levis seems to have been a man of facile charm and superficial attraction, moving quickly from job to job at small hotels in little North Country communities. Solid Canton citizenry thought he was after the widow Remington's money. So did the Sackriders, and so did Fred, who was suddenly transformed from unconventional artist into outraged Victorian at the first hint that his mother might bestow her affections on anyone other than his dead father.

Fred and Clara's relationship had never been the same after he made his stand for independence and his art in 1884 in Kansas City. As news came from the Sackriders in Canton about the middle-aged love affair, Fred erupted, seared by his loyalties to his dead father and the "scandal" he believed to be growing. A century later, values have changed so drastically that readers may have trouble comprehending Fred's reactions. In small-town, nineteenth-century Canton, widows were expected, at best, to remain true to their dead husbands and, at worst, to enter into a second marriage with someone of quite similar background and circumstances. Although Canton undoubtedly had its gossips, the whole village waited silently to see the outcome of Clara's second bid for a mate. Little is said directly when such an event occurs in an interdependent community like Canton. People await results with concern, but few with judgment. But the Sackrider family, so upright in its Presbyterian ethic, Victorian tradition, and position of village leadership, greeted Clara's new liaison with disbelief, pain, and even shame. Three hundred miles to the south, Clara's son was furious and frantic.

Eva and Fred had had Clara with them that past winter for a visit, and when Clara had a bout with a pesky cold, Eva had dosed her with a mustard plaster.[12] In answer to their probing queries, Fred's mother had assured them then that she did not intend to marry

Levis; that he had not even proposed. Eva and Fred wrote to relieve the anxious Sackriders about Clara's intentions. But by April's end, the unhappy Clara grasped at her chance to move out of her shadowy life of frustrating widowhood. A rash of angry letters flew back and forth between mother and son, with Eva's abetting Fred in his vain bid to keep Clara true to the sacred memory of his father. Fred's outraged, authoritarian demands were met by Clara's stubborn refusal to consider her son anything but an impudent upstart.

In outraged despair, Eva wrote to Horace Sackrider at the end of April 1888 that Mother had requested her to purchase dress goods for a gown (perhaps intended for her wedding apparel), then had canceled instructions after Eva had already sent the materials on by mail. A few days later, Rob Sackrider telegraphed them that Clara had defied the entire family (and most solid Cantonians) to marry the "darned old goose" Eva perceived Levis to be.[13] Clara and Fred's bitter acrimony ended their relationship for nearly a decade and a half; in a rage, Fred, who could be as pigheaded as Clara, vowed never again to speak to his mother. Eva, who knew Fred well, did not believe him, and, in the end, she was proved correct. Quietly and gently, she listened to her husband's eruptions, which gradually decreased in volume and violence.

As Mrs. Orrin Levis, Clara moved permanently away from Canton with her new husband, first to Carthage, then on at irregular intervals to other hotels in other New York State towns, eventually dying in 1912 in Geneva. She did return for yearly visits to her hometown, and over the years the schism between her and her son gradually healed, although they never became close. In the early twentieth century, Clara visited Fred and Eva at Ingleneuk, and in 1909 she attended Frederic's funeral and was so overcome with grief and pain that Eva, herself deeply shocked and grieving, was worried by her mother-in-law's distress.[14]

Apparently Canton's prediction that Levis would prove a weak and improvident husband would eventually prove correct. In 1912, young Pierre Remington, Mart's son, wrote to Eva to warn her that Clara was asking Remington and Sackrider relatives for money to pay mounting debts.[15] Clara's inheritance from Pierre Remington was dissipated, and the Levis couple moved from one job to another, leaving unpaid bills behind. Fred's younger cousin advised Eva not to advance funds to Clara, because no one could stem the tide of disaster, and Eva's own future at that time as a widow was uncertain. At Clara's death later that year, however, Eva made sure that her mother-in-law's body was taken to Evergreen Cemetery to rest near Pierre and Frederic.

Fortunately, Fred was busy with work commitments in 1888 when his mother remarried. He even cut short his numerous letters to friends. He was sent again by *Century* to the Southwest, first stopping to visit the Houghs in Kansas City. Frank Hough, whom he described to Eva as "a real friend," went on West with him. Fred later met Powhatan Clarke, who took him to the Apache reservation of San Carlos. After he returned home, Eva observed that "Fred is working as hard as he would if he had 40 children hanging on his coat tails crying for bread. He is making paintings now for the Fall Exhibition which go way ahead of anything he has ever yet done. He went to see Mr. Harper a week ago . . . [he] said they wanted all of Fred's work they could use. Quite a puff for the 'Fatty.' "[16] Fred's name and talk of his work had reached even to Paris, they learned. In addition, he received invitations to membership in private city clubs, such as Fellowcraft and the Players, the latter becoming his favorite.

That summer, Fred and Eva visited Canton from Gloversville with heads held high, despite Fred's outrage at his mother's marriage. He had written to his Uncle Rob, "I don't propose to 'bury myself.' I will face the music. . . . I am perfectly calm. Nothing can influence me one way or another now. The thing is done and I don't propose to skulk before the good people of Canton. I go to the Islands in a few days from Canton." In a postscript, Eva added, "We want to see the Gunnisons and we want to see George and you all and why should we not come there and do the way the rest of you are doing." If Fred was able to speak of heading for the Thousand Islands, Eva knew the storm was past. He was looking once more into the future, so to reassure Rob she added, "Fred feels anything but desperate and you need have no fear of him."[17] Eva never believed that Fred's rages would lead to violence, as some of his family and friends feared, upon occasion. They discovered that Canton was not as cruel as they had anticipated. No one approved of Clara's new husband, but the village grieved more for pained family pride than it did for the now absent Clara.

After a few weeks in the North Country, Fred hurried back to his Mott Avenue studio and approaching deadlines. His regular commitments to *Century* and *Harper's* kept him hard at work, and he had an added commitment to *Century* editor Richard Gilder to write a series of articles about Indian life, as he had observed it on his western travels. Fred chafed for exercise to relieve the pressures of work at his easel and writing table. He decided he had to have a horse, although he confessed that "it gives me a pain to see these 'bobbing chappies,'" who posted sedately on English saddles on Central Park bridle paths.[18] He wanted a Whitman (western) saddle for himself. He had his horse, which he named Beauty, by the end of October, and Eva was thankful that he had found a release for the growing tensions created by work pressures.

Unfortunately, the horse did not arrive in time to prevent Fred from penning a vitriolic condemnation of Theodore Roosevelt to his Canton friend and lawyer, W. A. Poste.[19] Measured against subsequent letters (both to and from Roosevelt), passages in letters to other friends, and entries in the journals of his final years, Remington's diatribe against a man he otherwise admired and respected seems baffling and inconsistent. In his journal of 1909, for instance, Fred commented on Teddy's thoughtfulness as a busy president who was barraged with requests, yet took a moment to express personal appreciation for Fred's writing and art in the note he had received.[20]

Extraordinarily creative individuals, such as Remington, often are, apparently, hard put to rein the emotions that they seem to experience with great intensity. When weighed against the evidence of Remington's occasional extreme depression and other mood changes, his infrequent tirades against individuals, although inexcusable, do make sense. The prestigious assignment had placed Fred in the difficult position of meeting his, his editor's, and Roosevelt's standards of excellence, and he may have feared failure. Roosevelt was also an extraordinary individual, who throughout his life kept up a pace that equaled Fred's in every respect. The products of his will, his pen, and his political activities were as noteworthy as Fred's art and writing. Undoubtedly, Teddy Roosevelt pushed Fred—either directly or through Richard Gilder at Century—to make changes to suit his own conceits for picturing what he, Teddy, had written. The pressure of too many deadlines, combined with Roosevelt's high-handed expectations, probably brought on the privately expressed outburst to Poste. (Some of his pent-up anger concerning his mother's marriage may have been siphoned off in the Poste letter, as well.) It is the only expression of hostility toward Roosevelt that we have found among the existing Remington papers, but we use it as an example of the inconsistent behavior and attitudes that made Fred enemies in his own lifetime and beyond, although Theodore Roosevelt never became one of these.

Fred's growing reputation as a top illustrator brought him a new assignment, in December 1888, that Eva knew was the fulfillment of a lifelong dream of Fred's.[21] Before Remington threw down his pens and brushes for a holiday respite in Canton, he took the train for Boston and the Houghton Mifflin Publishing Company. The firm wanted him to illustrate a new, book-length high-quality edition of Henry Wadsworth Longfellow's *The Song of Hiawatha*. Excitedly, Eva wrote to Uncle Horace. She, Fred, and every other nineteenth-century schoolchild had learned to declaim the sonorous lines of New England's poet laureate:

> By the shores of Gitche Gumee,
> By the shining Big Sea waters,
> Stood the wigwam of Nokomis,
> Daughter of the Moon, Nokomis. . . .
> There the wrinkled old Nokomis,
> Nursed the little Hiawatha. . . .

On his return, with pressures of the fall forgotten in enthusiasm for the new assignment, the Remingtons took the train to Canton for Christmas.

Thanksgiving and Christmas were big feast days for North Country people. Thanksgiving meant turkey and a re-creation of the legendary meal offered early settlers by their Indian friends. Christmas usually meant a fat goose, its skin roasted to a crackling brown, stuffed with sage, bread, and sausage, and the pan juices cooked with flour to fill gravy boats with rich, greasy goodness. Ham and roast beef often appeared on the table as well. Potatoes, turnips, slaw, home-canned vegetables, preserves, homemade breads and rolls, cranberry and apple "sass," pickles, plum pudding, mince and pumpkin pie, and slabs of cheddar cheese accompanied the festive fowl and meats. This was the kind of food Fred loved.

Often, friends joined the festivities. Harriet Ferry Appleton, as an old woman, remembered that "in Canton when the Remingtons were visiting at the Sackriders one Christmas, I recall having Christmas dinner [with them]." She also remembered that while she was visiting the Sackriders on Miner Street one Christmas season, a "log sled with lumber drove into the yard across from the Sackrider house and Remington penned a pen and ink sketch. . . . Eva said that it was the best he had done."[22] (This sketch later became a Remington Christmas card, and the original now hangs in Ogdensburg's Remington Art Museum.) Mrs. Appleton also mentioned that Remington gave the sketch to her father, who was visiting her in Canton that holiday season. This Canton holiday vacation of 1888 may well have been the occasion when Fred drew the sketch of a father and children tobogganing that is now in the collection at the Canton Free Library (see illustrations).

Christmas in Canton, the new *Hiawatha* assignment, and the anticipated January publication of his first *Century* article, "Horses of the Plains," sent Fred Remington into another burst of creativity. When he and Eva returned to Mott Avenue and the new year of 1889, he plunged into work on a large oil, which he named *The Lull in the Fight*. He had decided to enter it in the National Academy exhibition or to send it to the Paris Exposition in the spring. He wrote to Powhatan Clarke that his concept was "brutal," that he intended the painting to be a realistic portrayal of a battle between cowboys and Indians, with dead and wounded cowhands and their horses in the foreground, and Indians ranging on horseback in the background. He expected that the art critics would "give it hell," but he had the composition planned and worked hard to bring his inner vision to life on the canvas.[23]

The Lull went to France in March, while Fred went to Mexico. In April 1889, a jubilant Remington learned that his painting had won the second prize at the Paris Exposition. April was a good month for Fred's career also because his second article appeared in *Century*. Fred's writing was straightforward narrative, based on his journal entries, which he sometimes quoted verbatim. Editor Gilder took credit for launching Fred into journalism, and *Century* thereafter published his articles.[24] In actuality, however, the first Remington article in a periodical had appeared the year before in *Outing*. That first story, "Coursing Rabbits on the Prairies," had recounted that lighthearted day of sport during his short ranching days in Kansas. With *Outing* and *Century* willing to publish his writing, Fred continued to write occasional articles thereafter, most of which he also illustrated. Later, *Harper's* also printed some of his writing.

Illustrating *Hiawatha* filled Fred's mind and most of his working time that spring and summer. Not only did he plan to paint 22 full-page illustrations, he also expected to fill the book with 401 pen-and-ink drawings for which he would use his collection of Indian artifacts as models. Longfellow had combined two ancient Indian stories to produce the idealized Hiawatha of his poem. One was the historical figure of the Mohawk or Oneida chief, who was supposed to have persuaded five Indian nations to form the Iroquois confederacy in either the fourteenth or fifteenth century; the other was a mythical demigod of the Ojibways, called Manabozho, a name that Longfellow is supposed to have considered for his hero.[25] Longfellow's poetic license gave Frederic Remington free rein to blend a variety of native styles from the many Indian groups he had observed into his illustrations. By summer, he was deep into serious work and urgently needed an environment more inspiring than Mott Avenue and the city to free his imagination.

That July, on their annual visit to Canton, Fred and Eva settled on a perfect place to work on the *Hiawatha* drawings. They joined a party of Canton people camping at Witch Bay on Cranberry Lake in the Big South Woods of the western Adirondacks. Here, in the former Mohawk hunting grounds where the legendary Hiawatha himself may have stalked swift-running deer, Remington could listen to the sough of wind in the fir trees or rest his eyes from painting by gazing across the lake toward Buck Island and the distant shoreline.

Cranberry, which lies near the southern border of St. Lawrence County, is not located in the highest Adirondack mountains, which rise farther to the east. The lake was vastly larger in 1889 than it had been when Indian families fished its waters or followed the shoreline north toward the St. Lawrence River. Early in the 1870s, the state of New York had dammed Cranberry at the northern outlet that becomes the headwaters of the Oswegatchie River. As a result, the lake was now the largest body of water in the northern Adirondack tier, with a border of gaunt skeletons of drowned trees raising ghostly arms from the waters near the shoreline. A mile north of the outlet a swath of rotting forest giants could still be seen, the result of the 1845 tornado that had ripped through the Adirondacks on its northeast path toward Lake Champlain and Vermont.

The camp (a raw building with open rafters and no cellar) at Witch Bay originally belonged to John Keeler, a Canton lawyer and lumberman. Besides the Remingtons that summer at Witch Bay, the Keelers were entertaining another Canton family, State Senator and Mrs. Dolph Lynde, and their daughter Grace, a high school senior. In 1961, when Grace was almost eighty-eight, she told Atwood about that summer when Fred and Eva were at Witch Bay:

Fred would take Eva and myself out in a boat in the bay while he painted or sketched. We'd sit perched up forward just parboiling in the sun. Fred sat toward the stern, his drawing board resting on the gunwales, humming and painting, oblivious of our plight.

His favorite place to work, however, was a huge hemlock stump, out beside the camp, nearer the point. He'd perch his easel on the stump, lay out his paints and brushes, seat himself on a stout camp stool just as close to the stump as he could get his big self and go to work; one leg thrown across the other, diddling that foot up and down, up and down; and whistling by the hour. Oh, dear me, how we came to hate that whistle! It nearly drove us crazy.[26]

That was the same summer that Judge Ledyard Park Hale and other Canton men turned the table on Fred Remington, the prankster. Judge Hale was so tickled by the incident that he asked Will Manley whether he could write about it for the *Plaindealer*. Of course, Will said yes. Fred was always pretty bumptious, but the *Hiawatha* commission and the Paris Exposition prize made him brag even more. Canton's leading horse dealer, Elbert Stevens, had imported a mustang and Fred's cronies persuaded the artist to show them how to ride the untamed bronco. As Atwood described the event in earlier writing,

Word quickly spread about town, so when Remington appeared at the American House that afternoon, decked out in his best white Panama suit and hat, quite a crowd was on hand. The bronco was led around from Williams Brothers livery, all saddled and groomed. Fred's friends were enjoying themselves to the full, offering worldly advice and much encouragement, eager to watch Fred give a few pointers on . . . western horsemanship.

Fred hoisted a foot to the stirrup and with a mighty heave elevated his excess poundage upward. He was still quite agile for a man of his size. On the instant he swung into the saddle, that bronco took over without benefit of warning. With the bit in its teeth it bolted like a streak of lightning directly across Park Street and onto the village common. There it went into the most approved latest and neatest bucking operation on record. Remington went sailing over the bronco's laid-back ears, down to a . . . belly-bunt landing on the lush green carpet. . . . Roars of laughter came from the crowd in front of the hotel as Fred picked himself up, shook out his suit, and looked down at [the grass-stained] white linen. Leaning back and shaking with laughter he called out: "All right, all right, into the bar, the drinks are on me."[27]

Altogether, 1889 was a year when many dreams came true for Fred and Eva Remington. Although it held its share of unhappiness and stress, it bestowed welcome gifts on the couple. Fred's career was in full cry. His name was familiar to all periodical readers, and editors clamored for more of his work. He had breached the fortifications of national and international art exhibitions and had arrived as a popular fine artist. (Never mind that the classicists ignored him and his work.) He was now established as a journalist, and he had achieved a boyhood dream of illustrating the legend of Hiawatha. He and Eva made ready to enter the glittering final decade of the nineteenth century with every indication that his swift climb to fame would continue.

(*Courtesy of Frederic Remington Collection, Owen D. Young Library, St. Lawrence University, Canton, N.Y.*)

7

GOOD TIMES
AT ENDION

« 1890–1895 »

Fred was only twenty-eight that December and Eva twenty-nine, when Fred's growing success brought another dream close to fulfillment. "I have signed the contract for the purchase of an estate—estate is the proper term—" Frederic Remington reported gleefully to Powhatan Clarke in December 1889, "three acres—brick house—large stable—trees—granite gates—everything all hunk—lawn tennis in the front yard—garden—hen house—am going to try and pay $13,000 cold bones for it—located on the 'quality hill' of New Rochelle—30 minutes from 42nd (Grand Central Terminal)—with 2 horses—both good ones on the place—duck shooting on the bay in the Fall—good society—sailing & the finest country 'bout you ever saw—what more does one want. I wouldn't trade it for a chance at a Mohamedan paradise. . . ."[1]

As was her habit when her husband wrote to Clarke, Eva Remington added a postscript: "Our new home is perfectly charming. We are the happiest people you ever saw and just looking in anticipation of good times we are to have there." As an afterthought, she told the dashing bachelor, "you ought to leave the army, get married & come & live next to us. . . ."[2] (Eva was a persistent matchmaker for Fred's friend.)

Fred and Eva Remington had bought their dream home—a spacious house and grounds on Webster Avenue in New Rochelle. Once a country village, by late 1889 it was within commuting distance by rail to New York City. Part of the vanguard of New Yorkers who moved to future suburbs, the Remingtons had come a long way from the dismal period only four years before in Kansas City. Fred was riding the crest of popularity as one of the nation's best-known illustrators. Financial stress seemed far behind. Fred later told Clarke that although he still did not have capital, he now had plans to accumulate some. But he and Eva, in 1890 and throughout the remainder of their time together, were willing to take chances in order to enjoy fully all that life brought to them. In their purchase of the "estate" on Webster Avenue in New Rochelle, they followed the philosophy, expressed by Fred more than once in his life, that "since we only go through this life but once I propose to go easy."[3] They named their new home Endion, an Ojibway word Fred had learned on a Canadian hunting trip the previous year with his writer friend Julian Ralph; it means "the place where I am at."[4]

The Remingtons intended to move to New Rochelle in April 1890. This was only one venture in what was to prove a second busy year. The rented house on Mott Avenue became a hurricane of activity. Fred was already busy enough for two people, finishing up paintings he planned to show in two upcoming April exhibitions—one at the National Academy of Design and his own one-man show set to open at the American Art Galleries. In addition, he was scheduled to place paintings in the May exhibit of the Brooklyn Art Club, and, of course, he had his illustrating and writing commitments to *Harper's* and *Century*. Now Eva sent their hired girl scurrying about to pack their belongings, which she was dismayed to realize had accumulated shockingly in their short stay at the house.

Once they were installed in New Rochelle, after their April 7 move, Eva wrote gleefully to the Canton relatives that the new house had plenty of space for all their belongings. Fred's studio was a long, narrow room on the first floor. Above it, in a room of similar proportions, they planned to have a home art gallery. The lawn was surrounded by American elms. The brick house was fronted with an "immense piazza" shaded by vines.[5] The horses in the stable were a team of grays that Fred pronounced to be "excellent." They discovered a strawberry patch in the garden. Before long, ten Plymouth Rock biddies moved into the henhouse.[6]

The move to New Rochelle preceded a spate of new professional projects. Remington's recent military acquaintance, General Nelson Miles, wrote that April to invite Fred to accompany him on a journey through the Southwest the coming summer. Miles by now had attained the rank of major general and was in charge of the Division of Missouri of the upper Midwest for the Army. At nearly the same time, *Harper's Weekly* contacted Fred to propose a trip to the Canadian Northwest with Julian Ralph to gather materials for illustrated articles. Fred chortled at the chance to go into the field with Ralph, a magazine writer who had become a good friend and companion at the Players Club near Gramercy Park. Fred figured that the two trips could be combined and enthusiastically included Missie in the proposed venture. It would be one of the few times Eva accompanied him on his journeys to collect illustrative materials.

In May, with the new house somewhat put to rights and Fred's work successfully exhibited, the couple slipped away for a short respite in the North Country before their trip west. It was trout season in the Adirondacks and the lure of forest and stream was irresistible to the restless artist. By now, Eva had learned the ways of keeping her husband happy and at his work. As Atwood has recounted in previous writing, "She tamed him as much as any living mortal could. . . . But he could never hold himself down to work in his New Rochelle studio for longer than two or three months at a stretch. Then he would pack up and take off."[7] Eva usually traveled to Gloversville or Canton when Fred took to the Big South Woods to fish or hunt. That May, Fred headed for Cranberry Lake, jolting by wagon along the rutted road that led a day's journey from Canton through the Woods toward Bishop's Hotel, a favorite with North Country sportsmen.

The hotel was located on the long, narrow outlet at the north of the big lake, near the place where it flowed into the headwaters of the Oswegatchie River (which Fred later canoed and wrote about). Bishop's dominated a small huddle of buildings that later became the little village named after the lake. The unpainted building was owned by Riley Bishop and his wife, Eliza Jane, who was called "Auntie B" by one and all and who was a wonderful cook. Riley had taken over from his father, William, who had bought the original twenty-five-year-old log inn, built when the state dam was being constructed.

Canton shoe store owner Joseph B. Ellsworth, Aunt Minnie Ellsworth's brother-in-law, was one of the first to tramp into Cranberry in 1862, when Fred Remington was a baby. "Old Joe" and other North Country men who braved the rough forest trails before a road was cut into Cranberry returned home with enthusiastic tales of a virgin hunting and fishing paradise. Other men soon followed, including Deacon Sackrider and his sons and Colonel Pierre Remington and his Ogdensburg friends. Fred and Eva had first visited Cranberry Lake while they were courting, under the chaperonage of Fred's mother, in a party that included Canton friends.[8] In 1889, they spent most of July at the Witch Bay camp. Now, from 1890 on, Fred returned for annual or semiannual visits to Cranberry that continued until the turn of the century.

Game and fish at Cranberry were legendary. The idea of having to stock a lake with fish would have raised eyebrows among those nineteenth-century fishermen. In 1898, the *St. Lawrence Plaindealer* reported that Senator Dolph S. Lynde and John C. Keeler pulled from the lake twenty-seven trout, which tipped the scales at a total of thirty-two pounds, *after* they were dressed. (The *Plaindealer* was always careful to note the results of sporting trips to its readers. It was no coincidence that its new young editor, Williston Manley, was as ardent a trout fisherman as Fred Remington.) A year later, Will Manley wrote about a record catch he himself made while fishing at the old "V" hole not far from the dock at Barney Burns's camp at Brandy Brook, another favorite Cranberry haunt. In less than an hour, he had seven monsters, the smallest of which, when dressed, weighed two and a half pounds, the largest just under five.

Fred Remington was no different from other Canton fishermen. He loved to stow his fishing pole (in the North Country even the most supple fly rod is a "pole") into the rig he hired in Canton, along with his artist's gear, and head for the Big South Woods. One of Atwood's favorite Remington/Cranberry stories came from Nina Bishop Louks, niece of the innkeeper, who waited table at Bishop's Hotel under Auntie B's supervision. Word would come up the line, Mrs. Louks told Atwood, that "Remington is on the way in." As soon as Auntie B spotted Remington's buggy emerging from the forest near the state dam, she'd gear up the kitchen staff to make ready for the artist. "We'd hustle," recalled Mrs. Louks, an old woman when she spun her yarn for Atwood. "We'd put the two stoutest plank-bottom chairs just as close together before his place as we could get them. Remington's big bottom would fill them both, and how that man would eat. My, how he would eat!"[9]

Fred combined fishing, sketching, drinking, and eating in his usual Cranberry schedule. He and the others at the bar at Bishop's vied in telling the best fish stories, but one evening Fred had a real fish story, which he recorded in his own way. Jubilant at his catch of a huge five-pound trout, he strode into the barroom holding his big fish aloft. After a few celebratory libations, he pushed his way behind the bar, brushes and palette in hand, and painted a portrait of his big speckled beauty as a record for posterity. Instead of having a fly in his open mouth, however, Fred's painted fish held a jigger glass for whisky labeled "Bait," according to the memory of Marshall Howlett Durston, who was a lad visiting at Cranberry that summer.[10] Fred's painting of his big trout remained above the bar at Bishop's for years—as did the cowboy he painted on his barn wall in Kansas, and the Indian who later surprised visitors walking into the Strong boathouse in the Thousand Islands, all of which are now gone.

In May 1890, Fred's stay was pure pleasure. He had not hauled canvases and other painting paraphernalia into Bishop's, as he had in 1889, and as he almost always did throughout the next decade. On those later visits, Mark and Will Manley often saw him sitting on the porch at Bishop's Hotel in front of his easel. They remembered, and told us when they were old, how sketch after sketch grew from Fred's pencil on the pad before him. Time after time, he tore pages from the sketching pad, letting them fall on the hotel porch until he was surrounded with drifts of paper (Mark once gathered up a bunch of these sketches to take home, but, alas, they have long since disappeared). Will, who put everything that tickled him into words in the *Plaindealer* columns, wrote about watching Fred sit there sketching, his rifle propped against the porch pillar. Fred, Will wrote, used to grab his rifle to take potshots at loons diving out on the lake.*

After ten days of fishing that May, Remington collected Eva and headed back to Endion to make ready for the big trip west. It was arranged that Fred would meet General Miles and travel first with him through the Southwest territories that Miles now administered. Eva later joined them, and she and "Darlin'" (as she sometimes called Fred) traveled in the general's party throughout California as planned. Then the Remingtons bade their host farewell and headed north

---

*Loons are notoriously hard to shoot, and Fred never got one so far as anyone knows, but Mark Manley did and had it stuffed. It hung—collecting years of dust—in the front office of the *Plaindealer* over the *Hello, Old Boy!* Remington sketch (see illustrations) that Henry M. Sackrider gave the Manleys after Fred's death. Back in those days, nobody in the North Country thought much about owning a Remington sketch or painting, because Fred frequently handed them out to his friends, in bursts of generosity.

toward Canada to make contact with Julian Ralph. Fred was proud
of his "old lady," as he wrote to Powhatan Clarke.[11] He had arranged to have Eva "packed over the mountains on a 'cayuse' and
she stood the racket like a little man." Fortunately, Eva's health was
good that year or she could never have kept up with the two adventurers. Fred took a room for her in a Banff hotel in Alberta while he
and Ralph went on into the wilds. But Missie accompanied the men
when they visited Blackfoot and Ute Indians. She later wrote that
she "never tired of looking at the Blackfoot Indians" who were, to
her, "the most picturesque people in the world."[12] Eva never complained about the rigors she endured on her trips with Fred: it was
against her code to complain publicly about any discomfort, physical
disability, or pain of heart or soul.

The couple returned to New Rochelle at summer's end, expecting to
spend the rest of the year putting their new home to rights. That
plan was not to be realized. A tragedy was in the making in South
Dakota, where the government had relocated Sioux tribes who had
formerly lived as nomads on the midwestern Plains. After the Civil
War, Americans pressing westward squeezed the Plains Indians into
small areas, depriving the Sioux and other tribes of the great hunting
grounds fundamental to their survival. The young nation's preoccupation with its own "glorious" destiny largely ignored what became
the death knell of these Native Americans. Although here and there
an advocate spoke out, nineteenth-century American naïveté concluded that, of course, the Indian tribes would become "civilized"
agrarians. This had been happening for about two centuries with the
already relocated, missionized eastern Indians, who had received the
double "benefits" of European culture and Christianity.

The most insensitive among Americans believed, however, that
the western "savages" should be eradicated as murderous barbarians,
thus saving settlers' lives and the government's money. Few Americans believed that the Indians had a right to live in harmony on their
own land. Until America set out to "win the West," the Indian peoples had lived as an integral part of nature. Americans misinterpreted
the Biblical injunction of Genesis to become the steward/caretaker of
all creation. They assumed that they should conquer and subdue nature for their own ends. Remington, whose own soul sought harmony with nature, at least had the grace to know and to state that
no American could ever understand the Indian mind. He was one of

the few men of his time who made an effort to learn about the native peoples, and, for this, he won the respect of some of the Indians. The Remingtons entertained Fred's Indian acquaintances in their home, and Eva, in her diaries after Fred's death, spoke of meeting several others.

Remington and Miles had plenty of time to discuss the issues surrounding the government reservation system that was supposed to take care of the "Indian problem." Both men were knowledgeable enough to realize that herding the Sioux onto the Pine Ridge reservation could only create desperation among the nomadic hunters. By October, General Miles contacted Remington for the second time that year. Trouble was afoot at Pine Ridge, apparently rooted in the relationship of the U.S. agents responsible for the reservation and the unhappy Sioux themselves. Miles invited Remington to accompany him to South Dakota, where he intended to explore the roots of the problem. The general was under orders from President Benjamin Harrison that the army was to avoid open conflict. How thoroughly the general intended to carry out his inspection, we have not been able to discover. (He may have believed that the military authority vested in his own person or his verbal directives would quell the conflict. Or he may have expected an inevitable eruption of violence.) Fred returned from this inspection trip to write two articles for *Harper's*, in the first describing cavalry troopers, Cheyenne scouts, long hours spent on horseback by him and the general (both were well over two hundred pounds), and a visit to the site of the old battle of Little Bighorn and Custer's defeat.

The second article was Remington's apologia for the plight of America's Indians: an attempt to portray Indian character positively; to communicate what he called the "retrograding" influence of reservation life; and to contrast the Plains Indians' hunting culture with America's stereotype of Native Americans as "corn planters" and Christian converts. He extolled the daring, discipline, and virtue of Cheyenne cavalry recruits, as well as the moral rectitude of scouts and Indians in general. These men, he maintained, had values of equal worth to—although different from—any of the dominant white civilization. He cited the Cheyenne standard for absolute truth in any dealings they had with whites.

In mid-December, a detail of army soldiers sent to arrest Chief Sitting Bull killed the Sioux leader, despite presidential orders to the contrary. When he received word of the outbreak, Remington immediately requested permission from *Harper's* to cover the subsequent Sioux uprising. Through a quirk of circumstance, Fred did not actually see the battle known as the Wounded Knee Massacre, when U.S. Cavalry attacked a Sioux encampment that included women and children. Fred had learned from General Miles that some of the Sioux were wearing "ghost shirts," which the Indians believed could stop American bullets and which they donned for battle. Miles had ordered a detail to investigate, and Remington received permission from the general to accompany the group into the Indian territory. As a result, Fred was scurrying through another part of South Dakota when the battle of Wounded Knee occurred. The detail Fred rode with was led by an Indian scout named Red Bear, who had developed what Eva later termed a "great attachment" for Remington. "After penetrating the Indian lines about seven miles, they were suddenly surrounded," Eva said later in a public lecture in Ogdensburg. "Red Bear . . . saved his [Fred's] life when he was about to be struck down with a knife in the hands of a redskin. The appearance of a number of cowboys upon the scene saved the little band, compelling the Indians to take to their heels."[13] Red Bear's act won him the artist's lifelong loyalty. Fred remained in contact with the former scout, regularly sending him money, and even the gift of a rifle. In return, Red Bear sent Remington a fire bag, which had been made by his wife and was commonly used by Indians to carry tobacco and pipes. Remington kept the fire bag in his collection of Indian artifacts.

An exhausted Remington went home to Eva in late December with a bad cold and a host of mental images. At one point on this assignment, he had covered 248 miles on horseback in a day and a half.[14] Nevertheless, he pushed ahead to write and illustrate articles about the tragedy, which began to appear in *Harper's Weekly* at the end of January.

The frenetic pace set by events of 1890 carried over into 1891. Fred worked and traveled at such a speed that he might have been escaping demons. Author Allen Splete remarks in his commentary on Remington's correspondence of this period that "it gives the air . . . of a man so busy . . . that he barely had time to catch his breath."[15] That year, another invitation came from General Miles, this time to visit Mexico. Again, Eva was Fred's traveling companion, although when they set out in March, Eva went alone to Dayton first to visit her brother Will Caten and his family. She went on to

Chicago and Kansas City (her first time back to the scene of her first months of marriage), meeting Fred and General Miles later, to travel south in the general's private railroad car. Once more, Eva was fascinated with a new world, so totally different from suburban New Rochelle and small-town northern New York. In Mexico City, she basked in the reflected glory of General Miles's and Fred's reception by the country's president. They headed homeward by ship, stopping briefly in Havana. Neither Eva nor Frederic Remington dreamed, as they steamed out of the harbor at Havana, that Fred would be returning to Cuba before the end of the decade.

In June, Fred received word that he had been accepted as an associate by the National Academy. His glee was cut short at this latest success when Eva became severely ill. "My better half is very sick," he wrote hurriedly to Clarke, "dangerously so in fact and the house is crowded with doctors and nurses. Poor little soul I hope she pulls through all right because I wouldn't be of any more use than an old shoe if she weren't around to luff me off when the wind's too breezy." All Eva ever had to say, in a postscript to the letter, about that flirtation with death was, "I hope I will not have to go through such an illness again."[16]

Fred never the left the house in the ten days when Eva hovered near death. He sent word north to Emma Caten, who came posthaste to keep watch at Eva's bedside with Fred. Once Eva rounded the corner to recovery, Emma remained to comfort and cosset her through her convalescence. This was only the beginning of the long visits that increased in frequency and duration in the years ahead. Emma had finally found a purpose in her lonely life. Single, unhappy at home with father and stepmother, plagued by frequent crippling headaches and other illnesses (to which a modern physician might attribute emotional rather than physical origins), the younger woman basked in being needed, brightened perceptibly at Fred's rollicking ways when all was well with him, and learned to accept the artist's frantic pace and his bursts of anger. She finally could do something for the sister who had fostered and nurtured her after their mother's death, when Emma was only eleven.

As soon as his wife was strong enough, Fred took Eva home to the North Country for a long restful summer in Gloversville and Canton in the loving care of the family. Then he escaped the long weeks of anxiety and stress. He set off for the Woods, loaded down with fishing and painting gear, putting behind his fears for Eva and memories of nurses, sickroom, medicines, and doctors. He was ready for rough male companionship, the sound of wind in the forest, the laughing of loons, and the tug of a trout taking the fly.

Although enjoying other fishermen installed at Bishop's Hotel, Fred found real companionship among the Adirondack guides who worked for visiting sportsmen. His special friend was Has Rasbeck, one of the three Rasbeck brothers. Bill (William), Has (Harrison), and Gib (George) Rasbeck hailed from Porter Hill in the town of Hermon twenty-five miles northwest of Cranberry. They, and men like Chan Westcott, Fide Scott, Steve Ward, Barney Burns, and the Howland brothers, had either grown up on pioneer farms near the Woods or abandoned civilization by their own choice. Steve Ward, a Civil War veteran who had a game leg from a war wound, for instance, lived in solitude in his cabin deep in the Big South Woods until he died in his nineties.

Bill, the eldest Rasbeck, had gradually transferred his headquarters from a hunting camp he'd built near Clifton Mines to Cranberry. He made himself a cottage near Bishop's Hotel in 1888, where he lived in solitary comfort. All his life, Bill conscientiously kept a diary, which gives a unique picture of his world and the people he encountered.[17] Bill habitually helped Riley Bishop around the hotel, digging potatoes or hammering together a dock, supplying fresh trout for Auntie B's kitchen, or heading along the shores of the lake at night in a canoe to "jack" for deer feeding on lily pads. (Deer froze into brown statues when a jacklight was shined into their eyes, making an easy mark for Bill's or Has's rifle.) This provided the hotel table with "hog" or "mountain goat." Until 1890, Bill, Has, and Gib annually harvested deer, lugged the meat to the nearest railroad, and sent it off to city restaurateurs for a tidy profit. Later, state regulations to guard the dwindling deer herds put an end to their off-season enterprise.

The Rasbecks were practically adopted by the families who hired them, enjoying life at Tramp's Retreat with the Howletts, or at Witch Bay with the Keelers, or up Brandy Brook at Barney Burns's popular camp in the late 1890s. Bill and Has Rasbeck often teamed up to guide parties. They knew where the big trout lay, and what bait the monsters would rise to. They had grown up tracking deer and "painter" and bear, trapping mink and beaver in winters. They could follow a faint forest trail for hours in the loping, bent-kneed gait that some old-time North Country folk still automatically adopt. Bill and Has Rasbeck were courtly, polite men, with the kind of dignity sometimes found in people who live close to nature and away from humankind. Bill Rasbeck turned from guide into chef in a trice, producing quantities of hearty fare for their hungry "guests." He kept recipes for brown bread, baked beans, johnnycake, berry pie, biscuits, and the like, pasted in his diary. Bill's cooking ability helped endear him to Fred, who used both Has and Bill in some of his later illustrations and paintings of the Adirondacks.

"Has was the more dedicated hunter, trapper, and fisherman of the two," Atwood said in 1968, when he wrote about the Rasbecks for the Adirondack Museum's *Cranberry Lake*.[18] That, of course, is why Fred Remington got on so well with Has and hired him in 1890, before he and Eva went to stay on Cedar Island in the St. Lawrence for a time. Sometime that summer, Fred concocted a scheme to buy land near Cranberry for a permanent vacation retreat. Fred was a creature of enthusiasm and impulse, who was caught up by the swell of popularity for the North Country that was drawing affluent New Yorkers to build luxurious camps in the Adirondacks and Thousand Islands. Northern New York could be reached comfortably now on an overnight railroad trip in berths in Pullman sleeping cars. This is probably when Remington invested in the Witch Bay camp, which ultimately was owned by him, John Keeler, and Dolph Lynde.

Fred and Eva Remington finally settled in at Endion for the winter after Fred made a fall trip back north to hunt deer at Cranberry with Rob Sackrider and the two Rasbecks. As they returned to their usual activities at home and in the city, the couple found another Canton family added to the growing urban North Country network. That year Barton and Emily Hepburn had moved their family from Canton to Gramercy Park in Manhattan. In 1888, Barton had been appointed U.S. bank examiner for New York, then, in 1889, director of customs for the big port of entry there. At first, Barton tried living alone in winter in the city, with his family remaining in the big house on College Street in Canton. Reluctantly, he and Emily finally agreed that moving the boys and their new baby daughter, Beulah, to New York was the only solution. It was now clear that Barton's future lay in the city. Eva rejoiced when she heard that Emily would be nearby. And the Hepburns' Gramercy Park home was near Fred's favorite Players Club.[19]

As Eva's strength returned after her brush with death, she began to plan social affairs at Endion. Fred, by now, was great friends with their near neighbor, Augustus Thomas, the playwright, who rode, hiked, and played tennis with him. Eva and Virginia Thomas became

ABOVE RIGHT: *Portrait of Deacon Sackrider.* Remington painted his maternal grandfather circa 1886. *(Courtesy of Richard F. Brush Art Gallery, St. Lawrence University Collection, Canton, N.Y.)*

ABOVE LEFT: Detail of portrait of grandmother Mary Sackrider, the Deacon's wife, by an anonymous painter. *(Courtesy of Buffalo Bill Historical Center, Cody, Wyoming)*

RIGHT: Only known photo of Remington's father, Major Seth Pierpont ("Pierre") Remington, shows him between two fellow officers of Scott's 900, his Civil War cavalry regiment. *(Photo courtesy of Atwood Manley)*

LEFT: Fred Remington at two or three years old. *(Photo courtesy of Frederic Remington Art Museum, Ogdensburg, N.Y.)*

BELOW LEFT: Eleven-year-old mascot for Canton's St. Lawrence Fire Department, founded by his father. 1872. *(Photo courtesy of Atwood Manley and St. Lawrence Fire Department, Canton, N.Y.)*

BELOW RIGHT: A chubby teenager, Remington posed with his mother, Clara. *(Photo courtesy of Frederic Remington Art Museum, Ogdensburg, N.Y.)*

RIGHT: At Yale, Remington was a rusher on the football team for the 1879–1880 season. *(Photo courtesy of Atwood Manley and Frederic Remington Art Museum, Ogdensburg, N.Y.)*

BELOW: Remington met his wife, Eva Caten, at Canton's annual County Fair in 1879. This primitive oil of the fair hung in the Ebenezer Miner house around the corner from Grandfather Sackrider's home. Artist unknown. *(Courtesy of Richard F. Brush Art Gallery, St. Lawrence University Collection, Canton, N.Y.)*

ABOVE: Eva Caten when she came to St. Lawrence University in Canton, as a special student in 1879. *(Private collection)*

LEFT: Eva's sister Emma Caten, who much later played a crucial role in preserving Remington's works and reputation. *(Private collection)*

BELOW: Remington never painted or modeled women. Yet this small bronze nude woman was bequeathed to Emma Caten by her sister Eva Remington and stood in her Ogdensburg entrance hall until 1957. Never officially authenti-cated, Caten/Remington oral tradition affirms it is a Remington. The detail shows that scratched on the base are "Bitch" and "97." *(Private collection)*

In the summer of 1889, Remington set up an outdoor studio beside Witch Bay Camp at Cranberry Lake. He was illustrating a special edition of Longfellow's *Hiawatha*. *(Photo courtesy of Frederic Remington Art Museum, Ogdensburg, N.Y.)*

In Central Park on his Irish gelding, Beauty. Fred rode until he was too heavy. *(Photo courtesy of Frederic Remington Art Museum, Ogdensburg, N.Y.)*

Remington gave this painting to his Canton friend Dr. Joseph C. Willson. Atwood Manley discovered and identified it. *(Courtesy of Benton Board, Canton Free Library, Canton, N.Y.)*

ABOVE: Remington took daily canoe rides around his island, Ingleneuk, in the St. Lawrence in the early 1900s. Atwood Manley has a vivid memory of seeing the portly artist expertly wielding a double-bladed paddle of the Rushton canoe. *(Photo courtesy of Frederic Remington Art Museum, Ogdensburg, N.Y.)*

BELOW: Ingleneuk in the Thousand Islands of the St. Lawrence River became Fred and Eva's summer home in 1900. This photo was taken by Remington. *(Photo courtesy of Frederic Remington Art Museum, Ogdensburg, N.Y.)*

ABOVE: Hunting trips in the Big South Woods of the Adirondacks were an annual affair for Remington (left) with Canton relatives and friends. Atwood Manley identifies Uncle Rob Sackrider (next to Fred) and cousin George Remington (second from right). Jim Johnson is seated. *(Photo courtesy of Atwood Manley)*

BELOW: Fred and Eva pose on the Ingleneuk dock. *(Photo courtesy of Frederic Remington Art Museum, Ogdensburg, N.Y.)*

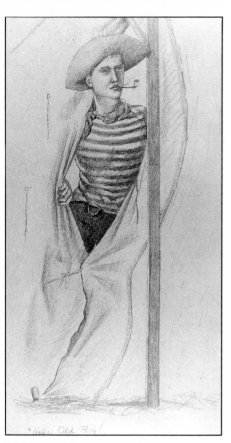

LEFT: *Hello, Old Boy!* *(Courtesy of Atwood Manley)*

BELOW: On his field trips to the frontier and to visit Indian tribes, the Artist of the Old West filled sketchbooks with quick studies and line drawings. This page illustrates his method of note-taking. Newly discovered, it has never before been published. *(Private collection)*

RIGHT: *A British Col. of Foot,* discovered in a North Country attic in late 1987. Probably sketched during Remington's 1892 two-week visit to England, it has never before been published. *(Private collection)*

BELOW: This untitled swashbuckling rifleman appeared on a cover of *Harper's Weekly* in the 1890s. One of sixteen newly discovered Remington sketches. *(Private collection)*

BELOW RIGHT: *Bartelle—2n Cav* is another recently discovered Remington sketch. *(Private collection)*

RIGHT: *Comin' Through the Rye* (1902) was an instant success when it went on sale at Tiffany's. Remington caught the four cowhands on a free-for-all, carousing gallop through a mythical western town in this intricately balanced composition. *(Courtesy of Frederic Remington Art Museum, Ogdensburg, N.Y.)*

LEFT: The famous *Broncho Buster,* Remington's first try at sculpture, was modeled in 1895 after Gus Thomas told Fred that he saw his subjects in the round and drew like a sculptor. *(Courtesy of Frederic Remington Art Museum, Ogdensburg, N.Y.)*

BELOW: *The Stampede* was Remington's final bronze. He began it in September 1909 but died before it was completed. Eva asked sculptor Sally Farnham to complete the piece. *(Courtesy of Frederic Remington Art Museum, Ogdensburg, N.Y.)*

Tobogganing in Canton. *(Courtesy of Benton Board, Canton Free Library, Canton, N.Y.)*

Remington used North Country people as models for his work far oftener than realized. He worked from this photo of Canton's John Morrow, Ben Bush, and Dave O'Brian, the mail carrier, for his *Financial Talk at a Nebraska Crossroads*. They are at the right in the painting (Atwood Manley has identified two of the others as Ezra Jackson, veterinarian, and Dr. John Bassett, physician, with raised arm). *(Painting courtesy of Frederic Remington Art Museum, Ogdensburg, N.Y.; photo courtesy of Atwood Manley)*

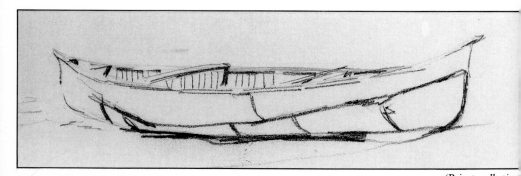

LEFT: *Coming to the Call* epitomizes the North Country wilderness. *(Private collection)*

BELOW: Remington burned the original oil paintings of his series *The Tragedy of the Trees,* along with others he did not want preserved. Fortunately, prints have survived. *(Courtesy of Frederic Remington Collection, Owen D. Young Library, St. Lawrence University, Canton, N.Y.)*

RIGHT: *The Howl of the Weather* catches the fury of North Country storms that Remington witnessed at Ingleneuk and on Adirondack lakes. *(Courtesy of Frederic Remington Art Museum, Ogdensburg, N.Y.)*

BELOW: Has and Bill Rasbeck, Remington's Adirondack hunting guides, are supposed to have been models for *A Good Day's Hunting in the Adirondacks*. *(Courtesy of The Adirondack Museum, Blue Mountain Lake, N.Y.)*

BELOW RIGHT: Remington discovered cowboys in Florida when he and Eva vacationed there one winter, then wrote and illustrated a *Harper's Weekly* article about them. *(Courtesy the "21" Club, New York, N.Y.)*

This was a common sight in the North Country during Remington's lifetime. The print is also from the destroyed *Tragedy of the Trees* series. *(Courtesy of Frederic Remington Collection, Owen D. Young Library, St. Lawrence University, Canton, N.Y.)*

Chippewa Bay's weedy shallows lay shoreward from Eva and Fred Remington's beloved island, Ingleneuk, in the St. Lawrence River. *(Courtesy of Buffalo Bill Historical Center, Cody, Wyoming)*

close friends also, and she was an adopted aunt to the Thomases' small son. Other New Rochelle neighbors included, for a time, the Jennings Coxes. "Jay," or "Jen," Cox was a banker who eventually moved to Cuba. The Kembles had also abandoned East Harlem, joining other new suburbanites in Westchester County, although they eventually bought a farm as a summer home farther away, in Massachusetts. Fred continued to see other friends from his Art Students League days. At the Players Club, he often met Julian Ralph, and their professional partnership flourished. Both were ardent sportsmen, and their first spontaneous Canadian hunting trip in 1889 was followed by a series of similar excursions. Julian liked to eat and drink as much as Fred, and they teased each other about their expanding girth.

About this time, Fred chanced on Irving Bacheller one day on Park Row. The two had not seen each other for some time. Irving said later:

> He had become a famous artist while I was building up my newspaper syndicate. [We] went into a café, and sat down together for a long talk. He wanted to know about my work and plans. Bliss Carman had just accepted a ballad of mine . . . I had a proof of it in my pocket.
>
> When we parted I gave him the proof and said: "Take that along with you, old man. I'll give you a license not to read it. You'll find it will burn as well as any other piece of paper." He saw and felt the pictures that I had tried to present in my phrasing, and wrote me a most encouraging letter about them. Frederic Remington was that kind of man. He liked to help some other fellow who was climbing the hill.[20]

Endion's spare bedrooms were often occupied. The Remingtons encouraged North Country relatives and Fred's military friends to stay with them when they visited New York. Cousin George Remington made buying trips to New York for the clothing store, which was expanding fast under his direction. Powhatan Clarke stopped in when he was on leave in the East and popped in for a few days in 1891 when he was en route to Germany to observe the kaiser's troops. By early 1892, he finally had good news for matchmaking Eva: at last the confirmed bachelor was courting seriously.

By late 1891, Fred Remington's convivial nature was leading him

more and more to eat and drink excessively. He kept up his whirlwind pace, immersing himself totally in current writing and painting
projects. He seems not to have listened to the warning message of
increased weight that his own body was sending him. Eva, however,
did. She had begun to call him "Fatty," with affection, and with the
bite of truth. She warned Canton relatives about every additional five
pounds Fred gained, and she enlisted Powhatan Clarke's aid by adding postscripts to Fred's letters about the additional poundage. Perhaps she hoped that the cavalry officer might be able to persuade her
husband of the benefits of moderation. In November, Fred himself
began to worry and wrote to Clarke, "There are a class of d——
fools in this world who don't know enough [but] drink whisky and
I'm one of them—I had always cherished a fond delusion that I was
one of the men who could but I ain't [sic] and henceforth 'no thank
you a little Appollusan's (sp?) please.' This is no drunkards afterclap
but a square deal if I have to join the 'Bicloride of Gold Club.' "21

Although they saw the Hepburns on a few occasions in 1891,
Eva Remington was engrossed in her suburban home, and Emily
was preoccupied with the growing health problems of her elder stepson, young Barton, who suffered severe and repeated asthma attacks.
Barton, Sr., was forever being called to Washington, and Fred was
at his easel or far afield on writing and illustrating assignments. Furthermore, the Hepburns had moved from Gramercy Park to Manhattan's Upper West Side. In 1892, Fred went off on his first European trip, and the Hepburns then moved to the nation's capital, after
young Barton's death, when the older Barton was named U.S. comp-
troller.

In 1892, Eva found herself thrown more and more upon her
inner resources. Poultney Bigelow, the former editor of *Outing*, proposed that Fred accompany him on a canoe trip in Russia, hopeful
that expenses might be paid by *Harper's* or other publications, in
return for writing and illustrations that he and Fred would produce.
Bigelow had taken a similar trip down the Danube with his and
Fred's friend artist Frank (Francis) Millet in 1890. Eva was opposed
to the trip, either because of fears generated by her own illness in
1891 or—and this seems more likely—because she was worried about
Fred's excesses. At first, Fred was hesitant, even though Powhatan
Clarke had written glowing details of his life in Germany. "I am
afraid I won't like Europe," Fred responded to Bigelow. "I was born
in the woods and the higher they get the buildings, the worse I like
them."22 But the exhilarating idea of canoeing on the Volga over-

came Fred's hesitation, and he tried to placate Eva by suggesting that she join him on the Continent after the canoe trip was completed. Eva, like it or not, had to accept Fred's decision, but she did not meet him in Europe.

But first, Remington took a quick trip west to gather more materials. He told Bigelow grandiosely, "I start for 'my people' . . . I go to the simple men—men with the bark on—the big mountains— the great deserts and the scrawny ponies—I'm happy."[23] He did not take his camera on the western trip. He was impatient with the slow and cumbersome process that photography still imposed. His photographic memory was accurate enough for his purposes, as unexpected events on the Russian trip later demonstrated.

Plans for the European voyage proceeded in the next months. Fred was in charge of ordering canoes from a Brooklyn boat shop. He also ordered paddles and canoe seats from his friend J. Henry Rushton, the Canton canoe builder. He kept up with illustrating and writing for his publishers. The picture *A Good Day's Hunting in the Adirondacks,* which included likenesses of the Adirondack guides Has and Bill Rasbeck, had appeared in *Harper's Weekly* in January (see illustrations). In addition, Fred finished three paintings for the annual National Academy exhibition. Before Fred joined Bigelow in Germany, he and Eva went north for their usual spring visit with relatives and Fred fished again at Cranberry. On May 9, the artist began his two-month adventure with his old college mate.

Poultney Bigelow and Fred Remington had met at Yale in the basement classroom where men art students were segregated from the women art students who attended the otherwise male institution. (The young ladies had their classroom on the first floor.) Bigelow was a college senior, taking an art course for pleasure (or credit). Fred was an underclassman and full-time art student. Professor John F. Weir, an artist in his own right, set his students to copying plaster casts, a discipline Fred disliked. Weir left them pretty much alone. After graduation, Bigelow moved into the periodical field in New York, becoming an editor of *Outing,* where his and Fred's paths crossed once more. Later Bigelow became a free-lance writer. Son of a former ambassador, he was far more cosmopolitan than Remington, and a frequent traveler abroad. While they were preparing for their trip, the two adventurers had found they had more in common than appeared on the surface.

The two adventurers finally arrived in Russia, via Berlin, laden with the two canoes, tents, sails, sleeping gear, and Fred's art paraphernalia and camera. They launched their canoes on the Volga and started downstream, only to be hauled ashore and taken before Russian authorities, who claimed that one or both were engaged in espionage. Fred's sketches were suspect, as were the glass photographic plates and their notes. They were escorted to the border and expelled, forced to surrender canoes, camera, and other equipment to the Russians. Returning to Germany, Poultney Bigelow fretted that there would be no pictorial record of this misadventure, but he need not have worried. Once in friendly territory, Fred set to work with pencil and sketch pad, drawing from memory and providing an accurate record of their short mission. Fred was angry about the loss of the canoes, which had been damaged, and for which they received compensation only after months of wrangling through official channels.

The two men spent the remainder of their time together at the horse farms owned by the German kaiser, articles and illustrations of which were duly published in *Harper's*. Whether the two traveled south to Algeria at this time has become a matter of conjecture among Remington scholars. Some researchers claim that Bigelow's 1894 and 1895 *Harper's Monthly* articles, illustrated by Remington, resulted from experiences in 1892; others claim that Remington and Bigelow took a trip together in 1894 to North Africa. We have found references to a later trip in some of Fred's letters but nothing absolutely conclusive. We do know for sure that in 1892 Fred went to Paris en route to England, where he found to his surprise that he enjoyed himself. He later wrote and illustrated two articles about the British military, based on his short stay in England. Because the entire trip took approximately six weeks in all, it seems highly unlikely that Remington could possibly have included a tour of Algeria in his schedule in 1892.

On July 9, Remington arrived back in New York and within three weeks was off again, this time to the North Country with Missie. They arrived in Canton on July 22 for a prolonged vacation, which culminated in Fred's canoe trip down the Oswegatchie River from Cranberry Lake with Has Rasbeck. The canoe in which the artist and his guide traveled was Fred's new Rushton canoe, the *Necoochee*, purchased from the now nationally renowned boat builder after he reached Canton. The people at Cranberry Lake thought Fred's proposed trip to be a harebrained scheme. "For many miles below the lake the river is shallow and rocky," Atwood explains.[24] "Has Rasbeck was among the skeptics, questioning, to begin with, his patron's good sense; and all through the voyage, as they chopped away at obstructing wind-falls, smashed against rocks, portaged around long stretches of rapids or waded downstream, slipping and sometimes falling neck-deep into holes, Has was 'wonderfully cynical at the caprices of the river.' "

Fred Remington, however, loved it; later, he wrote about the journey in "Black Waters and Shallows," which appeared in *Harper's Monthly* and then in his own anthology of his articles, *Pony Tracks*. Has would have preferred some fishing and some hunting. But Fred was pitting man against nature, and his fertile imagination created scenarios of Indian braves of bygone days slipping silently along in their birchbark canoes. Their trip took them fifty-one miles, about halfway down the Oswegatchie toward its mouth at Ogdensburg, where it empties into the St. Lawrence. In the short distance Has and Fred traversed, the river drops eleven hundred feet.

These were the years of Remington's prime. The pace set in the first year of the decade, when he turned twenty-nine, continued without lagging until nearly the end of the century. His work was in demand from the country's most popular publications, although as the decade progressed *Harper's* began to show a reluctance to publish everything he submitted. This was probably because Fred's demands increased in direct ratio to his feeling of worth, and partly because the first hints of approaching financial problems for the publishing house began to worry *Harper's* executives. Fred's paintings were exhibited in shows that represented the nation's artistic elite. His annual one-man exhibitions—Fred was a pioneer in this type of show—netted him more renown, as well as proving a splendid marketplace for his art. (In 1893, he made more than $7,000 in the sale of ninety-three out of the one hundred paintings in his one-man show and auction at the American Art Galleries.) He continued to travel extensively and often, for business or for pleasure, or a combination of both.

In February 1893, Fred was off to the Southwest again with General Miles. He returned home via Mexico, where he sketched bullfighters and aspects of Mexican life. It was probably during this absence of Fred's that motherly Eva—all of six years older than her friend Emily Hepburn—gave the younger woman a piece of her mind. The Hepburns were finally back in New York, this time permanently. Barton was the president of the ailing Third National Bank of New York and in charge of negotiations that would lead to the 1896 merger creating the National City Bank of New York. The family lived on West Fifty-seventh Street, and Emily was overwhelmed with her multitude of responsibilities, all of which she tackled with the intention of being the most perfect housekeeper and parent possible. Partially, Emily's problems lay in her own intelligence and lively curiosity. Her intellect craved exercise, and her social nature craved stimulating friends. However, Barton was engrossed in his professional life with its accumulating duties, leaving Emily alone at home.

Up to the point of Eva Remington's intervention, Emily followed the dictates of a stern New England conscience, which forced her to continue economies she had been brought up to practice in rural Vermont. She had one stepson remaining in her care, as well as her own little Beulah, still a toddler. That year, she gave birth to the second Hepburn daughter, Cordelia, named after Barton's older sister. Emily tried to supervise the children and to run the big household by herself and still somehow satisfy a few of her own needs. Somehow, immersed in her own problems, Emily forgot to think about Barton. One thing that Eva had had to learn to consider in her own wifely role was the care and scolding of Fred, a man who consistently abused his own health and energies. Emily had Fred's quality of rushing ahead over obstacles, and Eva could see that quiet Barton Hepburn was suffering from his wife's overwork.

When Eva dropped in one day at the Hepburn's home to visit informally, she found Emily hard at work. Eva, "finding her carrying on all the household duties herself, said crisply, 'Emily, you don't *have* to do all that work.' "[25] Eva's abrupt and forthright comment gave Emily Eaton Hepburn food for thought. There is no record of the conversation between the two women that afternoon. Later, Emily acknowledged that after her talk with Eva she viewed her life with her husband in broader perspective for the first time, thinking beyond the confines of house, children, and her own personal frustrations. During their talk together, Eva passed on some of her own hard-won wisdom. She had tried to keep up with Fred until her brush with death in 1891. Thereafter, she shared the parts of his life to which she was equal physically. Otherwise, she stayed at home and hoped for the best for Fred. When he was at Endion, she brought her own brand of discipline to bear on Fred and focused her energies to create the kind of home that welcomed his return.

Eva and Emily's talk that day changed life for the Hepburns. A woman of action once decisions were made, Emily immediately hired help: thereafter, three servants customarily did the work she had attempted. After that, although the demands of Barton's work allowed less time than ever before for them to be together, and even more responsibility for home and parenting rested upon Emily, Emily bent her energies and talents to improving the quality of both their lives. She learned to invite old North Country and Canton friends to dinner, as Eva did, although sometimes Barton sent word that bank work would keep him away. She often played the piano for her weary husband after dinner, finding that he listened and relaxed for as long as she played, no matter how preoccupied with business he might be. Their life together took on new and important dimensions through Emily's fresh insights. For his part, Barton came to recognize Emily's homebound isolation and her thirst for knowledge and action. He encouraged her to find women friends with whom to spend the hours when business kept him away. The couple freed each other to follow their individual lives; at the same time, from then on they were sensitive to each other's needs. Eva's pivotal role in bringing about the Hepburns' new direction firmly cemented a friendship that grew so close in years to come that the Hepburns followed the Remingtons to build a home in Connecticut, and even finally to a final resting place nearby in Canton's Evergreen Cemetery.

In 1893 and 1894, Fred traveled in the West, in the Southwest, and in Canada. On these trips, his companions were varied. He met and made friends, found new spots to explore, and revisited old acquaintances from past sojourns. At Yellowstone, he ran into Owen Wister, the Philadelphia-born writer, and the chance meeting began a new friendship and professional partnership. Fred and Julian Ralph went on assignment together again, traveling in the Southwest and ending up in California. With General Miles, he went hunting for grizzlies in the West, and, in 1894, he took a canoe trip into Canada. Everything was grist for his illustrating/writing career. Except when it was holding a rifle, rod, or paddle, Remington's hand contained a pen or pencil for sketching or recording, either tersely in his journal or buoyantly in his letters to friends, all that he experienced and observed.

In 1893, Fred's decade-long friendship and correspondence with cavalry officer Powhatan Clarke came to an abrupt and tragic end. In late 1892, Clarke had married a young cousin of Mark Twain's. Both Fred and Eva were delighted the next year to learn that the Clarkes had an infant son. Then, in mid-July 1893, Clarke died in a drowning accident while on duty in the West. Fred and Eva probably were in northern New York at the time of Clarke's death.

As year followed year, the Remingtons spent longer and longer

vacations each summer in the North Country. They stayed with relatives in Canton or at the Hodskin House, then traveled sixteen miles
to Ogdensburg to continue the round of visits. Here, they usually
engaged a room at the big Seymour House. Then they moved on
upriver to the Thousand Islands, where they occasionally rented a
camp on Cedar Island and, even, one year rented the Strongs' Snug
Island camp. Each year, Fred took to the Big South Woods and
Cranberry, to hunt or fish, work or loaf. Often, Emma Caten joined
them, going north by train from Syracuse, where she now lived with
her father and stepmother after the Catens moved there from Gloversville.

The void created by Powhatan Clarke's death gradually filled.
Although old friends held a special place in their associations, the
Remingtons welcomed new acquaintances into their widening circle.
In the mid- to late 1890s, Fred discovered another hunting and fishing partner in an old Yale college mate, Joel Burdick. They spent
time at Cranberry together, and Joel joined Fred's other cronies on
hunting trips in the Laurentian Mountains in Canada, or on canoe
trips on Lakes George and Champlain.[26] Fred still made sure to be
at Cranberry when Senator Dolph Lynde and John Keeler were at
Witch Bay. More and more sportsmen were discovering Cranberry:
the Howletts and Durstons from down Syracuse way now visited
regularly. So did Chester Lord, who was editor of the *New York Sun*.
There was much visiting back and forth between Witch Bay, the
Howlett's Tramp's Retreat, and Buck Island, where another Syracuse
family, the Vanns, had built their camp.

Fred wrote to Poultney Bigelow frequently, and his friendship
with Owen Wister ripened. Throughout the remaining years of the
Mauve Decade, Wister and Remington collaborated on articles and
illustrations. They met occasionally in New York, when Wister met
with his publishers. Fred read Wister's manuscripts and offered suggestions that could lend authenticity to the Philadelphia author's
portrayal of the West. Much of Fred's correspondence in the 1890s
included business notes to editors and officials on *Harper's* and the
other periodicals for which he worked. Of course, Fred frequently
took the train to Manhattan for business appointments and meetings
with friends at the Players Club, where he fell off the wagon regularly, returning to New Rochelle to repent and resume his struggle
toward moderation once again.

At home in New Rochelle, Eva Remington loved to entertain.
Friends and relatives gathered frequently at Endion for social eve-

nings, Sunday afternoon dinner parties, tennis matches, and other informal fun. Their guests represented a wide variety of people from many backgrounds: military men, writers and artists, people from the North Country network, and neighbors. Eva, despite recurring health problems (which are referred to as "ovaritis" in Fred's and her letters and may account for their childlessness), maintained her own circle of women friends. She was an executive of sorts, as she supervised the women hired to help with cooking and housework. Endion also required the services of an outdoor groundsman, who was supervised by Fred when he was home and who was added to Eva's list of responsibilities when he wasn't.

The Remingtons took great pains with their employees. They had the North Country attitude that the people they hired came to "help out" and happened to get paid for what they did. For instance, Fred went to great lengths to write to Bob Sackrider to make sure that Rob would purchase a mackinaw shirt for their groundsman, at the time a man named Tom. "Not loud colored," Fred added.[27] Eva fussed and worried over the women, rejoicing with them and sorrowing with them upon occasion. But she also could pull them up short, if they fell behind in the line of duty. In bursts of involvement with his home place, Remington supervised Tom, who was later replaced by Jim Keeler, in the stables and about the grounds. He made a big thing of this, but Eva was in charge during Fred's frequent absences and seemed able to run Endion with few problems all by herself. The Remingtons still practiced some Yankee-type economies. Although they could afford to pay city and suburban prices, they had butter and cheese, apples and potatoes sent from the North Country. (They tasted of home, besides being cheaper in spite of freight costs.)

Barton and Emily Hepburn frequently visited Endion. Barton was an outdoorsman with a love of the West like Fred Remington's. Both he and Emily watched Fred's career with interest and affection. Barton always loved a chance to see Remington's work in process. He was "immensely impressed" with Remington's paintings, drawings, and later his sculpture of Indians, cowboys, and U.S. cavalry.[28] He gave every encouragement to Fred in his work, eventually purchasing at least one painting for his own home. As a woman thirsty to experience all that life could hold for her, Emily had some sympathy for Fred Remington's voracious appetite for life. Years later, she said his philosophy had been "Nothing in moderation."[29]

One Sunday afternoon, when Emily and Barton were invited for dinner at Endion, they missed their train and arrived later than they were expected. When they finally arrived, Fred Remington was awaiting them with impatience. In his usual outspoken way, he scolded them for being late and keeping the other guests, and especially himself, waiting for dinner. Then Fred led the company to the dining room, where he immediately sat down to consume a gigantic steak, while the rest of the group—in the manner of Eva's serene hospitality—made their way in a more leisurely fashion through a five-course dinner.[30]

One New Year's Eve toward the end of the decade, the Remingtons entertained a large group of guests at a party. Harriet Ferry, the former Kansas City girl who had observed the young Fred Remington's early struggles, was one of the guests. Fred's beautiful "old maid cousin," Ella Remington, was another. Harriet was by that time married to Charles William Appleton, and they had moved to New York City. Harriet Appleton and Ella Remington always remembered that late evening dinner party and the other guests: the Gus Thomases and the Edward Kembles among them. Harriet was especially impressed with Virginia Thomas's beauty. But the conclusion of the party was what struck her most: "At midnight we went into the studio, down about five steps, and sat on the floor in front of the fire. We had delicious lunches from (Indian) bowls with wooden spoons. Mrs. R had robes for us to wear. Our music consisted of drums and musical instruments, all Indian. The placecards were comic sketches by Kemble, very amusing."[31]

Droll and irritating by turns, fired by enthusiasm for his current work or driven by his internal demons, Fred was never dull company. Eva had long before realized that she could not keep pace with his giant strides to experience everything life had to offer. She followed along in his wake, much as she had in Canton when his rapid strides on afternoon strolls left her well in the rear. Eva had found her own pace for living, and it was attuned to the rhythm of the rest of their world. She had learned, moreover, that gentle persuasion had far more effect on Fred than anger, which she reserved for rare occasions. Among their good friends, whose affection and support were always present, she found the allies she needed to make Fred sometimes stay within reasonable limits of energy.

And from the same group of friends, Fred, who seemed hard-pressed to bring his tensions under control, sensed affection for him and admiration for his talents—both of which he needed constantly although he hid these needs from the outside world. One of the men who perceived and understood Remington better than most was Augustus Thomas. In late 1894, the playwright, watching the artist sketch from a model, made a chance comment that brought a new direction to Remington's talent and a new joy into his life. For by the end of 1894, Fred had begun to "mess with mud," because Gus Thomas happened to say one day that Fred drew more like a sculptor than an illustrator.[32]

(Courtesy of Frederic Remington Collection, Owen D. Young Library, St. Lawrence University, Canton, N.Y.)

8

MESSING WITH MUD
AND SEEING A WAR

« 1895–1898 »

Although Remington had multiple commitments to illustrating and to writing, "messing with mud" became more and more his preoccupation as the winter of 1894 rounded the corner to become 1895. Even the anticipated publication of his first book, *Pony Tracks,* which Harper's brought out early in April 1895, played second fiddle to the lumps of plasteline (clay mixed with an oil base to keep it malleable) that drew him like a magnet whenever he entered his studio. Another major change was also in process: this was the first year that Remington did not plan to enter any paintings in the annual National Academy exhibition. True to his character, he had decided to go it on his own. In late fall 1895, he was to hold his own show, to which end he had to prepare a worthy body of work. With enthusiasms fueling creative energy, Fred breezed into the new year at full steam, ready to continue work and play at the same breathtaking pace he had followed in the first five years of the decade.

In his studio that January, Fred moved back and forth from easel to sculptor's stand, unable to resist substituting his new sculptor's tools and clay for brush and oils. As he slapped clay onto the skeletal armature of a man astride a rearing horse he had contrived, little by little a semblance of living muscle and flesh began to emerge. Working with clay was almost like molding life itself out of earth, water (or oil), and the fire of internal vision—not at all like his prior attempts to produce an illusion of three-dimensional life on flat paper or canvas.

Fred's new creative bent, however, could not fend off fatigue or winter's harshness. By the end of January 1895, he was sick, depressed, and ready to take off in full flight to new horizons in his usual escape pattern. He moaned to Owen Wister: "I feel that I may have grip and there is a riot in Brooklyn and I am tired out and two servants are sick and the old lady has to work and is out of temper and I am going to Florida for a month the very minute I can get the Doc. to say I can."[1] Poor Eva, what a trial Fred must have been that month! Having him refer to her as "the old lady" must really have made her hackles rise.

Fred and Eva headed south to Florida at the end of the month on what was to become their last extended trip together to unknown and unexplored parts. Fred had high hopes for saltwater fishing adventures. He and Eva wanted Owen Wister to join them, for Fred's and Wister's personal and professional friendship was flourishing. At Jacksonville, vacation plans were abruptly halted for a week when Eva took to her bed. Coping with Fred's grippe, sick servants, and a long journey had taken its toll on her never robust health. By the time they reached Punta Gorda, their destination, Fred had rebounded to ebullient anticipation, his January woes forgotten. "Come down," he urged Wister, still immured in Philadelphia's raw, icy winter. Fred was ready for "tarpon—red snapper—ducks—birds of paradise—curious cow-boys who shoot up the rail road trains."[2] He had sniffed out a huge cattle ranch that was located not far off and now, in full cry, was on the trail of a new story. As it turned out, Owen Wister was too ill to make it to Florida to fish with Fred. Fred gathered materials alone for "Cracker Cowboys of Florida," which appeared that August in *Harper's Monthly* with his illustrations. As Fred wryly acknowledged, "cowboys are cash with me."[3] His public demanded cowboys and he was bound to find them, even in Florida.

When the Remingtons returned home, Fred was bouncing with renewed energy and good spirits. He had stopped drinking when he and Eva departed New York, and throughout the spring he felt wonderfully well. Once back in his Endion studio, he returned to work on the two-foot-high clay model he had left draped in a dust cover. Slowly, as winter gave way reluctantly to spring, the form of a cowboy, balanced precariously on a bucking mustang, emerged. Altogether, Gus Thomas's instinctual observation about Fred's peculiar way of seeing his subjects "in the round" was correct. With no training at all except for sketchy art classes at Yale and the Art Students League, Remington had a winner—and he knew it. By the end of March, he could crow to Poultney Bigelow, "It's the biggest business I ever did and if some of these rich sinners over here will cough up and buy a couple of dozen I will go into the mud business."[4] His very first attempt at sculpture had produced the immortal *Broncho Buster* and he wanted it to be cast in bronze.

Fred's explorations into this new creative world were boosted that May. At Gus Thomas's invitation, established sculptor Frederic Ruckstull set up a tent in the Thomas backyard to house the huge and idealized equestrian statue of Civil War general William Hartranft, commissioned for Pennsylvania's capital in Harrisburg. Naturally, Fred spent considerable time watching Ruckstull work and learning more about his new artistic medium. Ruckstull may have guided Remington to the Henry-Bonnard Company, where, in August, Fred took his plasteline *Broncho Buster* to be transformed by sand casting into bronze. Or, perhaps, he had heard via the artists' grapevine that Augustus Saint-Gaudens, the most prestigious of American sculptors at this time, used the Bonnard works for the statues he had had cast in the United States.[5]

While officiating at the *Broncho Buster's* birth, Frederic Remington continued to illustrate, to paint, and to write. But his market was changing. At *Harper's* a new wind was blowing; the parent company of the prestigious *Monthly,* the popular *Weekly,* and their companion publications—in which Remington's work appeared sporadically—was rumored to be in troubled financial waters. Old, familiar faces disappeared and new staff members came aboard.

The year of 1894, although apparently a banner year for Fred's work in terms of the number of illustrations published by *Harper's,* had really been the watershed. For the first time, *Harper's* had rejected illustrations Remington had submitted. That year, the periodical had published sixty-five of his illustrations in the *Weekly* and ninety-eight in the *Monthly.* Many of these accompanied seven of his own articles in the former periodical, and three in the *Monthly.* But, in 1895, the total diminished to thirty-two illustrations in the *Weekly*— mostly for six articles he wrote—together with forty-two illustrations and two articles in the *Monthly.* During 1895, Fred and Owen Wister worked in partnership on three articles for the *Monthly.* Fred's story and illustrations, based on the western grizzly hunt with General Miles in 1894, had appeared in January, and now he had finished his article about Florida. The *Monthly,* also that year, hired him to illustrate two articles written by Caspar Whitney, a *Harper's Weekly* staff writer who was a good friend of Fred's.[6]

Two other old magazine standbys were falling by the wayside, too, although both would publish his work again in years to come. *The Century* had ceased to use Remington as an illustrator in 1894, and *Outing*, with Poultney Bigelow gone from its editorial staff, rarely asked for Remington's drawings now. Although he had work in the January issue and would appear in December 1895, *Outing* would not publish his work again until nearly century's end. *The Century* eventually began to buy his work again in 1897. Fred now looked to other periodicals to add to his list. *Cosmopolitan* was using his work consistently, having first published *Custer's Last Fight* in 1891 to accompany an article by General James G. Wilson. In 1895, he was working on illustrations scheduled for five issues of *Cosmo*, as he called the magazine. *Scribner's Magazine*, which had used Remington at the beginning of the decade, published him once more in 1899. Before 1900, he would be working for *Collier's* and, in 1897, he was sent on assignment for William Randolph Hearst's newspaper, the *Journal*, to report on the Spanish-American War.[7]

In middecade, Fred's correspondence was as prolific as ever. Poultney Bigelow, living in Europe, and Owen Wister, with whom Fred worked closely that year, heard from him frequently. Theodore Roosevelt, now in Washington, invited him to a dinner there in early April, at which Rudyard Kipling was to be an honored guest. Fred planned to go, even dashing off a note to Wister to propose that they take the same train together. But Fred did not make it to Washington, having been taken ill.[8] Afterward, Kipling, who was living temporarily in the United States, wrote to Remington, "It was great fun at Roosevelt's dinner: but I had counted a good deal on your also being there."[9]

Later that year, however, Kipling and Remington lunched in company with Poultney Bigelow, who was temporarily back from Europe. Fred was working with the British author to plan the illustrations for Kipling's "The Maltese Falcon," which appeared in *Cosmopolitan* in August 1895. Kipling and Fred that day engaged in a lively debate about the relative value of British and American systems, points of view, and contributions to world values and accomplishments. Fred was his usual bumptious self, speaking with "audacity, frankness and picturesqueness," Bigelow recalled in an article published shortly after Fred's death. Poultney thought Fred "the most unconventional, outspoken and delightful of companions." He was a good foil for Kipling, keeping that intrepid interpreter of the British "tommies" and their colonial tasks at his best. The exchange was full of wit and mental gymnastics.[10]

In 1895, Fred had recently discovered the bicycle. Trying to keep his weight under control, he rode regularly on the big-wheeled, new-fangled contraption—and so did Eva. He thought bicycling great fun and told both Wister and Bigelow so. True to form, he produced an article on the subject for *Harper's Weekly*, because "everyone in America" was riding cycles and it was a sure thing for the magazine.[11] When rested, on the wagon, working hard, and "up," Fred bounced along the currents of life like a helium-filled balloon in a high breeze. Life right then was full, exciting, successful. Forgotten were midwinter gloom, *Harper's* rejections, his own inner doubts. He was ready to conquer the world. He told Owen Wister in March, "I am riding a bike. I am happy. . . . I have just learned how to paint. I have invented a military appliance which will make me 'rich' . . . and I am going to have a book published called *Pony Tracks*."[12] Fred later repudiated his optimistic statement about learning to paint. In 1895, his painting was in its infancy, in comparison to his accomplishments a decade later.

Besides getting to know Ruckstull, May 1895 included a fishing trip to Canada. Fred seldom fished now, his huge girth making it a bit precarious to sit in a small rowboat or canoe and to fight a big one snagged at the end of a line. Instead, Fred either sat in the bow sketching, his weight sinking the craft perilously close to the water-line, or remained comfortably ashore at a scenic spot—say, at the edge of Quebec's Lake St. John, with drawing pad propped in front of him.

In May, Fred was still on the wagon. Of course, he let all his friends and sundry acquaintances know it. As a convert to teetotal-ism, he "reasoned that I had had all that kind of fun one man could expect to have and do anything else so I cut square off and feel better—but I am not a d—— bit sorry about any drink I ever had." In this gleeful mood that spring and summer, he concocted numer-ous plans for excursions later in the year. At one point, he decided to take a long trip, to start at Lake Superior and then to "come down by canoe." Another plan was to make a six-hundred-mile canoe trip on the Ottawa River.[13]

The "high" that Remington's life exhibited that spring, the im-mense amount of work he tackled, the number of letters he wrote, the high-flying trips he planned, the tumble of thoughts, words, and work that poured from him certainly bear out recent twentieth-century discoveries about similarities between creativity and the "manic" phase of bipolar personalities. Although most people experience ups and downs (or "normals" and downs, or "normals" and ups), Fred's swing upward without the depressive influences of alcohol during this teetotalling period certainly seems to have verged on or entered a realm of euphoria.[14] Fortunately for posterity, Fred Remington never swung completely away from reality and was able to harness these emotional highs to his artistic goals, continuing to produce a noteworthy body of paintings and bronzes. Unfortunately for his physical well-being, however, he also never completely abandoned the depressive effects of alcohol, which he continually and unsuccessfully fought to avoid for the rest of his life. Whether he had instinctually found that alcohol depressed his tendencies to "fly too high" or whether he really had an addictive personality (as we might call it today) is open to debate. Remington functioned for the last fifteen years of his life under the increasing physical handicaps of overweight and digestive problems, which may or may not have been caused by the deleterious effects of his years of excess. Because no medical records remain, we again enter the realm of speculation about the cause of his "dyspepsia" and the other illnesses mentioned in his journals during his final years.[15]

Remington had given up his flights of fantasy, such as his overly ambitious proposals for canoing trips, by midsummer. None of the glorious pipe dreams he planned materialized. Instead, he slowed down, returning to the hectic pace that was "normal" for him after his and Eva's usual July vacation in the North Country. Here, they divided their time among Canton, Cranberry Lake, and the Thousand Islands. The latter site attracted the artist as a vacation haunt more and more strongly each year. Fred's conversion to abstemiousness was no longer mentioned in his correspondence, and we suspect that he had returned to former habits again once he was in residence at Bishop's Hotel at Cranberry, and almost certainly when he was fraternizing with his Ogdensburg cronies on the River. In the fall, he did return to Canada on a hunting trip with Julian Ralph, but before that he saw to the casting of his first sculpture.

In August, Remington's *Broncho Buster* was immortalized in bronze. He had taken the plasteline model to the Henry-Bonnard works, where it was laboriously transformed into metal. The sand casting method employed there was a multistage process in common use in foundries of the nineteenth century. Fred was already somewhat familiar with the process because, back in Canton as an inquisitive youth, he and most other village lads had watched sand casting at the David Jones Water Street foundry that produced the St. Lawrence Box Stoves that had brought local fame to this Canton industry.[16] In sand casting, the clay model was first encased in plaster in such a way that the plaster, once hardened, could be neatly pried away in sections. The sectional hollow plaster mold thus created was oiled and reassembled to form the vessel for a plaster *Broncho Buster*. After having been freed from its plaster tomb, the plaster statue was in turn carefully cut into castable sections. Once more, molds were made of the sections, this time in hard-packed sand, in an intricate and time-consuming process.[17] With vents and canals added, the molten metal was then poured and allowed to cool. The last step in the long process, after the finished rough bronze appeared, was to file away extrusions and to treat the statue with one of several acid concoctions to "patinate," or color, the final product. Duplicates could be made in the sand molds, but, at best, sand casting did not allow for subtle detail.

Remington was aquiver with excitement and anxiety about his *Broncho Buster*. As an illustrator, he was successful. As a painter, he still had a way to go. But sculpture was something else again, and the first child of this talent was soon to be judged by the world. On August 22, he told Owen Wister, "Keep my name in stereotype in printer's cases. They will have to use it right along because if my model won't do I am going to be the most eminent market gardener in the suburbs of NY."[18]

The *Broncho Buster,* which Fred officially registered with the Copyright Office on October 15, made its public debut only days later at Tiffany's on West Sixteenth Street in New York. As its creator, Fred had all the qualms of a parent about to introduce an offspring into society. He need not have feared, because his instinct that he had a winner was correct. Critics acclaimed his first bronze, and knowledgeable New York flocked to see it. Fred received word from *The Century* that the magazine wished to publish a photograph of the sculpture, which sent the *Broncho Buster's* likeness abroad throughout the land. The postal service in New Rochelle did heavy duty that autumn as enthusiastic praises arrived at Endion.

"You will be great," wrote Al Brolley, his boxing partner from the old days when he worked in Albany. Brolley—now Judge A. A. Brolley of the Albany Court of Appeals—continued, "and I hope that as time [goes on] still more develops and multiplies fame's laurel wreaths about your brow . . . St. Gaudens [sic] says it is 'very good!' does He? I know he can't touch it. You wait!"[19]

"Where is the *Broncho Buster* to be seen?" William D. Howells, the revered dean of American letters, asked Remington. "The picture of the statue took me tremendously. You are such a whaler in every way that it would be no wonder if sculpture turned out to be one of your best holds."[20]

With such kudos at hand, Fred tried to explain to Owen Wister what *Broncho Buster* meant to its creator.

> I have only one idea now—I only have an idea every seven years & never more than one at a time but it's *mud*—all other forms of art are trivialities—mud—or it's sequence "bronze" is a thing to think of when you are doing it and afterwards too. It don't decay—the moth don't break through to steal—the rust & the idiot can not harm it for it is there to say by God one day I was not painted in another tone from this—one day anyone could read me now I am *black-letter*—I do not speak through a season on the stage—I am d—— near eternal if people want to know about the past and above all I am so simple that wise-men & fools of all ages can "get there" and know *whether or not*.[21]

"Dear Mud," Wister responded, "You are right. Only once in a while you'll still wash your hand to take hold of mine I hope. It would be an awful blow to one of this team if bronze was to be all, hereafter. I am going to own the broncho buster. The name is as splendid as the rest. . . . Tomorrow I shall see the BB at 430 W 16th St."[22]

The *Broncho Buster*'s appearance may have been the zenith of Fred Remington's art in the eye of the admiring public that year, but more success was yet to come. On November 14, Fred's one-man exhibition opened at the American Art Association on East Twenty-third Street with 114 paintings to be available for sale at the evening auction scheduled for November 19. That night, 20 paintings were sold to such dignitaries as William Randolph Hearst, Joseph Pulitzer, and his friend Owen Wister.[23] The rush of events had Fred in a daze: "I am d—— near crazy between illustrating. . . . That sale— the bronze, magazine Horse Show pictures—a patent I am trying to engineer—a story (good one) which I can't write about canoeing . . . and several other things make life perfectly *Chinese cookie*."[24]

Events and opportunities swirled about Fred Remington as 1895 drew to a close. After his illustrating career peaked in 1894, it was as if whole new dimensions were opening before him. He had success, if financial security, acceptance, and prestige constituted success. Only ten short years before, Remington had "lost everything" that he had inherited from the father he idolized. He had also lost his youthful fantasies about life, what had remained of his good name, the emotional support of his mother, and, temporarily, his wife. Thrown entirely upon his own inner resources, he had struggled through turbid waters to this present crest. If Fred had only been content to look backward, he could have balanced on the wave of his success and coasted. Instead, as always, he glimpsed new horizons ahead. Having discovered immortality in bronze, he now reached for the rainbow.

It was time to learn to paint, really to paint, to explore the nuances of color that the lens of his extraordinary eye sent inward to the restless creative pulse. It was as if, having heretofore perceived what lay before him in black and white, he now awoke to Technicolor. Ever the knight errant, he set out for the West again, as if somehow in those great, new, and still primal lands he would find what he sought. The "thing to which I am going to devote two months," he told Wister, "is *color*. . . . I have studied *form* so much that I never had a chance to '*let go*' and find if I can see with *the wide open eyes of a child* what I know has been pounded into me [that] I *had* to know—now I am going to see—[if] I am sufficiently idolic to have a *color sense*: and I am going to go loco for two months."[25] He wanted the reassurance of a companion who would understand. "I would like a man with me whom I know is crazy," he wrote to the Philadelphian. "Come come come come."

Instead, he went west alone. Owen Wister departed in the opposite direction to explore Europe. (Over the next two years most of Fred's friends seemed to be bent on exploring the world: Dana Gibson and Julian Ralph also went to Europe, Caspar Whitney to Siam, Poultney Bigelow to Egypt. Only Fred stayed home, vowing that finding America was far more exciting and important than any foreign travel.) On his return to Endion in March 1896, Fred was back to his frenetic, terse, breezy self. He was strangely silent about the original goal of his journey. Had he failed in his own mind, we wonder, or was he silent because he was so determined, because he could own only to himself how difficult a task he had set, how far he had to travel on this inward mission. All that he reported of the trip to others was that he had found a good story line and illustration ideas for an article about the legendary Texas Rangers.[26] He had painted, loafed, shot, and quit drinking (again). He had found some new ideas. He was going to do another sculpture, a companion piece for the *Broncho Buster,* and it was going to be better. Everything in art that he returned to remained safe, familiar ground that was already firm underfoot. He did not mention his quest for the unattained. Instead, Fred threw himself into work of the moment, life at Endion, reading and letter writing, his usual plans for excursions, and the annual North Country vacation. Life slipped quickly into its normal pace and routine, although Fred's pace was anything but average. What he considered a normal pace was what most would view as hectic pandemonium or high adventure.

In 1896, the Werner Company of Chicago published *The Personal Recollections of General Nelson Miles.* Fred had been asked by his old army friend to illustrate this book and had willingly acceded, little dreaming that this project would later bring headaches. The illustrations were drawn from Miles's and his own memories and experiences, as well as from earlier sketches he himself had made. Nothing in the book illustrations was outstandingly different from his earlier drawing. Throughout the 1890s, Fred maintained close contact with Miles and with other friends in the army. He wrote numerous and sometimes voluminous letters and, apparently, was of some influence on his friends' behalf in the egregious political infighting that was then rampant in this branch of the armed services. He always put in a good word for his friends, recommending them for specific jobs or promotions, assisting those with writing ability to realize their ambitions. He had been such a good friend to Powhatan Clarke, for instance, that the cavalry officer had been published in *Harper's Weekly* some years before his death.[27] Lieutenant Arthur Sydenham, with whose detail he rode during the Wounded Knee uprising, was so grateful to Remington that he later wrote a laudatory biographical sketch about the artist that was, finally, printed in 1942 in the New York Public Library's periodical publication.[28] Even Custer's widow had asked Fred to illustrate her biography of her husband (in 1886).

Fred's active imagination and inquisitive mind were always intrigued by all aspects of army life. He dashed off sketches showing his ideas for new army uniforms and, with his usual aplomb, then submitted them to army headquarters in Washington for consideration. Some of his ideas were good; he received commendatory letters from officialdom on occasion. When he had traveled to Europe and

Russia, he had in his pocket letters of commendation from Washington. In the 1890s, he played, off and on, with the idea of a new munitions carrier and eventually drew detailed designs. Fred did patent his invention and dreamed of a harvest of riches to swell his coffers, although he ultimately sold the patent to his good friend and fellow outdoor enthusiast, Joel Burdick.[29]

Besides his continuing army relationships, Fred was in the good graces of Washington through Teddy Roosevelt, now rising rapidly in government circles, and General Miles, who was appointed senior commander of the army. Roosevelt, still as ardent a sportsman, western enthusiast, and military buff as Fred, thoroughly approved of Remington's work and his writing. (Later when he became assistant secretary of the navy the bespectacled Roosevelt openly courted Remington's approval of the service, inviting him to inspect the fleet anchored off Virginia's eastern shores and take part in Washington social affairs.[30] Teddy may have had in mind to lure the artist into adding seascapes and naval paintings to his repertoire—thereby indirectly adding luster to Roosevelt's own reputation. Although Fred was never really interested, he did visit the fleet off the Virginia coast.[31] The Spanish-American War would help cement the mutual admiration the men held for each other.)

In July, after previous renovations to the big New Rochelle house had been completed, Fred and Eva decided to build an enlarged studio for Fred and a butler's pantry for Eva as a sizable addition to Endion. It would be worth the temporary mess for Fred to have room for his clay models, all his painting paraphernalia, and the growing collection of miscellany that served as props and costumes for his models. The studio plans included a big fireplace where Fred fancied he would warm his toes, cigar in hand, creating paintings and sculpture in his mind's eye with the help of flickering flames. It was to be like an "old Norman farmhouse," he told Poultney Bigelow tongue-in-cheek, because Bigelow was by now a confirmed expatriate and Fred liked to pull his friend's leg.[32] (The fireplace turned out to be a bane. It wouldn't draw right and Fred complained about this the next year during a raw, cold spell in early March. The studio, however, was a success. Reached by a series of six steps downward, it was large enough for all Fred's accoutrements.)

Another major project with which Fred busied himself in 1896 was beginning preparations to publish a book of his own artwork. Because Harper's did not print or market art books, he had to look elsewhere and found the smaller publishing house of Robert H. Russell. As he inventoried his mounting body of work to select pieces for the book, he played with the idea of asking Owen Wister to write the preface. *Drawings* did not appear until 1897, and during that next year Fred and Owen Wister tossed ideas for the proposed preface back and forth. Somehow during the course of events Wister did not get to the task when Fred wanted him to. Fred, who never was a patient man, fumed as publication time neared and no Wister preface was forthcoming. Wister did meet the deadline, but this became the first sour taste in an otherwise fruitful relationship.

The year of 1896 continued apace. Illustrations, drawings, and paintings flowed copiously from pen and brush, some as illustrations for his own articles. He finished his bronze *The Wounded Bunkie,* and began to model *The Wicked Pony,* which he finally copyrighted in 1898 along with *The Scalp,* his fourth piece of sculpture. In April, he went north to canoe on Lake George and Lake Champlain in company with Joel Burdick, George Wright (his New York attorney), and others.[33] In May, he and Eva spent a week in the Adirondacks. In June, he and Owen Wister went to New Mexico to gather materials for more illustrated joint articles. During the summer, he and Eva had their usual month's stay in the North Country.

Fred was haunted in the early and midnineties by an unfulfilled ambition of his youth. He wanted to see a war. The desperate fight for survival by the Western Indian tribes had ended in their sad defeat. The frontier was gone, and Fred, the recognized eulogizer of its passing, no longer had fresh subject matter to record and glorify for posterity. He may not have been entirely accurate as a reporter of historical fact, but he had transformed the players on the western stage to a larger-than-life stature that satisfied his public then and has since imbued the lost frontier with an aura of almost mystical idealism. Even in the winning of the West, if it could be counted winning to Fred's mind, he had never seen "real" warfare.

Somehow, Fred sandwiched a stupendous amount of reading into his busy life: books, periodicals, and newspapers taught him about the past and kept him abreast of the present. By 1895, he sensed with others that the winds of war were stirring, this time from a different direction. Fred had a keen sense for coming military conflict, from the 1890s until the end of his life.[34] Now his quick perceptions turned his attention southward, where the United States of America was beginning to flex its economic muscles. The tentacles of investment that crept toward Central America resulted from a growing desire to secure new sources of raw materials, as well as new markets to feed expanding industrial capacities. Washington official-dom supported the view that securing both sources and markets was in the national welfare. The nation moved away from its pattern of isolationism. James Monroe's doctrine was taken out of storage, dusted off, and reinterpreted.

Only ninety miles southeast of the tip of Florida lay the "Pearl of the Antilles," the Spanish colony Cuba. Here, at midcentury stretched miles of sugar cane and tobacco plantations, which had become the suppliers for the United States' growing sweet tooth and its growing addiction to nicotine. Cuba's government and laws fol-lowed the Roman code of the mother country, far away across the Atlantic. Cuba's Spanish rulers governed through a process that was primarily judicial; executive prerogatives were often unclear. Gradu-ally, a system had evolved that passed official powers down through a few families, who also happened to be the major landowners, and who had, by the 1880s, become a "sugar oligarchy."[35]

Intent on additional financial gain there, the Hispano-Cuban landholders in the mid-nineteenth century turned their eyes to the North American continent as the nearest, most profitable market. And, because the early Spanish masters had decimated the ranks of the indigenous Indian population, they turned to Africa to supply a slave labor force essential to swelling sugar cane production. Sparked by the abolitionist movement that filtered into Cuba in the mid-1800s, armed conflict existed between advocates of a free Cuba and those still loyal to Spain. A rebellion had started in what is now called Oriente Province (where Fidel Castro was later born). General Va-leriano Weyler, commissioned to subdue it, prevailed, and leaders of the rebellion were forced into exile in North America, where they continued to fight from the United States for Cuban independence.[36] These exiled Cuban leaders made every attempt to influence Ameri-ca's foreign policy.

With its own western frontiers defined and with the tools of the industrial revolution at hand, United States enterprise now turned south for raw materials and markets. Northern entrepreneurs arrived in Havana with new technologies for refining sugar. Following these economic pioneers were other American businessmen, industrialists and bankers, such as Fred and Eva's New Rochelle neighbor and friend, Jay Cox, whose father, "Pa Cox," was a national political force.[37] A free Cuba could prove to be a far better economic adjunct to America's welfare than a subject colony, one that still had to send "tribute" to its mother country. In addition, after subduing the freedom movement, General Weyler's harsh hand as a military tyrant earned him the nickname of "the butcher." Reports of his continuing brutality incensed the people of the rest of the hemisphere.

With growing fascination, Fred Remington watched the makings of "his" war. So did William Randolph Hearst, who had come to the newspaper scene in New York in 1895 when he acquired the *New York Journal,* whose editorial policy quickly changed to sensationalism. Joseph Pulitzer's *World* now had competition, because Hearst hired as many of the best writers, journalists, and illustrators as he could attract by paying the highest price going at the time. When *Harper's Weekly* published Fred's drawing *The Flag of Cuba,* in March 1896, there is little doubt that Hearst saw it and filed away in his mind the fact that Remington's eye, like his own, was on a sure-fire story to come. In fact, Hearst contacted Fred Remington in December 1896. He wanted to send him to Cuba to assess the situation there, in partnership with the debonair Richard Harding Davis, who was literally tall, dark, and handsome, as well as slim as a blade. Davis had never been a favorite with Fred when that popular journalist sat for a time in one of the editorial chairs at *Harper's.*[38] Davis, in turn, was not particularly fond of Fred. Perhaps the mutual personal dislike arose because each man liked dominating center stage. Perhaps Davis suffered a mite of jealousy at Fred's success, which, in illustration at least, equaled his own journalistic triumphs—and now Fred aspired to journalism, too. Both men were, however, professionals, and Fred's Cuba assignment was a journalist's dream, although it meant abandoning Eva over the Christmas holidays.

A Manley family myth about Hearst's summons to Fred Remington originated with Williston Manley, who, by 1896, was at the helm of the *St. Lawrence Plaindealer* in Canton. Will always insisted to Atwood, and later to Peg, that Hearst handed Fred a specially made money belt, well filled with the coin of the realm to see him on his way to Cuba.

"Here, take this to stake you," Hearst directed Remington, according to Will. "Get to Cuba as fast as you can and draw the war."

"But there is no war," Fred countered.

"You go and I will make the war," Will claimed Hearst told his man.

The original plan was for Davis and Remington to reach Cuba, via Florida, aboard Hearst's steam yacht, the *Vamoose.* The two journalists cooled their heels in Key West while the *Vamoose* was being repainted an appropriate wartime gray. Impatient as the refitting dragged on, the two correspondents traveled instead to Havana on the *Olivette,* a regular passenger steamer that plied back and forth between Cuba and Florida. Once in Havana, they viewed conditions there and interviewed General Weyler, the "butcher." Their trained eyes observed the unrest and oppression, the squalor and endemic disease rampant among the general population.[39]

Fred's reaction to what he saw was an acute discomfort. He told Poultney Bigelow after his return home that he "saw more hell there than I ever read about. . . .—small pox—typhoid—yellow jacket (or yellow fever)—dishonesty—suffering beyond measure."[40] Although he wrote to Eva that he was sure that war was coming, a time-honored legend exists that Fred wired Hearst, "Everything is quiet. There is no trouble. There will be no war. I wish to return." And it was now that Hearst was supposed to have cabled back, "Please remain. You furnish the pictures and I'll furnish the war."[41] No matter what the basis for the legend, Fred was back at Endion by the end of January 1897, just two weeks after Hearst's *Journal,* in its blatant style, had run a full-page announcement that the two correspondents were in Cuba. (Davis remained to explore and to garner more information for future articles.)

Late in January 1897, Fred's first illustrated article appeared in the *Journal.* On February 12, a second article about Cuba's condition was published. Richard Harding Davis was author of this story. It was about the coldhearted manner in which women leaving Cuba aboard the *Olivette* were searched by the military. Accompanying Davis's article was an illustration by Frederic S. Remington that showed an upended woman, bare buttocks in view, being callously searched. This scandalous and horrifying exposé helped fan the flames of war that had been smoldering in the United States. Hearst *was* furnishing the war, as promised, in his legendary comment. Remington, who was safely at home in Endion weeks before Davis reboarded the *Olivette* to return, abetted Hearst's promise with his sensational drawing. The furor the article and picture created obscured a later retraction printed in the *Journal*: Davis's article had not been founded on fact.

After Fred returned from Cuba, the weather was rotten as the late winter drew to a close. An ugly north wind staved off the advance of spring. Mrs. Harding, the Remington's cook/housekeeper, kept predicting that the weather would clear, but Fred was less hopeful. Even his new bicycle was idled by the same raw blasts that prevented Eva's Plymouth Rocks, huddled in the new henhouse, from laying fresh eggs. While the new fireplace smoked badly, Fred finished four full-page illustrations for the Hearst assignment, which appeared in mid-April, accompanying another Davis article.[42] In addition, Owen Wister had asked him to do the frontispiece of his western novel *Lin McLean,* which Harper's was set to publish that year.[43] His own book, *Drawings,* was also about to be published and he continued to push Wister to write the preface. He soon had less welcome news: Werner Company, publishers of the Miles memoirs, which Fred had illustrated, had just released *Frontier Sketches,* making use of illustrations from the Miles book without permission and with no promise of payment or royalties to the artist. Fred was irate and eventually sought legal redress.

Tense, frustrated by weather and work, and with rumbling thunder the only herald of impending war, Fred went early to fish in the Adirondacks that year, but winter still lingered in New Rochelle when he returned. Good weather did arrive, however, in time for Eva and Fred's annual summer vacation in the North Country. They stayed at John Keeler's Witch Bay camp. Nearby, at Fred Howlett's Tramps Retreat, teenage Marshall Howlett Durston that summer faithfully recorded life at Cranberry in a journal. As Atwood wrote earlier, Durston was "a callow youth of seventeen" then. One evening he crossed the lake to spend the night with Fred Remington and Eva at Witch Bay:

"It was crude, terribly crude, only two windows, and overrun with mice," Durston recalled over sixty years later for Albert Fowler, who was gathering material about early Cranberry.[44] "Remington would libate mornings, taper off for lunch, start painting and then work like a demon. He'd keep painting on into the night by lantern light, oblivious to the world.

"His camp was cluttered with 'dead Indians.' He didn't give a hoot what folks thought or said. He worked as though the devil were after him with a pitchfork."

Although he may have been prodded by the devil's pitchfork in the young Durston's eyes, Fred felt "bully" after his vacation, reporting that life in the open air and fishing for trout had brought his weight down to 240 pounds. He was rarin' to go. He decided to head for Montana in September to hunt elk and to find more nourishment for his talents. While in the western mountains, he visited Buffalo Bill Cody's ranch. He had met and written about Colonel Cody in 1892, when Buffalo Bill took his Wild West Show to London, where the British swarmed to see bucking broncos, Indians, and cowboys. (Years later he visited Cody's show when it played in Connecticut, hoping to capture some good action sketches for his paintings, but grumpily wrote in his journal that he had been frustrated by crowds and weather.[45])

Autumn 1897 followed the schedule of earlier years. Fred's new book finally had its Wister preface and was off the presses. He was moving between sculptor's stand and easel in his studio. His public still called for cowboys and Indians. His publishers kept buying his articles and drawings. In December, he received acclaim from yet another quarter: a request from the U.S. Postal Service to submit drawings for a special commemorative series of stamps to be issued in 1898. The occasion was the Omaha Exposition, which was to illustrate the "history, industrial development, and present importance of the country lying west of the Mississippi." Fred set to work with a will, quickly producing sketches from which the Post Office Department finally picked two. Remington's *Troops Guarding Train* appeared on the eight-cent stamp of the series, his *Mining Prospector* on the fifty-cent stamp.

Meanwhile, Remington finished more illustrations for Hearst about Cuba, which showed the horrors he had seen the previous year. One picture published in January 1898 had as its caption his own description of the actions of the Spanish "savages." Then, on February 15, 1898, Gus Thomas, near neighbor to Fred and Eva and Fred's hiking partner in New Rochelle, hurried to Endion with news that sent Fred scurrying. In Havana harbor, the United States battleship *Maine* had been mysteriously blown up and sunk. Fred was sure now that he would see his war. He contacted *Harper's* immediately, convincing his editors to sign him on as a war correspondent. He got in touch with Hearst, too, and became an official *Journal* war reporter. Eventually, he was hired to report on the war for the *New York Tribune* as well. Then he hastened first to Fort Slocum on David's Island, just off the coast of Westchester County, to sketch recruits drilling there, afterward traveling to Fort Myer, Virginia, where he watched cavalry troops training.[46]

As fast as he could, Fred moved on south. By April 1, he found himself once more at Key West, along with dozens of other writers and artists now designated as members of an official press corps, all also eager to see a war. There, sitting on rocking chairs on the veranda at the grandiose Tampa Bay Hotel, Fred and the others were made to wait for almost three weeks. On the afternoon of the twenty-second, as Richard Harding Davis wrote, "a small boy fell off his bicycle in front of the hotel and ran his eyes along the porch . . . handed a telegram, and, mounting his wheel again, rode away up the hot and dusty street."[47] The telegram the lad had delivered read, "Rain and hail." Once uncoded, the message announced that the United States had declared war on Spain. The fleet, which was lying off Key West, was ordered to sea to blockade Havana harbor.

In a trice, the somnolent war correspondents sprang to life again and Fred made haste to quarters assigned him on the battleship *Iowa*. For the next seven days and nights, he was at sea, as the ponderous vessel moved back and forth, back and forth, at the entrance to the Cuban harbor. As he wrote in "Wigwags from the Blockade" for the *Weekly,* "Nothing happened. . . . The appalling sameness of this pacing up and down before Havana works on the nerves of everyone, from captain to cook's police." One part of war, Fred was learning, was to "hurry up and wait." The only bright spot in the boring adventure was the companionship of Dr. Percy Crandell, ship's doctor. Inaction was anathema to Fred: "it's all horribly alike to me," he penned in his *Harper's* article, "so I managed to desert," sneaking aboard a torpedo boat that pulled alongside, and riding to the *New York,* where he found a jubilant Rufus Zogbaum and Richard Harding Davis. "Stiff with jealousy," he heard them describe the cruiser's shelling of Cuban working parties on the shore at Matanzas the previous day.[48]

Meanwhile, on Key West, the army was assembling its expeditionary force of cavalry and foot soldiers to invade Cuba. Army regulars were augmented with volunteers, who responded enthusiastically to the call to arms. Teddy Roosevelt, lately assistant secretary of the navy, had resigned to help organize the soon-to-be-famous Rough Riders under the doughty Colonel Leonard Wood, and the unit assembled at Key West. To Florida came General William Shafter, appointed commander of the expeditionary force through political influence. (Fred's friend, General Nelson Miles, who was now commander of the army, had been bypassed and remained in Washington.) To the Tampa Bay Hotel scurried military observers and attachés of Germany's and Britain's embassies. Clara Barton was on hand with her volunteer nurses. Bored by the navy's routine chase of elusive Spanish ships at sea, Remington, Davis, Zogbaum, and others hitched rides back to the Tampa Bay Hotel. Once again, they sat on the hotel piazza. The Cuban conflict had temporarily become a "rocking chair war."[49]

No one was quite sure why the monstrous Tampa Bay Hotel had been built (or so named). Florida was not yet invaded seasonally by the "snow birds" of the twentieth century. The hotel stood in isolated Baroque splendor on the sandy key. Its palatial accommodations and atmosphere were in marked contrast to the grim realities that the press correspondents were to report. Itching at inactivity, Fred Remington held court on the veranda, surrounded by men like novelist Stephen Crane; his friend Poultney Bigelow, who had arrived posthaste from Europe; and Caspar Whitney, just returned from the Far East. There was a charisma about Fred's personality that even Richard Harding Davis had to acknowledge. (Davis described the rocking chair war in his *The Cuban and Porto Rican Campaign,* in which he gave Fred's personal magnetism its due.) Everyone put in his opinion about the future course of the war, including John Jacob Astor (who had volunteered for Cuba's freedom forces and was now part of the U.S. Army); Ira Sankey, of religious revivalist fame, whose hymns were popular with the soldiers; and the ubiquitous Theodore Roosevelt, when he was not organizing his Rough Riders. The Tampa Bay Hotel porch had become the Spanish-American War's version of the old village well, where everyone met and where everyone knew everyone else.

In light of the number of people Fred knew who flocked to Key West, it was not surprising that at least one was from the North Country. Irving Bacheller, now head of the nation's first newspaper syndicate, the Bacheller Syndicate, arrived to see the Rough Riders and to garner information. After he had inspected the cavalry camp, "the sun was setting as I tramped back toward the entrance. I passed a line of officers' horses hitched to posts. One of them had got his neck under the hitching strap and was in trouble. I went to his head to relieve him when I heard a shouted command: 'Keep away from that horse.'

"The command was followed by a loud laugh near me. I turned and saw Frederic Remington. That kind of greeting was characteristic. We had a delightful hour together."[50]

When the invasion forces finally sailed to Cuba in late June, after weeks of drilling among the Key West palmettos and after three false starts, the correspondents, Fred Remington among them, finally found their war. They were headed toward the key port of Santiago de Cuba, located on the southern coast, its narrow-mouthed harbor reaching far inland. Santiago City at the harbor's innermost northeastern point was protected to the east by the north-south range of

the San Juan hills. Farther east on the coast lay the place marked
Siboney on the map, from which a jungle-infested mountain trail
ascended to Guasimas and thence inland farther still to El Poso, all
names that were to be immortalized through bloody conflict in the
weeks ahead. Rebel guerrilla forces under General Calixto Garcia y
Iñigus were hiding in this region.

The vastly overweight and lethargic General Shafter debarked
off Siboney for a prearranged strategy meeting with the Cuban rebel
general. With him went Fred Remington, Caspar Whitney, Stephen
Bonsal, and Richard Harding Davis. From their longboat, the correspondents viewed coconut palms fringing the little bay, with a
backdrop of mountains forested with manigua bushes stretching to
the skyline. Davis later said that every feature of the landscape was
highlighted: "There was no shading, it was all brilliant, gorgeous,
and glaring. The sea was . . . indigo . . . like the blue in a washtub;
the green of the mountains was . . . corroded copper; the scarlet
trees . . . the red of a (British) Tommy's jacket, and the sun was
like a lime-light in its fierceness."[51]

Waiting for them were Cuban officers with mules and ponies to
transport the American dignitaries up the rough cattle trail to meet
the white-haired, white-mustached Garcia. For the first time, the officers and correspondents faced the reality of the Cuban situation.
With no military escort or protection, the U.S. commander and his
aides struggled up the overgrown trail in the steaming heat. Once at
the Cuban campsite, the leaders discussed how and where to disem-
bark twelve thousand troopers and their horses, ammunition, and
supplies, all now waiting offshore on the transports. The decision
was made to land at Baiquiri still farther east.

None of the correspondents was allowed to land with the first
troops to hit the beach. When he did go ashore, Remington was
with the Sixth Cavalry. "The first night ashore it rained and I slept
all night wet," he wrote to Eva.[52] "I stayed with the 6th but found
they did not move . . . stalled—I got lifts for my pack most of the
day. . . . I have an awful cold and can't get over it . . . —by God
I haven't had enough to eat since I left Tampa—I am dirty—oh so
dirty. I have on a canvas suit and have 2 shirts—my other shirts as
the boys call them.—I have no baggage which I do not carry on my
back." Fred plowed along the trails that led the invaders to Siboney,
Las Guasimas, El Caney, El Poso, and San Juan—those hamlets,
junctions of mountain trails, or steep hills marking the battles of the
Santiago campaign. His erstwhile correspondent companions were

with other groups. Of the majority of the press corps—and most of
the army officers as well—only Davis and Fred Remington had any
conception of what lay ahead.

The troops were burdened with weapons and heavy packs, as
well as blankets and uniforms that were intended for more moderate
climes and colder weather, not the sweltering heat and humidity of
tropical Cuba. The dry winter months were yielding to the heavy
daily downpours of the island's yearly rainy season. Damp rot, mold
and mildew, mud and muck, pools that bred multitudes of mosquitoes, dripping jungle foliage, were the environment through which
troops slogged and horses plunged. Each footstep of the lines of
soldiers churned the mire deeper. Campsites turned into mucky
nightmares. Dampness invaded the most carefully guarded belongings. No one—except staff officers far back of the line of march—
was dry. Invisible dangers far more catastrophic than jungle rain or
enemy ambushes lurked everywhere: typhoid, yellow fever, malaria,
amebic dysentery were far more threatening to the ill-clothed, ill-
prepared Americans than the misery they endured twenty-four hours
of every day of the invasion. Harried medics and field doctors in
their crude stations were inundated with much more than the inju-
ries of battle. Enlisted men and officers alike shivered and sweated
alternately, felled by the ravages of tropical fevers.

At thirty-six, Fred Remington finally had his heroes and his war.
As he panted along in the wake of the troops, his quick eyes found
tales of action and gallantry that transcended the deeds of battle.
Although his knowledge had helped him to prepare better for the
Cuban campaign than many he encountered, Fred was burdened with
his girth and with other, invisible handicaps resulting from years of
overindulgence. Like the soldiers, he was forced to abandon most of
his gear. He was as grimy, his boots as muddy, his clothing as wet
and bedraggled as those of any of the men he acclaimed in the reports he sent back to the States. He was frustrated and hungry. He
was awed, disgusted, angry, bored, frightened, lonely, hot, tired. Like
the troops, he fell exhausted to rest at roadside during breaks. Like
the officers he knew, he was filled with loathing of General Shafter's
incompetence and his disregard for the orders he received from General Miles, his superior. At long last, the artist/observer was now a
full participant in the scenes he recorded. As he lay to rest beside the
muddy trail, with rain dripping from lush foliage above, he must
have reached in imagination to his long dead father, who had en-

dured four endless years of war no less arduous and horrifying, to communicate to that Civil War colonel that now he understood.

In the confusion that he learned to be the inevitable condition of warfare, Fred kept meeting men he knew. Beyond Siboney, he met up with novelist-turned-correspondent John Fox, with whom he could share the only blanket the two had between them, as well as the universal misery. Fox was someone with whom he could talk as a fellow recorder of this phase of history. Wherever he went, he recognized numbers of officers from his past, as well as members of his New York clubs, a Japanese major he had met, the Prussian attaché von Goetzen, British, and Cubans.[53]

Among the cavalry's elite, the Rough Riders of Colonels Leonard Wood and Teddy Roosevelt, Remington felt most at home. Here were cowboys from the western plains and mountains, and cosmopolitans from the Northeastern Ivy League elite. Before the Rough Riders' famous charge in the San Juan hills, Fred had bought a horse himself, one belonging to an officer now en route home as victim of a tropical fever. Fred lent a hand with the wounded, encouraging the confused; somewhere in the midst of the melee, he discovered that he had lost all traces of nervousness and apprehension, although he knew himself to be a nervous man. And he proved himself a man of compassion.

In Florida, at the Tampa Bay Hotel before the invasion, two young lads, at least twelve years his junior, had appeared among the crowd of journalists, officers, officials, and hangers-on. They were Teddy Burke and Teddy Miller, the former a New Englander, the latter an Ohioan. They had hastened south after war was declared to enlist. Young Teddy Burke had met Remington before, but where and when have never been established. These two youths joined the group that held court about Fred on the big hotel piazza—two "strong, bright-eyed . . . American schoolboy(s) . . . athletes, etc.," Remington said later. Later Fred wrote to Theodore Miller's father that he had done everything he could, even lied, to prevent the youngsters from volunteering for the Rough Riders. He had tried to persuade them that the cavalry unit's officers, Wood and Roosevelt, "were bad men and would certainly get them all killed." But it did no good: "it all went for nothing," Remington admitted.[54] The boys enlisted.

Teddy Burke fell ill en route to Cuba at the end of June on a transport called the *Yucatán*. Short on infantrymen, army headquarters shipped Rough Riders to Cuba minus their mounts to fight on foot. Although he was weak and ill when he arrived, the young man tried to keep up with the fighting in the San Juan hills. Finally he dropped by the wayside, where Fred Remington found him lying in a ditch. The burly artist picked up the slim younger man, who was only five feet seven; slung him over his shoulder; and carried him to the field hospital at Juragua. In one of the few letters we have that Fred wrote about his Cuban experiences, he gave Eva the bare bones of the story: "I found Eddie Burke sick—I nursed him up—got a d—— doctor to promise to invalid him and went on. Afterwards I found he had joined the Regt.—and was sick with Typhoid."[55] Fred had made sure that young Burke was cared for by a Captain Winter, as Teddy Miller found out the next day when he was able to visit his friend. Burke's niece, Patricia Hayes Howard, who carried on a correspondence with Atwood Manley in 1969, told him that "Fred Remington saved Teddy's life," words used by her mother in an oft-repeated family story Patricia heard as a child.

Young Ted Miller did die in Cuba. He was fatally wounded on July 1 at San Juan and taken to a nearby field hospital, where Fred Remington is supposed to have preceded him and to have reserved a bed. Here, Ted Miller succumbed a week later. Teddy Burke, who had returned to battle still weak and ill with fever, later described to Miller's father the grief he and his friends felt when the news of their comrade's death was passed along the picket line. Teddy Burke managed to hang on until the Spanish surrender, but then was shipped home in one of the first contingents of the wounded and ill, to spend many months convalescing. In years to come, he married and settled in Hartford, Connecticut, not far from Ridgefield, the town to which Fred and Eva Remington moved in early 1909.

Teddy Burke became one of Fred's hunting companions in later years, and Fred sketched the younger man. The drawing, titled *The Essex Trooper*, showing a small man in a woolen cap and carrying a gun, appeared in Remington's 1902 *Men with Bark On*, his second book of drawings published by R. H. Russell. The original signed sketch remains in the possession of Burke's descendants. The friendship between Remingtons and Burkes continued even after Fred's death in 1909. In her diaries Eva recounted visits made by Teddy and Madeleine Burke to Lorul Place, at Ridgefield, until Eva moved back north to Ogdensburg, in 1914, the year before Teddy Burke himself died.[56]

At the battle in the San Juan hills, Fred Remington later wrote that he personally was "stalking in between" the advance of the Rough

Riders and the rear. He missed the famous assault of Kettle Hill, when the indomitable Teddy Roosevelt led the Rough Riders to victory in the charge that made him a hero to his countrymen. Later, Fred memorialized the Rough Rider charge in a large (and not his most skillful) oil painting. *The Charge up San Juan Hill* included one of those lapses in accuracy that Fred considered part of his artistic license, but that have since drawn much criticism. Although the painting shows some men on horseback, their horses had never arrived in Cuba.

Throughout the steamy weeks of jungle fighting, Fred had been sick himself. His weight, lack of sleep and food, sleeping in the mud, the weary marches, and finally the loan of his horse to a wounded man left Remington "too weak to walk far," as he wrote in his article "With the Fifth Corps."[57] He headed for the rear, shaking with fever. "The sight of that road as I wound my way down it was something I cannot describe," he said. "All the broken spirits, bloody bodies, hopeless, helpless suffering which drags its weary length to the rear are so much more appalling than anything else in the world that words won't mean anything to one who has not seen it." Fred himself made it to headquarters at the rear that day, found some food, got some rest, and finally retrieved his mount. The next day he started forward again, but made it only to El Poso, where he lay down under a bank by the creek. He had the fever, and dizzily he rose to drink the dirty water. Somehow he found his way back to camp. That night he realized that he had truly finished seeing his war, which—although he did not realize it in his fevered state—was nearly done. By the time the Spanish surrendered Cuba, on August 12, 1898, Fred had already been at home for a month, with Eva nursing him back to health.

9

NEW
DIRECTIONS

« 1898–1907 »

As summer 1898 faded into autumn, Cuba and the Philippine Islands, half around the globe, were now the responsibility of the American victors. Injured and fever-ridden veterans of the Cuban and Puerto Rican campaigns returned to their homeland. By the end of August, the Rough Riders were being mustered out at Montauk on Long Island. Colonels Teddy Roosevelt and Leonard Wood took stock of the casualties among the volunteer corps of Rough Riders who had enlisted the previous spring. Roosevelt wrote personal letters to families of men who had fallen at San Juan, including that of young Ted Miller, whose father later gathered it and other letters into a memorial booklet. He also wrote with real appreciation to Fred Remington, who had arrived home at Endion on July 10. Unknown to Roosevelt, though, his officers had also contacted Frederic Remington in order to secure a gift of appreciation to present to their leader. At a farewell banquet in Roosevelt's honor that November, they presented the delighted Teddy with a Remington *Broncho Buster*.[1]

At Endion, Fred watched the hush of late summer invade lawn and garden. For once, he was idle, recuperating from the rigors of campaign life in Cuba, and not yet ready to return seriously to easel or clay. Instead, his tired mind worked through the slow process of externalizing events and sights that had bitten deeply into his psyche. On the lawn, shadow and sunlight created dappled designs that fed the artist's weary spirit. At the back of the Webster Avenue property, Eva's Plymouth Rock hens pecked busily for bugs hiding in grass behind the stable. Jim Keeler, the new handyman, moved methodically about his work. In the stable, the big grays munched from their mangers and Beauty, the Irish hunter Fred loved, tossed a sleek head to whisk flies away. On the lawn near the veranda, a litter of the Japanese spaniel puppies he and Eva bred romped and tumbled in furry joy. At his feet lay his old pointer, snoozing with nose on paws. In the kitchen where Eva supervised the annual canning and jelly making, steam rose from the big range as the fruits of summer were transformed into rows of jars on pantry shelves.

Although outwardly Remington's portly form was fast filling out to its former girth and beyond, his inner spirit still fasted, too weary with war to turn toward the arduous task of creation. Some spring of inner resilience had been stretched too tight in Cuba. Those few short weeks climbing mountain trails on the jungle island had taken him to the peak of his personal invisible mountain of vitality. Although his admiring public never realized it and acclaim for his work mounted steadily through the first decade of the twentieth century, from late 1898 onward, Fred Remington had begun to "come down the other side of the hill," as Atwood describes the waning of the life force. When his thirty-seventh birthday arrived that October 4, Remington entered his next year as a man whose youth was left behind him.

In the remaining months of the year, Frederic Remington began at last to regain his momentum. The beat of life quickened, his nervous and physical systems no longer faltering from the aftermath of war. As autumn waxed and maples on the Adirondack mountainsides sang their annual paean of scarlet joy to sky, Fred plunged again into the work from which he had been torn so abruptly at the sinking of the *Maine*. He had articles to write and illustrations to paint. He had upcoming exhibitions for which to prepare. The unformed lumps of clay still responded to his stubby, skillful fingers. He made sure to register his copyright for his two last bronzes, *The Wicked Pony* and *The Scalp*. By year's end in 1898, Fred was looking for another means to reproduce his sculpture in bronze, because the Henry-Bonnard foundry, razed by fire that year, was temporarily out of business. Although he continued to model, no new Remington bronzes were produced for sale until 1900.

During the fall, Fred described and illustrated his Cuban war experiences for *Harper's Weekly* and the *Monthly*. In addition, the *Monthly* that year had published stories about his first fictional character, Sun-Down LeFlare. In early January 1899, Harper's brought out his book *Sun-Down LeFlare*,[2] which contained these and other stories about the mythical Indian interpreter. In addition, Remington continued to scribble out war articles for *Collier's*, gradually switching subject matter and drawings to outdoor and western life. He was eager to work now for *Collier's* and other publications because he foresaw the end of his professional relationship with the financially troubled house of Harper. He was right. Fred was one of the most highly paid illustrators of his time, and in 1899, Harper's stopped using him as they economized. At the end of 1899, he wrote to Owen Wister that "they dropped me out the window over a year ago but I find a way to get printed."[3]

In early 1899, Remington returned briefly to Cuba to report on conditions there under U.S. Army occupation. Outwardly the island remained much the same, except for its army overseers. As the century ended, the United States became restive about its new territorial responsibilities far afield; the mood of the country changed, and voices were raised to make Cuba and the other Spanish-speaking territories independent. Meanwhile, in Havana, the population still threw slops from second-story windows onto the streets; open sewers remained common. Yellow fever, malaria, and typhoid were still rampant. Soon after Fred's brief return visit, a commission headed by army physician Walter Reed began to test the theory that mosquitoes bred yellow fever. [4]

It was in this period that a few perceptive colleagues began to sense nuances of inner turmoil in the artist, although Remington's behavior seemed much as before. War and vanished youth had created an inner vacuum that Remington needed to fill. Work, success, and the various occupations that had hitherto brought satisfaction now seemed empty. There was a need to change, to grow, to find new purposes and goals working deep within the artist. Howard Pyle of Delaware, the premier American illustrator of the time, was one of those who sensed the process in which Fred was engaged. The "father of American illustration," Pyle believed, like Remington, that viewers should be able to live within a picture. Both Pyle and Remington, observing the historical development of the nation's body of art, expected that America's truly great works would be created sometime in the future. In March 1899, Pyle responded to a letter from Remington:

I received your letter the other day and read it with no small amusement. At the same time, there was an undercurrent of something else than jocularity that caused me a feeling of real discomfort—a feeling that somehow you were not happy in your heart. I agree with you that one cannot be entirely successful when one departs out of one's line of work. Your line of work is very strong—both in painting and drawing—that is always a matter of respect with me. . . . Probably you do not know how many admirers you have and how great they regard and justly regard— your great art. I wish we lived nearer to one another so that I might see more of you but you never come on as far as Wilmington and I rarely come to New York nowadays. I find myself as the years go along becoming more and more a miser of my time. When I look ahead, the end seems so close and I have done so little that I almost despair of accomplishing anything. I feel as though I stood only on the threshold of art with almost nothing to show for twenty three years of effort. So it is true I judge every day lost to my art, almost never come to NY and lead a life that is that of a hermit. The evil of it is that I cannot unite myself to such friends as I might find in you. I wish it were otherwise![5]

What Pyle expressed in his letter must have struck at the heart of Fred's own dilemma. He was in transition and had not yet charted his course for the future. To his own eye, his art fell far short of his inner ideal vision. What the Wilmington artist described rang true for him, too. Pyle described a creative urge that some have called the divine discontent, which—if directed properly—could lead to further artistic development. If Pyle also suffered from a sense of being incomplete artistically and had chosen the rigorous and lonely discipline he described, then this might be one answer to what Frederic Remington himself sought. From that time on, Remington turned inward in his pursuit of artistic excellence, husbanding the strengths that remained from his profligate youth, aided and abetted by his wife, who guarded his privacy so that he might work toward becoming a true fine artist. As this new purpose became apparent, his friend Gus Thomas dubbed him a "mental hermit," a characterization Fred recorded in his journal.[6]

Remington did become more and more a man of solitude. Trips

to New York City became an arduous chore, although he had to travel there to deal with financial matters, his publishers, or the framing of his pictures and to continue essential relationships with others in his field. He began to shun the city cronies with whom he formerly caroused. New York club dinners became a duty, no longer an occasion for buffoonery and overindulgence. Instead, he chose books for his main companions and enjoyed the vagaries of Sandy, the young collie who had replaced his pointer. He had promised Eva and thereafter told his friends that generally he limited his alcoholic intake to an occasional glass of port or claret, and he continually tried to diet. This was a difficult discipline for one who had indulged freely—and North Country Remington lore does contain stories of lapses.

The new course somewhat modified Remington's earlier abrupt mood changes, typified formerly by spurts of euphoria or vitriolic anger. He no longer fantasized about six-hundred-mile canoeing trips; instead he guarded his strength, functioning within growing physical limitations and directing his total energies to his art with only an occasional trip west or north for sport and work. His outbursts against individuals or groups, such as those against his mother at the time of her second marriage or new immigrants with (to him) incomprehensible values, smoothed to low muttering swells. Indeed, as the years passed, he found compassion for his mother, with whom life had dealt so roughly. "She is certainly an old lady and can't stand much," he noted later in the new decade in his diary.[7]

From the war period onward, Remington seems to have begun a process of accepting himself and most of his world more realistically, although he tried to epitomize the mythic and preserve the ideal, as he perceived them, in frontier life and in his art. He worked as hard as ever for six days each week, but now on Sundays he rested. On the Sabbath, he loafed, visited neighbors, acted as host for Eva's Sunday afternoon dinner parties, and rebuilt energies for the week to come. His diary tells why: "For people who work hard this Sabbath calm is necessary to preserve us from the Nut House. When I started in Art I worked Sundays but I'm too old now for that pace."[8] He went to bed before the rest of the household, no matter who was present, whereas formerly he had never stopped working or playing.

Eva, and perhaps a few other family members, must have recognized these changes in her oversize husband. Mindful of his disregard of his health, she coaxed him constantly toward moderation. To this end, she invited old and new friends to Endion. The Remingtons' social life seems to have reverted to the small-town fun of Fred's and her own youth in Canton and Gloversville. On almost every weekend, the Thomases and Kembles, the Hepburns and other old North Country friends were invited to Webster Avenue to share food and conversation. With Eva's encouragement, Gus Thomas, their next-door neighbor and friend, lured Fred once more to take frequent rambles in the surrounding countryside. During these hikes they continued ongoing debates that covered everything from politics to art to philosophy to the animal kingdom. Fred, however, no longer had the energy or the need to prove his vigor. He never again challenged hiking chums to races as he had Edward Kemble, less than a decade before.

In 1899, his work was as popular as ever, more so if anything, as the western adventure faded into history and myth. In the midst of the nation's clamoring industrial expansion, many responded to Remington's portrayal of a more elemental time and place. That year his *The Dash for Timber,* which showed a group of horsemen riding pell-mell toward safety from pursuing Indians, won praise at the 1899 Annual National Academy exhibition. His *Broncho Buster* and other bronzes continued to sell steadily. But that spring, Remington was struggling deeply to chart a course for his own artistic growth, acknowledging that he was changing, and yet, all the while, still tugged by memories of activity that had satisfied in bygone years. He wrote to his uncle, Rob Sackrider, that spring:

> I want you and Em to go up to Cranberry with us . . . we used to have fun at C and I guess we ain't too old now. . . . We want to board with you for a month—will you take us as star boarders. . . . I am getting old and Frenchy and am going to send my own Claret up. . . . Eva is not very well and needs a change and I have worked so d—— hard and so d—— long. . . . I haven't had a drink of anything stronger than claret or beer since Feb. 1, '96 I weigh 295 lbs.—net. . . . Eva is grey—almost white—very skinny—careworn—but not yet in need of a maid—though I have to hook up her dresses and am in favor of the maid . . . *we* want mountain air. Did you ever imagine Rob that Canton ozone would rate as mountain air?[9]

Slowly, as the century ended, Remington moved into a new way of life, setting new goals for himself. Gradually, plans evolved that brought positive changes into his and Eva's life. The most significant decision for all of us who have received his artistic bequests was his renewed vow to attempt to become a "real" painter. This time, however, he set to work privately and stubbornly, without the hoopla of enthusiasm that he had previously communicated so readily. It is unlikely that even Fred's closest friends knew how serious his determination had become. Only when his first night scenes and other new paintings were hung in exhibitions in the new century did his public realize that the man who drew horses, Indians, and cowboys so facilely was attempting to communicate something new and different—and, of course, periodical readers continued to demand pictures in the old style. The art critics, however, observed subtle changes in subject matter, in painting techniques, and especially in the moods expressed in these new canvases. The artist of the Old West, they told the public, was surpassing his former skills.

To become a painter, not simply a storyteller, Fred Remington realized that he would have to follow a rigorous new discipline. Gradually, he set more and more exacting personal standards for his work. He no longer planned a whole series of pictures in a single day, then dashed them off in record time. Instead, his themes generated slowly in his imagination and he worked long and hard to preserve his inner visions on canvas. He moved from one painting to another, returning to struggle again and again with problems he sensed in former canvases. He was his own strict instructor and his own worst critic. Time and again he felt that he had missed the mark. Sometimes he abandoned the work of weeks completely; at other times, he returned to it with a blank canvas to begin the arduous process once more. It was during these years that he ignited several bonfires at Endion, destroying canvases of earlier years. Today, only prints remain of paintings like his series *The Tragedy of the Trees,* and other works that now would be priceless. Although some have ascribed the bonfires to Fred's hope for monetary gain through increased prices for his remaining paintings, evidence we found in his journals points instead to his desire for excellence.

Of course, to follow his new artistic star, Fred Remington needed to modify and redefine his management of financial affairs. He knew enough about improved photography and new printing techniques to realize that the market for his illustrations, already minus *Harper's* publications, might fade away. This part of his career had been built, after all, upon a form of illustrative journalism, the artist's interpretation of events or stories. Now photographs recorded modern history in the making with detailed accuracy. In the new century, mass-market color printing became a reality. Fred's illustrative metier had been his action line drawings and wash paintings in black and white. He had either to adapt or to find new ways to stay in the public eye. With no major independent income, he had heretofore relied on the illustrating market, and he still needed to foster and to guard it financially. His total energies, therefore, could not yet be directed solely toward fine art. Although major periodicals still vied for his work, the changing market and his new goals were in conflict. Ever the pragmatic and canny Yankee in most of his material affairs, Fred set out to resolve the problem.

In *Collier's,* now a leading magazine and growing in popularity, he found a partial answer; soon it became Fred's chief source of illustrating income. Fred relied on his persuasive bargaining powers to work out a yearly agreement with publisher "Bobbie" Collier that guaranteed the publication a quota of Remington drawings and ensured him a set income. In addition, Remington still intended to write and had already begun to think of attempting a novel. His bronzes brought income, via their sale at Tiffany's, but he must also continue to produce new sculpture. For these sculptures, he had an urgent need for a more efficient method of bronze making than the Bonnard company had previously supplied.

In addition, however, Fred had to supplement his professional income to accommodate his and Eva's needs and still provide time for him to improve his painting skills. Remington had been talking for years about investing some of his earnings, and now, under the tutelage of Fred Gunnison, who had risen rapidly in financial circles in Brooklyn, he took some fliers into the stock market and became a conscientious reader of financial news. Also at Gunnison's urging, he became a Brooklyn mortgage holder. In all these plans, Remington's wife was a full partner and even, perhaps, an initiator. Eva was intelligent, pragmatic, and a superb listener, and she had learned much from the conversations that took place around the Endion dining table or over coffee in front of the fireplace. Eva had funds in her own name, which she began to invest, although more modestly than did Fred. Eight years later, she used some of her own capital to help finance their final home at Ridgefield, Connecticut.

Whenever the Hepburns and Remingtons visited together, as they did more and more often because the Hepburns now owned a motorcar, Fred and Eva listened for gems of financial wisdom that might fall from Barton's lips. Hepburn had become a leader in the New York financial world. By 1902, his reputation had risen so that he was wooed and won by the Chase Bank, where he soon became president and a director of the prestigious institution's board. Before Fred's death, Barton had become chairman of the board.[10] Emily Hepburn was also an expert in finance and, believing that women should be full participants in society, may have encouraged Eva's interests. Emily's business acumen became legendary, in fact, and Atwood's favorite anecdote about her Yankee shrewdness is a good example.

Long after Barton's death in 1922, Emily, as a trustee of St. Lawrence University and a major benefactor of this and other North Country institutions, made frequent trips to Canton by automobile. Invariably, she found time to head for Bob Sparr's antique shop on Pine Street, where she drove a hard bargain with Bob, who was no slouch at bargaining himself. Puzzled because Emily had already furnished Dean Eaton Hall (the women's dormitory she had helped to provide for the university) with antiques, Atwood queried her, "Mrs. Hepburn, why do you continue to purchase antiques from Bob, when Dean Eaton is fully furnished?"

Ever stately, the gray-haired Emily drew herself up to her full height and, in her characteristically refined but forthright manner, replied, "Atwood, I always fill my car with furniture from Robert's shop. I take it to New York where I pass it on to my city friends— at a price twice what I have paid Robert. At that they are still getting a bargain."

With experts like the Hepburns and Fred Gunnison as advisers at the turn of the century, the Remingtons were able to found a financial base that helped Fred toward his goals. Fortunately for Fred and Eva, the turn of the century marked an upswing in the nation's economy. For several years thereafter, good fortune smiled upon them, their investments prospered and increased, and they looked ahead to financial independence. At the same time, they looked for other ways to enhance the quality of their life, and at the same time, to give Fred an environment that would further his artistic goals. Sometime in 1899, the Remingtons made another major decision that brought them both joy in years to come and provided a creative environment for Fred's work. The couple determined to buy a summer home in the Thousand Islands and to spend several months there each year.*

Remington's yearly schedule still included trips to the West to gather materials. In autumn 1899, Fred traveled to Montana and Wyoming to paint. In 1900, he was at Yellowstone again and later that year at the Ute Reservation and then in Taos, New Mexico. Still another year, he returned to Mexico, this time with John Howard of Ogdensburg as his traveling companion. One summer he went northeast to Newfoundland on a two-week trip, and still later, Fred Gunnison lured him back to Havana, where Gunnison attended a banking convention and Fred visited his old friend Jay Cox again. He was in South Dakota once more in 1906, and his final western trip took place in 1908, when he returned to paint the mountains in Wyoming and Montana. However, that trip taxed his failing physical powers almost beyond endurance, for the Golden Era (as journalist Mark Sullivan later called the first decade of the new century) brought more health problems to Fred's ever heavier form with each new year. He now tipped the scales at over three hundred pounds, far more weight than his frame could carry; wheezed when he tried to walk; and found that a good mount could no longer carry him!

Remington's twentieth-century western ventures were used now to collect a different kind of material for his work. No longer were actual episodes of western cowboy and Indian life his goal; only his imagination and memories could provide these in the 1900s. As early as 1899, he realized this, as he told Owen Wister, with whom he was still in contact: "that old cleaning up of the west [the final conflicts of the frontier]—that is the war I am going to put in the rest of my time at."[11] That year brought an abrupt end, however, to the friendship between these two men. Wister's *The Virginian,* which Fred had read in manuscript, had placed the Philadelphia writer in the public eye. The two had arranged to meet when Wister visited New York on business with his publishers. At the last minute, Fred wired that he could not make the appointment. Wister, who did not receive the

---

* Some confusion has persisted about the date the Remingtons purchased their small island in Chippewa Bay. According to Atwood's notes, the Remingtons bought Ingleneuk in 1899, although they did not vacation there until the following year. Other researchers have noted different dates. We believe that some of the confusion has arisen because Fred and Eva rented in the Thousand Islands during one or more previous summers, a fact confirmed in Irving Bacheller's reminiscences, *From Stores of Memory.*

message, waited in vain at the meeting place. When Fred made little of the missed appointment, Wister ended their five-year relationship. At first, Fred apparently did not hear the unvoiced rejection, but then he moved on with his life, never again looking for, and probably no longer needing, a male confidant.

Instead, he had his primary relationship with pigment and canvas, as he searched to understand color and capture nuances of light. That same year he dashed off a note to Howard Pyle: "Just back from a trip. . . . Trying to improve my color. Think I have made headway. Color is great—it isn't so great as drawing."[12] On later western forays, he saw color, felt color, sensed color, in hot sandy desert at noontide or dark, in forested mountain ranges outlined against the early morning sky. He commented upon the difficulty of painting in early morning in the rarefied air of the high mountains. The atmosphere had a shimmering quality quite impossible to re-create in oils. Never, for as long as he lived, was Remington satisfied that he could capture nature's subtle and extravagant palette on his own canvases.

At Ingleneuk in 1902, he tried to explain his dilemma to writer Edwin Wildman, who rode the train to Hammond and thence was delivered to Ingleneuk for one of the rare interviews Frederic Remington granted in his later years. Wildman's article, "Frederic Remington, the Man," appeared the following March in *Outlook*.

Fred had previously confided to Howard Pyle that neither color nor form was enough: "neither are in it with Imagination. Without that a fellow is out of luck." Now to Wildman, he explained another dimension he felt essential to his art. "Big art is a process of elimination," Fred now told his interviewer. "Cut down and out—do your hardest work outside the picture—let your audience take away something to think about, to imagine."[13] This from the man who had taken such delight in crowding into one illustration the mass of horses, Indians, and soldiers in the *Capture of Black Elk*, published in *Harper's Weekly* in 1888.

He still could not paint women, Remington admitted to Wildman, but what he really yearned for was to be able to put a sunset on canvas. As he talked to the writer, a spectacular North Country sunset stained the crystal clarity of the sky over the River and the islands. The brilliant, changing colors spread through the spectrum from lemon yellows to oranges to crimson and to violet. "It seems as if I must paint them," Fred said. "As if they'd never be so beautiful again, but people won't stand for my painting sunsets. They've got me pigeonholed in their minds, you see: cowboys, Indians, horses, the military."[14] Poor Remington was caught in the web he had spun for himself in those bygone days of youthful ambition and dreams of financial success.

Along with sunsets on the St. Lawrence, Fred became intrigued with nighttime's subtle nuances of shade and shadow. Some of his early efforts to paint night scenes, or nocturnes, were less than great, but they did have power. Not long ago, Peg visited the Addison Gallery at Phillips Andover Academy in eastern Massachusetts. Here, she looked silently at *The Wolf in Moonlight,* a Remington nocturne. The painting was crude, brusque, and frightening. Something awesome and terrifying glinted in the wolf's penetrating eyes, which were the only object of real light in the painting. Fred had caught a remorseless, stalking predator in them, perhaps his own inner vision of mortality.

Moonlight fascinated Remington more and more in those latter years. He spent hours looking into the night sky, soaking up the mystery of darkness that is full of subtle, hidden light. Ingleneuk was a perfect place to study moonlight. "We have first moon now. Clear nights and I studied until near 11 o'c last night. I rowed the women on the water . . . moonrise was shimmering at them."[15] Later he noted in his diary, "Saved my moonlight of the 'Cavalry at Ford.' " Back in New Rochelle, with his dog Sandy as his companion, he went out at night to study moonlight. Looking into the studio fire at Endion, he began to wonder how to paint firelight. One of his last paintings, which was never named, was of soldiers hunkered down around a campfire. It is now owned by the Remington Art Museum.

At the turn of the century, no work of Remington's had yet appeared to alert the critics, the public, or his friends to the artist's new intentions. Instead, observers could easily have decided that it was "business as usual" for Fred. His second anthology and fourth book came from the bindery in January: *Men with Bark On.* (Remington remembered the term he'd used offhandedly in a letter to Poultney Bigelow in the 1890s and used it as his title.) The likeness of Teddy Burke, *The Essex Trooper,* was included in this collection of illustrations. He also that year began to work on a series of pastels that ultimately was published as *The Buckskins. Collier's* soon reprinted them as a special portfolio, and lucky today are those individuals who still own these.*

---

*Recently, the Manley doorbell rang, to usher in a North Country woman who brought a pristine set of *The Buckskins* to show Atwood. She had discovered them in a bureau drawer when she was sorting through family belongings.

In 1900, Remington solved one of the remaining problems that hampered his new purposes. He joined forces with Ricardo Bertelli of the Roman Bronze Works to reproduce his "mud" models in bronze. The Roman Bronze Works, which was located across the Williamsburg Bridge from Manhattan in Greenpoint, just north of Brooklyn, helped to introduce the ancient "lost-wax" method of casting to American sculptors. First employed in Bertelli's native Italy during the Renaissance, this method was quicker, easier, and far more subtle than the sand-casting techniques employed by the Henry-Bonnard foundry, which had been rebuilt in Westchester County after the disastrous Manhattan fire in 1898. Although some of the nation's most prominent sculptors, including Augustus Saint-Gaudens, continued to employ the Bonnard casting method, Remington was delighted with the lost-wax process.

Instead of several ponderous steps of plaster casting prior to pouring the bronze alloy, Bertelli's men were able to create a shell of glue or wax around core materials in the exact likeness of the original plasteline model created by Remington. He could alter and refine the waxen surface in minute detail, the jubilant artist learned. Eventually, when it was encased and ready for casting, the mold was fired in a furnace, which melted out the glutinous wax skin through vents. The molten bronze was then poured in to replace the vanished, or lost, wax. Thereafter, Remington regularly crossed the Williamsburg Bridge to Bertelli's Greenpoint foundry to work on the wax models of his creations. The final steps of filing and smoothing then treating with acids to produce the desired metal hue were familiar to Fred from the old sand-casting process. The lost-wax method allowed him to produce an "original" with every casting made. This is why variations occur, for example, in the direction of the horse's tail on later castings of *Broncho Buster*.[16]

A bonus for Remington in finding the Roman Bronze Works and the lost-wax method was the partnership he and Bertelli established. It lasted for the remainder of Fred's life and became a working friendship. Bertelli was a frequent visitor at Endion and later at Lorul Place in Connecticut. He brought his future wife, actress Ida Conquest, to visit; Fred observed that Bertelli "was slick on" the striking woman, whom Fred also liked immediately.[17] Fred, who didn't give a rip about spelling anyhow, persistently wrote notes to "Bartelli," which was of no import to anyone, least of all to the partners, who soon discovered what a mutually satisfactory financial deal they had. Bertelli taught Fred what he needed to know about bronze.

Fred kept taking plasteline models to Greenpoint, turning a tidy profit for both artist and foundry owner. The culmination of their work together took place in 1908, when Fred's *The Cowboy,* his only large sculpture, was cast in sections at the works, shipped to Philadelphia, and placed on the rocky plinth in Fairmont Park on the east side of the Schuylkill not far north of the Philadelphia Art Museum.* In all, Remington produced a total of seventeen smaller sculptures that were replicated and sold during his lifetime.[18] The last, *The Stampede,* was completed after his death by Sally James Farnham, a young sculptor friend of the Remingtons.

Born in 1881, Sally James was a daughter of Ogdensburg's prominent Colonel Edward C. James, a younger political friend of Pierre Remington and one of the Ogdensburg lawyers under whom Barton Hepburn trained. Like many other North Country people, the Jameses became part of the New York City North Country network once Colonel James moved his family to the city, when Sally was a tiny child. There he became a well-known trial lawyer. Sally grew up to marry Paulding Farnham, a Tiffany staff member. Shortly thereafter, during hospitalization for a severe illness in 1901, she was given a lump of plasteline. She then modeled her first human figure and announced to unbelieving visitors that she intended to become a sculptor. She showed Remington her second attempt, a Spanish dancing girl, which he told her was "all-fired ugly, but very much alive."[19]

With Fred's encouragement, Sally Farnham began to study seriously, and the Remingtons watched her growing professional accomplishments with affection and pride. She eventually won national recognition for her work, which included a heroic statue of Simón Bolívar (the Venezuelan who had liberated much of South America from Spanish rule) given to New York City by Venezuela; the bas-relief bronzes for the Pan American Union in Washington, D.C.; as well as several public commemorative statues. One of these still stands in her home city of Ogdensburg, for—like other transplanted North Country people—the James family maintained lifelong Ogdensburg ties, and Sally's older sister married Dr. Grant C. Madill, who later headed Ogdensburg's Hepburn Hospital medical staff.

Sally also had her work cast by Bertelli at the Roman Bronze Works, probably because of Fred's recommendation. Sometimes these two sculptors from the North Country met at Greenpoint by chance, and when Fred saw her Ogdensburg war memorial statue there, dur-

*Fred's pet name for *The Cowboy* was *Big Horse*; many people call it *The Fairmont Cowboy.*

ing the casting process, he was enthusiastic. When Sally was executing her bronze reliefs for the Pan American Union, Fred noted this in his diary.[20] And he was concerned during the 1908 recession when Paul Farnham, Sally's husband, lost his position at Tiffany's, the Fifth Avenue store that sold Fred's bronzes.[21]

Fred Remington, sculptor, experienced one professional disappointment at the turn of the century. Canton's village fathers had decided to erect a memorial to the town's Civil War heroes, including Fred's own father, Colonel Pierre Remington. Fred heard of the project and offered to create a bronze memorial statue that could stand in Canton's Village Park. For local political reasons long forgotten, Fred's offer was never accepted. Instead, the contract for the Civil War memorial was awarded to a local cemetery monument dealer, who had also become a distributor of mass-produced "statues" and sold duplicates of the Canton statue throughout the North Country! That is why, on a polished granite pedestal at the corner of the Village Park, where Main and Park streets meet, the same lifeless soldier of the Grand Army of the Republic guards the Street with the same remote and vacant gaze that looks out over many small northern New York villages. Those politicians never realized that they deprived Frederic Remington's home village of a priceless art treasure. And Fred missed a chance to memorialize his father and other Canton Civil War heroes. Sally Farnham created the memorial for Ogdensburg, the other North Country community Fred loved, and Philadelphia, not Canton, is the location of Fred's only full-size bronze.

In 1901, an unpleasant event occurred: in April, Fred and his horse Beauty took a tumble, and the big Irish mount fell on Fred's foot. Remington had to take to his bed for a week, but his newly philosophical outlook seemed to help him, and soon he was able to hobble around and work at his easel, with injured foot propped up on a stool. Fred was too heavy now for his Irish beauty and he knew it. By the time that he and Eva moved to Ridgefield in early 1909, Fred's corpulence had forced him to ride a broad-backed mule, if it's correct to call jogging along on the back of those hybrids riding.[22]

The fall from his horse was only the first of many health problems that began to plague the artist. His years of high living had played havoc with his digestive system. The rich, heavy meals of pork he so loved now regularly brought on acute "dyspepsia." Although he yearned for a hearty breakfast of three or four eggs with a rasher of the bacon or fat sausages sent to Endion from the North Country, these foods often caused such acute discomfort that he could not work. Instead, he and Eva tried to eat simply. "Kid and I pale over oatmeal diet bravely," he noted in his diary.²³ Digestive problems, added to alcohol's deleterious effects, were an important reason that Fred began to shun the all-male parties he had previously enjoyed at the popular New York City clubs. Eva's gentle insistence had much to do with this, but, in addition, Fred was learning his own limitations. By the time 1907 rolled around he could confide to his journal, "I abhor night owling as much as I used to love it—oh, for a moderate man's ways but it's heck or nothing with me."²⁴

Despite his losing battle for physical health, Remington's professional accomplishments and reputation continued to soar. For the first time, in 1901, Remington's work was published in full color. That year, *Collier's* surprised the public on July 7 with its first four-color, two-page center spread, Remington's *Caught in the Circle*. In December 1901, he held his first successful exhibit as a fine artist. At Clausens' Gallery in Manhattan, critics and crowds swarmed to see his twenty-five new works. To their surprise, the fifteen paintings and ten pastels revealed a new and different Remington. His paintings had softer lines, suggestive of the earlier French Impressionists. Viewers could see that he was experimenting with new use of color. Although some paintings were similar in subject to his old work, they now evoked a different emotional response, as if the artist was searching for internal meaning rather than for superficial effect.

In 1902, Bobbie Russell published Fred's second book of illustrations, *Done in the Open*. That summer he spent his months at Ingleneuk writing his only novel, a romantic story of the part Indian, part Caucasian John Ermine, named for his hero. Eva's sister Emma Caten helped him edit the manuscript before it went off to Macmillan. True to his private and public image that he could not draw women, he had his friend Charles Dana Gibson (originator of the famed Gibson girl) make the full-page rendering of the book's heroine, whom Ermine loved, wooed, but never won. In October 1902, the first cast of Fred's *Comin' Through the Rye* was poured at the Roman Bronze Works. Four exuberant cowboys ride at full tilt astride galloping mounts in this bronze, their horses somehow balanced by Remington's genius, with only a few hooves' bearing the entire weight of the composition (see illustrations). The technically brilliant and action-packed bronze was greeted enthusiastically by the public.

Remington still sold to other magazines, such as *Cosmopolitan* and *Scribner's*. In addition, he did some advertising art. One experiment that has never been authenticated, as far as we can discover, was mentioned years later by the then popular illustrator N. C. Wyeth in a letter to his Massachusetts family. Wyeth had been a young student of Howard Pyle at the beginning of the twentieth century and was an ardent admirer of Remington. At the height of his own professional career, and long after Remington's death, Wyeth was commissioned to paint a series of murals in a public building. In a letter to his mother at that time, Wyeth said that he planned to travel to Utica in central New York State, to visit a hotel decorated with murals executed by Frederic Remington.[25] Unfortunately, Wyeth did not mention the name of the hotel and we have not be able to trace this clue, although Remington student Richard Myers of Canton states that he also has heard that Remington painted mural decorations in Utica.

In 1903, Remington switched to Knoedler's Art Gallery for his annual one-man painting exhibition. These new arrangements satisfied him so well that, starting in 1905, he used Knoedler's for his shows until his death. Working at a steady pace, he continued to produce new paintings each year, as well as working regularly in clay. His bronze *Mountain Man* came from Bertelli's works in 1903, the same year that his well-known *Fight for the Water Hole* appeared in the series of paintings he produced under contract for *Collier's*. In the meantime, his Players Club friend Louis Shipman had persuaded Fred that *John Ermine* could be a surefire dramatic success. With Shipman in charge, the novel was transformed into a stage script and *John Ermine* went into rehearsal. Fred and Eva both went up to Boston for the advance tryout there. They stayed in Rhode Island with their friends the Jack Summerhayeses. (Jack, whom Fred had met in the 1880s during the Indian uprisings and with whom he had maintained a friendship mainly through correspondence, had by this time retired from his army career.) Shipman then moved the play to Chicago, where it opened in the Globe Theater. In November, Shipman took *John Ermine* to New York, where the play died quickly and rather quietly. Remington seems to have viewed the whole project in a somewhat offhand manner, probably because his main energies and interest focused now on fine art.

The contract Fred and Bobbie Collier formulated in 1903 called for Remington to produce a series of illustrations commemorating the Louisiana Purchase. These began to appear in *Collier's* in February 1904. That same month, his annual exhibit at Knoedler's (Fred shortened the name to "Noe" sometimes in his diaries) was augmented by an auction of ten of his old paintings. In addition to painting exhibitions, in 1905 Knoedler's held a show of his bronzes, for which he was gaining ever more prestige. On the strength of the successful bronze exhibit, the Corcoran Gallery in Washington, D.C., purchased two of his best works: *Comin' Through the Rye* and *Mountain Man*. In March 1905, *Collier's* produced an all-Remington issue and in the autumn published Remington's *Great Explorers* series, in which the drawings were not really up to his old standards. More successful was the series published in *Cosmopolitan* that year, *The Way of an Indian*.

That spring of 1905 began a process that eventually led to Frederic Remington's only life-size sculpture, *The Cowboy*. In April, he received a request from a committee appointed by Philadelphia's Fairmont Park Commission to submit a model for committee consideration and possible approval. Fred set to work with a will, completing a clay model in mid-November, which he had crated and sent to Philadelphia. For the next seven months, endless business communications traveled back and forth between New Rochelle and Philadelphia. Fred fussed and fumed. He badly wanted the commission, a challenge that fired his imagination. The drawn-out negotiations irritated a man who chafed at any limitations, and who was now always physically uncomfortable, to boot. But, as is the way of committees, no contract was forthcoming until June 1906.

By that time, Fred had turned to other pursuits, producing for Bertelli's two new models, *The Outlaw* and *Paleolithic Man*. He and Eva had also begun to explore the possibility of acquiring a permanent country home, because New Rochelle was changing from the rural retreat of the early 1890s into a bustling, increasingly crowded suburb to which New Yorkers flocked. That summer at Ingleneuk, Fred pursued his painting goals and dreamed of building a home on the thirty acres of farmland he and Eva had discovered, either through Fred's friend Jimmie Finn or his former Art Students League teacher J. Alden Weir, in rural Connecticut near a tiny village called Ridgefield. Over the next three years, the execution of *The Cowboy*, the pursuit of excellence in painting, the problems of financial distress, and the creation of the dream house in Ridgefield would vie with Fred's burdens of obesity and poor health, as well as with his frustration with twentieth-century life in New Rochelle. If he and Eva had not had Ingleneuk in the St. Lawrence as an escape for four months each year, his work might well have declined in both quality and quantity.

10

INGLENEUK AND
THE PASSING PARADE

« 1900–1907 »

For almost ten years, the little island of Ingleneuk in the Thousand Islands was the focus of Frederic Remington's lifelong love affair with the land of his youth. There, in Chippewa Bay, with the deep, mysterious waters of the St. Lawrence River surrounding and protecting him, he could find beauty everywhere he looked. The mighty River had always beckoned Fred, in much the same way that the Big South Woods of Cranberry lured and regenerated him. Ingleneuk was a mere dot on a map, compared with larger islands that spangled the River, but it offered privacy, lying in the lee of Cedar Island. Cedar guards the small islets within Chippewa Bay like a mother hen hovering over a bevy of chicks.

Fred knew Chippewa Bay well. The Strong family, of which his Ogdensburg boyhood friend Ned was now head, had owned and summered on Snug Island in Chippewa Bay for years. John Howard's wife, Charlotte, was sister to Ned, so Howards and Remingtons habitually had spent part of vacations at Chippewa together once Fred and Eva settled in New York City. To be near their friends and yet to live independently, Eva and Fred for one summer, at least, and probably more often, stayed at the Cedar Island Phillips Inn or rented a cottage there. John and Charlotte soon purchased a tiny islet close to Snug Island. Across a short stretch of water lay another small island, complete with a large and comfortable house and the inevitable boathouse, which the Remingtons decided to buy in 1899 and later called Ingleneuk (another Indian name).

In the 1890s, when the Remingtons visited Chippewa Bay with the Howards, they soon were introduced to other North Country and New York City people summering in the bay area and became part of the casual social life there. Nothing delighted John Howard more than taking his friends on spray-spattering excursions on his naphtha launch, *Karma,* among the scenic islands dotting the River. *Karma* stopped off at this dock or that island to visit other Ogdensburgers, such as the Knaps, among the growing vacation population. Prominent New Yorkers had "discovered" the Islands in the 1880s, and all kinds of pleasant social and sporting activities proliferated. The American Canoe Association, a popular and prestigious organization among boating and canoing buffs, chose to hold some of its annual meets on the River.[1] The Thousand Island Yacht Club became a center for water-related sports, as well as a popular social center.

The outstanding feature of summering in the Islands is that individual desires of almost every kind can be satisifed: a crowded social life or complete isolation, loafing and fishing or more strenuous exercise, spendthrift enjoyment or a simple back-to-nature existence. At Ingleneuk, Fred found a haven in the midst of beauty where he was able to concentrate on painting in isolation; on fishing, resting, and reading; on visiting with friends and entertaining his New York colleagues with enjoyment and in comfort. Eva could follow her own pursuits, which included social outings that Fred usually preferred to ignore. The life they adopted for four months of each year at their island home was indicative of the deep changes in Fred, for he had changed in other areas, as well as in his artistic goals.

For the next nine years, from 1900 through 1908, as the first fat robins tugged at worms in the garden at Endion, or if early spring's raw winds set memories of the north running through his mind in New Rochelle, Fred Remington began to chafe for his island. "Raw with drizzle," he wrote one year in his diary. "We are beginning to home for the island."[2] He waited impatiently each year for word from the North Country that the ice was breaking up on the River, about the height of the spring floodwaters on the pilings that supported his dock. When Pete Smith's scrawled laconic notes arrived, he hurriedly penned instructions to his caretaker to replace a rotten board on the dock, to see that the house was safe and sound, to make sure that his Rushton canoe, the St. Lawrence skiff, and his launch

Missie had wintered well. While Eva, in company with Annie and the other maids, made temporary chaos at Endion with spring house-cleaning, Fred pushed to finish up his work on clay models and paintings in the clutter of his studio, his mind straying constantly toward the North Country.

Just as Ingleneuk replaced Endion and New York City as the "place" in Fred's life, Eva was now Fred's primary relational tie, except for occasional hours of camaraderie with someone like busy John Howard. Fred no longer looked outward to other family and friends for companionship and support. He relied instead on Eva, who, while busy with her own affairs, was always available to him. His correspondence consisted mostly of short business notes, not the long chatty epistles he once had penned to Powhatan Clarke, Poultney Bigelow, and Owen Wister.[3] Although he kept in close touch with Canton family and friends, the ranks were thinning and for Fred life in Canton consisted mainly of memories. Eva sometimes packed a valise and left the island for a visit with Emma Sackrider, Aunt Minnie Ellsworth, or Sarah Caldwell in Canton, but Fred, as often as not, remained on Ingleneuk with his easel and books as companions and Annie Lothier, the New Rochelle maid who accompanied them north for several summers, to feed him and keep the camp tidy.

The relationship emerging between Fred and Eva during the years at Ingleneuk seemed a reversal of their earlier roles. Previously, Fred was the initiator and leader, and Eva, the follower. Now she set the pace, lured Fred from his easel on outings, or invited guests to share their vacation island. She was a gentle taskmaster who prodded him to eat less in quantity and to eat more that was nutritional. She knew that sometimes his thirst for alcohol prompted him to secrete a bottle of whisky in some out-of-the-way corner to which he retreated for an occasional nip. But she firmly and carefully brought him around, persuading him to substitute the imported claret or port he took to the River each year from New York. He posed as a connoisseur of wine, claiming to have developed a palate, all with Eva's encouragement. Fred never called his wife "the old lady" now, reverting instead to an occasional "Kid," as in their early married years, but mostly she was "Missie." The journals Remington kept in the last three years of his life reveal deep affection and respect for Eva.[4]

The Ingleneuk camp was a commodious, well-built house with eight bedrooms that could accommodate Fred and Eva, their guests, and Annie, the cook/housekeeper. Wide verandas on three sides of the house held comfortable chairs and in fine weather became Ingleneuk's social center. The essential boathouse was large enough to store several boats, and a sturdy dock acted as a breakwater against whitecaps in rough weather, sheltering the big boathouse doors. The dock always needed repairs in spring after the ice "went out." There was land enough on Ingleneuk for a kitchen garden and a lawn tennis court. After they became accustomed to the island, Fred built himself a studio. And he soon hired Pete Smith to keep an eye on things in the long harsh North Country winters and to help with carpentry and odd jobs the rest of the year. Pete became the kind of handyman that first Tom had been, and now Jim Keeler was, in New Rochelle.

At Endion each year, as soon as word arrived from Pete that spring had finally reached the shores of the St. Lawrence, Fred would hurry to the New York Central ticket offices to book reservations on the sleeper for Hammond, near Chippewa Bay. There they would be met by W. C. Forester, owner of the store located at Chippewa Bay near Hammond, who loaded the Remingtons and their gear for the last leg of the trip. Forester's Store is still there at Chippewa and is still the message center and gathering place for vacationing islanders in the Bay.

The first annual ascent to the Remington's new summer home at Ingleneuk took place in late May 1900. That year, the two Remingtons, plus their dogs Nip and Sandy, who traveled in the baggage car, clanked north by railroad from Grand Central Terminal to Clayton. They had yet to discover the more convenient route to their island via Hammond and Forester's boat. In 1900, they steamed downriver from Clayton to Ingleneuk on the *Island Belle*. While Eva unpacked, put things to rights, and explored Ingleneuk's housekeeping amenities, Fred set up a temporary studio on the veranda for rainy days, and another in a tent on the lawn for fair weather. Then he worked in the boathouse and puttered about the island, getting used to the new terrain.

The first weeks at Ingleneuk were raw and chilly, true North Country spring weather. When milder temperatures finally arrived, Remington began the daily routine of an early morning swim around the island, modified later to a quick dip. Anyone who has tried swimming in the icy St. Lawrence River waters (between forty-five and sixty-five degrees in summer) knows the numbing cold that the first shock of submersion brings to every part of the body. If an individual can survive that first momentary paralysis, as Fred well knew, a hard swim produces a sense of blood-tingling well-being that cannot be duplicated. Perhaps the temporary euphoria that sent his swimmer's spirit soaring was the satisfaction of having survived the experience as much as it was this rare, for him, sense of physical well-being.

Fred later added a daily canoe ride around the island to his routine. He was a master of the double-bladed paddle. As Atwood remembers from that early childhood glimpse he had of the artist, his bulk came perilously close to foundering his vessel. But the Rushton cedar canoe never shipped water, so skillfully did Fred maneuver with graceful, seemingly effortless paddle strokes. When he fished, he used a St. Lawrence skiff or a rowboat, anchoring it above pickerel weed in some inlet if he wanted to angle for bony, but sweet-tasting, perch; or rocking on the swells near the edge of an underwater ledge when he was after bass. Like other North Country fishermen, he netted his own minnows for bait or else asked one of his men to get a pailful when he rowed to Ingleneuk on some errand. (As the weight of years and added flesh accrued, Fred was more and more inclined to let someone else do the arduous chores.)

The final boat purchase Fred made for the island was his "put." All North Country people called motorized launches "puts" or "put-puts" and found fanciful names for these mechanical pets. The *Missie's* motor was temperamental and its owner was neither mechanically minded nor patient. Fred preferred to use other craft rather than tinker with motorized gadgets. Like every other boat lover, he worried about his craft in winter. High water could be destructive, as could the cruel River ice, which, when it breaks up in the spring rains, piles up against any obstruction, exerting tons of pressure and crushing wooden boathouses and their contents like fragile matchboxes.

Fred played tennis on Ingleneuk's grass court in those first years with anyone he could corral, including the young Strong sons. Later he contented himself with tossing around a medicine ball. Missie liked medicine ball and was delighted when Fred's artist friend and an Ingleneuk visitor, Jimmie Finn, sent her a small one all her own. Badminton, sometimes called "shuttlecock and battledore" in those days, was another lawn game, as was the ever popular, more refined game of croquet. Eva was in charge of the flowers that were set out each year. Fred and she supervised the vegetable garden together. Like every other countryman, Fred watched the daily progress of his lettuces, onions, and tomatoes.

Every day, Fred tapped the barometer to determine whether it was falling or rising. The weather fascinated him, and he kept careful records of storms, sunsets, moonrise, wind, turning leaves, chill, and warmth. He watched the gulls and other River birds. One day he observed a group of gulls attacking a great blue heron feeding in the shallows, the gray-white birds trying to drive the heron away for some unknown reason. The heron ignored the pests, continuing to stalk the minnows cavorting between his stalklike legs. Remington concluded that the gulls were actually intimidated by the statuesque fisher. He worried about a muskrat that had invaded the island, afraid to take pot shots at it for fear of hitting his rambunctious and foolhardy young collie Sandy. He was fascinated that a weasel swam to the Knap island and killed off all their chickens. At summer's end, he always noted the departure of the cliff swallows.[5]

Getting supplies for Ingleneuk proved to be a bit troublesome. Sometimes Pete Smith picked up odds and ends at one of the general stores in Hammond or one of the other hamlets on either the American or Canadian river shore. Over the years, Fred found teenage boys to help with the numerous island tasks that took too much of his time or became too arduous. There was always wood to be fetched by boat to keep the house warm on the chilly summer evenings, eeds to be yanked from the garden and lawn, mowing, or odd jobs that took hammer, nails, and saw.

In 1961, when he was gathering anecdotes for his Remington Centennial booklet, Atwood traced down two of these helpers. Henry Denner was then sheriff of St. Lawrence County. Atwood found Denner at noontide dinner with his deputies at the jail in Canton and plied him with questions about the artist. Instead of answering, the sheriff kept eating. Finally, he wiped his mouth on his napkin and turned to Atwood. "I won't talk about him," he said. "He was no good. He drank like a fish." So that was that. At a Rotary Club meeting at about the same time, Atwood delivered a talk about his ongoing research for the Remington Centennial. After the meeting, he was approached by a fellow Rotarian visiting from nearby Potsdam. Charlie McClellan had also worked as a lad on Ingleneuk for Remington, and his memories were more positive, reinforcing anecdotes Atwood had already collected. North Country people had either loved and remained loyal to Remington or had little respect for, even loathed the artist, for whatever reasons.[6] Few of the northern folk of Fred's time appreciated or understood Remington's artistic accomplishments, considering him eccentric, rather than talented, for spending all his time with paintbrush and easel. Because they could not comprehend the man or his life, they looked for ways to find fault with a North Country man who did not fit into familiar patterns.

Eventually, Fred hired a second handyman, Horace Allen, who one day received a request from the artist that was incomprehensible to the Yankee handyman. (And at first also to Atwood, who collected the anecdote but never wrote it down. Atwood, a true Victorian in every sense of the word, had great trouble bringing himself to tell Peg this story.) Fred asked Allen to get him a pail of "horse piss" and promised him a dollar for it. Allen dutifully arrived with the redolent liquid, thinking secretly that Fred really had gone "galley-west," as the locals call it, or else was drinking again.[7] The real reason for the odd request was that Fred had learned, like other artists of bygone eras, that urine helped to fix pigments so that the colors on a canvas did not fade with the coming years.[*]

Eva solved the problem of getting the bulk of needed food and household supplies to the island by combining a day of shopping in Ogdensburg with visiting friends there, commuting back and forth on the *Island Belle* or the *Riverton*. Sometimes, she stayed overnight. Eva visited with Charlotte Howard, John Howard's wife and Ned Strong's sister, and Lizzie Herriman, wife of Fred's friend Al. She was good friend of Mrs. Grant Madill, wife of the city hospital's medical director, who was sculptor Sally Farnham's sister. Sally and her mother-in-law Julia Farnham often went north in summer and Eva always visited them.[8] The friendships forged during these years would be an important factor in Eva's decision to move from Connecticut to Ogdensburg six years after Fred's death.

When the muse failed him, or he felt lazy, or the bass weren't biting, Fred occasionally went along to town with Eva to meet Al Herriman, Jim Westbrook, and other old chums. Of course, John Howard remained Fred's special friend. By this time, John was the right-hand man of George Hall, the local shipping tycoon, who had a fleet of riverboats that carried basic goods needed for the North Country economy upriver. Hall also owned the George Hall Coal Company, and his business pursuits sent John Howard on frequent trips to New York, Montreal, and even farther afield. The old school

---

[*]Earlier artists had always used whatever nature provided to help them with their creations. Weavers in some South American Andes villages use llama or sheep urine when dying wool, for example. And Maria, the famed Pueblo potter of San Ildefonso in New Mexico, rediscovered a lost secret of her ancestors: adding sheep dung to the fuel with which they had fired their clay pots.

friends frequently met at Ogdensburg's Century Club to lunch together on hearty, multicourse, high-calorie fare that was a mark of the period's well-to-do. They dined in leisurely fashion, talking politics and fishing, business and weather.

At that time, thick homemade soup began a meal, after the men had lingered in the barroom. Several meats were offered after a fish course of bass or trout or salmon. Fred loved ham and other forms of pork, although a beef roast sometimes satisfied him. Fowl was always on the menu, especially St. Lawrence County turkey. Fresh vegetables were available in summer, of course. Corn was drenched in butter or served "cream-style." Tomatoes and lettuce could be had in their season, with homemade sweet-sour "boiled" dressing—made with eggs, vinegar, and sugar—or mayonnaise. Cabbage and potatoes were North Country staples. Fred smothered a heap of salted, buttered mashed potatoes with gravies made of pan juices, plus fat and flour to thicken them. Parker House rolls, named for the famous hotel that first served them, had become popular, and other hot breads were part of every meal, with plenty of good North Country butter to coat them. North Country people liked deep-fried fritters in a side dish, to be set afloat in a pool of golden maple syrup. Some people liked a dab of an ice or a lemon sherbet (made with county cream, of course) to clear the palette between courses. Desserts included berry pies and hearty cakes, all confected with plenty of butter or lard, sugar, eggs, and cream. Ice creams were becoming popular: real cream an essential ingredient in the egg custard base, all frozen in hand-turned freezers. Cheddar cheese was a northern New York must to accompany pie. Fred always promised himself that he would stay "dry" on these Ogdensburg trips, and sometimes he did. He was not the only one of the old Ogdensburg gang who had problems with drinking. At least one of the others, according to his correspondence with John Howard and Eva's later diaries, had an alcohol problem severe enough that he spent periods in sanatoriums.[9]

Using the steamers for transportation was common practice. When the Remingtons' New York friends and Fred's business colleagues trekked north on the railroad to the Thousand Islands and Ingleneuk, they often sailed on the *Island Belle* on the final leg of the trip. So did relatives and friends from Canton. Sometimes, however, Pete Smith or Fred met guests in Hammond or at Clayton with the *Missie*. Although summer entertaining was informal and infinitely easier than at Endion, Eva didn't want to spend all her time cooking and cleaning. Annie Lothier or another of the hired girls from New Rochelle accompanied the Remingtons to the island to help. The Remingtons made sure that their employees had summer fun, too. On their days off, the girls went blueberrying or took a jaunt to Ogdensburg or other river points on the steamer. Annie Lothier was a black woman for whom both Eva and Fred had much affection. She finally left their employ to marry, but missed them so much that eventually she returned.[10]

Emma Caten spent the summer of 1902 on the island with her sister and brother-in-law, as well as visiting for a couple of weeks almost every summer. She kept a diary the summer she stayed with Fred and Eva, which is primarily a record of her struggle to accept her lot in life, to find good health, and to discover meaning in her existence. She was increasingly unhappy with her family in Syracuse. Fred and some of his visitors, his New York lawyer George Wright included, encouraged Emma to write, and the diary was her first attempt. She read Fred's manuscript of his only novel, *John Ermine of the Yellowstone,* and considered herself to be a better editor than her brother-in-law.[11] Fred was notorious for casual spelling, and his punctuation often consisted mainly of dashes.

Although it was hard to pry Fred off Ingleneuk, he and Eva sometimes traveled by buggy down the "river road" to see the Jim Westbrook family at their camp on an island in the middle of the Galloup rapids below Ogdensburg. The Westbrooks had a lively brood of children, one of whom lived in Canton as an adult. Frances Westbrook Bates, whose husband headed the St. Lawrence University Mathematics Department, told Atwood that she and her brothers and sisters dreaded Frederic Remington's visits. "We used to evaporate when the Remingtons came," Fran said. "Fred Remington just did not know how to get along with us youngsters. The minute he arrived at our cottage, he'd grab one of us kids and throw us off the wharf into the river. Then he'd jump in, clothes and all, and pull us out. He thought that was great sport. We didn't. He'd laugh uproariously at our discomfort. We all sneaked off to hide to get away from him." Frances did not mention Eva to Atwood, although she was present, probably visiting on the porch with Jim Westbrook's wife.[12]

Irving Bacheller took his friend Hamlin Garland, who was also a popular regional writer of the time, to visit at Ingleneuk.[13] Later, Garland alone spent a weekend with Fred and Eva.[14] Bertelli visited several times, ostensibly on business, but when that was completed he was a restless guest who needed entertaining. He wanted to fish, he wanted to meet people, he wanted to handle the *Missie*. Artist friends, like the Kembles and their daughter Beth, arrived. In 1908, Mrs. Kemble visited alone, because her husband, who was active politically, as was Gus Thomas, had traveled to the Democratic Convention in Colorado. Henry and Virginia Little visited from New York, too. Henry was a longtime friend and a New York businessman. Virginia Little put on a pair of Fred's voluminous pants in lieu of the then popular bloomers, roping them tight around her middle, and ran around the tennis court twelve times daily in an effort to lose weight. Now, this was pretty strenuous exercise for a city woman in an era when ladies usually strolled about the lawn or at most indulged in croquet.[15]

The Madills, the Herrimans, George Hall, the Newells, Sally Farnham, and her mother-in-law Julia often took the steamer to Ingleneuk for a day. The Remingtons and their guests then rowed or "putted" to the island homes of other friends to visit. Eva became proficient with paddle and oars and, if Fred chose otherwise, took her friends on excursions by herself. Other summer people in the islands, such as the Sudds family from Gouverneur, whose island home was on the tip of Cedar Island across from Ingleneuk, visited back and forth with Ingleneuk's inhabitants. Life usually was casual and informal, but Eva, who liked social affairs more than Fred, sometimes took guests for luncheon at the Thousand Islands Club. The most Fred would do was to attend motorlaunch or sailing races at the club. He offered a prize for a motorboat race between George Hall and the admiral of the Thousand Island Yacht Club, a man named Inglis. Hall won and took possession of the small cup amid much badinage.

With all this social and other activity, it was a wonder that Fred did any painting. But he finished some of his best later work at Ingleneuk. He made his night studies, the nocturnes that became a hallmark of his last works. He finished up canvases begun in New Rochelle and shipped in a railroad baggage car to Ingleneuk. Some of these won acclaim in his later exhibitions. He started many a painting only to throw it out. He had become particular about his work and he would not save less than what he considered to be his best efforts. The journals he kept are full of comments about his struggles for perfection.

Fred's mother, Clara, lived downstate, of course, with her second husband, but she visited Canton every summer. The breach between her and her son partially healed. Clara, it was clear to any observer, was aging, prey to a variety of ills. Life had not been kind to her, nor she to life, but now her headstrong nature was subdued. Observing her failing health, Fred was able to relegate to the past the anger and bitterness that her second marriage had roused in him. Eva, ever the healer, doubtless played a major role in reconciling mother and son. Clara repeatedly visited the artist and his wife, both at Endion in New Rochelle and at Ingleneuk on the River. Orrin Levis, Clara's husband, was never invited, however, although Fred did note, in 1908, that he had heard from his mother that her husband suffered from diabetes.

As the summers at Ingleneuk progressed through the Golden Decade, Fred and Eva watched more changes occur among Canton family members. Their ties to Canton had mostly ended, now that only Uncle Bill Remington's family and the Rob Sackriders remained there. Uncle Horace Sackrider had died in 1890, before his own parents' deaths. Mary Sackrider was buried in 1894, and Deacon Henry Sackrider followed his wife to Evergreen Cemetery the next year. Of Fred's own generation, only Ella Remington remained in Canton—and even Ella married and departed in 1904. Young Henry Sackrider had tried a year at St. Lawrence, then departed for Pratt Institute in Brooklyn to learn engineering.[16]

Emma and Rob Sackrider remained in the old Sackrider home on Miner Street. Rob had become something of a dandy as the years progressed, even adopting a pince-nez. His outer style may have been established to hide his ineffectual personality, for he was the retiring member of a family of male achievers. He remained a bookkeeper/clerk at the bank, but working in that respected and conservative institution could not save him from money problems. In the economic crunch that squeezed the whole population—including Fred and Eva—in 1907 and 1908, Rob was in enough financial trouble to need help. Fred and his cousin Henry had inherited Horace Sackrider's estate, so Fred waived his rights to most of his share, even deeding his property on Judson Street over to Rob.[17] (Today this property is a prosperous housing development across from the Manley home.) Among Canton people Rob had a tendency to coast on his family's reputation and to put other folks down, Atwood recalls. Emma, on the other hand, was remembered long after her death in 1935 as "a lovely woman."

Of the Remington clan, only Uncle Bill, Aunt Lavilla, and Ella remained in Canton after 1900. Cousin George was only sixty miles away in Watertown, managing the branch of the Remington Clothing Store, but that was quite a distance in those days, at least two to two and a half hours by railroad. Fred and George kept in touch, but Fred had almost no contacts with his Uncle Mart's sons, Charles and Pierre. Charlie had drifted off to become a newspaperman of sorts. In the early 1890s, Fred had tried to help him find a job on Herbert Gunnison's *Brooklyn Eagle*. In a note to Gunnison, a loyal member of the North Country network, Fred confided that he had little hope for Charlie's future.[18] Young Pierre, he believed, was the more stable of Mart's two boys. With his uncle Mart's widow, Aunt Florence, remarried, young Pierre moved with his mother to Syracuse, where his stepfather was a prominent businessman. He and Fred seldom met, although family ties remained and they knew each other's whereabouts. Pierre had a beautiful voice and made singing his career, appearing in opera road companies that traveled from city to city to perform in opera houses like the one in Canton's Town Hall.[19] After Fred's death, Eva heard from young Pierre, who apparently kept track of all family affairs. His letter to Remington researcher Robert Taft in the 1950s provided us with information used in this narrative.[20]

Fred's only woman cousin, Ella Remington, seemed to be on her way toward becoming in actual fact the "old maid cousin" Fred used teasingly to call her. She kept house for her aging parents in the gracious new Remington home that Uncle Bill had built on Main Street between the Baptist meetinghouse and Grace Episcopal Church. She was an attractive woman in her late thirties, who seemed content in her role, busy with family and friends. Suddenly, in 1904, she surprised her family and the entire village, when she accepted the proposal of St. Lawrence geology professor Frank Mills, a handsome Cornell graduate some years her junior. Her uncle, Dr. Almon Gunnison, was asked to perform Ella's wedding at Canton's Universalist Church. Dr. Gunnison was now St. Lawrence University president, having assumed the position in 1899.[21]

After the wedding ceremony, W. R. Remington, who was a man of political stature and served on the University Board of Trustees, threw a big wedding reception at the Hodskin House.[22] At the reception, another family schism, almost as bitter as that old feud between Fred and his mother, began. The rambunctious triumvirate of Fred Gunnison, Fred Remington, and George Remington inadvertently was at the root of the trouble. All three, naturally, were in Canton for their beloved Ella's wedding, and each was in the mood to celebrate. In the Hodskin House barroom, away from the more sedate festivities being held elsewhere in the hotel, they invited Frank Mills to raise more than one glass to his and Ella's happiness. They did not know that the groom was unused to alcohol (but if they had, it probably would not have deterred them). The liquor went to Frank Mills's head. As he left the barroom to return to the reception, he encountered a commercial hotel visitor and jovially jammed the stranger's hat down over the man's ears in tipsy hilarity. This dire episode was observed by St. Lawrence University President Gunnison, who summarily terminated his new nephew's association with the university. Ella was furious at her uncle and refused to have anything to do with the Gunnisons for several years thereafter.[23]

Frank Mills easily obtained a teaching job at Phillips Academy at Andover, Massachusetts, and the newlyweds left Canton. Mills's brief lapse from grace and dignity was not repeated. He and Ella purchased a large "gentleman's farm" near Andover (Frank apparently had independent income), living out their days there in comparative luxury. Frank later changed profession from teacher to businessman, becoming an executive in a coal and steel business whose headquarters were in Pittsburgh, Pennsylvania, although the couple remained in Massachusetts.[24] For over three years, Ella refused to have anything to do with her maternal uncle. Fred duly recorded the course of Ella's and Almon Gunnison's feud in his journal, noting that it ended only at her mother's death, which occurred early in 1908.*

Soon after Ella's 1904 marriage, her brother George's health began to fail. Although we have no confirmation, we suspect that he was a victim of Bright's disease (a kidney ailment). He was forced to quit the management of the Remington Clothing Stores, now a North Country institution, and was a patient in a sanatorium not far from New York City. His closest friend and cousin, Fred Gunnison, looked after his welfare and his finances, and all seemed well for a time. Then, at the end of February 1907, word was sent to the far-flung relatives, by family friend Jim Johnson in Canton, that William Reese Remington, "Uncle Bill" to Fred, was dying.

Jim Johnson was a close family friend who visited the River on fishing trips with Fred and also occasionally popped into Endion in

---

*We are privy to this unrecorded incident only because Williston Manley had also seen Frank Mills's escapade. He reported it that evening to his wife Mary Atwood Manley, Ella's best friend. For this reason alone, we are able to interpret Fred's oblique journal references to the Mills-Gunnison feud.

New Rochelle when he was in the big city. Jim and his widowed mother had moved to Canton when he was a boy. When electricity was introduced in the North Country, Jim set up and owned Canton's electric company, later to become a part of Niagara Mohawk. Jim had some special quality of friendship and loyalty, for he was important to both Fred and Eva. He was a lifelong bachelor and a favorite with many Canton families, to whom he endeared himself. With almost no family of his own, he looked after his friends' old folks for them, including Fred's Uncle Bill and Aunt Lavilla in their final days.

When George Remington learned that his father was dying, he took the New York Central north, against doctor's orders, to bid farewell to W. R. On March 8, 1907, after George was back in the sanatorium, Fred was called to the wall telephone at Endion to learn from Jim Johnson that Uncle Bill had died of heart disease. Fred and Eva traveled north into the teeth of a late winter blizzard for Uncle Bill's funeral. Fred Gunnison remained in New York to watch over George, whose condition was worsening rapidly after the strenuous trip north. Fred and Eva found Canton a dismal place with this final member of the old Remington brothers gone.[25]

With the presence of death so prominent, Fred called on his friend, Dr. Joseph Clarence Willson, the Canton physician, with a project he had long had in mind: he wanted his father's remains moved to a larger lot so that he and Eva could rest beside the Colonel when their own time came. Joseph was one of his closer Canton friends. The two men had a special bond. Willson, who was only a few years Fred's senior, was one of the few North Country people who had actually experienced life among the cowhands of the Southwest.

When he received his medical degree in 1880, young Willson had headed for Texas for adventure and set up practice among cowhands in the Lone Star State. Although he never had held a gun in his hand, the young doctor—as he told Fred later on the Street in Canton—hit the bull's-eye with the first shot fired from the six-shooter his new Texas friends gave him. After ingratiating himself with his cowhand patients, Dr. Willson finally returned to Canton to practice medicine there for a time. But in later years, he quit doctoring to take over the beautification of Canton's Evergreen Cemetery, which had begun as a hobby and had evolved into a major passion.[26]

Remington and the physician studied Evergreen's maps, and Fred decided to buy a big lot in the northeast section of the big cemetery's acreage, which Dr. Willson promised to plant with some of the native fir trees both men loved. In addition, Dr. Willson agreed to make final arrangements to have the Colonel moved to the new lot. In appreciation for his help, sometime later Fred gave Dr. Willson the small oil painting of a cowboy that Atwood found in 1960 in the attic of the old Kip homestead.

On March 24, back at Endion and weary from the strain of the past weeks, Fred was once more called to the phone with bad news. Fred Gunnison reported that Cousin George was dead. This time Fred and Eva remained quietly in New Rochelle, and Fred Gunnison made the long trip north to help Ella Mills arrange for the second Remington funeral that month. Shortly thereafter, not long after Ella returned to her own home, more bad news arrived in New Rochelle. Jim Johnson reported that Aunt Lavilla, W. R.'s wife, had broken under the double tragedy. Fred's words in his journal were that his aunt was "hopelessly insane." She required round-the-clock care, which Jim Johnson arranged and supervised, and eventually was institutionalized. Fred was shocked that nursing cost more than one hundred dollars a week. Lavilla died in the following January, in 1908. With her passing, the Remington name was gone from Canton life. Ella Mills sold the Remington home, and the last family link was broken for Fred. Only the Robert Sackriders remained. At Lavilla's funeral, Ella Remington Mills and the Almon Gunnisons ended their three-and-a-half-year feud.

11

BIG HORSE
AND BIG PLANS

« 1907–1908 »

Work now became Frederic Remington's panacea for pain of flesh and ache of spirit. For the rest of 1907 and on into 1908, he plodded steadily ahead with painting and modeling, concentrating on improving his skills, husbanding his dwindling physical strength, and refueling his creative fires through reading. He was able to surmount the multiple family losses and to confront the challenge of modeling his first large-scale equestrian statue, a complex task that became his major preoccupation in 1907.

The request from the Fairmont Park Art Association to submit a model based on a Western theme for them to consider for one of the nation's largest city parks was the culmination of Fred Remington's ten years of "messing with mud." He had first been approached by representatives of the Philadelphia committee in 1905. By mid-1906, negotiations had progressed far enough that Fred could begin to develop a concept that could be transformed into a heroic-size composition. By the beginning of 1907, the inner vision was ready to be worked out in a scaled-down plasteline model to be submitted for the Fairmont committee's approval. Remington worked furiously to complete his four-foot-high model during the first two months of 1907, before news arrived about the family tragedies. To meet the Fairmont committee's March deadline, in February Fred sent word to his sportsman crony Joel Burdick that he needed help. Burdick, who had already proved to Fred that he had talent in working in clay, traveled to Endion immediately, and the two men worked feverishly to finish the model.

Fred was by now as skillful in modeling as he had become in the 1890s in producing his best illustrations. After completing the *Broncho Buster* in 1895, he had produced three more major bronzes by 1900: *The Wounded Bunkie*; the *Broncho Buster's* companion piece, *The Wicked Pony*; and *The Scalp*. Since the turn of the century, models for fourteen more bronzes had come from his studio, including a reworked *Broncho Buster* and a second rendering of *The Rattlesnake*. The technically difficult and immediately popular *Comin' Through the Rye,* the group of four cowboys riding hell-bent for leather, shooting pistols, and carousing, was among the fourteen later bronzes. Although these offspring of his talent partially satisfied Fred's driving ambitions to achieve, he had always longed to create a life-size equestrian statue. Now, that tantalizing chance hovered before him.

As he strove to finish the clay model for the Fairmont Park committee with Joel Burdick's help, Fred learned that month from eminent American sculptor Daniel Chester French that New York's Metropolitan Museum of Art wished to add four Remington bronzes to its collection.[1] The selection committee of the nation's foremost museum, French wrote, had chosen *Broncho Buster, The Cheyenne, Mountain Man,* and *Dragoons—1850,* as representative of Remington's work. In his letter, French was highly complimentary to Fred, and Remington, for once, could not pretend nonchalance in the face of this honor. The selection placed him firmly among the elite of American sculptors, including French and the famed Augustus Saint-Gaudens, whose work Fred valued highly.[2] Remington's four bronzes went on display at the Metropolitan later in the spring, and Fred and Eva traveled to town to see them displayed in the great museum.[3]

Despite this important recognition of his work, the Remington family tragedies of that year and Fred's anxieties about the Fairmont Park committee's coming decision overshadowed his satisfaction. He finished the four-foot scale model of *The Cowboy* (also known as *Big Horse*); had it cast in plaster, then crated, and finally sent it off to Philadelphia only a day before the phone call brought news of Uncle Bill Remington's death. After the family crises, Fred turned to the worrisome task of planning how to construct a life-size horse and cowboy rider in a studio that, although he had had it enlarged only a few years before, was not nearly big enough to accommodate a structure that would rise eighteen feet high.

At Endion that spring, he paced the studio and lawn outside, measured distances, pored over sketches, and pondered ways to expand the studio so that it could hold the gigantic form. For two months he continued to plan and to fret. Finally, he began inquiries among colleagues to find able assistants who could engineer and build the equipment necessary to create the Philadelphia cowboy. Before traveling to the Thousand Islands with Eva in late May, Fred left final detailed instructions for having the studio remodeled and enlarged. The walls were to be pushed outward and a huge barnlike door was to be installed. Fred had decided that the main work on the equestrian statue must be done outdoors, in the light of day in which it would eventually stand. In this decision, he had the examples of sculptors Frederic Ruckstull, whom he had watched at work in 1894, and Saint-Gaudens, who habitually worked outdoors beside his New Hampshire studio.[4]

When the Remingtons returned from Ingleneuk in September 1907, Fred began final preparations for work on the actual life-size plasteline model that would eventually be cast in bronze. It was a mammoth undertaking, which he approached with trepidation, and, as usual, his anxieties brought on acute digestive problems. The enlarged studio could now accommodate the gigantic armature that must be built, and Fred also had room to store some of the one-hundred-pound bags of plasteline needed for the great task. In addition, the studio held his other sculpturing paraphernalia, as well as painting equipment and a miscellany of props used when he set up models for his work. In the final stages of production, Fred knew he would have to have the gigantic clay form entombed in plaster on the spot where he had modeled it, then have the ponderous plaster-coated object transported safely to Brooklyn to the Roman Bronze Works. What troubled him most, however, was that he had never modeled in such large proportions. Even the idea of the size gave him dyspepsia.[5]

As he pondered the problems of *The Cowboy* that he must solve, Fred also wondered what to do for his Canton friend Jim Johnson, who had been such a stalwart support during the Remington family crises of the previous spring. Usually, Fred gave a drawing or painting to people who had been kind and helpful to him and Eva. This time, however, meeting Jim in New York, he invited his friend to New Rochelle for a short visit. Jim was taking a well-earned rest after caring for his own mother in her final illness, as well as helping the

Remingtons. At Endion, the two men spent most of Jim's visit discussing the technical problems still to be solved before actual work on *The Cowboy* began.

As always, a visit with someone from home lifted Fred's spirits. After Jim departed, Remington contracted with a man from Hoboken named Paine, who agreed to superintend engineering and construction details of the mammoth armature. First came construction of a track upon which to wheel the gigantic structure-to-be outside on a "car" (a sturdy wheeled platform), so that work could take place in the best possible light. Here, in the yard beside the studio, Remington and Joel Burdick would add clay to the eighteen-foot skeletal structure of the horse. The horse and cowboy would be constructed separately, covered roughly with the oil-base clay, and then assembled for final modeling. As work progressed, Fred put in his first order for several hundred pounds of plasteline and sent once more for Joel Burdick. With Paine and a specialist named Marchetti, who was hired to add lathe to the armature, the team decided on their strategies and schedule. All that October, Marchetti and his Japanese assistant worked on the skeletal forms of the horse and rider, under Fred's anxious supervision. Finally, the rough forms were ready for Remington and Burdick to begin work.

On October 31, 1907, Fred wrote in his journal: "My first day on Big Horse Job. I rolled the thug out on the track. It looked all right after fixing a weak hind leg and quarter. . . . I am getting over my fear of the big surfaces. Got two 15 ft. planks and ordered a new step ladder. I expect to break my neck working."

Except for preparing for his annual late autumn exhibition at Knoedler's Gallery, all Fred's energies and time went into the two large figures that rested each night in his studio. When he was not actually working, he was thinking through problems about Big Horse and its cowboy rider. He curtailed correspondence, except for business letters about Big Horse to Professor Leslie Miller, who headed the Fairmont committee. Joel Burdick followed along after Fred's swift work, modeling well but slowly. As the final deadline for the completion neared, pressures mounted, and Fred fumed at Burdick's plodding pace. There were plenty of difficulties: the cowboy's chaps would not come right. The horse's head was out of proportion, so that Fred had to rehire the "fool horse" that had served as his model for the original four-foot sculpture the previous winter. Fred could not climb the high staging because of his weight. Then they had more trouble with a hind leg.

As autumn progressed, the entries in Fred's journal changed from anxiety to jubilation: "Had great time tackling big horse outside modeling—suffered greatly but am getting a whole figure and hope to establish final style as I finish. B worked and does well on upper figure." "Are rapidly getting horse in shape." "Beautiful day. B and I worked—he on man and I on horse head. Doing splendidly." Ricardo Bertelli phoned to ask about progress, and then went out to New Rochelle to see the big figure on which, Fred had written him, they were "working like tigers." By November 29, Fred crowed, "I have got a splendid external horse treatment and now see my finish. I will be successful."

By mid-December, the job was finished, except for minor details. Fred sent word to Bertelli, who promised to arrive on the sixteenth with his plaster man, Contini. Only Contini showed up at the appointment, but later Bertelli arrived to finalize casting plans with Fred. On December 18, Fred and Joel Burdick finished the last detail of *The Cowboy*. By a coincidence, they received a telegram that same day from the Philadelphia Park Committee, requesting permission for the committee to view the finished work the day after Christmas. When they arrived to see the sculpture on December 26, the Philadelphia men were enthusiastic. On January 14, 1908, Remington received official notice from Professor Miller that *Big Horse* had been accepted and that advance payments would begin in May. Fred's reaction was a big "Hurrah!" in his diary, not only because the child of his talent had been accepted and a sure success, but because he badly needed money to finance construction of the new home he and Eva had determined to build in Connecticut.

Since the beginning of the new century, Frederic Remington had chafed at the influx of people into New Rochelle. The town had mushroomed to a population of twenty-three thousand and gave every indication of becoming even more crowded. Yearning for real country, Fred's eye had turned northward, and, sometime in 1906, he and Eva had chanced on the village of Ridgefield, nestled in the western Connecticut hills near the New York border and complete with railroad service to the city.

Fred Remington had first learned about Ridgefield from his former Art Students League teacher Julian A. Weir, who wrote to their mutual friend Childe Hassam that he had recommended the village to Fred as a likely place for the Remingtons to settle.[6] Jimmie Finn, a fellow artist, a Players Club crony (whom Fred with his penchant for nicknames had of course dubbed "Mickey"), and a friend of Remington neighbor Gus Thomas and of Hassam, was also considering buying land in the Ridgefield vicinity.[7]

In addition, and of equal importance to Fred and Eva, the Hepburns were looking northward for property to buy and build on, or at least Emily was. For some summers, Emily had leased a summer home in Norfolk, Connecticut, so that her children could enjoy country life and to provide some respite from city responsibilities for Barton. Her stepson, Fisher Hepburn, was a student at Williams College in the Berkshires, and Emily yearned for the Green Mountains of her own Vermont youth. At first, Emily had hoped to find a summer home in Vermont, but it proved to be too far from Barton's work. So Emily, like Fred, was searching closer to New York for a summer home.[8]

In mid-March 1907, Fred reported in his journal that he had received a survey of a thirteen-and-a-half-acre tract of former Ridgefield farm land. A week later, he purchased the property for $4,250. At nearly the same time, Emily Hepburn also bought land at Ridgefield; her purchase was a large property at the top of a ridge of hills that had a magnificent view westward into New York State. The land of the two new Ridgefield property owners lay less than two miles apart.[9] In 1909, at lunch together in New York, Barton told his friend Remington that the Hepburns had decided on Ridgefield because they wanted to be close to the Remingtons.[10]

Once her mind was made up, Emily Hepburn always plunged swiftly ahead. She hired an architect immediately and began to describe the kind of house she envisioned. The front that faced the world was to be handsome and strikingly formal, as Barton desired, and the final result was a broad portico, flanked by four great Ionic-capped pillars, above which rose the peaked porch roof. In contrast, Emily insisted that the back of the house, which looked out over the neighboring hills, was to be friendly and informal. Inside, the contrasting themes were also used. A series of formal reception rooms, one of which was often used as a ballroom, contrasted with comfortable family living quarters and a big servants' wing. Emily, who always made sure that any project of hers was carried out properly, went to Ridgefield regularly to check on building progress at Altnacraig, or "high crag," as the Hepburns named their estate.[11]

Often on weekends that spring of 1907, Emily and Barton rattled up to 301 Webster Avenue in New Rochelle to pick up the Remingtons for a Saturday drive to Ridgefield in their automobile. The two couples were swaddled in dustcoats and the women swathed in veils against the suffocating clouds of dust churned up as the car carried them along the rural dirt roads.

Automobile travel in those days was fraught with adventure. The Hepburns were invariably late because Emily always overscheduled her life. The car broke down regularly or else one or more tires blew out because country roads were rutted and unpaved, meant only for horses and wagons. The travelers jolted along, cushioned on elliptical springs and primitive shock absorbers on which the car body was suspended. They often dropped into a deep pothole, which all too often broke the spring leaves, making immediate repairs a necessity.[12] Fortunately, Barton had maintained the mechanical skills of his farm-family youth, and like all drivers in those days, never set out without necessary tools and repair materials. Sometimes the foursome arrived at Ridgefield after dark, having to stop to light kerosene headlamps that illuminated the road only a few feet ahead. If Fred was impatient or Eva was uncomfortable, they did not complain. By day the scenery was magnificent; their talk was of future homes and good times; and not far ahead at journey's end was the Ridgefield Inn, which had comfortable beds and good food.[13]

Although they were as eager to move as the Hepburns, the Remingtons were in nowhere near the comfortable financial position of their friends. They could not begin to build until Endion was sold, and the new home they had in mind would be far more modest than the imposing Hepburn mansion. Fred hired a less well known architect to draw up plans for the Remington "farm," as he took to calling his Connecticut acreage. The land had indeed been farmed by previous owners, and the life he and Eva planned at Ridgefield would be almost that of farmers. A barn stood on the Remington property and, while Emily Hepburn conferred with her architect and builders, Fred made arrangements with a local man, Warren Keeler, to do the haying and to keep up the Remingtons' fields, in return for their pasturing Keeler's cow. Eva was as enthusiastic as Fred; she looked forward to having her own cows and to churning her own butter. Later in the year, they lured the Kembles to Ridgefield to show them their future home, and it was not long before these friends bought their own farm nearby in Massachusetts. Within months, Fred put Endion on the market.

The Hepburns were already in residence at Altnacraig by the time the Remingtons began to build Lorul Place, near the end of 1908. In fact, by then Emily had bought additional property from her neighbor, publisher E. P. Dutton, for a huge vegetable garden and then had purchased a farm twelve miles away to raise livestock and fowl for the Hepburn home in New York, as well as for Altnacraig. From then on, the Hepburn schedule revolved around milking, egg gathering, plowing, sowing, and reaping, as much as it did around Barton's financial and banking interests and the nation's economy.[14]

At the beginning of 1907, that national economy was hesitating. By midspring, a major recession was in the making. By summer, when Emily was in the midst of creating Altnacraig, the economic scene was so bleak that Fred Remington had to admit that chances of selling Endion were dim, and he almost gave up the idea of building at Ridgefield. However, once Fred made up his mind, with Eva's active support and help, he was outwardly as decisive as Emily Hepburn. He prodded his architect to keep on with the plans for a house that would include a big studio and plenty of room for guests. Before summer's end, he and Eva accepted a bid for $16,700 to build their house. At the end of September, Fred took the train to Ridgefield to chortle over a barn full of hay and oats and was hoping to buy additional acreage. He instructed Warren Keeler to sell the hay by the "stack," for $60 or $75, and to sell the oat crop, too. He and Eva ordered four barrels of apples to be sent to New Rochelle, where they figured they would have to live at least one more year, but Frederic Remington, would-be farmer, was entering well into his new role.

The recession grew worse as 1907 ended. Stock prices fell drastically and the banking industry quivered in dismay. However, Fred believed he had security in his continuing *Collier's* contract, which had been formalized in a letter the previous March and which netted him a thousand dollars a month. In addition, his paintings and bronzes were selling well, partly because of his popular western subjects, partly because of his increasing skill as a fine artist, one the critics viewed more positively with each new exhibition. In large part, however, his success in art sales resulted from his association with the Knoedler Gallery; he first exhibited there in 1903, and had shows there annually from 1905 on. Roland Knoedler, Fred discovered, was a master at marketing his new client's work. In addition, that December, *The Cowboy* was finished and the Philadelphia committee was scheduled to view it. Despite the economy's downturn, Fred looked forward to building soon at Ridgefield when he stopped in at Scribner's Bookshop, in New York, just before Christmas to buy his new journal.[15]

On January 1, 1908, Remington opened that new diary, then paused to weigh optimism against reality. The prediction of Eva's New York friend Mrs. Elizabeth Cochran, who—Eva assured him—was invariably correct in her psychic glimpses of the future, flashed into his mind. Picking up his pen, he wrote, "According to the Cochran theory, this is my year—we shall see. I am laying out my *Collier* pictures for the year. Have *The Thunder Fighter* and the *Long Horn Cattle Sign* thought out. . . . I am in great hopes to sell this place this year but the prospects are poor in these hard times. The country is most thoroughly unsettled and a hard Presidential battle coming which will do more to unsettle them."

Immediately after New Year's Day, Fred sent for Contini and the Roman Bronze crew to begin encasing *Big Horse* in plaster made from the twelve big bundles of the dry white dust that he had ready in the studio. It was time to prepare the huge statue for its journey to the Roman Bronze Works in Greenpoint, where Ricardo Bertelli planned to cast it in sections. Fred's role as creator of *The Cowboy* was finished. During the months ahead, until it was crated and sent to Philadelphia, he had only to travel to Greenpoint to work on final details, and to make sure that the base he had designed would harmonize with the rocky hillock in Fairmont Park where *Big Horse* would finally stand. To this end, he traveled to Philadelphia in early March to examine the chosen site: a spot north of the Philadelphia Museum and just east of the East River Drive.

By the time Bertelli's skilled artisans had finished casting, chasing, and patinating *The Cowboy,* Fred and Eva were far to the north at Ingleneuk. The Philadelphia committee invited Fred to attend the formal unveiling of this, his first (and, as it turned out, his only) large sculpture, but he declined. No one was really interested in a sculptor, he believed.[16] *Big Horse* was what counted. So, when an excited crowd of Philadelphians, complete with Indians and cowboys in full regalia, took part in the unveiling ceremonies in Fairmont Park on June 20, 1908, Remington was taking his daily canoe ride and working at his easel in the Thousand Islands.[17] The challenge of *Big Horse* had lain in its conception and its execution. Fred had met each design and engineering obstacle and conquered it. Now, for him, the bronze cowboy and his big horse were relegated to the past, and Fred was back at his easel and worried about how to finance his proposed house at Ridgefield.

In mid-January 1908, Remington had confided to the new journal, "It seems to . . . me a little hard getting back into the painting mood after modeling so long—4 months and 1/2. I sometimes feel that I am trying to do the impossible in my pictures in not having a chance to work direct but as there are no people such as I paint, it's 'studio' or nothing."[18] Nevertheless, the artist turned away from the challenge and pressures of his equestrian statue to the medium he was determined to master. As he had worked on *Big Horse,* at times his mind had conjured up new mythic visions of the Old West, and now was the time to paint them.

He continued to follow reports of growing economic crisis and picked up financial tips in the city from Fred Gunnison or Barton Hepburn. Although he usually reacted with anxiety when he sensed a gathering storm like this difficult financial situation, now he was calm, confident that his friends' advice and his own business acumen would see him through. Although Endion might not sell immediately, he had his income from *Collier's,* more from his investments (although dividends were down), and increasing demand for his paintings. Perhaps he would receive other commissions like *The Cowboy.* Gus Thomas told him that Jimmie Finn and Childe Hassam were impressed that Fred could complete a work in three months (really four and a half) while Saint-Gaudens had taken twelve years to finish a comparable piece. (Saint-Gaudens was in the thoughts of the art world at the time, because he had recently died, in late 1907, and a commemorative exhibition was being planned, to which New York artists—including Fred—contributed funds.)

With each new day and week of 1908, Fred's and Eva's enthusiasm for Ridgefield increased as plans became firmer. Then, in February, Fred received a disturbing communication from *Collier's,* his major source of revenue. The publication's new art director—Fred called him "Sad Eyed" Bradley—wrote that he was rejecting three of the paintings Fred had sent in to fulfill his yearly commitment. Reverting to current slang, Fred wrote, " 'and twenty-three to me' or words to that effect."[19] Bradley's words were ambiguous, Fred felt, so he immediately phoned publisher Bobbie Collier to clear up the matter.

Now began a month of constant conflict and tangled communications, which drove Fred's tender digestive system into chronic turmoil and caused so much mental distress that he could not work consistently. In response to his call, Collier told him to disregard Bradley's comments and to forward the letter in question to him. "Having your daily bread cut out in so summary a fashion is nervous in these hard times" was the way Fred put it. An interchange of telephone calls, appointments in town, and more letters followed. At first, Bobbie Collier said that Bradley did not "understand the situation" and that Fred should continue working. Then Bradley and Remington talked face to face and Bradley stated firmly and clearly that he did not want to use Fred's work; that as far as he was concerned, Remington was fired. Fred fought back, once more trailing Collier to his lair to get the final word straight from the top. The publisher proved to be elusive, never where he said he would be, but finally Fred faced him in his publishing office. Again, Collier maintained that Fred was not to worry; that he had neglected to "tell Bradley about my case," Fred said in his journal. Fred later wrote to the publisher that the situation was humiliating. Collier's response was a telegram that told Fred, "you can count on me."[20]

On March 19, however, Fred stopped in at *Collier's* to ask the business office for his monthly check. The publication's treasurer stated that Bradley had stopped payment. This was the final straw. Fred stormed out in humiliation and raged inwardly all the way home to Endion on the train. Once there, he sat down to write to Bobbie Collier for a formal release from his contract. The next day he wrote in his journal: "I am empty. I d—— near lost my identity let alone everything else."[21] Although he received a contrite letter from Bobbie Collier only three days later, asking for forgiveness and stating his willingness to accumulate Fred's pictures for the future, Fred's eyes fastened on one statement. Collier explained that "Bradley's point is a falling off in advertising." The magazine's income was the bottom line, not placating words or promises or personalities.

The 1908 national economic crisis (which old-timers who survived both this and the 1929 stock market crash recalled as being the worse of the disasters), in combination with the evaporation of his major revenue source, was now about to affect Frederic and Eva Remington in a dramatic and frightening way. For over twenty years, Fred and Eva had been able to live securely and well. From that day in December 1885, when Fred walked into J. Henry Harper's office with his western drawings and his cock-and-bull story about getting to New York City from the West, Remington's financial success had run parallel with his ascending professional reputation. Both the artist and his wife loved the good things in life, and they had been able to indulge their desires, although they never were grossly extravagant. Except for the first two years in Brooklyn, they had not been forced to economize. For the past eighteen years, they had lived comfortably and securely at Endion in New Rochelle. Fred had had the courage to change his professional goals and to grow as an artist. It seemed ironic now that, with his painting hovering on the brink of a real breakthrough—to depths and heights he himself would never comprehend—their dream for a life at Ridgefield, where he could paint without financial pressures to produce commercial illustrations, seemed to be slipping away.

Neither Fred nor Eva allowed despair to end their dream, and each believed that life could still be full and good. Over the years, Fred's optimistic nature and Eva's pragmatism had stood them in good stead, and they had weathered difficult periods together. So the couple set about adjusting to the impending situation. Fred continued to negotiate with *Collier's* through the spring of 1908. These conversations eventually ended on June 29, when *Collier's* agreed to complete Fred's contract for the current year.[22] No contract would be forthcoming in 1909, however, so that the tidy annual sum of twelve thousand dollars (a substantial amount at that time) would vanish with the new year. Like the rest of the nation, the Remingtons waited to see the outcome of the presidential election. They had lived long enough to realize that the economy was often affected by politics and that perhaps after Election Day the nation's financial downswing would slow. While Fred's friends Edward Kemble and Gus Thomas both attended the upcoming Democratic Convention, where William Jennings Bryan was nominated, Fred believed that the Republican nominee, William Howard Taft, was the better candidate.

Word reached Endion that spring that Fred Gunnison, now president of the Brooklyn Home Trust Company, was seriously ill. It was no wonder, considering the strains imposed by the financial panic that had followed hard on the heels of two years of family responsibilities and conflicts. Ordinarily, in the financial crunch in which Fred and Eva found themselves, they would have sought Fred Gunnison's advice. Now, however, Fred and Eva were forced to make financial decisions affecting their future at Ridgefield without him. Although their New Rochelle home was on the market, they had received no serious offer.

As the national economy dipped closer to disaster, the Remingtons continued to plan to build. However, Fred's diary shows that they vacillated about how and when to commit themselves to action. First they thought they would build that spring, then in the autumn. At one point, Fred threw up his hands in despair and was ready to give up. The Hepburns, in their secure financial position and having a cooperative, competent architect, already had Altna-craig near completion.[23] Fred, though, was having trouble prying action out of his architect. Finally, near the end of the summer he dismissed the man and hired a new architect, Frank Rooke. Rooke immediately came through. On November 9, 1908, Fred and Eva accepted a contractor's bid to build the Ridgefield house for $27,743 (almost $10,000 more than the first architect's 1907 estimate). Rooke guaranteed to have their house finished in six months, barring an unusually severe winter. With Endion remaining unsold in 1908, Fred had cast about to find financial resources to meet projected expenses. Now, he must hasten to do so in earnest.

12

"AN UNCERTAIN CAREER AS A PAINTER"

« 1908–1909 »

One person who may have helped Fred move toward a firm decision to build that year in Ridgefield was Jimmie Finn, whose name now appeared with growing frequency in Fred's diaries. Finn was eager to buy land that backed on the Remington's Connecticut property, and Fred was delighted at the prospect of having another friend close to him. Throughout the early months of 1908, the Hassams and Finns were often at New Rochelle, visiting the Thomases or Remingtons. Both these professional colleagues approved of Fred's work on the Philadelphia cowboy, and both were impressed with the new land-scapes Fred showed them that year. Childe Hassam voted for Fred in the academy's elections that spring, although once more Fred did not succeed in gaining membership. One spring day, "Charlie" Has-sam and Fred, in company with another artist friend, Henry Smith, met publisher Bobbie Collier by chance in Greenwich, Connecticut. During the conversation, Hassam and Smith tried to explain to Col-lier what was "good" in art. Fred wisely did not participate in the discussion, which was just as well, since the conflict between him and *Collier's* had not yet been resolved. Bobbie told the artists he would take their viewpoint "under advisement."[1]

Although preoccupied with the *Collier's* problem of ailing fi-nances and with whether or not to build at Ridgefield, in the first months of 1908 Fred planned new paintings, reworked his model of the *Rattlesnake,* traveled often to Greenpoint to put finishing touches on *Big Horse,* retouched his oils *Winter Night in the Corral* and *Where the Sun Goes,* and struggled to catch moonlight on canvas. He revised *Thunder Fighter* three times and was still dissatisfied. He laid in *Saving the Wounded Buck* and felt it had promise; it might, he speculated, even be the painting to be picked by the Corcoran Gallery, which was considering adding one of his oils to its painting collection. That February, he burned a stack of old canvases, including *Bringing Home the New Cook, Apache Water Hole,* and *Drifting Before the Storm.* They would no longer haunt him with their imperfections, but, he admitted in his journal, "God knows I have left enough that will."[2] His painting goals for the year focused on the annual late autumn Knoedler show, and he intended that the public would see only his best work. As his reputation spread, Doll and Richards, art dealers from Boston, sent word that they wanted to carry his work and perhaps to arrange an exhibit there. He would thus be represented by dealers in three major cities, because he still sold work through a Chicago dealer.

Remington went often to the city that year to view exhibitions of the works of fellow artists, some of which he liked and others he found wanting. He had definite ideas about artistic excellence. Albert Bierstadt was one artist he did not respect; Fred thought he "knew nothing of Harmony." He considered the work of "The Eight," painters who were then popular, "a joke" when he saw their exhibition at the MacBeth Galleries. The only one worth seeing, he thought, was the landscapist Lawson. He admired some paintings he saw that year, however, and wished he could add them to his private collection: Arthur Dow's *Haystack at Ipswich,* Carl Rungius's *Elk on Mountainside,* and Francis Millet's *Thunder Storm* were among those he would have liked to hang in the upstairs Endion gallery. In February at Greenpoint, he saw Sally Farnham's Ogdensburg war memorial statue and thought it splendid. He and Eva attended the Saint-Gaudens' memorial exhibit at the Metropolitan, which he viewed with respect.

By the end of April, Fred was tired and nervous. His chronic dyspepsia was bothering him, and that year introduced him and Eva to a new diet food, puffed rice, a concoction that was nothing but air, so far as Fred was concerned. His journal that spring was his "wailing wall." He yearned for Ingleneuk, but still had too much work to finish to leave for the North Country. He chafed at the confines of his studio and longed for a change of scene. His eyes were tired from painting: in February, he had thought that the winter sun, into which he squinted as he attempted to catch the violet light of bare tree trunks, would blind him. His aging, scatterbrained collie Sandy, who still acted like a pup, was continually running off or getting into fights. One night, the dog failed to come home and Fred found him the next day in the New Rochelle pound. Dogs had to have licenses now in New Rochelle, he was informed, so he bought licenses for the recalcitrant Sandy and for Eva's dog, Nap. Fred loved Sandy but considered him a fool.

Fred's nervous exhaustion lifted in early May when an old North Country boyhood friendship was renewed. Will Wheelock, now a prestigious attorney in Indianapolis and Chicago who had served a term in the Illinois legislature during the 1890s, dined and spent the evening at Endion. Fred and Will Wheelock reminisced and laughed together about old times. Both of them had been devil-may-care youths. Their paths had not crossed since a mysteriously engineered prank that ousted Will from St. Lawrence University over twenty years before. Will filled Fred in on the details of that disastrous night on the third floor of the university's Richardson Hall, where some of the male students lived. The high jinks that began moderately had got out of hand, Will explained. Someone—even in 1908 Will wouldn't admit to being the ringleader—had the idea of tipping one of the old box wood stoves that heated students' rooms in winter over the edge of the circular staircase that rose from the first floor in the center of the building. No one, he assured Fred, had had the least idea that the iron stove was so heavy it would crash through the solid planks of the first floor right through to the basement.

"We were caught," Will told Fred, who was reminded of the spitball escapade in Kansas that had ended in a magistrate's court. Like Fred at the end of his ranching days, Will had had to leave the scene of his "crime" precipitously the next day, because he had dishonored his father, Washington Wheelock, who was custodian for the St. Lawrence University buildings. All had turned out well, Remington and Wheelock reassured Eva, who found it hard to believe that the impressive lawyer had been as harebrained a youth as Fred. Here was Will Wheelock with a law degree from Northwestern and an impressive record in Chicago governmental affairs, active in politics and legal counsel for the Rock Island Railroad.[3]

That evening with Will Wheelock helped lift Fred's spirits. Free of depression, he set about cleaning up his work in the studio. Memories of North Country days with Will helped to set his sights on their island. "All our thoughts and doings are now for the island," he confided to his journal the next week. "I do not know what we would do without that island at this time of year. We would go crazy if we had to stay here."[4] They made their train reservations; packed up clothes, painting gear, and dogs; and headed north by month's end to find that Pete Smith had painted the Ingleneuk house a dark green, repaired the dock, and made sure the boats were all watertight.

Once again, the River wove its healing spell. Settled into the summer routine of work and rest, Fred was able to complete his self-assigned quota of summer paintings by mid-July and dedicated the rest of the summer to soaking up every loved detail of island and River life. That whole summer at Ingleneuk was joyful but touched with pain and nostalgia, for, by June 3, Fred and Eva had reached the necessary but difficult decision to put Ingleneuk on the market. Its sale would generate the funds they needed for the house at Ridgefield, and they could see no alternative. During the summer, they invited the family of Fred's old Canton attorney, W. A. Poste, for a visit. The Postes were talking about buying an island on the River, as the Almon Gunnisons had, and the Remingtons may have hoped that they would become interested in purchasing Ingleneuk, but this did not happen.

All Fred said in his journal about the need to sell was "Very dismal, this breaking up of Ingleneuk."[5] The rest of his diary that summer detailed island life, both human events and those of its natural inhabitants. Sentimentally, Fred had called Ingleneuk "A Temple of Rest," a "Hoboes' Dream."[6] Then, on August 30, he wrote, "Now begins the last week . . . at Ingleneuk. LAST OF THE SWALLOWS."[7] On September 5, they packed and shipped their boxes, and Fred worried over a small "tip-up" that did not follow the migration of his fellow birds and that Fred was sure would perish. The next day, in the teeth of a heavy gale, the Remingtons nailed up the woodshed, locked the house, and put the Ingleneuk key into the mail bag to go to John Howard, who had promised to help them sell. Now both their homes were up for sale, and with the stagnant national economy it looked as if neither would attract new owners in time to help the artist and his wife finance the Ridgefield house.

Immediately after leaving the island, Fred hurried to Wyoming for what was to be his last western trip. Eva, as usual, went to Gloversville to her sister Clara. Remington was physically miserable during his three-week trip but was successful with some of the studies he attempted. On the way home, Kermit Roosevelt, Teddy's son, and another acquaintance boarded the train at Chicago, and there Fred learned of Theodore Roosevelt's anticipated year-long trip to Africa. Once returned to New Rochelle, Fred plunged into new paintings, working on *Cavalry on the Southern Plains, Lost Warriors,* and *Saving the Wounded Buck* (which he abbreviated to *Plugged Buck*). He began another clay model, this time of a cavalry trooper, and hired a horse as a model. He decided to sketch his Philadelphia cowboy as a memento of his first large equestrian statue, driven by a need to take part of his past with him to Connecticut.

October and November were full of preparations for both the December Knoedler's exhibition and decision making necessary to the projected house. For the latter, Fred lunched with Fred Gunnison, now recovered and back in harness, to ask advice about ways to finance Ridgefield. Gunnison told Fred he could help, and thereafter both Remingtons breathed more easily. In October, Fred tried a game of tennis with Virginia Thomas but lasted only two sets: "even my feet gave out," he confided to his diary. "I cannot stand it for long."[8] He became more enthusiastic about his cavalry trooper and modeled it with the studio doors open to enjoy the warm, smoky yellow autumn weather. On Election Day, he voted a straight Republican ticket but, with no fast communications media in that era, went early to bed without knowing much more than early news that returns seemed promising for his party. The next day Jim Keeler, their general factotum, woke Fred and Eva with the news that Bryan had been elected. Fred jumped out of bed in dismay, then found that Jim had been enjoying his little joke: Taft had been elected, as Fred had hoped.

The projected costs for building Ridgefield caused Eva and Fred deep misgivings. They studied two bids their architect had obtained from builders, finally realizing the scope of their undertaking. Fred was philosophical about the risk: "It's like getting married—same either way we decide."[9] He went once more to Frank Rooke's office, where he learned of two additional construction bids that were more reasonable and immediately decided upon the more expensive of the two. Frank Rooke assured him that that bid had come from the more desirable builder. Greatly excited, he called Eva to meet him, and they hastened by train to Ridgefield, where they, their architect, and the builder staked out the site for their own home and a tenant house.

A few days later, Remington met Fred Gunnison to set up a process that would assure paying necessary building costs as they occurred. Gunnison requested that Remington start an account at his bank through which loan moneys would be funneled to meet building expenses. Although Gunnison said there was no problem in financing Ridgefield, he said that Remington and Eva were "damn fools" to put so much money into the Connecticut place. When Fred reported their banker's comment to Eva, she bristled that "Fred is an idiot with bells on."[10] Fred personally felt that both Gunnison and Eva were wrong, but he was in for it, "so let her go Galligher."

With his financial commitment assured, Remington looked optimistically toward the next spring when his household would move to the country, former fears forgotten. Eva, in the meantime, touched her husband deeply by insisting on using her own income and some capital to meet the first payments. She wanted Ridgefield as much as Fred did; being near the Hepburns and having her husband live a quiet, healthy country existence were as important priorities to her as was the hip-roofed house now rising on the Connecticut hillside. Once he had made his commitment, Fred's finances took an upturn. Stock market sales crept upward; John Howard wrote that there was a chance that Tom Strong might buy the island; if Remington's intuition and artist's eye were correct, his Knoedler show promised to be successful.

On a fine Saturday, November 28, Fred went to town to supervise the hanging of his paintings at the Knoedler Gallery. They looked fine in the effective frames created under his close supervision by Ashler and Stabb. The Knoedler staff were enthusiastic. On Monday, the public echoed their praise for the nineteen works that included landscapes and North Country scenes, as well as Remington's traditional western themes. Every one of the canvases glowed with Remington's newly emerging style, reflecting the self-taught techniques he had worked so hard to master.

The *Herald* was the first newspaper to review Fred's show, and its comments were positive. Gilder of *The Century* complimented him, and by the following Wednesday he learned via the artistic grapevine that even free-lance art critic Royal Cortissoz, whose good opinion the art world sought above all others, was much impressed. Praise and congratulations began to pour in. Cartoonist Homer Davenport and the Edward Kembles appeared at the door at Endion, and the group spent "a wildly enjoyable evening" (Fred's words) celebrating until Eva firmly ushered out their guests and she and Fred went wearily upstairs to bed at 11:30 P.M. "Nice write up in mail," Fred wrote before falling into bed, but ended on a slightly anxious note: "In two weeks $7000 payment due on house."[11]

Fred need not have worried about the coming bills. Although each day brought more expenditures to meet from the shrinking bank account, Roland Knoedler sent word that Remington's paintings were selling. New York Judge Charles Russell, another member of the urban North Country network and a relative of Harriet Ferry Appleton, bought *Shot-gun Hospitality* to give to Dartmouth College. Press clippings continued to arrive at Endion with glowing reviews. Letters arrived from Royal Cortissoz, Caspar Whitney, and Teddy Burke. Judge Russell called. By the following Tuesday, December 8, eight of the paintings had sold. When his show closed December 12, Fred rejoiced, "I have landed among the painters, and well up too."[12]

The glow of well-being brought about by his successful exhibit continued. Released from anxieties about the merit of his art, Fred now appeared to be free of his financial worries, as well. By mid-December, the two Freds had worked through arrangements to finance payments for Ridgefield, with Remington's placing a block of stock with the Home Trust as security on the loan. Then, only three days before Christmas, Professor Leslie Miller's letter arrived from the Philadelphia Committee, stating that the Fairmont Association would pay a total of $11,004 for *Big Horse*. Although they spent Christmas alone (Emma Caten was in Europe and all other hoped-for guests had declined Eva's invitations), Christmas 1908 was a joyous occasion. Carefully, Fred noted the thoughtfulness of his friends: Gus Thomas gave him a French palette; his lawyer George Wright, a Perrills whistle; Henry Smith, *Egypt: Its Monuments* (Fred's record here is somewhat mysterious, but we assume this was a book); Eva, a *History of the World*; Will Wheelock, a foot-long Havana cigar. Frederic Ruckstull had told him "they will cover my paintings with gold some day."[13]

The day after Christmas, the Remingtons started out early to see their new home. It was stunning, far more than they had hoped, the hip roof ready for shingles, the chimneys rising. "We are tickled to death with view," wrote Fred. "My studio window is magnificent."[14] On December 29, Fred traveled to Philadelphia, where Professor Miller handed him the check for $11,004, which Fred deposited that same day when he arrived back in New York: "and thus closes the Fairmont Cow Boy," he wrote that night.[15] On New Year's Eve, he looked back over the year that Mrs. Cochran had predicted would be "his." Carefully Fred listed 1908's accomplishments:

This year
> I unveiled a monument of a cowboy in Fairmont Park
> I painted a lot of pictures which made a great hit at
> Knoedlers
> I started building a house in Ridgefield Conn
> And my gross results in money were $36614.87 and
> money from Knoedlers $6800
> And I kept on the water wagon.[16]

The next day, New Year's, he continued in the same vein: "I am no longer on salary and fully embarqued on the uncertain career of a painter. . . . 'Who does not see that I have taken a road, in which incessantly and without labor I shall proceed so long as there shall be ink and paper in the world.'—Montaigne."[17]

Hard on the heels of the Knoedler success came other offers. His Chicago art dealer wanted a Remington show; there were offers to reproduce his paintings. Knoedler wrote to set the date for his 1909 show, November 29 to December 11. But all was not clouds of glory for Fred professionally. Doll and Richards's Boston Remington exhibition resulted in a roasting from art critics there. They called his night scenes "monochromes." In addition, his bronzes had not sold in 1908, a fact Fred attributed to the national straits: "things have slowed down commercially . . . until you can't get a rabbit to run from a dog."[18] But life was too full of other events for Fred to fret: a friend, Bob Mulford, wrote to inquire about the price of Ingleneuk; the Remingtons were invited to be guests of honor at a Hepburn dinner on West Fifty-seventh Street to meet their future Ridgefield neighbors; Fred was in demand among his cronies to lunch at the Players Club or the Waldorf; and the couple accepted an invitation to the Berkshires in northwest Massachusetts to visit Fred's artist friend Bob Emmett and for Fred to paint snowscapes.

Fred had formed the habit of clipping tidbits that struck his fancy from newspapers and pasting them in his journal. One of these was "That a good man, though in the dark he strives, Hath still an instinct for the truer way." A more cynical maxim that tickled his fancy was "Nothing is new—nothing is true and nothing matters." He was working steadily at painting, having in the works *Buffalo Runners in the Big Horn Basin, Blanket Signal,* and *Sleeping Village.* Eva made Fred a big blue painting smock that he thought was as big as a "three ring circus tent," but it protected him from his absent-minded habit of wiping brushes and hands on his clothes. Prophetically, he insisted that he and Eva draw up wills.[19]

The trip to Massachusetts proved an exhilarating experience. The Remingtons stayed in a little hotel at Deerfield and walked over the snowy roads to the Emmetts' old farmhouse. Eva and her hostess went on a sleigh ride, and later during the visit Fred sketched Emmett's sugar house. "Snow is grand stuff to paint," he remarked, "but one must wait for moderate days to work in."[20] The view of nearby mountains—one of which Fred mistook for Mount Monadnock—at sunset, life in the little village, the farm folk he talked with, and the sight of a big gray fox all added to his sense of fulfillment. Once the Remingtons were back in New Rochelle, the Chicago reviews of his work more than compensated for his Boston reviews. From the *Chicago Record Herald*: "Possibly no man is developing into painterlike workmanship with greater strides than is Frederick [sic] Remington at the present time. His tight, dry handling, due to the dictates of reproduction, is giving way to a velvety touch possible of all sorts of mysterious depths."[21]

Then in mid-February came word from John Howard, who thought he could sell the island. A check for five hundred dollars soon followed, and Fred went off to get attorney George Wright to deal with the legalities of selling Ingleneuk to Tom Strong. He was touched when "dear old John Howard" sent him an original poem, "When Rem He Left the Bay." The sale of the island was a wonderful excuse for a day trip to Ridgefield, which revealed that Rathgeb, Fred's builder, and architect Frank Rooke were rapidly progressing toward completion of the big house, the tenant house, and the barn. Fred still thought at times that "we are crazy to get this," when he let himself think of bills piling upon bills, but he was excited to see the progress. Later, as arrangements for the island sale neared completion, Fred confided in his journal that "if Tom gets as much pleasure out of Ingleneuk as we have, it is the worst I wish him."[22]

In what was becoming an annual offering to oblivion, in late winter Fred once more made a bonfire of old canvases he could no longer tolerate. This completed, he turned toward spring, which came early that year, and arrangements for the impending move. He and Eva had purchased a carriage, and Emily Hepburn volunteered to store it at Altnacraig until the Remingtons' barn was finished. Fred was concerned that Endion was still not sold and went to Fred Gunnison to arrange for a mortgage on Endion to meet the Ridgefield expenses. Gunnison persuaded him to put more securities up for bond and to take, instead, a short-term loan. All these uncertainties about meeting financial obligations for Ridgefield, the pressures of his work, and the many details involved in preparing to move brought Fred's sensitive digestive system to the boil. He began to suffer from chronic dyspepsia and diarrhea, caught a cold, and had to cancel social obligations.

One social obligation, which had professional undertones, Fred did attend that March. Bobbie Collier invited him to attend a formal "breakfast," to be held to honor President Theodore Roosevelt, who had just left office. Although *Collier's* continued to publish Remington's work, even after his death, these were reproductions of paintings purchased and accumulated under the expired contract. Fred's official contract with the periodical had finished at the end of 1908. On New Year's Day 1909, Fred noted that the magazine continued "to advertise me exclusively although I am fired." He did not intend to let his anger at this rejection fester or become public knowledge, however, so he accepted his former publisher's invitation. He had a good time in company with old colleagues, who included Colonel Leonard Wood and Caspar Whitney. Afterward, he philosophically remarked in his journal, "Some little talk awhile of me and thee, there was—and then no more of thee and me."[23]

With this obligation behind, and despite his anxieties about the coming move, Remington embarked on painting *Sun Dance,* his interpretation of the Indian religious ritual, during which chosen braves have spikes driven through their chests behind pectoral muscles and are suspended from the spikes by thongs from a high pole for an entire day. He chose to depict the ending of the rite, lit by flickering campfire flames, some participants hanging unconscious, the rest of the tribe watching from the background. Fred felt compelled to paint the painful rite, but "I'll never sell it—it will give everyone the horrors. It is in my system and it's got to come out." The more he worked on *Sun Dance,* the more he found it to be "a horror, but a great thing—the biggest thing most significant of the western Indians."[24] He struggled with the painting, which was as difficult to organize and execute technically as its concept and meaning were to convey.

He asked young Schuyler Kemble, son of his artist friend, to pose for *Sun Dance.* Fred was enthusiastic about the youngster's ability and decided to use him again. As it turned out, the lad was a better model than he was a worker, for when Fred hired him later that spring to help with packing and cleaning up at Endion, he decided that the boy was lazy. Fred always had trouble relating to or directing the young, perhaps because he still had too much of the child in himself.

As they organized for the move at Endion that year, Fred and Eva traveled to Ridgefield to inspect their new home almost weekly. Bit by bit, they saw their house take shape: chimneys finished, walls lathed and then plastered, the barn's cement floor laid, sewer installed, blinds ordered and delivered and painted. Excitedly, the artist and his wife kept adding more buildings to the original plans. They sent word to Frank Rooke to build a shed and a chicken coop. Eva ordered seeds for the big vegetable garden she wanted laid out, and Fred wrote to a nursery in New Canaan to plant fruit trees. The farm wagon Fred had ordered was delivered: "bottle green good wood—iron-brake . . . spring seat." And there would be a hay rack added. Fred began to buy farm implements, determined to have his new "farm" fully supplied and in prime condition for production. In late March, Frank Rooke sent word that their man-of-all-work, Jim Keeler, could move his family from New Rochelle to the new Ridgefield tenant house in early April, but that the big house would not be ready until mid-May. By the end of March, Fred and Eva had named their country home Lorul Place (the origin of which has never been determined).

On April 7, exactly nineteen years to the day after they had moved to New Rochelle, the Remingtons began seriously to pack. The bronzes were crated up, Fred's collection of guns was packed, and Endion began to look barren. On April 10, a New Rochelle house agent appeared with a prospect who seemed seriously interested in Endion. It was the last remaining property in the Lathers Hill section of the suburb with a whole acre of land. On April 13, rain began to fall, although the weather was warm. Fred hurried to New York on business and returned, before the gentle rain turned to a downpour, to continue packing. By April 17, all was in readiness for the first moving expedition to Connecticut. Then, on April 20, in another driving rainstorm, Jim Keeler's house goods were added to the loaded moving van, and Jim and an additional man loaded up the new wagon and started off in the rain for Ridgefield, with Eva's Nip and Jim's dogs aboard in boxes. Fred and Eva, whose anxiety mounted with each gust of the east wind that drove sheets of rain sideways, took the train to Ridgefield, their minds on their hired man and on their dogs. Fred hoped that Jim would turn back, but in the evening at the Ridgefield Inn, they received a telephone call from Jim, who reported that the wagoners had had a "most awful day" and had luckily found a place to stay near Bedford when they were ready to give out from exhaustion.

The wagon and its exhausted drivers arrived at Lorul Place at noon the following day. Relieved, Eva returned to New Rochelle by train to continue packing at Endion, leaving Fred and Jim to camp out in the stable, to unpack and give a semblance of order to the stacks of boxes and goods. As usual, Fred could not resist the hearty country breakfasts of bacon and eggs Jim prepared each morning, and he suffered for his indiscretion. From then on, Fred went back and forth to Ridgefield every few days and gave up all thoughts of serious painting until the move was completed.

Moving day was set for May 17. Eva invited a few friends for a farewell dinner at Endion. Fred supervised packing, continued to direct details of finishing up the new house, ate more fried eggs and suffered indigestion, then took over entirely when Eva's physical reserves gave out and he was forced to send her to her bed. He hired Schuyler Kemble to help with the packing and fumed at the boy's adolescent slowness. By May 13, four vans were filled, and Endion was nearly empty. Then, on May 15, only two days before they left New Rochelle for good, word came that Endion was sold. Gratefully, the Remingtons agreed to take twenty-five-thousand dollars in cash, signing a contract to close the coming July. On their last night in New Rochelle, Fred wrote, "We have lived here 19 years last March—the best days of our lives and we go with very few regrets. The charm of New Rochelle as a living place has long departed."[25]

For the next month, life was unbelievably difficult. The excitement of the move changed to dismay at the conditions Fred and Eva discovered they must live in temporarily, until their house was completely finished. In fact, they had to move into the tenant house with Jim and Nora Keeler. Nip bit Jim's little girl. In the big house, in each room, stacks of boxes and furniture were piled helter-skelter. Carpenters and painters were still at work in the midst of this chaos. The banisters were not yet up on the stairway. The paperhangers were working in the library. Somehow, however, order was imposed bit by bit. Jim had the barn's inhabitants under control, including a fine, new red Guernsey. The fields were planted and Jim put the hens to setting. Fred tackled setting his studio to rights. Eva settled the library and directed their maids in placing furniture, working around the carpenters. On May 21, they ate their first meal in their own house—in the kitchen—and, on May 24, Eva churned her first pound and a half of butter. Eva's sister Emma arrived to help, but bad weather and absent workmen conspired to hold up progress, so that Fred remarked, "The plot thickens and I do not think the house on Lorul Hill will ever be done."[26]

Not until June did Fred find time to return to painting. Somehow, with infinitesimal movement each day, he and Eva began to settle into a routine of country living. People called; the Hepburns invited them for meals; Fred began to take daily hikes again, sometimes with Barton Hepburn. Eva overcame her fear of driving the new pony cart and began to return calls. Fred went to the city for a day, beginning a weekly habit, and commuted back with his former teacher Julian Weir, who also lived in the area. Both the Remingtons enjoyed the weather, the growth of their garden, the antics of piglets, and a fight among the cows when the new red Guernsey was allowed to join the herd.

Fred and Barton Hepburn talked stocks and finance. Emily and Eva attended musicales and Emily talked about the importance of getting the voting franchise for women. Before long, their old friends began to visit, first the Kembles, then cartoonist Homer Davenport. The Hepburns gave a formal tea to introduce Fred and Eva to Ridgefield. Eva enjoyed herself, but Fred, as usual, found a formal social occasion, no matter how cordial the people, a trying event. On another day, they went with the Hepburns by motor to Daniel Beard's farm near Danbury. The naturalist, a founder of the American boy scouting movement, was already an acquaintance of Fred's, who found the Beards' colonial home, filled with furniture of the period, a "lived in" place. Beard showed them a hooded adder, which he kept in a box, but quieted Eva's fears by saying that copperheads and rattlers were the poisonous snakes of the area. And slowly, Fred began to regain "the mental vision of an artist instead of a constructor of buildings."[27]

Life was so full that summer that Fred had only occasional thoughts of former summers in the North Country and the Thousand Islands. He could not, however, get the region out of his blood, and, that spring, John Howard persuaded him to join the Canadian Pontiac Club, a private sportsman's haunt. Fred paid the dues from the sale of the *Missie*. He and Eva planned a trip to Canada to the club for late that summer. In the meantime, he found that his new home environment was paying off in his painting. "I worked to great advantage—the color vibrated for me," he recorded in July. He finished one painting, which he named *The Love Call*; worked out a concept for a new work; and finally was able to bring into focus the harmonious composition that had eluded him so long in *Buffalo Runners in the Big Horn Basin*. In July, the Cass Gilberts came to call. Gilbert was one of the outstanding architects of that time. Occasionally, Fred heard gossip from New York. Jimmie Finn and Nick Biddle, another artist, came for dinner. Fred became an honorary member of the New Roosevelt Rough Riders. At the end of July, he decided to give the Hepburns one of his small landscapes as a gift, "a small intimate eastern thing which will sit as a friend at their elbows." The many kindnesses Emily and Barton showered on him and Eva touched him deeply.

Fred and Eva set forth the last day of July for Canada, feeling the need for a change after the strenuous events of the past year. Fred noted in his journal that "this will be the first time I have left the pilot house since I stood on Hepburn's steps last October and said, 'I will build a house on that hill if Taft is elected.' "[28] For the next three weeks, they loafed and enjoyed the water and woods, the few other guests, and the cabin they were assigned at the Pontiac Club. Fred sketched once in a while. At the end of their stay, they went to Ottawa for the first time; there Eva enjoyed sight-seeing and shopping for Irish linens. But each was happy to return home to Lorul Hill and their new contentment.

Throughout the remaining summer days and on into the autumn, Fred worked hard to prepare for his 1909 Knoedler's exhibition. He was pleased with his Pontiac sketches, which, when they were varnished, "came true and strong." He made arrangements with General Leonard Wood to paint an equestrian portrait of this military man whom he respected and who had become a friend. Wood was to visit Ridgefield, with his saddle horse, to pose for the painting. As he doctored the results of his year's work, he wondered whether "this bunch will make artistic New York sit up."[29] Then he began to worry about the Canadian pictures but, with the arrival of General Wood, a gracious and charming guest, whom they introduced to the Hepburns at a dinner in his honor, Fred forgot his momentary worries. As soon as Wood's horse arrived, Fred dug into the portrait. He was as pleased with this painting as he was with his other work that summer of 1909.

The only cloud in the sky at Lorul Hill appeared late that summer, when Jim Keeler announced that he would no work longer for the Remingtons, apparently giving as his reasons that he was imposed upon in the rural environment and duties, as well as being homesick for New Rochelle. Fred, who had thought that life was finally in order, was furious. At first, he cajoled, then spoke his mind. As Jim continued to complain, Fred went to local farmer Warren Keeler and hired him on the spot, then sent Jim Keeler and his family packing by mid-September. Usually loyal to his employees, Fred had a sudden change of attitude toward Jim Keeler that must have been caused by some crucial incident. All he said after the man had left was that Jim had "discharged himself," and that he had become "an imprudent, dissatisfied fellow."[30] The truth must have been somewhere in between the charges of employer and employee: Jim was competent to be groundsman on a suburban estate but not a real farmer; Remington's expectations were probably too high and, preoccupied with his art and new acquaintances, as well as suffering from poor health, he may not have provided adequate supervision.

More and more, as fall progressed, Fred found himself pulled into the informal social life of Ridgefield. The Hepburns, Gilberts, Emmetts and others—all affluent and socially prominent—he found as congenial as any of the small-town friends of his youth. These families, too, lived in harmony with the rural environment around them, enjoying simple pastimes and pleasurable outings. This was not at all what Fred had formerly pictured to be the life-style of these people, who were considered financial and cultural leaders in New York. And, it appeared, they accepted and enjoyed him as much as he did them. With the passage of weeks and months at Ridgefield, work and relaxation, exercise and sociability, all merged into an even, serene flow.

Remington had been thinking about starting another clay model. On September 26, a quiet Sunday, he decided to model a group of cowboys and steers in sculpture. He named it *The Stampede,* and, on Monday, he began to lay clay upon his armature. Working with clay right then was more satisfying than trying to finish his oil *The Outlier,* with which he was having trouble. That Wednesday, he drove to the home farm of E. P. Dutton, where he negotiated with the publisher's farmer to purchase another cow. A week later, when he turned the Jersey into the meadow with the rest of his herd, "a regular Spanish bull fight" followed, with "cows and men yelling and bawling through the dewey grass."[31]

As autumn progressed, Fred worked off and on at his new clay model or painted, sometimes successfully and sometimes unable to attain the effects he sought. He was not working at the high pitch of energy of years past. Instead, he found himself more and more involved in the joys of country living. His old friend Poultney Bige-low dropped in to visit, the Hassams asked Fred and Eva to their home and visited Lorul Hill. Bertelli made the trip out from Brook-lyn, and later the Remingtons visited the Julian Weirs. Eventually Remington returned to work on *The Outlier,* a night scene of an Indian sentinel, this time successfully. Later he commented that Childe Hassam had told him that he considered the oil to be the best of Remington's paintings.

On October 4, Fred Remington turned forty-eight. A few days later, he carefully pasted into his journal a birthday jingle, written in his honor, that had appeared in a newspaper:

> The moose, the deer, the caribou,
> O Reming, have been good to you,
> The flight of horses on the plain,
> The running stream, the forest main,
> The open sky, the earth below
> Have been your chosen studio.

> Would you have done better in cities, to the dulcet murmur of some anemic model? We doubt it. You are a primitive man, born a few centuries after your time. Instead of paint-ing on rocks you have used a canvas. Here's a health to thee, in pure crystal mountain dew, double distilled—the kind that inspires but does not inebriate salute.[32]

Two days later, Fred had all but three of his paintings boxed and shipped to Knoedler for the coming show. At home in Ridge-field, he continued to work on *The Stampede,* finally getting its com-position right after one of the bulls disintegrated. He made sure his frames for the Knoedler show were finished and delivered, and then he went to town to see that all was in order at the gallery. He could hardly believe his ears when Roland Knoedler told him that his show would have to wait its turn—after Knoedler's exhibit of their "big-gest thing," which Roland did not name but alluded to as an Old Master. Fred left Knoedler's stunned and not knowing what to think. A week and a half afterward, it was announced that Knoedler's was going to exhibit the Frick collection of Van Dykes.

Instead of raging as he would have in the past, Fred arranged with Bertelli to send to Ridgefield a *Broncho Buster* that needed work, and for Bertelli's man, Contini, to cast *The Stampede* the day before Thanksgiving. On that blizzardy Thursday, the Remingtons ate one of their own geese for Thanksgiving dinner.

Then, a few days later, Fred took to his bed with what he called "a bad rheumatic foot." Invitation cards came for him to address for the postponed Knoedler's exhibition. Laid up, he had to write Knoedler's staff instructions about hanging his paintings. On December 4, Remington's show opened with great crowds pushing in to see the latest Remington paintings. Six pictures sold immediately, three at a thousand dollars apiece. Impatiently, Remington awaited word on the show from friends and art critics. Finally, on December 7, he read the first review and carefully pasted it in his journal (Fred did not identify the New York newspaper): "It must be extremely trying for those commentators on pictorial art who always insisted that [Frederic Remington] was only an illustrator and decried his ability to paint. . . . By this time they must be impressed with the facts that Remington's work is at once splendid in its technique, epic in its imaginative qualities, and historically important in its permanent contributions to the records of the most romantic epoch in the making of the West."

Other laudatory reviews followed fast on the heels of the first. Fred carefully pasted each one in his journal. Of *The Winter Campaign,* one reviewer wrote, "—a group of soldiers squatting about a fire, with their horses huddling close to them to keep them warm— expresses, as only Remington can the oneness of feeling of animals and men in the face of nature's menace of death."[33]

Then the writer added, "Indeed, in all of Remington's pictures the shadow of death seems not far away. . . . The presence, in Mr. Remington's characteristic work, of a great central motive like this, derived from the actual conditions of that vast, hungry region whose jewel and symbol is the dry skull reposing on the desert's breast, is an indication of power, and the ability to express the motive in a hundred vivid forms is a proof of genius."

Those phrases contained both commentary and prophecy. Five days after his exhibition closed, on December 20, a terrible pain caught Fred in his belly as the artist stood before his easel. At first, Fred feared he had an intestinal stoppage and dosed himself with Tarrants, a patent medicine. Later, he wondered whether the trouble had been caused when he turned the corn sheller two days before. He finally went to bed so stiff and sore that he could hardly move, but by December 22 he insisted he was enough better for a trip to the city.

The remaining entries in Frederic Remington's 1909 journal, written in Eva Remington's hand, recount subsequent events:

Wednesday, December 22, 1909—
Frederic and I started for town on 8:26 A.M. train. Going to the station Frederic felt the jar of the wagon very much and when he got to the station felt he must or ought to come back but kept on and went to town. When we arrived in town he was so ill we decided to come back on 12 o'clock train. . . . We arrived home about 3 o'clock. Frederic immediately went to bed. I called Dr. Lorre who came . . . but nothing definite developed til Thursday morning. He was very restless all night and in pain at times. . . .

Thursday, December 23, 1909—
The doctor came about nine o'clock and after a thorough examination said he must have council. . . . [it was] agreed an operation for appendicitis was necessary . . . so we got Dr. Abbe who arrived at 8 P.M. It was decided to operate immediately. The three doctors and 2 nurses were here. . . . When Dr. Abbe told him he must operate—he said—"cut her loose, Dr." in his usual brave way. He had a comfortable night considering.

Friday, December 24, 1909—
Frederic spent a comfortable day and seemed strong and helped the nurse when he wanted to move himself. . . . He was very cheerful. Clara and Horatio [Burr; her sister and brother-in-law from Gloversville, New York; Eva's other sister, Emma Caten, had also hastened to be at her sister's side] arrived on the 2:15 P.M. train.

Saturday, December 25, 1909—
Frederic seemed comfortable and cheerful—about one o'clock a change came for the worst and the doctor said it was the beginning of the end—and after midnight he sank rapidly. He was cheerful and felt he was better. It was probably the lack of pain that made him so. . . . We opened a few small packages before the change for the worst took place—His system was so full of poison he cd not throw it off.

Sunday, December 26, 1909—

At 9:30 A.M. Frederic passed away. The doctor remained here till all arrangements for the funeral were made. Fred Gunnison took care of the affairs in Canton and Horatio here. I kept up wonderfully—Telegrams were sent. . . . — The storm was over but the wind blew very hard.[34]

Frederic Remington's funeral was held in Canton, New York, on December 28, 1909. Dr. Almon Gunnison, president of St. Lawrence University, preached the funeral sermon in the Universalist Church on a bright, clear, cold winter's day. Somehow, Eva got through the service, although she almost fainted.

Frederic had been at his work only a week before. Now he was dead. Friends had flocked to Ridgefield the day after his death: Hepburns, Emmetts, Thomases, Kembles, Irving Bacheller, Jimmie Finn, the Hassams, Alden Weir, Fred Gunnison, George Wright. Henry Smith's wife and Almon Gunnison traveled the long overnight ride with Eva to the North Country, with Fred's body in the baggage car. In Canton, Jim Johnson, Rob Sackrider and Emma, Fred's mother and her second husband, and all the Canton friends were at hand. In the semicircle of blond oak pews rising from the front of the Universalist Church, village and North Country people and some of the most notable figures of the Golden Decade sat side by side to honor the boisterous fat man who had mythologized the passing of their nation's frontier.

After the funeral, despite her own shock, fatigue, and strain, Eva Remington feared for her mother-in-law, who was in a state of nervous excitability. Long walks seemed to help Eva, and twice the day of the funeral she and dear old friends walked the snowy, elm-lined village streets: to Aunt Minnie Ellsworth's, to the library, to the station for train tickets. That same evening, Eva and Henry Smith's wife boarded the evening train, arriving in New York two hours late the following morning, to be met by Remington's lawyer, George Wright. Eva returned to Ridgefield on the 3:32 P.M. train to be confronted with a flood of letters and telegrams and frozen water pipes.

On December 31, Eva Remington carefully wrote the last entry in her husband's journal. "We all rested being tired after the terrible shock. . . . We found the pipes had frozen and busted and plumber came to fix them. All water turned off on the north side of house. We three girls [Eva, Clara Burr, Emma Caten] walked about the place. Cold and clear."[35]

13

EVA AFTERWARD

« 1910–1918 »

Fortunately for posterity, Eva Caten Remington possessed fortitude, intelligence, and common sense. In addition, she truly believed that the ebullient man who had been her husband for twenty-five years deserved a niche in American history as an exceptional artist and sculptor. Throughout the turbulent but never dull years as his wife, Eva had bent all her energies to supporting and nurturing Remington's unique combination of whirlwind energy, driving ambition, alternating moods of elation and anger, self-destructive overindulgence, and the sensitivity hidden behind his ideal vision of life's potential.

If she had been less intuitive or less staunch in her belief in his talents, it is unlikely that Remington, the illustrator, would have risen so quickly to prominence. If she had not stood by his dream from the beginning, the artist of the Old West might never have persevered as a sculptor and then struggled on to arrive at the pinnacle of excellence as a painter that he sought. Eva had always been honest about her own desires for the good life, as she—a woman of her temperament and status in the late nineteenth century—saw it. As we have seen, under her proper and gracious Victorian exterior, Eva turned out to be accepting, yet firm and forthright. Otherwise, the childless marriage might never have grown into the partnership that culminated, in its last years, in Fred's respect for and dependence on Eva.

If Eva Remington had been less loyal, practical, and perceptive, priceless information about the artist and valuable products of Remington's talent that make up our historical record and our artistic heritage might have been destroyed in the years following his death. Eva was able, for the most part, to push aside the shock and grief of Frederic's sudden death in order to attend to a multitude of business details that involved his work. She was able also to withstand innumerable pressures from self-appointed, and mostly well-meaning, advisers who sought to influence her disposal of her husband's paintings, bronzes, writing, copyrights, and other effects. Always the gentlewoman, courteous and even demure in dealing with her husband's agents and business colleagues, she nevertheless exhibited that hidden vein of iron that Fred had first met abruptly in Kansas City, when he used her as his first and only female model.

Although her husband had departed from life quickly and tragically, his presence lingered in every nook and cranny of the Ridgefield farm and house that they had built together. In the first weeks of 1910, a flood of letters, telegrams, and cables of condolence arrived, all of which had to be acknowledged. Clara and Horatio Burr had left on New Year's Day for their home in Gloversville; Eva's younger sister Emma remained to help the sister she loved so deeply, even then establishing what was to become a basic thread in the new fabric of life Eva was to fashion. Together, the two sisters adjusted Eva's wardrobe to the conventional garb of mourning of that day. When the weather allowed, they walked about the grounds of Lorul Place. Only a few close friends, such as the Hepburns and the Thomases, came to call, because turn-of-the-century society respected the right of the widow to her private grief. On January 3 came a cablegram from the German kaiser and the crown prince expressing their sympathy to the fifty-year-old widow. Soon, she received newspaper clippings with laudatory articles about Remington and his work. In the diary for 1910 that Fred had purchased but never lived to fill, Eva wrote, "Am so glad his work is so highly appreciated." As for her own grief, she had Emma, Emily Hepburn, Virginia Thomas, and the empty pages of the diary in which to confide her loss and feeling of emptiness. "Virginia misses Frederic every minute as we do," Eva wrote, "and we constantly talk about him."[1] However, the inner discipline that she set for herself rarely allowed Eva to admit, even in the privacy of her journal, the extent of her loss.

Instead of looking backward or inward, Eva immediately confronted important business decisions and well-meaning advisers. In addition, she firmly grasped every opportunity that was presented to prepare a place of honor for Frederic Remington's work in the annals of art and history, staunchly supported in this goal by Emma. Eva's actions and thoughts, preserved in her diaries over the next several years, often directly contradict our stereotypes of the mourning Victorian widow; the purposeful life Eva thereafter adopted certainly became her anchor for dealing with private despair and grief.

Only two weeks after Remington's funeral Eva began to search through the contents of his studio. She also began to learn the many details about marketing paintings and bronzes that Frederic himself had formerly handled briskly and easily. That first week in January, Eva and Emma began the arduous, yet fascinating task of methodically sorting the artist's sketchbooks and looking over the stacks of photographs he had collected for use in his paintings, so that they might determine what to do with them. Until now, Eva had not been sure of what the studio contained. So began a strange new life for the woman whose days had been filled with social and cultural interests and with acting as hostess and supporting and nurturing her husband.

By mid-January, the new widow was deep in the midst of negotiations with her husband's agents, while reviewing the pressing recommendations of colleagues or friends. Ronald Knoedler, head of the gallery where Remington exhibited, advised Eva to sell all the paintings immediately, during the period of intense interest in his work that his sudden death had aroused. John Howard wrote from Ogdensburg to ask permission to find a way to dispose of the outstanding collection of Indian artifacts, which he believed should be preserved in a national museum; Eva sent him word to proceed. Will Wheelock wrote to ask about the disposition of Fred's bronzes— later, Eva discovered that Will wanted to purchase one of Fred's *Broncho Busters,* which she directed Bertelli to send him. Later on, Barton Hepburn recommended selling all the remaining bronzes, paintings, and sketches at auction. Wisely, Eva consulted attorney George Wright often, and the two worked closely during the months to come. With Fred's will in probate at once, she began to take over all business matters, including managing the disposition of his remaining art and their investments. As the year progressed, she discovered that many problems existed and that she was less well off than she had assumed. In addition, she began to receive inquiries about selling off livestock and Lorul Place itself and, before she had fully adjusted to her new circumstances, was confronted with deciding about her own living plans.

As she sorted papers, Eva found that Knoedler's had failed to return three Remington paintings (*Sun Dance, Episodes of Buffalo Inn,* and *Buffalo Runners in the Big Horn Basin*) that had appeared in Frederic's final exhibition. She notified the gallery immediately. Another art agent arrived to consult about Fred's drawings. Still another wished to reproduce drawings from the sketchbooks. *Collier's* wrote to ask permission to reproduce any painting that the magazine had not heretofore published. Buffalo Bill Cody's manager wanted a photograph of the artist for publication. Eva wanted to make sure that the paintings Remington had stored at the Lincoln National Bank in the city tallied with the list she found. She needed access to Fred's safety-deposit box. Thus began a routine that lasted well into the year. Almost daily for several weeks, and at least once weekly thereafter, Eva commuted to New York to meet George Wright and to conduct business with Knoedler's, Tiffany's, or the banks.

In the welter of unfamiliar details confronting her in 1910, Eva kept sight of her purpose: making sure Frederic's work was remembered and memorialized. At the same time, she quietly and firmly maintained control of all decision making about his artworks and possessions. She persuaded *Collier's* to send her prints of all her husband's works that had appeared there. She planned gifts to St. Lawrence University of prints, books, sketches, and even the cap and gown and master's hood Fred had honorarily received from Yale. She was in regular contact with Ricardo Bertelli about completion of the enlarged *Broncho Buster,* which was to go on sale at Tiffany's in March, and she made a special trip to the city to make sure the bronze was displayed properly in Tiffany's Fifth Avenue window. That same day, she conferred with the Knoedler staff about any pictures being sold by the gallery for reproduction. At home, she and Emma catalogued the Indian collection, and throughout the spring she made appointments with museum officials from Washington, Philadelphia, Brooklyn, and New York's Museum of Natural History, who reviewed the collection, made recommendations, and tendered offers. She met Sally Farnham at the Roman Bronze Works to confer about *Caught in the Stampede,* which Sally had finished and which now would be cast. She and artist Henry Smith conferred about the Metropolitan's interest in securing a Remington painting for its collection.

One March day, after busy hours in town, Eva found two prospects for memorializing her husband. As she sank wearily into her seat aboard the train for Ridgefield, she was greeted by architect Cass Gilbert and his wife. That night, she wrote in her journal, that [Gilbert] "advised me to get together a book about Frederic and to do it at once. . . . Also said he would see if he could induce the government of Texas to have a *Broncho Buster* put up in monumental size."[2] The next day, Eva began to write a series of letters to Fred's many notable colleagues and acquaintances: General Leonard Wood, Gus Thomas, Edward Kemble, Ricardo Bertelli, Owen Wister, Louis Shipman, Royal Cortissoz, Barton Hepburn, his former boyhood friends, famed football coach Walter Camp at Yale, and Julian Weir. As the year progressed, she continued conscientiously to post similar letters until almost everyone who had known Remington had received her earnest supplication for material for the book. In return, a flood of replies arrived with promises to help, as well as personal recollections and amusing anecdotes, old letters to and from Fred (the latter often illustrated with quick, humorous sketches by the artist). Eagerly, Eva began to seek a writer/editor and a publisher. With Frederic's demise fresh in the public mind, she was confident that Owen Wister, Royal Cortissoz, or some other writer who had known her husband and his work would respond favorably.

The second memorial Cass Gilbert had suggested also seemed promising in 1910. In April, she learned from Homer Davenport, the cartoonist who had often visited New Rochelle and Lorul Place, that important plans were afoot to start a memorial fund to finance a large Remington statue, probably a gigantic *Broncho Buster,* to be erected in Washington, D.C., to honor its creator. Davenport explained that Theodore Roosevelt was to initiate the fund drive during a trip to Cheyenne in August of that year. The former president and those organizing the memorial wanted Eva to be present on the trip. By May, when Emma returned to Syracuse and Eva proceeded on north to Canton, plans were well under way for the proposed Western tour (train fare for which was $67.80 round-trip!).

On August 24, Eva met her escort, Homer Davenport, at Grand Central Terminal to board the sleeper for Chicago, anticipating hearing the speech Roosevelt would deliver to launch the memorial fund campaign for her husband. At midnight in Utica, she learned, their train was scheduled to pick up Roosevelt's private cars and then proceed west. She climbed into her berth that night, looking forward to a full and exciting trip. Soon after daybreak the next morning, Eva awoke to the squawks, jerks, and grindings of brakes on wheels as the train ground to a halt, and then heard voices shouting outside. Raising the shade at the window of her berth, she peeked out cautiously. Above an immense, milling crowd that thronged the station platform, Eva made out a sign that read Buffalo. Then, she watched Colonel Teddy Roosevelt push through the crowd to a stone wall and crawl up it to gain a promising place to address the crowd. "They all seemed to love him," she observed.

Soon thereafter, Eva had her first glimmering that all was not to proceed as she had been encouraged to believe. First, the former president's entourage of cars was unhooked from her train. His political managers had routed Teddy to Chicago via Toledo, where another great crowd hailed the man they wished to see return to the White House. In Chicago, the two groups of travelers were pulled into different stations. Then Eva's train chugged through the Midwest to Omaha, while Eva watched miles of waving corn and wheat out her window. In Omaha, Eva and the party with whom she traveled once more glimpsed Roosevelt as his train pulled out of the railroad yards. Teddy would reach Cheyenne in advance of Eva. Farther west, the flat land through which Eva's train steamed was lonely and desolate, but soon the clack of wheels on rails slowed as the engine began its labored climb into the Rockies. Eva's spirits rose again.

Eva Remington reached Cheyenne in midmorning on August 27 to discover a great parade moving along the main street, passing in review before Theodore Roosevelt. "It was all thoroughly western and picturesque," she wrote later in the diary. "There were the governor, actors and citizens in the grandstand, cowboys, Indians, cowgirls, citizens on horseback and in motorcars. A pair of buffalo harnessed to a wagon, a unique sight. . . . After lunch at the Independence Club we rode to Fremont Park. We were seated with the reporters. Fremont Park is high, overlooking the mountains and the entire city. Thousands were here to greet Col. R. We were directly under the Col. when he spoke. It was very impressive."[3]

Roosevelt made no mention of the Remington memorial fund, however. After Teddy's political oration, Eva and the multitude were treated to an authentic western rodeo, which in her diary Eva called "cowboy sports," commenting on the fierceness of a bucking buffalo. As she made ready for bed that evening, she wrote her only comment about the proposed memorial: "At the governor's dinner Col. R said a lot about Frederic." Almost as an afterthought, she added that

Roosevelt "had mentioned that I was in town."[4] For these brief moments, she had traveled all those weary miles to Cheyenne, had waited
so eagerly to hear with her own ears what the man Fred had honored
and revered would say about her husband.

Although Eva did not yet realize it, Frederic Remington's slide
to oblivion had begun. Eva, who had no pretensions about her own
importance, was not disappointed for herself. Her purpose was to
make sure Frederic's memory was honored. And he certainly was
remembered, so far as she could tell, by the people she met, or whose
acquaintance she renewed in Cheyenne and later in Denver. She met
Mrs. James Garfield, the widow of the slain president, and talked
with Gifford Pinchot, proclaimed the father of the American conser-
vation movement. She did see Roosevelt in Denver for a few minutes; "he is very busy" was her only observation on the interview.
Before she left the Brown Palace Hotel in Denver for her return
home, the proprietor promised to make a contribution to the Remington memorial fund and said that the hotel would hold an exhibition of Frederic's work, if Eva would send the paintings west at her
own expense. This, she found as soon as she reviewed her financial
condition, was impossible.

As the months dragged on, Eva was yet to find a biographer to
record her husband's life and to see fruition of the fine schemes that
his friends had helped to set in motion. Many contributed to the
memorial fund, which Davenport was managing, and all seemed enthusiastic about the biography. For a time, Eva consulted with the
Century Company about their sponsoring and publishing the biography, but this also came to nothing. At year's end, she still was
making inquiries, and so far no writer or publisher had come forward. She conscientiously continued to compile information for the
book and to approach people for contributions to the fund. But, by
the beginning of 1911, the world would turn its attentions elsewhere.

In 1910 and each year thereafter while she remained at Ridgefield, Eva traveled north to spend time in Canton and Ogdensburg.
That first year of widowhood, prior to her trip west, Eva began to
emerge a little from her mourning when she was in the North Country. In Canton at the Sackrider home, she struggled with the still
nearly impossible concept that Frederic lay beneath the big tree in
the cemetery, with its carefully tended gravesite and the wreaths of
everlastings placed near his headstone. As she visited Aunt Minnie
Ellsworth, talked with Jim Johnson, or walked up the Hill to see Dr.
Gunnison at St. Lawrence about giving the college Fred's cap and

gown, it seemed more likely that her husband was away on one of his western jaunts.

It was somewhat easier in Ogdensburg. Here, she visited quietly with friends; went with Mrs. Grant Madill to see the additions to the city hospital made possible by Barton Hepburn; dined with the Howards. She could not bear the idea of making a trip upriver to the islands or of seeing Ingleneuk again. But all her friends and acquaintances in Ogdensburg made her feel welcome, and the first stray thoughts about eventually moving north flickered in her mind.

Back at Ridgefield in 1910, she learned from George Wright that it would be unwise to move from Lorul Place before she sold the house. "I must keep it attractive," she reminded herself and firmly set about seeing that the place was properly kept, the fields harvested, the pigs sold, the butter churned, the garden produce canned and preserved.[5] She read a great deal in her lonely hours, even dipping into the Swedish mystic Emanuel Swedenborg. Occasionally, she entertained friends in a modest way. With her sister Emma gone, Ridgefield was a hauntingly lonely place. She could hardly wait for word that Emma would return. Emily Hepburn's frequent visits became ever more important. The Hepburns were thoughtful people, calling often together or dropping in alone or with one of the children. Eva was delighted to see Barton and his daughter Cordelia one particularly difficult day: "It's not agreeable to stay alone. It's not good for one. I shall be glad when Emma gets here." And, when Emma finally did arrive, "I am awfully glad to have her here."[6]

Her financial affairs were far from secure. Fred and she had not even had time to adjust their economics to life in Ridgefield after their move to Lorul Place in May 1909. She had no realistic basis on which to determine exactly what life there would cost. And now she was without her former provider. Knoedler's wrote to say they had an offer of eighteen hundred dollars for a painting (not identified in her diary), but "I refused it. Will NOT sell them cheap."[7] She needed every dollar such sales could reap and realized that the paintings would increase in value with no new Remingtons forthcoming to swell the market ever again. She had made the decision that she and Bertelli would keep the molds for the bronzes and that the Roman Bronze Works would continue to produce (and Tiffany to sell) the Remington sculptures. When she eventually drew up a new and final will, Eva included a clause that on her own death all the forms from which the bronzes were cast should be smashed and destroyed.

Eva thought carefully about how to thank good friends who had helped her through the difficult first months of widowhood. Once the *Broncho Buster* had been sent to Will Wheelock, she turned her mind to determining how to show her appreciation for her lawyer, George Wright. She decided to give him a sketch Frederic had made of author Julian Ralph. George had accompanied Ralph and Remington on a hunting and fishing trip to Canada one winter. She also could not resist the plea of a St. Louis schoolboy who begged for a sketch by her husband. And she continued methodically to sort her husband's books and other belongings. Remington had never bothered to organize his library, and this complicated her own orderly methods.

By late 1910, Eva began to go about a bit socially. She lunched at the Hepburns' New York home in company with the Cass Gilberts and Howard Pyle, who turned out to be "much different than I expected . . . a perfect society gentleman in the way of good manners, breeding, etc."[8] Pyle charmed her and she met him several times thereafter when he was visiting friends in the art community. Eva saw the Emmetts and Biddles (both men artist friends of her husband) and Dana Gibson. Pa and Jen (Jennings) Cox visited. The friends she and Fred had made through the years remained loyal, and these other artists knew Remington's artistic worth.

However, she found others were not true to a memory. She had one disturbing piece of news, sent by her mother-in-law: a plagiarism of *John Ermine* was on the road, playing theaters in small upstate villages. Louie Shipman, who had persuaded Remington to let him turn the novel into a mediocre play, failed to answer her frantic queries for advice. Another disappointment soon followed. She had hoped that Knoedler's would hold another Remington exhibition that December, but Roland Knoedler gently ushered her out the door. As Christmas approached, she gratefully accepted Ella and Frank Mills's invitation to spend that first holiday period without Fred on their Massachusetts farm. On December 25 at their house she wrote in her diary, "I have gotten through the day very well," but she could not help but recall events of just a year before, when Frederic lay dying, no matter how sternly she chided herself "to be as cheerful as possible" and "not to make other people unhappy or pour out . . . troubles on other people."[9]

On New Year's Eve, Eva confided to her journal, "The year has been one of great moment for me. . . . Frederic has been taken away . . . and all my life entirely changed. . . . The year has not been one of financial success . . . there has been a general exposure of business and things not having been conducted along honest lines."[10]

Her old world continued to slip away in the years ahead. In May 1912, she wrote in her diary: "so many men of the artistic world have passed away in the last three years—Frederic, [Edwin] Abbey, [Howard] Pyle, Frank Millet, [Homer] Davenport, [Charles] Schreyvogel."[11] Davenport had died penniless, and the small moneys collected for the ill-fated illusory Remington monument were forwarded to Eva, who conscientiously returned them to the donors. Knoedler's continued to sell the paintings, and Tiffany continued to sell the bronzes. No home had been found for the Indian collection, nor had a writer emerged for the biography. Eva had been hurt to receive only a curt note from Owen Wister's secretary when she again asked him to write her husband's life story. Eva's last desperate ploy to have the biography written was to beg Frederic's cousin Charles Remington, the elder of Uncle Mart's two sons, to agree to take on the task. Charlie had wandered west and was working on a newspaper in southern California.[12] Nothing came of her request, even when she contacted him in person while touring the South and West with the John Howards and Emma that year.

Ironically, now that Frederic was gone, Eva herself became a traveler. During his lifetime, she seldom had accompanied him on his trips, the whirlwind pace with which he moved having proved too strenuous for her lesser energies. Between 1910 and 1915, Eva and her sister Emma Caten traveled together first to Europe, and then on the trip through the South and West with John and Charlotte Howard. Sometimes, Eva took short trips, such as a five-day vacation in Atlantic City or a short visit in Pittsburgh and on to Dayton, Ohio, to stay with her brother Frederick's family. While in Dayton in 1913, she received a clipping from her maid, Annie, about the burning of the Hepburn's Ridgefield home (Altnacraig was restored immediately thereafter). She continued making her usual summer trips to Canton and to Ogdensburg. On one such visit, she was serenaded late one night by members of a St. Lawrence fraternity and lay abed, watching the moonlight Frederic had so loved to paint filter softly through the open window while the young men's voices filled the night air.

As time passed, Eva gradually reentered the circle of friends in Ridgefield who welcomed her return to social life. Emily Hepburn, as usual up to her dignified neck in all kinds of worthy causes, inveigled Eva to attend local women's suffrage meetings. From these, Eva emerged a convert and followed the struggles of the cause closely thereafter, although she did not live to vote herself. She also read about national politics with close attention, and as war became imminent in Europe voiced her dismay at that "awful European war." She still went to New York City to see friends, conduct business, and attend plays and the opera. But the richness and flavor of bygone years eluded her; none of the delicious excitement and enjoyment spiced life as it had when Frederic was alive. Although Eva took pleasure in many of the small events at Ridgefield, she lived now on a dreary gray plateau, compared with the peaks and valleys of excitement and separation, pleasure and pain, of the whirlwind days with Fred.

Small happenings loomed large in her quiet life. Betsey Caten Deuval, Eva's great-niece, the grandaughter of Will Caten, is one of the surviving members of the Remington/Caten tribe. Betsey was able to elaborate on one of the small, but to Eva and Emma momentous, events that Eva noted in her diary. Young Leonard Caten became engaged to Adelaide McAllister (Betsey's mother) in 1914 and took his fiancée to meet his two aunts in Ridgefield. Leonard, who was attending St. Lawrence (as his father Will Caten had in the 1880s), had met Adelaide at college. The young couple arrived on a late afternoon train at the Ridgefield depot, one wintry day, just as a soft snowstorm enveloped the countryside.

"Mother never forgot the sight," Betsey relates. "Up to the station drove two tiny ladies, bundled in furs and hats and a fur robe, drawn in a sleigh pulled by the stout pony, named Pinto. Aunt Eva and Aunt Emma softly embraced, kissed and patted my father and my mother over and over again in their excited pleasure. They were such ladies. My mother told me they were darlings, both of them."[13] In addition to knowing the Remingtons only through the memory of other family members, Betsey can hardly recall her own father, Leonard, who died during her childhood. But Betsey knew Emma well, and she often traveled from her home in Gouverneur to visit her great-aunt in Ogdensburg. Through Emma Caten's eyes, Betsey learned to know and love both the long dead Eva and her artist uncle. Emma impressed on young Betsey the need to memorialize Remington, and she charged her young great-niece to carry on Eva's and her own mission. Betsey was shown her Uncle Frederic and Aunt Eva's wills by Emma, who explained in detail what Eva really wished the North Country world to remember about her husband. For, as the years slowly moved by after Frederic's death, it became clear to Eva that the greater world no longer cared about either her husband or his art.

At Ridgefield, by 1914, the remaining visible ties to Frederic had all but disappeared. Sandy, the collie that Fred complained about continuously but so loved, died. Despite the supportive ministrations of the Hepburns and other friends, Lorul Place became more and more of an emotional and financial burden. As the strain of keeping it up grew, Eva was drawn more strongly to the North Country, where Frederic was still remembered. She finally decided to lend the Indian collection to Ogdensburg's Public Library. Always loyal to Frederic's memory, John Howard and his professional superior, George Hall, agreed to help raise the necessary funds so that the Indian artifacts could be displayed attractively. Eva herself asked friends of Frederic's to contribute.

It was decided that the Indian collection would be moved to its new home in 1915. One room at the Ogdensburg Public Library was to be renovated to hold the collection and a carpenter hired to construct display cases. Early that year, Eva journeyed north twice to oversee the project, supervising the final arrangements and hanging some of the objects herself. It was an exhausting but satisfying labor of love; she was well satisfied with the results. Gleefully, in early summer 1915, Eva personally conducted a tour of the exhibit before its official opening for Fred's Ogdensburg friend, Ned Strong, and for Will Wheelock, who was visiting the North Country and had come to Ogdensburg especially to see her.

The Lorul Place house had been on the market most of the time since Frederic Remington's death. By early spring 1915, as she planned the packing of the Indian collection, the house was sold to a Miss Louisa Hauser, who arrived to inspect her new property and to purchase some of Eva's unneeded furniture. Eva wrote to John Howard to find a home for her in Ogdensburg and returned to packing, not only the Indian collection but her own belongings as well. When she walked out of the front door of Lorul Place for the last time, it was with no regret. The Ridgefield home that Eva and Frederic had dreamed of, planned for, and worked so hard to bring to fruition through three long difficult years had been a happy place for only a few months. Since her husband's death, it had been a financial burden and an overwhelming responsibility.

With Eva's departure from their midst, Remington's memory

faded quickly from both the community at Ridgefield and the art world in New York. Ridgefield friends sincerely mourned the Remingtons, especially Barton and Emily Hepburn, who could—after all—visit Eva only on their trips to the North Country. New York City was different. After the famed Armory Show in 1913, which marked the arrival of a new and different approach to art, the artist of the Old West and his works were soon relegated to a forgotten past. Only in the little North Country city of Ogdensburg did excitement remain for St. Lawrence County's most prominent artist, and even here he had detractors who criticized his personality and largely ignored his work. The acclaim Remington's work did receive in the North Country came largely through Eva and Emma's efforts and from his old friends' loyalty to his memory.

John Howard was able to find a home for Eva and her sister Emma. This loyal friend persuaded George Hall to lease the Parish Mansion on Washington Street, which Hall owned and where he had once lived, to Eva for a nominal sum. Thus, the two women took up residence in the historic mansion that stands across from the public library where Eva had so carefully arranged Frederic's Indian collection. Eva and Emma placed their furniture and Frederic's remaining paintings and bronzes in the high-ceilinged rooms where George Parish and his mysterious Ameriga Vespucci had once maintained their discreet relationship.

Here, Eva and Emma lived for the next two years. At first, Eva took part in community affairs, occasionally delivering lectures about her husband's life and work to library or other groups. At times, she traveled to Canton for a visit with old friends, but Frederic's relatives were gone and the village was a place of bittersweet memories. Now, she and Emma centered their affections on their nieces and nephews, of whom only Will's son Leonard was nearby, still a student at St. Lawrence University. The advent of World War I in Europe added to the strains that already had sapped Eva's strength. Leonard Caten enlisted in the army after graduating from St. Lawrence and married Adelaide McAllister, the girl he had taken to visit at Ridgefield that snowy day three years before. Leonard, now in uniform, and Adelaide again arrived for a visit. Proudly, the little ladies showed the young couple through the stately rooms where Frederic's paintings hung and his bronzes stood on stands and tables. Then Leonard went off to fight in that dreadful war.

Eva's life waned quickly. Although she had not completed her self-imposed mission to achieve lasting recognition for her husband, she had found a home for Frederic's works and a place of repose for herself. Soon, the mansion proved to be unwieldy and expensive to maintain. In early 1918, the sisters moved to a house on the Crescent, and there Eva succumbed to her final illness. On November 2, only nine days before the Armistice, Eva died of cancer at fifty-eight. After funeral services at her home, her relatives and friends buried Eva beside Frederic under the big tree in Evergreen Cemetery in Canton, and Emma was left alone to carry on the mission to save Remington's name and work for posterity.[14]

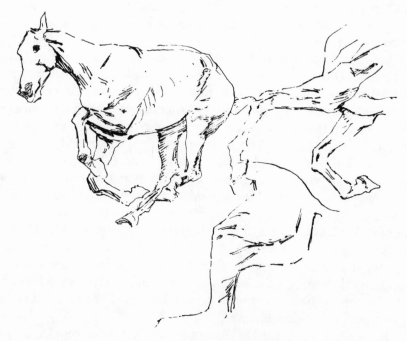

(Courtesy of Benton Board, Canton Free Library, Canton, N.Y.)

POSTLUDE

REMINGTON'S REBIRTH

Emma Caten never gave up working to ensure Frederic Remington's rightful place in history. After Eva's death, she moved into a small house in Ogdensburg, where she lived until her own death in 1957. She penned endless letters to publishing houses, continuing Eva's search for a biographer. She kept a careful eye on the Indian collection and the other Remington treasures now entrusted to the community. This once frail little woman was indomitable and, over the years, won the respect of Ogdensburg for her rectitude and abilities.

The Remington Museum opened in 1923 in the former Parish Mansion. Thanks once again to John Howard, funds were raised to augment the terms of Eva's will, which had bequeathed Remington bronzes, paintings, and other memorabilia remaining in her possession to the Ogdensburg Free Library. The Indian collection was moved from the library to the new Remington Museum, along with other Remington papers and mementos, including Fred's journals of the last three years of his life. Emma kept some of Eva's effects, including her private diaries, which covered the years after her husband's death, and a small, unsigned bronze of a nude woman (see illustrations), which always thereafter remained on a stand in Emma's entrance hall.

With the advent of the Great Depression, Ogdensburg's Remington Museum, along with other North Country institutions, struggled to survive. Eva's bequest to the public library helped to cover only a modicum of staff and maintenance. Ogdensburg's city government, which allocated money to the institution, had to tighten the city budget drastically in the 1930s, and the museum, despite the best intentions of community leaders, was not a high governmental priority. If it had not been for a coterie of faithful people, dedicated to preserving and passing on the North Country's cultural and historical tradition, the little institution's doors might have closed forever.

For the next thirty years, North Country people traveled to Ogdensburg to show their children the paintings, bronzes, and Indian relics left by the Remingtons. Stray tourists found the largely unpublicized museum by chance or through word of mouth. World War II invaded the North Country as its people struggled to recover from the Depression. The patriotic spirit that had prevailed through nearly 150 years of North Country history once again asserted itself, and most North Country boys went off to war. During those stressful years, there was neither time nor energy to pay attention to long ago battles for a vanished frontier memorialized by Frederic Remington. The Ogdensburg museum languished almost unnoted except for the ministrations of Emma Caten and the interest of a few local people.

Farther afield, Frederic Remington and his art were almost forgotten. In Hollywood in those years, producers of Westerns sometimes looked to old Remington paintings to provide inspiration for the black-and-white movies they churned out, especially the B productions. Across America at Saturday matinees youngsters often gained a stereotypical knowledge of the Old West from these pictures, where the cowboys were "good" and the Indians "bad."

Here and there, a few devotees of the Old West looked more deeply into the myths and heroes of the vanished frontier and remembered the nineteenth-century men who had recorded them. Walter Latendorf, a western devotee, opened a small secondhand bookstore in Manhattan in the early 1940s featuring Western Americana, which he named Manados.[1]

A trickle of people began to frequent Manados, mostly men living or working in New York who had become intrigued with the history and legends of the West. By the mid-1940s, a circle of men gathered around a big table in the main room each Thursday at the end of the workday to trade western stories, to drink generously of Walter's good whisky supply, to sing old Western songs to a mandolin, and then to eat together in a nearby restaurant.[2]

The core group was small, but other buffs who heard about the group, such as Jeff Dykes of College Park, Maryland, sat at Latendorf's round table every time business took them to New York or a day off allowed them to indulge their hobby. A spry and alert eighty-seven when interviewed in 1987, Dykes recalled the men he met at Latendorf's when he joined the regulars. Among the circle were Nick Eggenhofer, a latter-day western illustrator, and artist/sculptor Mahonri Young, grandson of Brigham Young. The mandolin player was a banker from New Jersey. Another regular was Douglas Allen, a public relations man in a New York–based oil company. A Columbia University professor named Harold McCracken was also in the group, along with Latendorf, and the only woman among them, Helen (Teri) Card, a free-lance writer and dealer in western Americana, and Walter Latendorf's assistant and girlfriend.[3]

Interest in the Old West was growing in other places. In 1944, in Chicago, a group of western enthusiasts organized themselves into a "Corral." Within the next two years, similar groups formed in St. Louis, Denver, and Los Angeles, and, in 1952, a New York Corral was formed, its nucleus the Latendorf roundtable group. From this beginning grew Westerners International, which now has its headquarters in Tucson, and lists among its members many prominent people across the country who are enthusiastic students and supporters of the western heritage.[4]

After World War II, the times were ripe for Western art to achieve a place of prominence. The country enjoyed an economic boom and money was plentiful. In Texas and the Southwest, the expanding oil industry produced new wealth. Tourism became a national industry, and travelers learned about the western past as America began to seek its roots. Interest in local and regional history sharpened, encouraged by new leisure for all as well as by public funding and private philanthropy. The newly affluent were eager to indulge new hobbies such as collecting Western art, to avoid taxes through gifts to charity, and later to hedge against inflation.

Frederic Remington's art became "collectible," in part through efforts of art dealers in New York and in the West whom the new collectors consulted. The dealers began to search diligently for original Remington paintings and bronzes, still extant in remote places. The writing of Harold McCracken and Douglas Allen of the original Latendorf bookstore circle helped to increase public interest in Western art and particularly in Frederic Remington.

In the 1940s, Emma Caten's long search for a biographer of her brother-in-law ended. She wrote yet another letter to a Philadelphia publisher, requesting that a book be written about Frederic Remington. An alert staff member at J. B. Lippincott forwarded her letter to Harold McCracken in New York, where, in addition to his teaching duties and his weekly visits to the Latendorf circle, he did freelance editorial work for the Philadelphia publishing firm. The vital connection was finally made, almost thirty years after Eva Remington had first begun her search for a way to memorialize Frederic.

McCracken traveled to the North Country to obtain information for a Remington biography from Emma Caten and other sources she recommended. By then, Emma was aging and relied on her memory, sometimes unable to recall sources of certain details that she passed on to McCracken. In addition, little cataloging of Remington archival information, much of which was still stored in boxes in the museum, had been done. While many pieces of Remington art still lay forgotten in musty North Country attics (and other bits of information lay untapped in the minds of people who still remembered Remington or in yellowed newspaper files or clippings and memorabilia in many of those same attics), McCracken gathered what information he could. With the publication of his biography of Remington in 1947 and with growing interest in the artist's works, the revival of Frederic Remington began.

McCracken, as literary midwife, became an authority on Remington and was later named director of the Whitney Gallery of Western Art in Cody, Wyoming*—now a part of the Buffalo Bill Historical Center—where he remained until his retirement. Other authors, including McCracken's Manados colleague Douglas Allen, soon added to the written record.[5] (With his son, Allen compiled the first complete listing of the then known published illustrations and bronzes by Frederic Remington and, like McCracken, visited the North Country, where for a short time he served as director of the Ogdensburg museum.[6])

In 1983 when the idea of our book was born, other biographies and books had been written about Frederic Remington and his art. Scholars and biographers had already said much about the man Remington, and more about his works and western experiences. We felt that the books and articles about Fred Remington that we had read were two-dimensional, still lacking another background against which more

---

*When the financially pressed Remington Museum in Ogdensburg was forced to sell Remington's Indian artifacts and some of the paintings, McCracken arranged for the Whitney Gallery to purchase them. Now much of Eva's bequest to Ogdensburg is displayed in the Far West.

of Remington's personality could be revealed. In none of them, for instance, was Eva more than a shadow.

As Peg scurried here and there at Atwood's behest, wrote countless letters, and made endless phone calls to ferret out information necessary to authenticate Atwood's leads for this book, both Frederic and Eva began to take on new dimensions. (And so did their families and their North Country friends.) They emerged finally as vital, living people in the Gouverneur living room of Betsey Caten Deuval.

As a little girl, Betsey Caten went often with her widowed mother to visit Emma, her great-aunt whom she loved dearly, and by whom she was dearly loved in return. Through Aunt Em, the persons of Uncle Fred and Aunt Eva became more and more real as she heard old stories repeated, stories that revealed yet another aspect of these two with each telling. As Emma grew old, Betsey also received instructions to continue Eva's and Emma's mission. And it was for this that Betsey Caten Deuval opened these hidden and private doors of Emma's memories to us, so that we could find out more about who Frederic and Eva Remington really were and are.

One question remains, however, that neither Betsey's memories from Aunt Em nor research nor speculation can answer: How did Frederic Remington himself view his work, his life, and himself? He did not live in an introspective age and was not an introspective man. We have, however, perhaps a partial answer. It is from a letter owned by Corning's Rockwell Museum of Western Art. In 1891, Fred wrote to a young Californian, Maynard Dixon, who wanted his advice about becoming an artist: "Art is not a profession which will make you rich but it might make you happy. Its voteries are all sacrifices, but you are the master of your own destinies."[7]

CHRONOLOGY AND GENEALOGY

1861   January 8—Seth Pierpont Remington, Clara B. Sackrider marry

October 4—Frederic Sackrider Remington born

1866   Remingtons move to Albany

1867   Remingtons move to Bloomington, Illinois

1868   Remingtons return to Canton

Colonel Remington rebuys *Plaindealer*

1870   Colonel Remington appointed collector of the port of Oswegatchie, Ogdensburg

1872   Remingtons move to Ogdensburg

1873   Colonel Remington sells *Plaindealer*

1875   Frederic Remington attends Vermont Episcopal Institute

1876   Attends Highland Military Academy

1878   Enters Yale University Art School

1879   Meets Eva A. Caten at Canton's annual county fair

1880   February 20—Colonel Pierre Remington dies

Spring—Remington moves to Albany, works in government offices

1881   August—Travels to Montana on two-month trip

1883   March—Buys ranch at Peabody, Butler County, Kansas

1884   April—Is established in business in Kansas City

October 1—Marries Eva Caten in Gloversville; couple lives in Kansas City in Pendleton Heights

December—Eva returns east

1885   Summer—Travels in Southwest

September—Returns east, takes Eva to Canton

October—Couple moves to Brooklyn

December—Sells first two illustrations to *Harper's Weekly*

1886   January—First signed illustration published in *Harper's Weekly*

Spring—Travels to Southwest

1887   February—Enters painting in annual exhibition of American Watercolor Society

Spring—Has painting in National Academy of Design Exhibition

—Travels to Canadian Northwest

Midyear—*Century* assignment to illustrate Roosevelt serial

Late fall—Moves to Manhattan

1888   March—National Academy of Design Exhibition

May—Travels to Southwest and Colorado

June—Travels to Texas

December—Houghton Mifflin hires to illustrate *Hiawatha*

1889   Winter—Travels in Mexico

Spring—*The Lull in the Fight* wins second prize at Paris International Exposition

June—Remingtons spend month at Witch Bay, Cranberry Lake, where Remington works on *Hiawatha* illustrations

1890   April—Moves to Webster Avenue, New Rochelle

—Holds one-man exhibition at American Art Galleries

—Painting hung in National Academy of Design

Summer—Travels in Southwest, California, and Canadian Northwest

December—Accompanies General Miles to South Dakota, Wounded Knee

1891   Spring—To Mexico with Miles and Eva

1892   Spring—Travels to Europe with Poultney Bigelow

Summer—Canoes on Oswegatchie River

1893   February—Travels to the Southwest and Mexico

Late summer—Meets Owen Wister

December—Travels to Southwest

1894   Canoe trip to Canada, fishing and hunting at Cranberry, possible trip to North Africa

1895   January—Begins *Broncho Buster*

October—Exhibition of copyrighted *Broncho Buster*

November—One-man exhibition of 114 paintings at National Academy of Design

1896   General Miles publishes memoirs with Remington illustrations

Publishes first book of drawings

December—Leaves for Cuba with Davis at Hearst's request

1897   Hearst publishes Davis/Remington reports and illustration that cause public uproar

	Spends vacation periods in North Country

Spends vacation periods in North Country
September—Travels to Wyoming as Buffalo Bill Cody's guest

1898   April through June—Reports on Spanish-American War from Flor-
         ida and Cuba
       July—Returns to New Rochelle ill

1899   *Harper's* ceases to use Remington
       Travels in West

1900   February—Travels to Yellowstone
       Begins to use Roman Bronze Works, Greenpoint, for bronze cast-
         ings
       Buys Ingleneuk in Thousand Islands, spends summer there
       October—Travels in Southwest

1901   Contract with *Collier's* assures annual income
       June through August—At Ingleneuk
       December—Exhibits fifteen paintings, ten pastels at Clausens

1902   Writes *John Ermine*
       Publishes *Done in the Open*
       Summers at Ingleneuk
       Collier's publishes four-color Remington art
       Produces *Comin' Through the Rye*

1903   Has first Knoedler's Art Gallery exhibit
       Fight for the Waterhole published in *Collier's*
       Produces bronze *Mountain Man*

1904   Travels to Mexico with John Howard in spring, to Newfoundland
         in July
       Summers at Ingleneuk
       Late fall—Returns to Cuba

1905   Second Knoedler exhibit, auction of ten old paintings
       Corcoran Gallery buys *Comin' Through the Rye* and *Mountain Man*
       Summers at Ingleneuk
       Cosmopolitan publishes *Way of an Indian* series
       Collier's publishes *Great Explorers* series
       Travels in Southwest
       Knoedler's holds annual exhibit of paintings, plus another one for
         Remington bronzes
       Is approached to create large statue for Fairmont Park, Philadelphia;
         makes preliminary model

1906   Models *The Outlaw* and *Paleolithic Man*

1907   Models small-scale *The Cowboy*
       Metropolitan Museum purchases four bronzes
       Travels in Southwest
       Summers at Ingleneuk
       Buys land in Ridgefield, Connecticut; hires architect

1908   Has mounting trouble over *Collier's* contract
        The Cowboy cast, opening in Philadelphia
        Decides to build on Ridgefield property
        Spends last summer at Ingleneuk
        Travels in West
        Highly sucessful Knoedler's painting exhibition
1909   Sells Ingleneuk and New Rochelle home
        Moves to Ridgefield, Connecticut, in mid-May
        Visits Canadian sportsman's club, Pontiac Club, with Eva
        Begins *The Stampede* in September
        November—Knoedler's exhibit
        December 20—Experiences severe stomach pains
        December 23—Emergency appendectomy at Ridgefield home
        December 26—Dies at 9:30 A.M.
        December 28—Funeral held in Canton

«————————————————»

THE REMINGTONS

Seth Williston Remington (1807–1881), married in 1826 to Maria Pickering (1809–1878); 6 children—Amanda M. (ca. 1827–ca. 1828), Chauncey P. (1829–1902), Maria L. (ca. 1831–183?), Seth Pierpont (see below), William Reese (see below), Lamartine Zetto (see below), and Josephine C. (1849–??).

Seth Pierpont (Pierre; the Colonel) Remington (1834–1880), married in 1861 to Clara (Clarissa) Bascomb Sackrider (1836–1912); 1 child—Frederic Sackrider (see below).

William Reese (Uncle Bill; W. R.) Remington (1839–1907), married in 1862 to Lavilla Everest (1844–1908); 2 children—George H. (1864–1907) and Ella (1867–19??; married in 1904 to Frank Mills).

Lamartine Zetto (Mart) Remington (1848–1884), married to Florence Stevens; 2 children—Charles (1876–1929) and Pierre (1882–1958).

Frederic Sackrider Remington (1861–1909), married in 1884 to Eva Adele Caten (1859–1918).

THE SACKRIDERS

Henry Lewis Sackrider (1809–1895), married in 1832 to Mary Hutchins (1815–1894); 4 children—Horace D. (see below), Clarissa Bascomb (see below), Robert H. (see below), and Frances (1860–1861).

Horace D. (Uncle Horace; Dude) Sackrider (1834–1890), married in 1863 to Marcia Haseltine (1836–1882).

Clara (Clarissa) Bascomb Sackrider (1836–1912), married in 1861 to Seth Pierpont Remington (1834–1880); 1 child—Frederic Sackrider (see above). Remarried in 1888 to Orrin Levis.

Robert H. (Uncle Yob; Rob; Bob) Sackrider (1845–1924), married in 1873 to Emma Merkley (1851–1935); 1 child—Henry M. (1877–19??).

THE CATENS

Lawton (1835–1905), married Flora Hoyt (1836–1880); 5 children—Eva Adele Caten (see Frederic Remington entry above), William L. (1861–1917; married to Adelaide McCallister), Clara Ella (1866–1930; married to Horatio L. Burr), Frederick A. (1866–1891), and Emma Louise (1869–1957). Lawton remarried to Sarah B. McCollum.

REFERENCE NOTES

Facts of publication for most books cited in these Notes can be found in the Bibliography.

The following abbreviations are used throughout the notes.

CORRESPONDENCE

fsr	Frederic Remington
ecr	Eva Caten Remington
hfa	Harriet Ferry Appleton
pb	Poultney Bigelow
pc	Lt. Powhatan Clarke
jh	John C. Howard
wap	William A. Poste
hp	Howard Pyle
tr	Theodore Roosevelt
hs	Horace Sackrider
ms	Marcia Sackrider
rs	Robert Sackrider
rt	Dr. Robert Taft
ow	Owen Wister

DIARIES OR JOURNALS

frj	Frederic Remington Journals
erj	Eva C. Remington Diaries
ecj	Emma L. Caten Diary

INDIVIDUALS AND INSTITUTIONS WITH OWNERSHIP OF SOURCES

BCD   Betsey Caten Deuval, Gouverneur, New York
CM   Rockwell Museum of Western Art, Corning, New York
GAM   G. Atwood Manley, Canton, New York
KSH   Kansas State Historical Society, Topeka, Kansas
LC   Library of Congress, Washington, D.C.
MMM   Margaret Manley Mangum, Henryville, Pennsylvania
OFL   Ogdensburg Free Library, Ogdensburg, New York
SLH   St. Lawrence County Historical Association, Canton, New York
SLU   St. Lawrence University, Canton, New York
RAM   Remington Art Museum, Ogdensburg, New York

INTRODUCTION

1. frj 1908, RAM.
2. Irving Bacheller, *From Stores of Memory,* pp. 10–12.
3. Ibid.
4. Ibid.

1: CALAMITY IN KANSAS CITY

1. Nellie Hough Boyd, "Remington at Twenty-three," *International Studio,* February 1923.
2. Ibid.
3. fsr to Arthur F. Merkley, December 29, 1883. McCracken collection, SLU.
4. Last will and testament of Seth Pierpont Remington, St. Lawrence County Surrogate's Office, Canton, New York.
5. fsr to Merkley, December 29, 1883.
6. hfa to rt, circa 1950, KSH.
7. Boyd, "Remington at Twenty-three."
8. Interview with BCD; also, erj 1910, BCD.
9. Boyd, "Remington at Twenty-three."
10. Ibid.
11. Ibid.
12. hfa to rt, circa 1950.
13. Ibid.
14. David Dary, "Kansas City, Cradle of Remington's Art," *Kansas City Star Magazine,* May 3, 1925. OFL.
15. hfa to rt, circa 1950.
16. Undated clipping, *Carthage Evening Press,* OFL.
17. Boyd, "Remington at Twenty-three."
18. Ibid.

19. Ibid.
20. "Dim Beginnings of Remington," *Kansas City Star Magazine*, February 5, 1911. OFL.
21. "Kansas City, Cradle of Remington's Art."
22. Ibid.

2: EARLY CHILDHOOD: "I ALWAYS LIKED HORSES" (1861–1869)

1. Irving Bacheller, *From Stores of Memory*.
2. Ibid.
3. Letter of Arthur B. Holmes to *Ogdensburg Journal*, February 28, 1880.
4. The entire account of this action comes from Thomas West Smith, *The Story of a Cavalry Regiment: Scott's 900*. (The specific copy of the book that we consulted is carefully preserved at Canton's Free Library; it, and others in the collection, belonged to Frederic Remington.)
5. Emma L. Caten, *Remington-Caten Family Histories*.
6. Holmes to *Ogdensburg Journal*, February 28, 1880.
7. fsr to Scott Turner, in *Collier's Weekly*, 1910.
8. Atwood Manley, *Frederic Remington in the Land of His Youth*.
9. Ibid.
10. Atwood Manley interview with Henry Merkley Sackrider, 1961.
11. Manley, *Frederic Remington in the Land of His Youth*.
12. William A. Poste, unpublished memoirs, SLH.
13. Helmut Lehmann-Haupt, *The Book in America*.

3: THE YOUTH: ENDINGS MAKE NEW BEGINNINGS (1861–1879)

1. Atwood Manley, *Frederic Remington in the Land of His Youth*.
2. Ibid.
3. Ibid.
4. Ibid; also *Ogdensburg Journal*, OFL.
5. Seth Pierpont Remington to fsr, 1873, RAM.
6. Manley, *Frederic Remington in the Land of His Youth*.
7. Daughters of the American Revolution, Swe-Kat-Si Chapter, *Reminiscences of Ogdensburg: 1749–1907*.
8. Original invoices, 1870s–1880s, SLH.
9. Mary Barnett, *A Random Scoot*.
10. William A. Poste, unpublished memoirs, SLH.
11. Barnett, *A Random Scoot*.
12. Irving Bacheller, *From Stores of Memory*.
13. *Ogdensburg Journal*, August 4, 1930, OFL.
14. Ibid.
15. *Ogdensburg Advance*, November 1916, OFL.

16. Ibid.
17. Robert Taft, unpublished manuscript, KSH.
18. *Ogdensburg Advance,* November 1916, OFL.
19. fsr to jh, 1875, RAM.
20. Taft, manuscript.
21. *Collier's Weekly,* September 17, 1910.
22. fsr to hs, 1878, SLU.
23. Ibid. Here and throughout, Frederic Remington's spelling and punctuation have occasionally been corrected for the sake of clarity.
24. *New York Herald,* January 14, 1894, in Taft Papers, KSH.

4: EXIT CHILDHOOD; ENTER EVA (1879–1884)

1. St. Lawrence University, *General Catalog of the Officers, Graduates, and Non-Graduates: 1856–1926,* SLU.
2. *St. Lawrence Plaindealer* files.
3. St. Lawrence University, *General Catalog.*
4. *St. Lawrence Plaindealer* and *Commercial Advertiser* files.
5. *Ogdensburg Journal,* March 1915.
6. *Ogdensburg Journal,* March 7, 1880.
7. fsr to ms and hs, 1880, SLU.
8. St. Lawrence County Surrogate's Office records.
9. *Ogdensburg Journal,* 1891.
10. fsr to Lawton Caten, August 25, 1880, RAM.
11. fsr to hs, 1882, SLU.
12. Peter H. Hassrick, *Frederic Remington: Paintings, Drawings and Sculpture in the Amon Carter Museum and the Sid W. Richardson Foundation Collections.*
13. William Rasbeck, unpublished diaries, SLU.
14. Painting owned by RAM.
15. fsr to hs, 1883–1889, SLU.
16. *Albany Morning Express,* 1883, GAM and OFL.
17. *Malone* [N.Y.] *Palladium,* 1884, OFL.
18. fsr to Arthur F. Merkley, 1883, SLU.
19. Peggy and Harold Samuels, "Frederic Remington's Stirrings in Kansas City," KSH.

5: "HE GOES LIKE THE WIND" (1885–1886)

1. J. Henry Harper, *The House of Harper: A History.*
2. Joseph Bucklin Bishop, *A. Barton Hepburn: His Life and Service to His Time*; and Isabelle Keating Savell, *Daughter of Vermont: A Biography of Emily Eaton Hepburn.*
3. Ibid.

4. St. Lawrence University, *General Catalog of the Officers, Graduates, and Non-Graduates: 1856–1926*, SLU; GAM notes.
5. Irving Bacheller, *From Stores of Memory*.
6. Brooklyn Museum, *The American Renaissance: 1876–1917*.
7. Quotation from letter of William James in ibid.
8. Quotation from letter of Henry Adams in ibid.
9. Interview with BCD.
10. erj, 1910–1915, BCD.
11. Ibid.
12. Brooklyn Museum, *American Renaissance*.
13. Ibid.
14. Mark Sullivan, *Our Times: The United States 1900–1925*.
15. GAM notes; Helmut Lehmann-Haupt, *The Book in America*.
16. hfa to rt, KSH.
17. Peter H. Hassrick, *Frederic Remington: Paintings, Drawings and Sculpture in the Amon Carter Museum and the Sid W. Richardson Foundation Collections*.
18. Peggy and Harold Samuels, eds., *The Collected Writings of Frederic Remington*.
19. Harper, *The House of Harper*.
20. ecr to hs, 1890, SLU.
21. Nelson A. Miles, *Personal Recollections and Observations of General Nelson A. Miles*.
22. Savell, *Daughter of Vermont*.
23. ecr to hs, SLU.
24. fsr to pc, RAM.
25. Lehmann-Haupt, *The Book in America*.
26. erj, 1910–1915, BCD.
27. frj, 1909, RAM.
28. Savell, *Daughter of Vermont*.
29. frj, 1909, RAM.
30. Nellie Hough Boyd, "Remington at Twenty-three." *International Studio*, February 1923.
31. fsr to ecr, 1880s and 1890s, SLU.
32. hfa to rt, KSH; ecr to hs, SLU; interviews with BCD.

6: DREAMS SOMETIMES COME TRUE (1886–1890)

1. erj, 1910, BCD.
2. ecr to hs, 1888–1890, SLU.
3. ecr to hs, 1888–1890, SLU.
4. Irving Bacheller, *From Stores of Memory*.
5. ecr to hs, 1888–1890, SLU.

6. Isabelle Keating Savell, *Daughter of Vermont: A Biography of Emily Eaton Hepburn.*
7. hfa to rt, KSH; telephone interview with Charles W. Appleton.
8. Bacheller, *From Stores of Memory.*
9. fsr to pc, RAM.
10. Ibid.
11. fsr to pc, RAM.
12. ecr to hs, SLU.
13. Ibid.
14. erj, 1909, BCD.
15. erj, 1912, BCD.
16. ecr to hs, 1888, SLU.
17. fsr to rs, 1888, SLU.
18. fsr to pc, RAM.
19. fsr to wap, SLU.
20. frj, 1909, RAM.
21. ecr to hs, SLU.
22. hfa to rt, KSH, and telephone interview with Charles W. Appleton.
23. fsr to pc, RAM.
24. Van Wyck Brooks, *The Confident Years: 1885–1915*; Peggy and Harold Samuels, eds., *The Collected Writings of Frederic Remington.*
25. Lewis Spence, *North American Indians: Myths and Legends.*
26. Atwood Manley, *Frederic Remington in the Land of His Youth.*
27. Ibid.

7: GOOD TIMES AT ENDION (1890–1895)

1. fsr to pc, RAM.
2. Ibid.
3. fsr to ms, SLU.
4. *Ogdensburg Journal*, OFL.
5. ecr to hs, SLU.
6. fsr to pc, RAM.
7. Atwood Manley, "Frederic Remington," in *Cranberry Lake, from Wilderness to Adirondack Park*, ed. Albert Fowler.
8. *St. Lawrence Plaindealer*, 1881.
9. Manley, "Frederic Remington."
10. Marshall Howlett Durston, "The Durston Diaries," in *Cranberry Lake*, ed. Fowler.
11. fsr to pc, RAM.
12. ecr to hs, SLU.
13. *Ogdensburg Journal*, March 1915, report on ecr lecture.
14. fsr to pc, RAM.

15. Allen P. Splete and Marilyn D. Splete, eds., *Frederic Remington— Selected Letters*.
16. fsr to pc, RAM.
17. William Rasbeck, unpublished diaries, SLU; Atwood Manley, "Bill Rasbeck's Diaries," in *Cranberry Lake,* ed. Fowler.
18. Manley, "Bill Rasbeck's Diaries."
19. Isabelle Keating Savell, *Daughter of Vermont: A Biography of Emily Eaton Hepburn*; Joseph Bucklin Bishop, *A. Barton Hepburn: His Life and Service to His Time*.
20. Irving Bacheller, *From Stores of Memory*.
21. fsr to pc, SLU.
22. fsr to pb, SLU.
23. Ibid.
24. William Rasbeck, unpublished diaries, SLU; Manley, chap. 3, "Bill Rasbeck's Diaries."
25. Savell, *Daughter of Vermont*.
26. fsr to Joel Burdick, in *Adirondack Life,* 1987.
27. fsr to rs, SLU.
28. Bishop, *A. Barton Hepburn*.
29. Savell, *Daughter of Vermont*.
30. Ibid.
31. hfa to rt, KSH.
32. fsr to pb, SLU.

8: MESSING WITH MUD AND SEEING A WAR (1895–1898)

1. fsr to ow, LC.
2. Ibid.
3. fsr to pb, SLU.
4. Ibid.
5. Michael Edward Shapiro, *Bronze Casting and American Sculpture*.
6. Douglas Allen, *Frederic Remington's Own Outdoors*.
7. Ibid.
8. fsr to ow, LC.
9. Rudyard Kipling to fsr, SLU.
10. Poultney Bigelow, article in *Outlook,* January 8, 1910.
11. fsr to pb, SLU.
12. fsr to ow, LC.
13. fsr to pb, SLU.
14. Ronald F. Fieve, *Mood Swings*.
15. frj, 1907–1909, RAM.
16. GAM notes.
17. Shapiro, *Bronze Casting*.
18. fsr to ow, LC.

19. A. A. Brolley to fsr, 1895, SLU.
20. William D. Howells to fsr, 1895, SLU.
21. fsr to ow, LC.
22. ow to fsr, 1895, LC.
23. 1895 American Art Association Catalog, *Frederic Remington*, RAM.
24. fsr to pb, SLU.
25. fsr to ow, LC.
26. Ibid.
27. fsr to pc, RAM.
28. Allen P. Splete and Marilyn D. Splete, eds., *Frederic Remington—Selected Letters*.
29. Ibid.
30. tr to fsr, SLU.
31. Splete and Splete, *Letters*.
32. fsr to pb, SLU.
33. fsr to Joel Burdick, in *Adirondack Life,* 1987.
34. frj, 1908–1909, RAM.
35. All materials included about Cuban history, except where indicated in specific notes, are from Margaret M. Mangum, *History and Culture of Cuba.*
36. Splete and Splete, *Letters*.
37. fsr and ecr correspondence, SLU; interview with BCD.
38. fsr to pc, RAM.
39. fsr to ecr, SLU.
40. fsr to pb, SLU.
41. *Ogdensburg Journal* clipping, n.d., OFL.
42. fsr to pb, SLU; Splete and Splete, *Letters*.
43. fsr to ow, LC.
44. Marshall Howlett Durston, "The Durston Diaries," in *Cranberry Lake, from Wilderness to Adirondack Park,* ed. Albert Fowler.
45. frj, 1908, RAM.
46. Peggy and Harold Samuels, eds., *The Collected Writings of Frederic Remington.*
47. Richard Harding Davis, *The Cuban and Porto Rican Campaigns.*
48. Frederic Remington, "Wigwags from the Blockade," *Harper's Weekly,* May 7, 1898.
49. Davis, *Campaigns.*
50. Irving Bacheller, *From Stores of Memory.*
51. Davis, *Campaigns.*
52. fsr to ecr, 1898, SLU.
53. fsr to ecr, 1898, SLU; Frederic Remington, "With the Fifth Corps," *Harper's Monthly,* November 1898.
54. GAM research notes, correspondence, unpublished writing.
55. fsr to ecr, SLU.

56. erj, 1910–1915, BCD.
57. Remington, "With the Fifth Corps."

9: NEW DIRECTIONS (1898–1907)

1. tr to fsr, SLU.
2. Frederic Remington, *Sun-Down LeFlare*; Peggy and Harold Samuels, eds., *The Collected Writings of Frederic Remington,* notes.
3. fsr to ow, 1899, LC.
4. Mark Sullivan, *Our Times: The United States 1900–1925.*
5. hp to fsr, SLU.
6. frj, 1908, RAM.
7. Ibid.
8. Ibid.
9. fsr to rs, 1899, SLU.
10. Joseph Bucklin Bishop, *A. Barton Hepburn: His Life and Service to His Time.*
11. fsr to ow, 1899, LC.
12. fsr to hp, SLU.
13. Edwin Wildman, "Frederic Remington, the Man," *Outlook,* March 1903.
14. Ibid.
15. frj, 1908, RAM.
16. Michael Edward Shapiro, *Bronze Casting and American Sculpture.*
17. frj, 1907, RAM.
18. Douglas Allen, ed., *Frederic Remington's Own Outdoors*; Bruce Wear, *The Bronze World of Frederic Remington.*
19. "Sarah J. Farnham, Sculptor, Is Dead," *The New York Times,* April 29, 1943.
20. frj, 1907, RAM.
21. frj, 1908, RAM.
22. Isabelle Keating Savell, *Daughter of Vermont: A Biography of Emily Eaton Hepburn.*
23. frj, 1907, RAM.
24. Ibid.
25. N. C. Wyeth, *The Wyeths,* ed. Betsy James Wyeth.

10: INGLENEUK AND THE PASSING PARADE (1900–1907)

1. GAM; Atwood Manley, *Rushton and His Times in American Canoeing.*
2. frj, 1908, RAM.
3. Allen P. Splete and Marilyn D. Splete, eds., *Frederic Remington— Selected Letters.*
4. frj, 1907–1909, RAM.

5. Ibid.
6. GAM, unpublished notes.
7. Ibid.
8. frj, 1907–1909, RAM; erj, 1910–1915, BCD.
9. fsr to jh, RAM; erj, 1910–1915, BCD.
10. frj, 1907–1909, RAM; erj, 1910–1915, BCD.
11. ecj, 1902, BCD.
12. GAM, MMM notes; conversation with Dr. O. Kenneth Bates.
13. Irving Bacheller, *From Stores of Memory.*
14. frj, 1907–1909, RAM; erj, 1910–1915, BCD.
15. frj, 1908, RAM.
16. GAM notes.
17. frj, 1907–1908, RAM.
18. fsr to Herbert Gunnison, SLU.
19. GAM research and notes; assorted newspaper files and clippings.
20. Pierre Remington to rt, KSH.
21. St. Lawrence University, *General Catalog of the Officers, Graduates, and Non-Graduates: 1856–1926,* SLU.
22. Ibid.
23. GAM notes.
24. frj 1907–1908, RAM.
25. frj, 1907, RAM.
26. GAM notes.

11: BIG HORSE AND BIG PLANS (1907–1908)

1. Daniel Chester French to fsr, SLU.
2. frj, 1908, RAM.
3. frj, 1907, RAM.
4. Michael Edward Shapiro, *Bronze Casting and American Sculpture.*
5. frj, 1907, RAM.
6. Peter H. Hassrick, *Frederic Remington.*
7. frj, 1907, RAM.
8. Isabelle Keating Savell, *Daughter of Vermont: A Biography of Emily Eaton Hepburn.*
9. Ibid.
10. frj, 1909, RAM.
11. Savell, *Daughter of Vermont.*
12. GAM unpublished writing, notes.
13. frj, 1907, RAM.
14. Savell, *Daughter of Vermont.*
15. frj, 1907, RAM.
16. frj, 1908, RAM.

17. *Ogdensburg Journal,* 1908; Allen P. Splete and Marilyn D. Splete, eds., *Frederic Remington—Selected Letters.*
18. frj, 1908, RAM.
19. Ibid.
20. Ibid.
21. Ibid.
22. Ibid.
23. Savell, *Daughter of Vermont.*

12: "AN UNCERTAIN CAREER AS A PAINTER" (1908–1909)

1. frj, 1908, RAM.
2. Ibid.
3. GAM notes.
4. frj, 1908, RAM.
5. Ibid.
6. frj, 1907, RAM.
7. frj, 1908, RAM.
8. Ibid.
9. Ibid.
10. Ibid.
11. Ibid.
12. Ibid.
13. Ibid.
14. Ibid.
15. Ibid.
16. Ibid.
17. frj, 1909, RAM.
18. frj, 1908, RAM.
19. frj, 1909, RAM.
20. Ibid.
21. Unidentified clipping pasted into frj, 1909, RAM.
22. frj, 1909, RAM.
23. Ibid.
24. Ibid.
25. Ibid.
26. Ibid.
27. Ibid.
28. Ibid.
29. Ibid.
30. Ibid.
31. Ibid.
32. Unidentified clipping pasted into ibid.
33. Unidentified clipping pasted into ibid.

34. frj, 1909, RAM, in Eva Remington's handwriting.
35. Ibid.

13: EVA AFTERWARD (1910–1918)

1. erj, 1910, BCD.
2. Ibid.
3. Ibid.
4. Ibid.
5. Ibid.
6. Ibid.
7. Ibid.
8. Ibid.
9. Ibid.
10. Ibid.
11. erj, 1912, BCD.
12. Charles Remington Obituaries, *Malone* [N.Y.] *Palladium* and unidentified newspaper, 1929.
13. Interviews with BCD.
14. All other information in this chapter about Eva Remington and Emma Caten is obtained from erj journals or BCD; historical data have been obtained from newspaper clippings of the *Ogdensburg Journal,* interviews with Ogdensburg and other North Country people, or Manley family oral tradition.

POSTLUDE: REMINGTON'S REBIRTH

1. GAM notes.
2. Information about the Latendorf bookstore obtained from a telephone interview with Jeff Dykes, 1987.
3. Ibid.
4. Telephone interview with David Dary, University of Kansas, Lawrence, Kansas, 1987 president of Westerners International.
5. Douglas Allen, ed., *Frederic Remington's Own Outdoors.*
6. Historical overview and information related to twentieth-century collectors is based on conversations and a formal interview with Robert Rockwell, Western art collector and founder of the Corning, New York, Rockwell Museum of Western Art.
7. fsr to Maynard Dixon, September 3, 1891, CM.

BIBLIOGRAPHY

BOOKS AND MANUSCRIPTS

ALLEN, DOUGLAS. *Frederic Remington and the Spanish-American War*. New York: Crown, 1971.

ALLEN, DOUGLAS, ed. *Frederic Remington's Own Outdoors*. Introduction by Harold McCracken. New York: Dial Press, 1964.

ALLEN, DOUGLAS, and DOUGLAS ALLEN JR. *N. C. Wyeth: Collected Paintings, Illustrations and Murals*. New York: Bonanza Books/Crown, 1972.

BACHELLER, IRVING. *Coming Up the Road: Memories of a North Country Boyhood*. Indianapolis, Ind.: Bobbs-Merrill, 1928.

———. *From Stores of Memory*. New York: Farrar & Rinehart, 1938.

———. *Opinions of a Cheerful Yankee*. Indianapolis, Ind.: Bobbs-Merrill, 1926.

BARRY, JANE. *A Time in the Sun*. Garden City, N.Y.: Doubleday, 1962.

BEERS, THOMAS. *The Mauve Decade*. New York: Knopf, 1926.

BISHOP, JOSEPH BUCKLIN. *A. Barton Hepburn: His Life and Service to His Time*. New York: Scribner's, 1923.

BOYER, PAUL. *Urban Masses and Moral Order in America, 1820–1920*. Cambridge, Mass.: Harvard University Press, 1978.

Brooklyn Museum. *The American Renaissance: 1876–1917*. Brooklyn: 1970.

BROOKS, VAN WYCK. *The Confident Years: 1885–1915*. New York: Dutton, 1952.

BROWN, CHARLES H. *The Correspondent's War*. New York: Scribner's, 1967.

BURKE, MARY BARNETT. *A Random Scoot*. Jericho, N.Y.: Exposition Press, 1969.

CASSANDRA, ERNEST. *Universalism in America*. 2d ed. Boston: Skinner House, 1984.

CATEN, EMMA L. "Remington-Caten Family Histories." 1936. Collection of the Remington Art Museum, Ogdensburg, N.Y.

CORTISSOZ, ROYAL. *American Artists*. New York: Scribner's, 1920.

CURTIS, GATES, ed. *Our County and Its People: A Memorial Record of St. Lawrence County, N.Y.* Syracuse: D. Mason, 1894.

CUSTER, ELIZABETH B. *Tenting on the Plains, or General Custer in Kansas and Texas*. New York: Charles L. Webster, 1887.

Daughters of the American Revolution, Swe-Kat-Si Chapter. *Reminiscences of Ogdensburg: 1749–1907*. New York, Boston, and Chicago: Silver, Burdett, 1907.

DAVIS, RICHARD HARDING. *The Cuban and Porto Rican Campaigns*. New York: Scribner's, 1898.

DESORMO, MAITLAND C. *The Heydays of the Adirondacks*. Saranac Lake, N.Y.: Adirondack Yesteryears, 1974.

DIPPIE, BRIAN W. *Remington and Russell*. Austin: University of Texas Press, 1982.

DONALDSON, ALFRED W. *A History of the Adirondacks*, Vols. 1 and 2. New York: Century, 1921.

DORRA, HENRI. *The American Muse: Parallel Trends in Literature and Art*. Washington, D.C.: The Corcoran Gallery of Art, 1959.

DRYFOUT, JOHN H. *The Work of Augustus Saint-Gaudens*. Hanover, N.H.: University Press of New England, 1982.

EVERTS, L. H., and J. M. HOLCOMB. *History of St. Lawrence County, New York*. Philadelphia: Everts, 1878.

FIEVE, RONALD R. *Mood Swings*. New York: Bantam Books, 1981.

FOWLER, ALBERT, ed. *Cranberry Lake, From Wilderness to Adirondack Park*. Syracuse: The Adirondack Museum/Syracuse University Press, 1968.

GROSS, SALLY. "Beyond American Impressionism: The Transition Years 1893–1913." Paper presented at Boston University Symposium on the History of Art, March 23, 1985.

HARPER, J. HENRY. *The House of Harper, A History*. New York: Harper Brothers, 1900.

HASSRICK, PETER H. *Frederic Remington*. Fort Worth: Amon Carter Museum, 1973.

———. *Frederic Remington: Paintings, Drawings and Sculpture in the Amon Carter Museum and the Sid W. Richardson Foundation Collections*. New York: Abrams, 1973.

———. *The Remington Studies*. Cody, Wyo.: Buffalo Bill Historical Center, 1981.

HOUGH, FRANKLIN B. *A History of St. Lawrence and Franklin Counties*. Albany: Little and Co., 1853 (facsimile edition, published by St. Lawrence

County Historical Association, Franklin County Historical and Museum Society; Baltimore: Regional Publishing, 1970).

JUSSIM, ESTELLE. *Frederic Remington: The Camera and the Old West*. Fort Worth: Amon Carter Museum, 1983.

KAISER, HARVEY H. *Great Camps of the Adirondacks*. Boston: David R. Godine, 1982.

KELLOGG, WALTER GUEST. *Parish's Fancy*. New York: John Day, 1926.

LEHMANN-HAUPT, HELMUT. *The Book in America*. New York: Bowker, 1952.

LEWIS, ALFRED HENRY. *Wolfville*. Illustrated by Frederic Remington. New York: Grosset & Dunlap, 1897.

LEWIS, R. W. B. *The American Adam: Innocence, Tragedy and Tradition in the Nineteenth Century*. Chicago: The University of Chicago Press, 1955.

LONGFELLOW, HENRY WADSWORTH. *The Song of Hiawatha*. New York: Bounty Books/Crown, 1968.

MCCRACKEN, HAROLD. *The Charles M. Russell Book*. Garden City, N.Y.: Doubleday, 1967.

———. *Frederic Remington: Artist of the Old West*. Philadelphia and New York: Lippincott Company, 1947.

———. *The Frederic Remington Book*. Garden City, N.Y.: Doubleday, 1966.

MCCRACKEN, HAROLD, ed. *Frederic Remington's Own West*. New York: Dial Press, 1960.

MCKOWN, ROBIN. *Painter of the Wild West: Frederic Remington*. New York: Julian Messner, 1959.

MANGUM, MARGARET MANLEY. *History and Culture of Cuba*. New York: Lutheran Immigration and Refugee Service, 1980.

MANLEY, ATWOOD. *Frederic Remington in the Land of His Youth*. Ogdensburg, N.Y.: privately published, 1961.

———. *Rushton and His Times in American Canoeing*. Syracuse: The Adirondack Museum/Syracuse University Press, 1968.

MARDEN, ORISON SWETT. *Little Visits with the Great Americans*. New York: Success Co., 1905.

MARX, LEO. *The Machine in the Garden*. New York: Oxford University Press, 1964.

MILES, NELSON A. *Personal Recollections and Observations of General Nelson A. Miles*. Chicago and New York: Werner, 1896.

MORGAN, H. WAYNE. *New Muses: Art in American Culture 1865–1920*. Norman, Okla.: University of Oklahoma, 1978.

MORRIS, EDMUND. *The Rise of Theodore Roosevelt*. New York: Coward, McCann & Geoghegan, 1979.

NOBLE, DAVID W. *The Eternal Adam and the New World Garden: The Central Myth in the American Novel Since 1830*. New York: George Braziller, 1968.

REED, WALT. *The Illustrator in America*. New York: Society of Illustrators, 1966.

REMINGTON, FREDERIC. *Crooked Trails.* New York: Grosset & Dunlap, 1898.

————. *Drawings.* Introduction by Owen Wister. New York: R. H. Russell, 1898.

————. *Done in the Open: Drawings by Frederic Remington.* New York: P. F. Collier, 1902.

————. *The Illustrations of Frederic Remington.* Commentary by Owen Wister. New York: Bounty Books/Crown, 1970.

————. *John Ermine of the Yellowstone.* New York: Macmillan, 1903.

————. *Pony Tracks.* New York: Harper Brothers, 1895.

————. *Sun-Down LeFlare.* New York: Harper Brothers, 1899.

RHEIMS, MAURICE. *19th Century Sculpture.* New York: Abrams, 1977.

ROOSEVELT, THEODORE. *Ranch Life and the Hunting Trail.* New York: Century, 1887.

RUSSELL, CHARLES M. *Good Medicine Memories of the Real West.* Garden City, N.Y.: Doubleday, 1930.

SAMUELS, HAROLD, and PEGGY SAMUELS. *Frederic Remington: A Biography.* Garden City, N.Y.: Doubleday, 1982.

SAMUELS, PEGGY, and HAROLD SAMUELS, eds. *The Collected Writings of Frederic Remington.* Garden City, N.Y.: Doubleday, 1979.

SAVELL, ISABELLE KEATING. *Daughter of Vermont: A Biography of Emily Eaton Hepburn.* New York: North River Press, 1952.

SCOTT, CLINTON LEE. *The Universalist Church in America: A Short History.* Boston: Universalist Historical Society, 1957.

SHAPIRO, MICHAEL E. *Bronze Casting and American Sculpture.* Cranberry, N.J.: Association of University Presses, 1985.

SMITH, THOMAS WEST. *The Story of a Cavalry Regiment: Scott's 900.* Chicago: Veteran Association of the Regiment, 1897.

SPENCE, LEWIS. *North American Indians: Myths and Legends.* George Harrap, ca. 1912; New York: Avenel, 1986.

SPLETE, ALLEN P., and SPLETE, MARILYN D., eds. *Frederic Remington—Selected Letters.* New York: Abbeville, forthcoming.

St. Lawrence University. *General Catalog of the Officers, Graduates, and Non-Graduates, 1856–1926.* Canton, N.Y.: St. Lawrence University, 1926.

STODDARD, SENECA RAY. *Old Times in the Adirondacks.* Saranac Lake, N.Y.: n.p., 1971.

SULLIVAN, MARK. *Our Times: The United States 1900–1925.* New York and London: Scribner's, 1926–1935.

TAFT, ROBERT. *Artists and Illustrators of the Old West, 1850–1900.* New York: Scribner's, 1963.

VORPAHL, BEN MERCHANT. *Frederic Remington and the West: With the Eye of the Mind.* Austin: University of Texas Press, 1978.

————. *My Dear Wister: The Frederic Remington–Owen Wister Letters.* Palo Alto, Calif.: American West, 1972.

WEAR, BRUCE. *The Bronze World of Frederic Remington*. Tulsa, Okla.: Gaylord Ltd., Art Americana, 1966.

———. *The Second Bronze World of Frederic Remington*. Upper Montclair, N.J.: Ranch, 1976.

WESSELS, WILLIAM L. *Adirondack Profiles*. Lake George, N.Y.: Adirondacks Resorts, 1961.

WYETH, N. C. *The Wyeths*. Edited by Betsy James Wyeth. Boston: Gambit, 1971.

YOUNG, MAHONRI SHARP. *American Realists: Homer to Hopper*. New York: Watson/Guptill, 1977.

ARTICLES, PAMPHLETS, AND PERIODICALS

"The American Scene Presents Frederic Remington." Special issue published by the Gilcrease Institute, Tulsa, Okla., Summer 1961.

Art Museum of South Texas. *Remington and Russell*. Corpus Christi, Tex.: 1974.

BAXTER, ELIZABETH. *Historic Ogdensburg*. Ogdensburg, N.Y.: Ryan Press.

BLANKMAN, EDWARD J. "The Lure of the Red Gods." *Adirondack Life*, January/February, 1973.

BOYD, NELLIE HOUGH. "Remington at Twenty-three." *International Studio*, February 1923.

The Cadet Fine Arts Forum. *Frederic Remington: The Soldier Artist*. West Point, N.Y.: The United States Military Academy, 1979.

DARY, DAVID. "Kansas City, Cradle of Remington's Art." *Kansas City Star Magazine*, May 3, 1925.

———. "The Kansas Prankster Who Won Fame in Art." *Kansas City Star Magazine*, December 6, 1970.

DYKES, JEFF. *Great Western Illustrators*. College Park, Md.: 1978, 1981, 1982.

———. "Tentative Bibliographic Check Lists of Western Illustrators." *American Book Collector* 16 (November 1965).

FORBIS, WILLIAM H. *The Cowboys*. New York: Time-Life Books, n.d.

Frederic Remington Art Museum and The Adirondack Museum. *The North Country Art of Frederic Remington, Artist in Residence*. A catalog for Frederic Remington exhibition. Exhibition Curator, William Crowley. Contributing Authors: David Tathum and Atwood Manley. Syracuse: 1985.

HANSON, IRVIN W. *101 Frederic Remington Drawings of the Old West*. Willmar, Minn.: Color Press, 1968.

HASSRICK, PETER H. "Remington in the Southwest." *Southwestern Historical Quarterly* 76 (January 1973).

Museum of Fine Arts. *A New World: Masterpieces of American Painting. 1760– 1910*. Boston: 1983.

MYERS, RICHARD. *A Guide to Old Remington Prints from 1888 Through 1914.* Ogdensburg, N.Y.: Ryan Press, 1975.

Persimmon Hill 6 (no. 1, 1976) and 10 (no. 3, 1980).

Rockwell-Corning Museum. *The Painter's West, A Selection from the Rockwell Collection of Western Art.* Introduction by Harold McCracken.

SAMUELS, PEGGY, and HAROLD SAMUELS. "Frederic Remington's Stirrings in Kansas City." October 1978. Kansas State Historical Society files.

SCHIMMEL, JULIE. *Stark Museum of Art: The Western Collection, 1978.* Orange, Tex.: Stark Museum of Art, 1978.

Special issue on Frederic Remington. *Cobblestone* 3 (November 1982).

"Up America." *Time Magazine,* November 20, 1972.

We consulted back issues of the following newspapers: *The St. Lawrence Plaindealer,* Canton, N.Y.; *The Commercial Advertiser,* Canton, N.Y.; *The Ogdensburg Journal,* Ogdensburg, N.Y.; *The Ogdensburg Advance,* Ogdensburg, N.Y.; *Watertown Daily Times,* Watertown, N.Y.; *The New York Times; Brooklyn Eagle,* Brooklyn, N.Y.; and *Kansas City Star,* Kansas City, Mo.

We also consulted the following periodicals: *Harper's Weekly, Harper's Monthly, Collier's Magazine, The Century Magazine, Outing Magazine, Outlook Magazine, The New York Times Sunday Magazine, Life Magazine, Time Magazine,* and *Adirondack Life.*

INDEX